MAY 1 7 2022			

the La Motte Woman

Mary Martin Devlin

Cuidono • Brooklyn

ISBN: 978-1-9444531-2-1
eISBN: 978-1-9444531-3-8

Cover image: Detail of Portrait of Empress Maria Fyodor by Konstantin Egorovich Makovsky, Regional Art Museum, Irkutsk/Bridgeman Images

Cuidono Press
Brooklyn NY
www.cuidono.com

Author's Note

Every character in this novel played a part in the extraordinary story of the extraordinary La Motte woman and the Diamond Necklace Affair, one of the most abundantly documented events in French history. The details of this pivotal event emerge in personal memoirs, letters, newspaper accounts from all over Europe, the official records and documents of the Diamond Necklace trial, and even in bills from a London jeweler. I have respected the facts of the event and, whenever possible, have allowed the players to speak in their own words.

The Queen's death must be dated from the Diamond Necklace Trial.

— Napoleon Bonaparte

1

The two girls, their arms encircling heavy gutter pipes, dangled precariously from the attic window of a fashionable dressmaker's workroom in the Palais-Royal. For over an hour they had been waiting for the fanfare that would announce the passage of the royal carriages with the Dauphin and his bride, the Austrian Archduchess Marie Antoinette. The newlyweds would proceed down the rue de Rivoli, past the Tuileries, to the Place Louis XV, where the day's festivities would begin.

It was a bright spring day in 1770, and Paris was in a delirium of joy. By night the city was a fairyland with lanterns strung along the rooftops, around windows, across streets. Notre-Dame Cathedral shimmered, a gauzy, glittering phantasm on the Seine; fountains in every square overflowed with red and white wine; loaves of bread lay so thick on the streets that even the poor did not bother to stoop and pick them up.

France was alive with hope: Louis-Auguste, the Dauphin, was sixteen years old, pious, frugal, and reserved; Marie Antoinette, fifteen, a golden child glowing with innocence, and these two when they reached the throne would surely right the wrongs and cure the miseries of the reign of the Dauphin's grandfather, the pleasure-besotted Louis XV.

"They aren't coming, Jeanne," one of the girls said, shrilling above the babble of the crowd in the street below. "It's gone ten o'clock." She looked leaden with disappointment.

The girl called Jeanne freed one arm and smoothed back a lock of hair. "Of course, they'll come, you ninny. They're royalty. And I should know what royal blood is all about."

"*Mesdemoiselles!*"

The girls looked at each other. Jeanne lifted her chin defiantly and turned her head away from the window. Clotilde, the other seamstress, ducked her head and scrambled back into the workroom.

"Jeanne de Saint-Rémy! Get back in here! With all the work that's to be done this day!" Mademoiselle Lamarche placed her hands on her broad hips and waited. She was a tall, imposing woman with a panoply of warts and moles disposed across her severe face, the premier dressmaker in Paris and accustomed to having her way. Especially with the young apprentice dressmakers who beavered away at their poorly lit tables in the low-ceilinged workroom up under the eaves of Mademoiselle Lamarche's elegant shop. Mademoiselle Lamarche would have shown herself proud and arrogant on almost any occasion but particularly now when the demand for her dresses for the Dauphin's nuptial parties had extravagantly bolstered her self-esteem. It was a heady experience watching seasoned courtiers mortgage a chateau or prize river-bottom acreage for the purchase of her latest sketchbook caprices.

Jeanne de Saint-Rémy stepped daintily down into the room, stretched and yawned theatrically, arching her back like a pampered cat, well aware that she was the center of attention and enjoying it. She was a striking young woman, not exactly a beauty, but she was exquisitely shaped. Her chestnut brown hair curled thickly about her shoulders, and her delicate complexion radiated youthful energy.

"Pathetic creature! Hanging out of windows, gawking at your betters! What kind of hoydenish behavior is that?"

"They're not my betters," Jeanne snapped crisply. "They're my cousins."

"Ah, yes," Mademoiselle Lamarche threw back her head and snorted contemptuously. "How could I have forgotten? Dear me, the Bourbons and the Valois. Why, of course, and you, their Valois cousin, the last of the descendants of our glorious Valois king, Henri II!"

Mademoiselle Lamarche felt exasperation gnawing at her nerves. This impertinent girl, this monster of impertinence, with her mulish pride. Had the girl's foster mother, the Marquise de Boulainvilliers, not been one of the shop's most valued customers, a profligate spender, and, naturally, had the Marquis de Boulainvilliers not been the Provost of Paris, Mademoiselle Lamarche would never have agreed to take the girl on as an apprentice.

At the first sight of Jeanne de Saint-Rémy, standing regally to one side of the shop, her deep blue eyes staring into space, Mademoiselle Lamarche had sensed trouble. And she had been right. For two years the girl had kept the workroom in a turmoil with her puffed-up pride, refusing to do work because it was beneath her, a princess of the blood royal, pulling hysterical fainting fits when the mood suited her.

It had been a difficult decision, but the Marquise had pleaded an urgent need to get the girl out of the Boulainvilliers chateau in Passy, and Mademoiselle had felt obliged to acquiesce. She could only speculate, but her instincts led her straight to some nasty business with that randy old goat, the Marquis. At fourteen Jeanne de Saint-Rémy was a full-blown woman. And attractive. Even Mademoiselle Lamarche would admit that. If the truth be told, there was a bit of the trollop about Jeanne. Men sensed that she was a hot-blooded woman and went weak in the knees when they were around her. Mademoiselle had seen quite enough of that when on occasion Jeanne had been allowed to help out in the shop below.

"Back to work, Jeanne," Mademoiselle said sharply. "The Comtesse de Broussard expects her gown before the sun goes down. And only your clever little hands can satisfy her." It was true. The girl was a genius with her needle.

Jeanne, her eyes a disconcerting glassy blue, stared at her mistress for a moment before returning, without a word, to her worktable. Mademoiselle Lamarche shrugged. There was no understanding that one. With considerable satisfaction she turned and surveyed the low, dusky room before going downstairs to her shop. The seventeen girls in apprenticeship were bent over their precious silks and taffetas, which whispered and gasped as the girls turned the garments to and fro.

Mademoiselle Lamarche had no sooner reached the second floor landing when the crashing sound of overturned tables and girlish shrieks filled the stairwell.

"*Mon dieu, mon dieu!* Will those girls never leave me any peace!" She lifted her skirts and hurried back up the stairs. "A mouse, most like. They've seen a rat, those dreadful females. *Mon dieu, mon dieu!*"

But when the dressmaker reached the attic and entered the workroom, the girls were clustered in awed silence around the overturned worktable of Jeanne de Saint-Rémy. Clutching a russet silk bodice to her breast, Jeanne lay rigid on the floor, her eyes fixed in a vacant stare, her limbs twitching convulsively.

"Send for my carriage!" Mademoiselle Lamarche cried. "Quickly!"

The Marquise de Boulainvilliers had just returned from overseeing the work of a dozen footmen arranging chairs along the walls of the great rectangular ballroom when the carriage bearing her foster daughter Jeanne arrived in the courtyard. That evening the Boulainvilliers would be celebrating the royal nuptials with a ball and fireworks. No expense had been spared, for the Marquise prided herself on the bounty of her receptions and the high caliber of her court connections.

When the Marquise saw the fashionable carriage pull into the courtyard, she had a moment of panic, fearing that some misguided guests had already begun to arrive for the ball and supper party. Down below, she saw her majordomo, rushing forward to open the carriage door.

"Jeanne? Is it Jeanne?" she cried, as Mademoiselle Lamarche's footman helped the girl out of the carriage. The Marquise was a soft-hearted woman, quick to shed a tear, of a loving, maternal disposition. She cherished her three daughters in a desperate kind of way, as if they were some heavenly gift that might be snatched away from her at any minute. It came, therefore, as no surprise to her acquaintances when they learned that she had picked up a child beggar on the king's highroad to Passy and had brought the girl and her brother into her family to be raised and educated as her own.

To be sure, the seven-year-old beggar had an exotic story to tell, an extraordinary story, really, which appealed to the Marquise's romantic bent. The child called herself Jeanne de Saint-Rémy and claimed to be one of the three remaining children of the last descendant of a legitimized son of King Henri II and his mistress. The Marquise, being passionate about royalty and genealogy, pursued the girl's outlandish assertions and found them to be true. To have plucked off the dusty highroad a beggar with the blood of French kings coursing through her veins seemed to the Marquise a dazzling *trouvaille*, not unlike finding a genuine jade brooch in the jumbled bin of an antiquarian.

To rescue royalty in distress, the noble Valois children fallen to beggary, became the Marquise's mission in life. She had a long political nose and had always been busy in the corridors of Versailles. She fully intended to have the children's genealogy confirmed by Chérin, the King's official genealogist. For her guests' amusement the Marquise found in Jeanne a deft little storyteller, who could make touching even the sordid details of the misery of her childhood. Jeanne's father, the Baron de Rémy, had married a servant wench and fallen into dissolute ways, finally resorting to poaching to support his growing family. The family properties at one time numbered seven but had been reduced to the chateau de Fontette, crumbling into its pestilent moat.

Eventually, the Baron mortgaged Fontette, set off for Paris with his wife and his two oldest children to plead for relief from the King, and ended his wretched life in a pauper's hospital in Paris. At this point in the story, the Marquise would ask, "And

what happened to your little sister when you set off for Paris?"
And Jeanne would reply brightly, "Why, my mother put baby
Marianne in a basket and hung her at Farmer Durand's window."
Her audience would raise their fans and titter and roll their eyes in
amusement at the droll antics of country folk.

As a child of six, Jeanne was put out to beg on the streets of
Paris, while her brother Jacques made a few sols each day as a boot-
black, and their slatternly mother supported her vicious habits by
plying the ancient horizontal trade. This depraved creature soon
deserted her small children, leaving them alone in an attic room
with only a sackful of chestnuts to stave off starvation. One day
Jeanne took her begging to the king's highroad to Passy, hoping to
reap a better harvest from wealthy courtiers on their way to their
country estates. And there, Jeanne hopped up onto the step of the
slow-moving Boulainvilliers carriage and began her beggar's prattle.

The Marquise had found the little beggar irresistible. Despite
her husband's objections, she took up the little wretches, cleaned
them up, got rid of their vermin, and sent them off to be educated.
It was only when Jeanne, a striking young lady of twelve, returned
home for her first communion that trouble began. The Marquise
had only the word of Giselle, the backstairs maid and a terrible
gossip, but she had seen enough with her own eyes to be suspicious about her husband's extravagant gifts—a repeater watch, a
string of huge South Sea pearls, reticules beaded in precious stones
that even a court lady would envy, a cameo ring—to their foster
daughter. Having made no progress in advancing the Valois claims,
the Marquise felt obliged to place Jeanne, for her own sake, in
apprenticeship to Mademoiselle Lamarche.

"Oh, my dear child," she said, taking Jeanne into her arms.
Jeanne was able to walk, but her head lolled to one side, and she
was extremely pale.

"It's only another malaise, maman," Jeanne said, reassured by
the look of fear in the Marquise's pale blue eyes. There would be no
return to the hated workroom this day. Not for many more days,
if Jeanne had her way.

"Another! Mademoiselle Lamarche must be quite vexed. Oh, Jeanne, what are we to do? And our nuptial ball this evening! Did you know? But, of course not, how could you? I must send for Doctor Perrault immediately. You must be bled and put to bed. Oh, and our ball this very evening!"

Servants appeared from all sides to prepare a large apartment of rooms on the second floor for the use of the invalid. Over the past few years, since her apprenticeship had begun, Jeanne had grown quite used to convalescing in these sunny, airy rooms, to being pampered by the Marquise, to lying in bed until late morning, gossiping about the latest fashions in clothes, coiffures, and beauty patches. After all, she said to herself as she climbed the stairs, remembering to drag one leg slightly, what was the point in toiling away in a cramped, stuffy workroom if she couldn't watch the wedding party pass by with the Dauphine, who was said to look like a beautiful angel, though Jeanne supposed that she was merely a girl just like herself? Only a year older than Jeanne and far luckier.

Soon Jeanne lay prettily installed midst a profusion of lacy blue and ivory pillows. The Marquise looked down at her. Already the color had returned to Jeanne's cheeks. It was such a mystery, these nervous spells, when the girl looked in the best of health. No doubt after a day of two of rest she would be as right as rain. And back to the workroom, she must go, the Marquise thought with a pang, for she always missed the girl's saucy prattle. Back to the workroom out of harm's way.

"It's Monsieur Perrault, my child," the Marquise said. "He's come to bleed you. You mustn't be afraid, *n'est-ce pas, docteur?*" The Marquise herself had a dreadful fear of doctors, and in moments of anxiety, such as this, she was afflicted with a noticeable head tremor.

Monsieur Perrault was a short, portly man, whose wig gave off an odor of perspiration and stale powder. He had spent the morning administering poultices and emetics to the aging and coleric Duc d'Aigremont, nasty work, and he looked forward to a quick and simple bloodletting. With a polite cough, he slipped his hands under the covers, lifted one of Jeanne's feet, and with a quick twist of his wrists slashed a rather large *x* in the tender instep of her slender foot.

Perrault drew out a none-too-clean handkerchief from his pocket and wiped the blade of his razor. Jeanne had closed her eyes, a contented look on her face.

"Brave girl, Madame," Perrault said.

"Yes, indeed, Monsieur. And always has been. Haven't you, my dear?"

Jeanne opened her eyes and frowned. "I never even got a glimpse of the wedding party. They were to pass just beneath our windows. I could have seen their faces as clearly as I see yours," she said.

Monsieur Perrault shook his head. A few dusty specks of wig powder drifted onto his shoulders. "Oh, the wedding . . . Sad times, Madame, I'm sorry to say." The afternoon sun slanted wanly across the large room. "Sad times," he said again.

The Marquise looked fearfully toward the doctor. "But what is it, Monsieur?" she whispered.

"Haven't you heard?" he asked, lowering his voice ominously.

"What?"

"On the Place Louis XV this morning. During the ceremonies for the Dauphin and his Austrian bride. The scaffolding, a whole section of it collapsed. Hundreds killed . . ."

"Not the royals?" the Marquise said.

"No, no. The Dauphin and the Dauphine were not hurt. So many crushed, though. Hundreds, they say. Blood flowing in every direction on the Place." Monsieur Perrault bowed to the invalid and headed toward the door. "Such a terrible omen in the midst of our jubilation, Madame. I see it as a sign from above."

"Surely not, Monsieur," the Marquise said, crossing herself. "God has sent us a beautiful princess from one of our oldest enemies, now our friend. We must rejoice. I wouldn't think of canceling our ball tonight."

2

On the fashionable rue Vendôme in a dusky backroom in the shop of the jewelers to King Louis XV, a pale, very blond man named Bassenge sat on a high stool and studied an ink drawing of an enormous, highly complicated diamond necklace. His head tilted slightly forward, his eyes narrowed as he reached out and slowly traced one of the long, cascading festoons of the necklace, his doughy white hand lingering over each diamond as if fervently praying over ancient beads. His face glowed with pleasure; he pursed his lips with a moist cluck of satisfaction.

With their daring creations Claude-Auguste Bassenge and his partner Paul Böhmer had become the most sought-after jewelers in Europe, being appointed court jewelers to the King of Poland as well as to the King of France. They were a formidable pair, these young and energetic Germans. Of the two, Bassenge was the aesthete, the designer, the obsessive dreamer; Böhmer the hard-headed businessman, the salesman, the worrier. They quickly made their mark in the fashion-crazed world of Paris and the court, where Louis XV's mistress, Madame Du Barry, had been stockpiling diamond jewelry for years, foreseeing the days when she would no longer have an addled, sex-crazed king around to squander the nation's gold on her.

Böhmer and Bassenge had conceived of this stupendous diamond necklace with the Comtesse Du Barry in mind, for only a king's treasury could afford this lavish outlay of jewels. Bassenge called the style of the necklace the *rivière* because it flowed gracefully over a woman's bosom down to her navel.

They had been patiently buying up diamonds for two years. The design of the already celebrated necklace called for 647 brilliants, amounting to 2,800 carats of the finest-cut diamonds collected from all over the world. The seventeen diamonds on the choker alone were as big as hazelnuts. Besides a choker with festoons and pendants, there were three other tiers of diamonds fifteen inches deep with four knotted tassels, each culminating in an eleven-carat button diamond surrounded by a cluster of eight diamonds of three carats each.

Böhmer, ostensibly watching the clerks in the front room, stood with his back turned to his partner and tried to sound a casual, conversational note as he said, "I've no good news from our cousins in Brazil. They've combed all the markets there for diamonds over ten carats and have come up with nothing promising. I think you should reconsider some of the stones we've already bought, Bassenge."

Bassenge's small ears flushed red with anger. "Not one of them will do! How many times do I have to tell you? Look, just look at this!" He gestured impatiently toward the drawing. "I'm working on my masterpiece! Our names will go down in history as the creators of the most spectacular necklace ever designed. Don't you see? Every diamond must be perfect. Perfect in every way. Perfectly cut. The color as white as ice. I need only a few more stones, but they must be perfect!"

He turned away abruptly and studied the drawing again. "We must simply be patient. A work of art cannot be rushed."

"Oh, if it's patience we're talking about," Böhmer said sourly, "I have all the patience in the world, indeed I do. It's our creditors who are in short supply of patience these days." Bassenge did not appear to be listening. "It would mean everything financially if we could put a stop to purchasing more and more diamonds. As if the next one or the next batch contained the perfect stone."

Bassenge sat stubbornly staring at the drawing. Böhmer pulled up a small wooden chair and sat down.

"Bassenge, listen to me," he said, "We've got to mortgage our showrooms here on the rue Vendôme. The interest on these dozen loans is eating us up. If you insist on buying more diamonds, we'll have to take out another loan of at least two hundred thousand francs. Just to keep the shop going from day to day."

"Where will you get that kind of loan?" Bassenge asked half-heartedly. He hated it when Böhmer forced him to listen to these details about money, always the same these days.

"From the financier Boudard de Saint-James. My good wife has kindly offered her beloved country place as collateral." Böhmer waited for some expression of surprise or gratitude at Madame Böhmer's generosity, but Bassenge sat lost in his reveries again. "So you see, it's to spare my wife this sacrifice that I thought you might perhaps reconsider, look again at the fifteen stones we received last month from our cutters in Amsterdam."

Bassenge grunted disparagingly. "Those? Why, they're too pink!" He drew himself up and took a deep breath. "I couldn't sleep again last night. I'm tortured by an aesthetic dilemma. I originally intended the clasp and the four bowknots from which the tassels depend to be made of gold. Now I can't help thinking that gold would be too common. Why not *émail* which our French workmen do so well? What do you think, Böhmer? The clasp and bowknots fashioned in enamel—Du Barry rose enamel to please the King?"

"Or Nattier blue. They say it's the young Dauphine's favorite color," Böhmer said.

"Even better! I like blue with diamonds. They also say Marie Antoinette has a passion for diamonds."

Böhmer, an affable, easy-going man popular in society, smiled genially, pleased that Bassenge had liked his suggestion. "We'll know soon enough."

"I'll bet she'll go crazy for this necklace. Any woman would. Especially a beautiful and spoiled princess."

"Who's never been denied anything in her whole life," Böhmer said, his spirits buoyed by the mere idea of another spendthrift woman in the palace at Versailles. "She just might buy it right out from under the nose of the King's fancy woman."

"I wouldn't be at all surprised," Bassenge said.

3

"What is it now, Monsieur l'Abbé?" Cardinal-Prince Louis de Rohan, his deep, mellow voice, usually so kindly when dealing with his secretary, had a sharp edge this morning. His head felt heavy, his tongue thick, his stomach uneasy. Useless and stupid to vow never to carouse again with the Emperor Joseph, he thought. One owes oneself some amusement in this cold, dank country. He looked at the Abbé Georgel's solemn face. "The Empress would . . . what? The Empress would like to remind me that this will be my fourth supper party in a fortnight? Is that it?"

Only seven months installed in Vienna as the French Ambassador to the Austria court and not a single day passed without some criticism from the Empress Maria Theresa regarding his establishment. This staid, unimaginative old woman was sorely trying his patience. He had been more than a little pleased by Louis XV's appointment, not that everyone at court hadn't expected it, for the Cardinal-Prince saw himself at the beginning of a long and brilliant political career. And he was determined that no amount of ill will on the Empress's part would spoil it for him.

"I'm afraid it's rather more serious than that, Your Eminence." The Abbé Georgel, his face gaunt and careworn, his shoulders stooped, shuffled forward over the fine Persian carpet, his dingy old soutane fraying about the hem a startling contrast to the radiantly youthful Cardinal-Prince's silken scarlet robes. The Abbé had gone straight from his Jesuit seminary to his position on the Cardinal's staff, and sometimes the Abbé thought that he could lay down his life for the Cardinal, such was his devotion to him.

The Prince arched his eyebrows in mock horror. "More serious, you say!"

The Abbé allowed himself a moment of disapproving silence before replying somberly. "Indeed, Your Eminence. It appears that . . . I understand that the Empress Maria Theresa has accused certain members of your embassy staff of smuggling silk stockings into Austria . . ."

"Silk stockings! Not muskets, not swords, not gunpowder. But silk stockings?" The Cardinal threw back his handsome head and exploded with laughter. "Silk stockings! What will that harridan think of next?"

The Abbé rubbed the bridge of his nose thoughtfully. Much as he admired the Cardinal, he deplored what he considered the man's frivolity, his inability to look at life as more than a delightful game. To the Abbé's unending dismay, the Cardinal had a painfully rosy view of life.

"I'm afraid the charge is all too true, Your Eminence."

"Even so, Georgel. Even so. Where's the harm in that? This is a backward country. One misses one's luxuries. What Frenchman could bear to wear those coarse things the Viennese put on their legs every day? I trust the Empress has noticed that her precious little Marie Antoinette has done her share of enriching the shopkeepers in the Palais-Royal and the Faubourg Saint-Honoré. The Dauphine is digging into the national treasury with both hands."

"Be that as it may," the Abbé continued, pursing his lips, "the Empress believes these individuals—I'm sorry to tell you, Prince, that your good friend the Comte de Villeroy is among them—in any event, these individuals are smuggling in silk stockings from Lyons to use as gifts to . . . well, buy influence. I believe that is the phrase she used."

The Cardinal sighed with annoyance and shifted his papers about the desk. There was no point in trying to appease the old harridan. The Empress thoroughly disapproved of him, and he knew it. From the very beginning, upon his arrival in 1772, she had thrown up her hands in alarm at the magnificence of his entrance into Vienna and his establishment there: One hundred and twenty outriders in red and gold livery! The Prince had brought along his own family Sèvres and crystal and silver, his own orchestra, his own stable of two hundred Arabian horses. Two hundred horses, she had exclaimed! The man must take himself for a prince. Exactly, the Cardinal had murmured when he heard the outcry. And the parties. The Empress despised the embassy's Gallic *joie de vivre*. Is it because her daughter in Versailles loves that *joie de vivre* all too much, the Prince wondered. Is that why the Empress raises such a stink about my parties? Because she knows that her own daughter is out in Paris night after night with the King's brother dancing, gambling, and cavorting until dawn. Is that it?

"What does the dreadful woman intend to do?" Prince Louis asked wearily.

She will have them arrested this evening. They will be imprisoned."

"House arrest?"

"I fear not, Your Eminence."

The Cardinal angrily swept a thick lock of hair back from his forehead. "The old cow is pushing me too hard, Georgel. Imprison my officials! She must know that it is too much, that I cannot and will not countenance this kind of action."

"I believe she does know, Your Eminence. It is my opinion that the Empress would like to have you recalled to France."

"Recalled! She must have gone mad. Does she forget who I am?"

"She favors the Baron de Breteuil, I have reason to think."

The Cardinal laughed. "Oh, *bien sûr*, if she wants a fat, boorish oaf to stand around and pay her court. Yes, Breteuil would suit her. Undoubtedly. But she will have to be patient. I shall never be recalled, so long as Louis XV is alive."

"The King is old. He is dissolute. And the Empress *is* patient. Her daughter will one day be Queen of France. Perhaps one day soon. I understand that she is already preparing the ground for the appointment of Breteuil. The Empress is turning her daughter's head against you, I fear."

"Ah, there she goes too far, Georgel. She doesn't know her daughter. Marie Antoinette and I are . . . how shall I say it, why, we are wonderfully alike in ways her mother would never understand. On the three or four occasions we met before my departure for Vienna, Marie Antoinette could not have been more charming."

Nonetheless, the Cardinal felt his spirits droop. His head had begun to pound again. He knew only too well the ways of the court, especially its perverse fickleness. In favor today, out of favor tomorrow. *L'absent a toujours tort*, Louis XIV used to say. Leaving the court was always a risk, and the Cardinal-Prince knew it. But to serve as His Majesty's ambassador to the court of Austria, what better preparation for the glorious political future the Cardinal intended for himself? If he were recalled, why, he would never be able to recover from such a humiliation.

"Are you certain of this, Monsieur l'Abbé? You have this information from your customary source?"

"Indeed. From my usual source. And I am pleased to inform Your Eminence that I have secured another informant. One who will be able to supply us with a copy of every letter the Empress sends to France." The Abbé squared his shoulders and smiled timidly.

"My God, man, you are a treasure. I shan't ask how you've managed to nab this latest one," the Cardinal said, his mood brightening.

The Cardinal sat back in his chair and studied his secretary. Georgel, a drab, insignificant cleric, daily wove his way in and around the Austrian court, unnoticed, probably scorned, yet in only a matter of months he had recruited an informant from the highest circle of the Empress's ministers. And now another. Georgel was a marvel. The Cardinal could scarcely contain his glee. An informant who could supply the Cardinal with the old cow's correspondence. Letters to her daughter. Letters to the Austrian ambassador to Versailles, the Count de Mercy, that presumptuous little spy, that viper in the French court. Letters to the Abbé de Vermond, Marie Antoinette's tutor. Another spy. And all of them plotting against the Cardinal-Prince.

"No need to worry, then, is there? We shall have the situation well under control. Thanks to you. You know, Monsieur l'Abbé, you must never forget how much I am indebted to you and your work on my behalf. I flatter myself that no French ambassador has ever sent more valuable dispatches to his sovereign. Without you our dispatches would be the usual endless conjugation of the weather: it is raining, it will rain, it has snowed. That sort of drivel. How is your mother, by the way? I always think of Auvergne when it snows."

"Not well, I fear. If the truth be told, she is rapidly going blind." The Abbé felt enormous responsibility for his family and never missed an opportunity to use the Prince's influence to the advantage of his family members.

"Dear lady. We must do something for her, Georgel. What shall we do? A reader, perhaps. Someone to keep her company during the long winter nights in La Chaise-Dieu."

The Cardinal shuddered. Among his many benefices he was the Abbot of the Abbaye de La Chaise-Dieu, and the very name, "Seat of God," was enough to strike a chill in his heart. Hard, flinty Auvergne. He visited the Abbaye seldom, as seldom as possible. He remembered the forbidding peasants, twisted and gnarled by hard work scrabbling over an ungrateful soil, filing meekly to the altar rail for Holy Communion. When there was so much color and gaiety in the world! And those medieval frescoes in the Abbaye, *la danse macabre*, the Cardinal could not look at them without recoiling. The dance of death, who could escape that dance partner? Sly death stepping on the train of a high-born lady in her finery and pitching her forward into a gaping grave. The smile on the face of the lady, all unsuspecting, joy in her beauty, her youth, feelings of immortality. And death, the eternal trickster, waiting his moment, the skeletal foot stealing forward, as the lady smiles and smiles.

The Cardinal shook his head and looked out the window. Only ten o'clock, and already the morning looked like late afternoon. Snow had begun to fall. A barren branch, frail and frozen, rubbed insistently against the windowpane.

"I should be most grateful, Your Eminence," the Abbé said, startling the Cardinal from his reverie.

Prince Louis rubbed his hands energetically. "I've fallen into a disagreeable mood. Such nonsense. There's serious work to be done, Monsieur l'Abbé. We must give Schreiber his final instructions for the party tonight. Let's see now. There will be twenty tables of ten guests each."

"You can't be serious, Your Eminence. The Empress will be outraged."

"Let her be outraged. By all means, let her fall into an apoplectic fit. I shall not have that vile woman telling me how to arrange my guests at table."

The Abbé could tell by the malicious glint in the Prince's eyes that it was pointless to argue with him. Yet he should. It was his duty to counsel the Prince, to prevent him from flying in the face of the Empress's opinion. To keep him from courting her displeasure. To the Abbé's mind, the Cardinal misjudged Maria Theresa. She was a relentless opponent who ran the country like a tough general. A ruthless general. Everyone knew the story of Marie Antoinette's birth. When the Empress went into labor with this her thirteenth child, she was sitting in an armchair reading and correcting state papers. Being comfortably installed, she was loath to quit the armchair for her bed. The child was delivered—a girl who was to become her favorite child—and after a bit of perfunctory clucking and cooing, the Empress handed the child over to a nurse, picked up her papers, and resumed her work. The Cardinal had no idea that he was taunting a tiger.

"I should think that, for just this supper party—and not for any others, mind you—Your Eminence might do well to follow the Empress's protocol of one long table, yourself at the head and your two hundred guests facing each other on either side."

"Why, you sound exactly like the Empress's minion who came to inform me of her displeasure with my little round tables. Don't tell me you've joined the opposition, Georgel," said the Cardinal, a broad smile spreading over his face.

"I only meant that the Empress does have a point. The little tables *are* somewhat intimate. Not too intimate, as the Empress maintains, only somewhat intimate, and for a formal dinner party . . ."

"I *never* have formal dinner parties. I despise the word. And I love intimacy. Her son the Emperor Joseph found the arrangement delightful. The whole court has vowed to take it up in their entertainments." The Cardinal-Prince laughed. "Tell Schreiber to arrange the seating according to this list."

The Abbé persisted. "It *is* a violation of court protocol, Your Eminence, one certain to displease the Empress."

"If it comes to that, I shall tell the old bitch that I am simply following her daughter's example at Versailles. Marie Antoinette has the entire court reeling in shock over her constant abuse of ceremony. She's like a wild child. I shall cite the Empress chapter and verse, never fear. Here, take this list to Schreiber. He will know what to do with it."

4

Now it was Böhmer's turn to be angry. In Böhmer's world catastrophe lay ever in wait, ready to spring upon and destroy the unprepared, the unsuspecting. On this day in early May of 1774 Böhmer felt fully vindicated in his fretful gloom. Two days before, disaster had blazed anew in the Böhmer and Bassenge establishment when the old King Louis XV had died and forever whisked his bottomless purse beyond the crown jewelers' grasp. Böhmer and Bassenge had been in the palace at Versailles since sunrise, dragging along despondently from one antechamber to another in the futile hope of paying their respects to the new King and Queen. The late afternoon sun had begun to settle over the gardens, and the vast antechambers smelled of damp and decay. In the distance they could hear the high-heeled clatter of courtiers swarming noisily around the young King and Queen like hungry geese in a barnyard at feeding time.

"His Majesty is on his way to the King's Chapel," Böhmer said dully.

"He's very pious, they say," Bassenge sighed.

"Indeed. Pious kings don't buy jewelry for their mistresses. Pious kings don't have mistresses. Do they, Bassenge?"

Bassenge pretended to be listening to the waning sound of the courtiers' heels on the marble floors. He knew that at any minute Böhmer would lash out at him for having let the Comtesse Du Barry slip through their fingers. "You should have shown her the design! You should have secured the King's word! He would have bought anything the slut told him to buy," Böhmer had stormed when they first heard the terrible news. But Böhmer had no real understanding of the artistic temperament. He was a journeyman designer, not to put too fine a point on it. Bassenge knew in his heart that if he had shown the drawing of the diamond necklace to the Comtesse Du Barry at any point before its completion, she would have left him no peace until she had it fastened around her neck. Bassenge had insisted on taking his time; he had insisted on perfection. And now the spectacular necklace was complete in all its glory, and the old king was dead, and the necklace languished in the jewelers' vault in a gold-tooled red Cardan leather case slightly larger than a doormat.

"The young King dotes on Queen Marie Antoinette," Bassenge said hopefully. "He thinks nothing is too good for her."

"The problem is, he can't pay her gambling debts *and* buy her jewelry." Böhmer glanced sullenly around the vast room. "He has only just finished paying us for the diamond bracelets she bought two years ago. He's a dull man, to be sure, but even he may figure out that he can ill afford a necklace that costs a king's ransom.

"Well, there are occasions when a gift of some splendor is mandatory for a Queen." Bassenge was not about to assume full responsibility for being left high and dry with the most expensive piece of jewelry ever created. "The birth of a child of France, for example. A son, an heir."

Böhmer laughed and laughed, a high, explosive laugh full of despair and frustration. "You've been stuck away in your workroom too long, my friend. It's been four years now, and the King has not yet been able to consummate the marriage! I wouldn't look for a son and heir any time soon if I were you. The King needs an operation and refuses to have it. He says that if it had been God's will that he have a son and heir, God would not have given him this . . . handicap. Or whatever it is. Pious prig! We'll get no maternity gifts out of him." Impatiently, Böhmer rubbed his clammy wet hands with a fine lace handkerchief.

"Miracles do happen," Bassenge said meekly.

"Perhaps. But I haven't seen many lately. In the meantime, we must think seriously of breaking up the diamond necklace and selling some of the stones separately to begin paying our creditors."

"Never! Never! Never!" Bassenge wailed.

5

A fine, chilling rain seeped from the lowering clouds. The six horses strained and slipped, the heavy carriage rolled and pitched as it made its way slowly up the hill. Cardinal-Prince Louis de Rohan pushed aside the curtain and stared at the empty fields where tattered fragments of mist drifted here and there over the stubble. He could not remember when he had ever been so angry. Recalled! Not even allowed to say goodbye to his friends. To his hosts of friends. All Vienna loved him. Especially those larkish, bedworthy Austrian women. Recalled! Hot, throttling rage that made his ears ring and his heart pound swept over him. His anger kept him from falling into a despondent torpor.

In the distance he could make out the spindly steeple of a village church. Surely they would find a decent inn there, some hot food, a bottle of wine, a change of horses. He was hungry.

The Abbé Georgel muttered and turned in his sleep. His breviary slipped off his lap and fell to the floor of the carriage. The Cardinal leaned forward and covered the Abbé's knees with a fur lap rug. It was a brisk spring afternoon, the Cardinal's foot brazier had gone cold, and his feet, in thin leather boots, ached.

The carriage lurched and began to slide down the other side of the hill. He would push on until he reached his estates at Ettenheim, in Baden, across the Rhine from Strasbourg. With letters already en route to his uncle the Prince de Soubise, he could reasonably expect most of the members of his family to gather at the chateau as early as the beginning of the following week. His niece, the Comtesse de Guémenée, one of Marie Antoinette's ladies-in-waiting, would be among them, and he counted on her to give him a better idea of how much his letter had damaged him in the Queen's eyes.

He rubbed his forehead and closed his eyes. The damage his letter had done? Wasn't it obvious? The way the Baron de Bretueil had strutted around the embassy in Vienna, like a fat cock taking over the barnyard, crowing about how much Marie Antoinette counted on him to set matters right after such grievous offense to the Empress Maria Theresa, and of course to her daughter. Bretueil, large, oafish, porcine, could never forgive the Cardinal his virile beauty, his easy charm, his joyous love of life. The Cardinal remembered Bretueil's gloating face and shuddered. Damn, damn, damn.

But how in God's name, he asked himself, did his letter making fun of Maria Theresa's sham of weeping over the partition of Poland fall into the hands of the Comtesse Du Barry? From the Duc d'Aiguillon, for a certainty. As thick as thieves, those two, the Duc and La Du Barry. How could Louis XV have made a man as weak-headed as the Duc d'Aiguillon Minister of Foreign Affairs? That letter meant only for the Minister and the King never should have fallen into the Comtesse's hands in the first place. There was no point in blaming La Du Barry for pulling out the letter and reading it aloud at a dinner party. She meant no harm. Mindless women do stupid, thoughtless things. She found the letter witty. Everyone did. It *was* witty.

And now the old king was dead, his black and bloated corpse sealed in a coffin and spirited away one dark night in 1774 to Saint Denis for burial. Even so, along the way enough people had realized who was in the plain pine box to cover it with spittle before it reached its resting place among the kings of France. And that pious bigot of a grandson who still had not figured out how to fulfill his marital duty to his lovely wife now sat on the old king's throne.

"I do beg your pardon, Your Eminence," the Abbé said, straightening his back. He looked more careworn than ever, his deep-set, hooded eyes doleful.

"Why?"

"I fell asleep. I hadn't meant to."

"There's nothing wrong with sleep, Georgel. Not yet. I understand that even members of the Austrian court are known to indulge from time to time. I wish that I . . ." He could not trust himself to continue. He hated self-pity, a loathsome weakness. "I've been thinking about that damned letter."

"It wasn't *just* the letter, Prince," the Abbé said gently. "You know that. You've read enough of the Empress's letters over the past year to realize that the unfortunate letter was simply an *occasion*, an opportunity not to be missed to do what the Empress has wanted to do since the day you arrived in Vienna."

"Of course. You're quite right. I still can't understand why the old bitch hound hated me so much." The Cardinal, surrounded by love and affection since the day he was born, had a difficult time comprehending the mechanics of hatred. "I was a *good* ambassador for France, Georgel." The Cardinal could see the village taking shape out of the damp mists. He felt suddenly overwhelmed by his humiliation. "But what does that matter now? What does any of it matter now that the new Queen despises me?" He turned to Abbé Georgel with a puzzled look and said, "But they adored me in Vienna! They idolized me. The Emperor Joseph, the Chancellor, they couldn't wait for invitations to my parties."

"I'm afraid that's what alarmed the Empress. You've read her letters, Prince. You know what she told her daughter about you. The Empress was nervous about her Viennese ladies; she thought you had bewitched them. She feared you were corrupting her nobility."

"But they loved France, and everything French, because of me. Isn't that what an ambassador is supposed to do? Turn old enemies into warm friends? I did that, Monsieur l'Abbé. The new King cannot fault me on that."

"Certainly not, Your Eminence."

The Prince closed his eyes and rested his head against a cushion. His lean, refined face seemed to the Abbé the very epitome of noble beauty. The Abbé studied him with growing melancholy. A fatal gift, this charming physical presence, a terrible distraction from the illustrious future the Cardinal should be preparing for himself. Instead, here he was, returning in ignominy to France. And the Cardinal would never truly understand why he had excited the Empress's animosity.

"I believe, however," the Abbé said, "that the King, who appears to be extremely pious, will be offended by some aspects of your life in Austria."

"What on earth are you talking about?" the Cardinal said, his dark eyes alert.

For a moment the Abbé lost his courage. What was the use, really? The Cardinal would never understand. Feigning a cramped muscle, the Abbé bent over and began to rub the calf of his left leg. "The Empress, if you recall, repeatedly refers—in censorious terms— to the conduct of a certain young woman in your entourage."

"You mean the Marquise de Marigny?"

"Naturally. The young woman who dressed as a choir boy and insisted on accompanying you on your travels." The Abbé flushed. "The Empress found the behavior of the Marquise de Marigny scandalous."

The Cardinal shrugged. "The Marquise is a passionate woman. She cared most deeply for me. Besides, she's French. What concern is she to the Empress of Austria?"

The wheels of the carriage rang out as they hit the wet cobblestoned streets of the village, shuttered tightly against the damp cold.

"Where is the Marquise, by the way?" the Cardinal said with a yawn. "I've completely lost track of her." He had grown careless with the Marquise, to be sure. She had a terrible habit of clinging to him that had turned her into a burden he no longer cared to bear. What he needed was a spirited woman, a daring, spitfire of a beauty who would make him laugh and never bore him with her tears.

6

The circular courtyard of the Boulainvilliers mansion in Passy had been bustling with carriages all afternoon. Lackeys scurried about in all directions searching for additional stables and fodder. Stableboys busily scooped and raked fresh horse droppings from the courtyard gravel as white and golden blossoms drifted down from the linden trees.

Everyone at court, it seemed, wanted to congratulate the Marquise de Boulainvilliers on her success in securing full honors of the Valois name for her foster children, those charming little beggars rescued from the streets of Paris. Rumors were rife that the King had awarded a pension to each of them, though how much no one could say for sure. More than a hundred guests, anxious to be present at this latest diverting spectacle, crowded into the elongated dining room overlooking the park. Footmen in the silver and blue livery of the Boulainvilliers household had to change their white serving gloves twice during the five-hour dinner party that had begun at two o'clock.

Jeanne surveyed the table triumphantly. At last, she thought, I've found the world my aristocratic nature craves. And this is where I intend to stay. Or soar higher. Why not? It is my due. As a Valois. Her heart was racing. She must forget all those years of humiliation hunched over a worktable in this or that modiste's shop. Buffeted back and forth, from one wretched establishment to another because of her fragile nerves. Who ever heard of a princess of the blood royal being forced to cut and stitch for any upstart stranger who happened to have a fat purse? What would those who had scoffed at her aristocratic pretensions say now? She smiled to herself and adjusted her pearl necklace.

The Marquise had placed her at the head of the table, at the place of honor, and her brother Jacques, who had just that day—May 6, 1775—been presented to young King Louis XVI and given the title of Baron de Valois, sat at the other end of the table. Soon he would be an officer in the navy, for the Marquis had purchased a commission for him. Her brother caught her eye and grinned. A tall, fair-haired young man, he cut a handsome figure in his presentation suit: a dark blue velvet coat with large red satin lapels, a pure white brocade waistcoat, and canary-yellow pants with white silk stockings. He wore black satin shoes with red high heels and large, floppy red satin bows. Jeanne watched him with pride. His table manners were excellent. True nobility, she said to herself.

"You look quite lovely, my dear," the Marquis de Boulainvilliers said, reaching out to take Jeanne's hand. He was a short, ample man with vivid purple and red grog blossoms spread over his large nose and broad cheeks. "Emerald green. It suits you. Sets off that glorious head of hair, Mademoiselle de Valois."

Jeanne felt a thrill, a sudden breathlessness, at the sound of her new title, her right to use the Valois name. So it was not a dream, after all. She freed her hand and lifted a wine glass. "Will you be sending for our sister Marianne now that the King has awarded us titles? You promised."

"The country lass? The one your charming mother put in a basket and left on a doorstep?" the Marquis said in a loud voice, lolling in his chair and glancing around to see whether he had an appreciative audience. No one looked his way.

"Put in a basket and hung at a window. That's the way the story goes," Jeanne said coldly. "My unfortunate sister, Mademoiselle de Saint-Rémy." From now on, it would be important to emphasize their new titles, even with the Boulainvilliers.

The Marquis leaned forward and lowered his voice. "I've been told that your sister is quite attractive. Blond. Rather too plump. But pretty as a picture." He winked and pinched Jeanne's arm.

"And stupid," Jeanne said sharply. "I shall have a deal of work in this house, keeping my sister out of harm's way."

The Marquis's eyes flashed with anger. His wig had slipped back on his head, and his forehead gleamed with perspiration. "I don't know what you mean. I should say that you've done rather well in this house, missy."

Jeanne studied his florid, congested face. She knew she had to be careful. This little toad of a man could be venomous when he cared to be. Thus far, she had played him like an accomplished musician at a clavichord. Timing was all.

"My foster mother has worked tirelessly on our behalf. Today we have the rewards. I am most grateful," she said.

"Rewards, indeed, yes, missy. Titles for the three of you, and a pension of eight hundred francs a year!"

"Eight hundred francs a year," Jeanne said scornfully, "Not exactly a princely sum. I wonder that the King thinks it sufficient for a Valois. It's insulting." She lifted her hand and fingered the glossy curl at her ear. "Oh, dear sir, I fear I shall need you now more than ever!" She lowered her eyes and looked up at him through her lashes.

The Marquis took her hand and squeezed it. "Never mind, my beauty," he whispered. "I shall always be there with a helping hand. You must never trouble your pretty head about money." He sighed. "Oh, Jeanne, I love it when you smile at me like that!"

Jeanne and her sister Marianne moved slowly down the broad avenue leading from the Bassin d'Apollon to the Grand Canal. The Queen had ordered a mock naval battle on the waterway for the afternoon's entertainment, and one of Jeanne's admirers, the young Comte de Blagny, had promised to save places for them. It had been a perfect summer, Jeanne thought, every day brought another promenade at Versailles and more admirers, eager to hear her story, fawning over her, anxious to take her arm for a stroll down the Galérie des Glaces. Once, standing in the Oeil de Boeuf salon, she had glimpsed the King coming out of Mass, though, to her mind, he looked nothing like a king. He was dressed in a snuff-brown ratteen suit, like a frugal bourgeois or maybe even a tradesman, and he wore no wig, only his own hair curled and powdered. He looked sturdy and athletic, it was said that he was a great hunter, but his sloped forehead gave him a common look, and his lips were too full and glossy.

"Can you imagine, Jeanne, the Queen! I shall see the Queen!" Marianne said, squeezing her sister's arm.

Jeanne tried not to be annoyed with Marianne. After all, she had never before been out of Champagne. Everything she saw was a sensation, a marvel, every sentence that came out of her mouth began, *Can you imagine!* After a while, it was tiresome, especially now that the novelty of her reunion with Marianne had faded. They had exhausted their common topics about people and places in their hometown, Bar-sur-Aube, though Jeanne never tired of reminiscing about life in the chateau de Fontette before that fearful night when their mother rousted them out of bed for the long walk to Paris. At Fontette she and Jacques had roved the fields, herding back and forth to pasture what few cows remained in their tumble-down barns, pinching fruit from the orchards of neighbors. But Marianne knew nothing of that life. She had been only a baby.

Jeanne affected a yawn, before replying. "You shall see the Queen *if* she attends. She's known to be capricious. You heard what the Marquis de Gramont said. The Queen is flighty." There was no reason to let Marianne know how excited she herself was. She could feel the vein throbbing at the base of her throat. The Queen! Why, it was almost unthinkable that she would see the Queen. This creature everyone talked about. Whose clothes and coiffures everyone imitated. All the stories, all the rumors. The courtiers gossiped that the King was impotent and that the Queen surrounded herself with her lovers. The King's brother, the Comte d'Artois, wasn't he one of them?

It was a long walk down the broad paths and stairway to the

canals. They could see the two ships, tacking slowly up the Grand Canal. The mock battle would take place at the intersection of the Petit Canal with the Grand Canal.

"You look superb, Jeanne. You always do. Just like a grand lady," Marianne said. She was a pleasant, easygoing young woman, quite happy to play the dumb country girl to her older sister.

"So do you. I should think we ought to look like grand ladies. Mademoiselle Lamarche doesn't give these frocks away, you know." Jeanne had experienced quite a few moments of triumph during the past months, but none as satisfying as her return as a titled customer to Mademoiselle Lamarche's shop. She had feasted on the look in Mademoiselle Lamarche's eyes for days.

True to his word, the Comte de Blagny had saved the two young women choice spots on the east bank of the Grand Canal.

"From this point we can see the two ships *and* the Queen and her party," said the Comte, a dark-haired Norman with a slight drawl and a tendency to fan the air with his hands. Jeanne tolerated his foppish affectations because he was so clearly infatuated with her. And his excited admiration had attracted other admirers. She had taken due note of that. A typical courtier, the Comte de Blagny had a resounding name, many debts, and no money.

"Work your elbows, dear child," he said to Marianne, "Or you'll lose your place. Here, Mademoiselle de Valois, stand next to me. You'll have a better view. They say that the crew of the *England* is quite determined to win, despite the fact that etiquette must have the *France* win for the Queen."

The two ships had drawn up facing each other. When the Queen and her party arrived, they would give a five-gun salute and begin the battle. The younger set at court made up the crowd. Though few would like to admit it, they trailed around after the Queen, hoping to catch her eye and eventually her favor. Her power was like a great magnet drawing them along. Only the Queen, it was said, had the power to name ambassadors, hand out preferments, and secure promotions. The King doted on her and could refuse her nothing.

The crowd was growing impatient when, in the distance, a brightly colored group of courtiers appeared at the very top of the stairs leading down from the chateau.

"It's the Queen," de Blagny said. "The one in the middle. Taller than the rest."

"The Queen?" Jeanne said, straining to see.

De Blagny tugged at her sleeve. "Do you know those letters they paint on houses in Paris? *M.A.C.L.*? Do you know what those letters mean?"

"Of course, I do," Jeanne said, annoyed. She did not want to be distracted. She had her eyes fixed on the tall, slim figure slowly descending the stairs. "They mean *maison assurée contre l'incendie*. All the houses insured against fire have those letters on the walls."

The Comte raised his voice. "No, my dear. Those letters actually stand for *Marie Antoinette cocufie Louis*. Marie Antoinette is cuckolding Louis!"

The group around them laughed, and there were a few scattered *bravos*. The Comte giggled proudly and nodded. Jeanne gave him a bright smile and poked him familiarly in the ribs with her elbow.

"What does *cocufie* mean?" Marianne whispered to Jeanne, and they laughed again.

"Take a guess," de Blagny said, but at that moment, as the Queen and her party came into full view, the crowd fell silent.

A young woman with the fresh, rosy scars of small pox whispered. "Do look! Aren't those the new diamond earrings the Queen is wearing? The chandelier earrings?"

"She wouldn't dare wear them in public yet," de Blagny said. "The King is not supposed to know she bought them. Poor fellow, if he finds out, he might even lose his head and try to reason with her. The national treasury will soon be empty if he can't keep her away from the gaming tables by night and Böhmer and Bassenge's jewelry shop by day."

The young woman said, "Those *are* the chandelier earrings! Why, they're enormous! The court jewelers say the Queen bargains like a fishwife. Quite a haggler."

"That's because she's passionate about diamonds and . . ." de Blagny rolled his eyes lewdly and the little group fanned themselves and smiled. Jeanne took de Blagny's arm and moved closer to his side. He seemed to know everything she wanted to learn about the court.

The Queen was walking toward them arm-in-arm with a pretty young woman dressed to perfection. The two women were deep in conversation and from time to time the Queen would take the pretty young woman's hand and bring it to her lips.

Jeanne was transfixed. "Who is that person with the Queen?"

"Ah, well, that is Yolande de Polignac," the Comte said with a wink.

A courtier on her left leaned forward and whispered in her ear, "The Queen's favorite."

"The favorite who has brought the whole impoverished Polignac clan into court in her wake. It's an infestation," de Blagny said bitterly. "The rest of us don't count anymore, those of us whose families have been at Versailles for generations. Without the Queen's generosity those petty schemers would still be hovering around their barren hearths in the provinces, shivering in their outmoded Louis XIV rags."

"Still, she's very pretty, isn't she?" Jeanne said.

"Ah, yes, the Queen is passing fond of pretty young women," de Blagny said and with a knowing look sniffed his handkerchief daintily.

The party turned at the bottom of the steps, and Jeanne could see the Queen quite clearly. She was dressed simply in pale yellow, a popular color called *cheveux de reine*, because it mimicked the blond and silver tones of the Queen's hair. As the party moved across the grass to a small, slightly elevated dais, the Queen put her arm around Yolande de Polignac's waist and led her forward to a chair. With a dismissive but charming smile the Queen refused a chair for herself, preferring to stand behind her friend, resting her hands on her shoulders.

The Queen's favorite, Jeanne repeated to herself, as if it were some magic incantation. She watched every move Yolande de Polignac made. Each time the Queen leaned down to whisper something to her friend, Jeanne felt sick with envy. What a fool I am, she thought, what a perfect fool. I imagined I had come so far. Congratulating myself on my new title, my pension. What a naive fool. When there is so much more to be had! Ambition, like a blinding flare, lit up her inner world and revealed its empty spaces.

During the entire afternoon, as the "battle" raged midst shouts, laughter, and catcalls, as guns boomed, sails snapped, and the two ships pitched and maneuvered, as officers fell merrily into the water, Jeanne, watching the Queen and her favorite, who seemed more interested in each other than in the battle, heard only a steady voice of discontent.

ᔑᘺᔓ

In the middle of the night Jeanne awakened to a sudden thump—or was it a roar?—somewhere in the house. She opened her eyes and stared into the darkness. She thought she heard footsteps running down below.

"Marianne! Wake up." Her sister slept heavily, her mouth gaping, snoring softly. Jeanne pushed at her shoulders. "Something's happened. I heard a noise."

Jeanne pulled on a shawl and opened the door to the hallway. A suffocating odor made her cough and gag. At the far end of the corridor she saw the Marquise, her nightcap askew, a shawl thrown over her nightgown, a bedside candle held aloft, groping her way in the darkness.

"What is it, maman? A fire? The smell, agggh, the smell. Like rotting plums."

"What could it be, Jeanne?" Her head bobbed furiously from side to side. Her gentle, weak eyes bulged in fear. "Something's happened in the wine cellar. I heard a loud noise. An explosion, it seemed."

"A thump. I heard a loud thump," Jeanne said. "I can't breathe. That smell!"

They stumbled toward the great marble staircase leading to the ground floor. Steam filled the grand foyer; the putrid odor of rotten fruit hovered in the air like a suffocating blanket.

Through the dense steam they saw the Marquis, his red face glistening, running up the stairs toward them.

"Get back, Madame! Back to bed, ladies." He stopped to catch his breath.

Cries of "Monsieur! Monsieur!" came from far below in the cellar.

"Never you mind, Madame. None of your affair," the Marquis said, turning to run back down the steps. "Coming, Gaston!"

"But, Monsieur! What is it? Monsieur!" The Marquise coughed and peered through the steam billowing up the staircase. Her husband had disappeared.

"Come along. I'll help you back to bed, maman," Jeanne took the candle from the Marquise and led her to her room. Jeanne knew very well what the pandemonium in the basement was about: the Marquis's illegal distillery had exploded.

"The house must be aired out from top to bottom! It's enough to make you sick," the Marquise said, "And the Comte de Clermont-Tonnerre is coming to call on our Gabrielle tomorrow. With my other two darlings married and settled, I have only my Gabrielle to worry about. Whatever will he think when he smells the house? Oh, I do so want a marriage contract from that one, Jeanne. It's my heart's only desire."

"Worry about that tomorrow," Jeanne said.

The sound of shouts and crashes resounded throughout the house. Jeanne could make out the high-pitched squeal of the Marquis. Well, he would be squealing even more when the King got through with him.

She found her sister Marianne sitting up in bed, her eyes still heavy with sleep. "That awful smell! What is it, Jeanne?"

"A disaster," Jeanne said. "Go back to sleep."

Jeanne sat beside the Marquise's bed after Dr. Perrault left. The curtains had been drawn, and a heavy silence, broken only by the Marquise's sobs, hung over the room.

"You mustn't cry, maman, you'll only make yourself sick," Jeanne said, her voice trembling. She wanted to break into sobs herself. She wanted to scream, yell, throw things, break things. Then she wanted to sit down and cry her heart out.

"I *am* sick, my dear. The scandal has broken me. My heart is broken. I shall never recover. Exile! The King is sending us into exile!" She began to sob again, her round face screwed up into a mask of pain. "Did the Comte de Clermont-Tonnerre call?"

"No."

"Did he at least send round his card? His footman? With perhaps some flowers for Gabrielle?"

"No. There have been no calls. No cards. No flowers. The street is quiet, as you can hear," Jeanne said. Yesterday at Versailles Jeanne and Marianne had twice crossed the path of the Comte de Blagny. He had looked straight past them, as if he had never seen them before. Jeanne had called his name, "Blaise!" she said, and he had colored a little and walked away to join a group of friends in the Princes Court.

"Gabrielle must be prostrate with grief," the Marquise said. "To have her family disgraced. Sent into exile by the King. To our estate at Montgéron, Jeanne! It's at the back of beyond. We shall all die of boredom within a fortnight. The Marquis finds the country intolerable. Those endless fields, the sheep, the cows, the toiling peasants, they depress him."

"He should have thought of that before he rigged up an illegal distillery in the cellar," Jeanne said. She could barely contain her rage. That little toad, what could he have been thinking of? Smashing her dreams. Just when everything seemed to be going beautifully. No one would ever know what dreams she had dreamed, even before the King acknowledged the Valois claims. She had imagined herself back at her dear Fontette, sumptuously installed, a little queen of her dominion, a true Valois princess. It was all over now. Why promenade in the gardens at Versailles if no one would look at you, or if they raised their fans and smirked? For Marianne the King's anger was just a part of this new world she didn't quite understand. She could go right back to the country and never feel the difference. A little adventure in Paris—can you imagine, I actually saw the Queen!—that's about all it would amount to. Jeanne's stomach turned over, and she began to cry softly.

"Please don't cry, Jeanne. If you cry, it only makes it worse for me." The Marquise tried to sit up against her pillows, then fell back dispiritedly. "I believe the Marquis simply wanted more money. He made quite a lot of it, he says, from the . . . the machine in the cellar. There's never enough money, Jeanne! The money seems already spoken for by the time it comes in from the estates. We must always be searching about for more and more. And there's the dowry for Gabrielle. Where's it to come from? My darling will have a nervous breakdown."

"Not yet," Jeanne said. "That peculiar American, Dr. Franklin, was in her boudoir this morning with another bagatelle he wrote for her. When I saw her last, she was giggling and cooing like a chambermaid." Gabrielle, or Mademoiselle de Passy as she was known at court, had the placid, self-assured beauty of a privileged aristocrat. Everyone loved her. Everyone found her adorable. Jeanne was not overly fond of her foster sister.

"Oh, our clever neighbor, the good Dr. Franklin. Such a friend. He dotes on Gabrielle like a father."

"Like a grandfather, you mean. The man is ancient. At his age running around writing verses for young ladies; it's ridiculous. Wearing those awful brown suits and that fur hat. Or cap. I can't tell which," Jeanne said.

"The ladies of Paris adore him. He's singular, Jeanne. A man of genius. The court is at his feet."

"Not the King. The King can't stand the sight of him. The Comte de Blagny told me so. The King has had a chamberpot especially made at Sèvres with a portrait of Benjamin Franklin painted on the bottom."

The Marquise hiccupped, then laughed merrily. "How malicious! How delightful! Is it really true, my dear? I've always said the King can be as witty as the next man when he chooses. A Sèvres chamberpot! Oh, my dear, how I shall miss the court! Such sweet slander! Such cruelty! I shall never find it in the country!" The Marquise turned her head into the pillows and began to weep again.

Jeanne got up and walked over to the window. Down below the courtyard was deserted. Not a single lackey to be seen, not even stirring around the stables beyond the grove of linden trees. The silence in the house was appalling. At this hour the house should have been bustling with footmen laying out the service for the dinner hour, and the kitchen and scullery noisy with chopping, stirring, baking. And in the drawing room scores of guests should have been milling about chatting, gossiping, peacocking around in their sumptuous clothes. Already the servants had begun to shroud the drawingroom in heavy linen dust covers, the mirrors, the pictures, the furniture.

Jeanne turned slowly away from the window. She looked at the Marquise apprehensively. "You've said nothing about Marianne and me."

"You will be all right, my dear. Never fear."

Jeanne bit her underlip. "I'm not afraid. Why should I be? I simply want to know, what's to become of me and my sister?"

The Marquise had rolled over toward the wall and kept her back turned to Jeanne. "Taking you with us into exile, well, of course, that's not possible, is it? And the house must be closed up here in Passy, for we can't possibly manage to keep it up, can we? Not with having to reduce our expenses now that . . . the, ah, machine in the cellar is quite . . . ah, ruined. We must . . ."

"So where shall we go. Marianne and I?"

"I'm afraid, dear child, there is really nothing . . ." The Marquise turned to face her foster daughter. "You're to go into a convent."

"A convent!"

"Yes, with your pension, you'll be able to live there rather comfortably, I would say. The Abbaye de Longchamps, my dear. The very best. You'll find only the cream of the aristocracy there. The King himself has secured your place. Now, don't start in with your angry looks, Jeanne. Listen to me. The Abbaye de Longchamps is not some dingy cloister in the provinces. You're going to find titled young widows retired there, and wives whose husbands are away on military campaigns will be there to while away a few months or years. It will be lively, gay. There will be music, amateur theatricals, fashionable visitors, gossip. Doesn't it sound like the perfect place for you and Marianne? What do you think?"

"What does it matter what I think?" Jeanne said.

7

"Claude, are you absolutely sure there is a *particule?* After all, you never can tell about these country folk. I mean, sometimes they make themselves aristocrats just by adding a *de* to their name, and nobody knows the difference." Surrounded by sunlight, Jeanne sat writing at a small, rickety table near the window of the low, dingy room.

"I'm certain of it. *Monsieur et Madame de Surmont.* They would be outraged if anyone even presumed to doubt their blue blood. They take themselves for the *crème de la crème* of Bar society," Beugnot said.

When Claude Beugnot and his friends heard that two princesses had leapt their convent walls and pitched up in Bar-sur-Aube at the Auberge de la Tête-Rouge, ostensibly an inn with cheap lodgings but in reality the local brothel, they hooted with laughter, then decided to call on these so-called princesses.

What started out as a joke left Beugnot as perplexed as he had ever been. He went away from his first meeting with Jeanne reeling with an excitement that refused to leave him, night or day. He lost his appetite and slept poorly. And since nothing relieved his tormenting symptoms like being with Jeanne, he began to spend his every waking moment with her and her sister, much to his bourgeois family's concern.

"The point is, do you think the Surmonts will take Marianne and me in? I'm desperate," Jeanne said, sealing the letter.

"Without question. This morning Madame de Surmont herself assured me that it would be an honor to welcome you to her home."

Beugnot did not tell Jeanne how difficult it had been to persuade Madame de Surmont's husband to take in two strangers known around Bar-sur-Aube as the offspring of the Baron de Saint-Rémy, a good-for-nothing poacher who had married a slatternly serving woman of appalling fecundity. Beugnot, however, was a young man determined to rescue his damsel in distress.

"Well, I haven't had much luck with the local aristocrats. Not one even deigned to answer my letters. Stupid clods. They'll never have another princess of the blood royal begging their hospitality."

"Never mind, the Surmonts are ready to welcome you with open arms," Beugnot said, hoping that it would be so. Madame de Surmont was, in truth, in a twitter and duly impressed by Jeanne's Valois title. "But I warn you, Madame de Surmont is the nosy sort. She may ask you why you left the convent."

Jeanne laughed and smoothed her hair in long, graceful strokes. Those two years in the convent after the explosion, the exposure, and the Boulainvilliers' fall from grace had been a nightmare for Jeanne, though Marianne had been content enough. "Why, Mother Superior punished me one time too many by making me kneel on beans to say my prayers. I tell you, my knees are a sight to see," Jeanne said with a pretty pout and a look that was like a bolt of lightning to Beugnot's overheated system.

"Shall we go for our walk?" she asked, reaching for her shawl. "To our favorite spot in the willow grove along the river?"

Marianne was cranky and tired of her older sister's bullying. "I don't think we should ever have left the convent," she said, reluctantly unpacking her bags. "I was perfectly happy there. The food was wonderful, and Sister Lucie promised that next year I could help her in the infirmary."

"Hmmph! Sister Lucie and her promises! How can you be such a simpleton?" Jeanne said. Marianne was proving to be an exasperating burden, a plump, pretty lump. "We're far better off back in the world. Another year in that convent, and they would have had to cart me off to the madhouse!"

Jeanne had known from the beginning that the convent, no matter how fashionable, would be a disaster. To be sure, there were plenty of titled ladies moving in and out, endless gossip about the young Queen and her racy friends, but the constant patter about life in Paris and the court had merely whetted Jeanne's appetite to get back to Versailles. What use were her new title and a royal pension if she had no estates from which to draw income? No, there was still a battle to be won, obstacles to be overcome. Marianne was such a child. She had no idea of what made the world go round. Why waste time in a convent when they could be out in the world, more precisely back in Bar-sur-Aube, making powerful allies in the quest to regain their ancestral Valois domain of Fontette?

"Where shall I put my gowns?" Marianne said, her voice edged with a whine. "You've taken all the space in the armoire."

"Then we'll have Monsieur de Surmont give us another armoire," Jeanne said.

"How long are we going to stay here? I'd rather stay with Monsieur Durand. He's like a father to me," Marianne said.

"*Seigneur!* What nonsense! What kind of social connections does Farmer Durand have, pray? The Surmonts may not be much, but at least they're the best Bar-sur-Aube has to offer. We aren't here to please ourselves, Marianne, I keep reminding you. We're here to find out how to reclaim Fontette. Now, are you ready? Monsieur de Surmont has agreed to drive us to Mass at Fontette."

Monsieur de Surmont felt quite proud of himself, squiring around two Valois princesses in his spanking-new berline. No one else in Bar had one like it, of course. Everyone expected the Surmonts to be at the vanguard of the latest fashion. After all, he was the town Provost, the head of the police and judge of civil and criminal court, and a member of the King's council for the province. In short, Monsieur de Surmont was First Citizen of Bar-sur-Aube, and when young Claude Beugnot had prevailed upon the Surmonts to take in the young Valois princesses stranded without a sou at the Auberge de la Tête Rouge, Monsieur de Surmont had been reluctant, to say the least. Now here he was escorting them to High Mass at the little church of Fontette, where Jeanne and Marianne had been baptized.

Personally, Monsieur de Surmont felt twenty years younger since the vivacious Jeanne de Valois had come into his house and into his life. Somehow each day opened up with exciting possibilities, and he knew that he would do just about anything to see that wicked smile of hers unfurl across her face. She was a devil of a girl, all right, and the prettiest thing he ever hoped to see, no matter that her mouth was a bit too broad and her features a trifle too irregular to be a bonafide beauty. But those bewitching blue eyes!

With a sigh Monsieur de Surmont pulled the berline to a halt and surrendered the reins to a peasant standing outside the small church of Fontette, the ruins of the ancient chateau, its crumbling roof visible across the sunny fields.

"Come along, my dears," Monsieur de Surmont said, gathering the two girls under his arms.

When they entered the musty little church and all the peasants rose to pay their respects, Monsieur de Surmont swelled with pride. One of the landed gentry, dressed in his Sunday best black ratteen, came forward and ushered them to the pew that the lords of Fontette had always occupied. Jeanne turned to Monsieur de Surmont with a dazzling smile.

"Are you happy now, Jeanne de Valois?" Monsieur de Surmont asked in a whisper.

"Oh, yes! Dear Fontette! This is my destined place!" she said and crossed herself.

After the consecration of the bread and wine, the curate, a wizened old man with a rheumy wheeze, stepped down from the altar and brought the sacraments to their seats so that they could take communion like aristocrats without leaving their pew.

Just as tradition decrees, Jeanne thought, trembling with excitement. After Mass, outside the church, the peasants crowded around the splendidly dressed young girls, doffing their hats, grinning and bobbing obsequiously.

"You must give our good villagers a *pourboire* to drink to our continued health and happiness!" Jeanne whispered, tugging at Monsieur de Surmont's sleeve.

"What? How much?"

"Six francs," she said grandly. "It's the royal custom."

🙠

"I won't have it under my roof!" Madame de Surmont raged. "People all over town are talking. I can't very well tell the Bishop de Langres never to set foot in this house again, you know that as well as I do! So it is up to you to discourage the man."

Madame de Surmont, a broad, ruddy-faced woman enormously proud of her social standing, bitterly rued the day she had ever gone to the Auberge de la Tête Rouge and begged Jeanne de Valois and her sister to accept the hospitality of her home. She had expected the girls to stay a week, possibly two, but it would soon be a year since this blue-eyed hellion had darkened her door, turned her husband into an infatuated, drooling fool, and set tongues wagging about her frequent, prolonged outings in the Bishop de Langres's carriage. Finally, Madame de Surmont had had enough. As soon as she finished her morning croissant and jam, she stormed out to the orangery, a new sunroom added to the house on Jeanne's insistence that it was a necessity for any house of distinction.

Jeanne looked up from her sewing, her deep blue eyes wide with bewilderment. "Discourage my spiritual adviser? Be rude to this wonderful man who has been kindness itself to me and my unfortunate sister? Is that what you are asking?"

"I am asking that you put an end to this nasty gossip circulating around town. This is my home, young lady! I can ill afford . . ."

"Nasty gossip? About me and the Bishop?" Jeanne said, her voice laden with innocent incredulity.

"You know exactly what I mean, and don't sit there pretending to be a vestal virgin! You can't fool me, Jeanne de Valois. The Bishop de Langres has a certain reputation . . . as far as women are concerned. He's forever getting someone in a scrape. And you're just the sort of woman . . ."

"Aaagh! This town is such a boring place!" Jeanne said, throwing aside her sewing and getting to her feet. "There's nothing to do! Why shouldn't I go for drives with the charming Bishop? He's certainly more entertaining than the yokels who frequent this gloomy house."

"*This gloomy house!* Why, you impudent little ingrate!"

"Please, dear Madame de Surmont, calm yourself," Jeanne said sweetly. "I only meant that no one has a private theater here. In all the grand houses of Paris and Versailles we entertain ourselves with amateur theatricals. We put on plays by our favorite authors and make our own costumes and have rehearsals, but here in Bar, what is there to look forward to in the evenings?"

"The Duc de Penthièvre has a private theater," Madame de Surmont said after a moment.

"You see?"

"And at the Chateau de Brienne someone told me they're rehearsing another Molière. The Michaux, you know, they're terribly refined and discriminating, were invited to see *Tartuffe* and loved it."

"Of course! Quite frankly, not having a private theater—let's see, how can I put this politely?—well, as far as I'm concerned, I would find not having a private theater a terrible embarrassment!"

Decidedly, the citizens of Bar-sur-Aube never ceased to be amazed by the prodigious "smartness" of Monsieur and Madame de

Surmont. Who would have thought that anyone without the space and resources of a chateau could install such a charming little theater in his residence? In the twinkle of an eye and at extortionary expense, the capacious attic of the Surmont townhouse had been turned into a perfect jewel of a stage, and now the fashionable set in town waited nervously for their invitations to the first Surmont production, a Molière comedy, of course.

As far as Jeanne de Valois was concerned, Madame de Surmont had drawn in her claws somewhat. This latest success with the private theater had plunged the whole town and even some of the local aristocracy into a serious state of envy. There was no way Madame de Surmont could avoid giving Jeanne credit for that, much as she tried. Jeanne's long afternoon drives with the Bishop de Langres continued, though more erratically now that her time was taken up with the forthcoming play.

"I do believe, my dear, that Mademoiselle de Valois's enthusiasm for the Bishop is waning. Pray to God that it is so," Madame de Surmont said to her husband one evening as they prepared for bed.

"Oh, what makes you say that? Not that I ever believed for one minute that the Bishop de Langres could ever turn the head of a young beauty like Jeanne," Monsieur de Surmont said.

"A beauty? Jeanne?" Madame de Surmont said. "Well, I myself would never go that far. At any rate, I do believe she's got her eye on my nephew."

"Nicolas de La Motte! That loafer! Jeanne has more sense than to tie herself down with that drone!"

"Nicolas has brilliant prospects for advancement in the cavalry. Everyone says so. He has wonderful manners. He's a man of the world. Just the sort of man Jeanne needs. Mark my words, many a woman would envy her if she lands him. I've seen the women eyeing him. He cuts a dashing figure in his scarlet uniform. Women go mad for uniforms! That silver-brimmed hat! Swaggering around with his red cape draped over his broad shoulders! Oh, Jeanne knows a fine figure of a man when she sees one, I've no doubt."

Monsieur de Surmont yawned. "The fact of the matter is: Nicolas de La Motte is a wastrel, and Jeanne is a proud woman. Look at her treatment of young Beugnot, who's been mooning around her since she came to town. The Beugnots are as rich as Croesus, but they're bourgeois, so that's an end to it. Jeanne would never stoop to marry a man like La Motte, so far beneath her socially."

"Hmmph," Madame de Surmont said, "Beggars can't be choosers."

❦

A smattering of cherry blossoms drifted across the garden and landed on the terrace at Jeanne's feet. She stooped and picked up a blossom and sat staring straight ahead, tearing the blossom apart, petal by petal. The Bishop de Langres, a tall man with fine, strangely vulpine features, paced the terrace, his hands behind his back.

"I'm exhausted," he said, flinging himself into a chair opposite Jeanne. "I can't bear the idea of another trip to Paris to argue with your foster father, the Marquis. Such a pig-headed man!"

Jeanne said nothing as she crushed another cherry blossom and rubbed the petals between her fingers. It was a cool, sunny afternoon in late May. Jeanne wore a pale cream cashmere shawl, a gift from the Bishop, around her shoulders. Her thick chestnut hair fell loosely down her back.

"Do you think the Marquise de Boulainvilliers would be more amenable to your marriage? Would she agree to sign the contract?" the Bishop asked, his youthful face strained.

"I should think not," Jeanne said, lifting her chin imperiously, turning away from him.

"It's too exasperating!" the Bishop said angrily. "Why not?"

"Because Nicolas de La Motte is low," Jeanne said with a contemptuous toss of her head.

The Bishop leaned forward and cradled his head in his hands.

"My dearest Jeanne," he said finally, "Talk to me, please. Tell me what you're thinking."

Jeanne turned around and looked at him coldly. "I'm thinking that I will never be able to endure waking up every morning and having to look at Nicolas de La Motte's dreadful nose lying on the pillow next to mine."

"Jeanne! Jeanne!" the Bishop pleaded. "This is no time to talk about noses. Please be serious."

"I *am* serious," Jeanne said angrily. "I have such dreams! You cannot imagine the plans I have, such glorious schemes, of one day regaining Fontette, and possibly the other estates, too—why not?— of returning to Versailles in fine frocks and handsome carriages and knowing all the right people and dining with them and going about with them and having the Queen take my hand and fawn over me as we stroll through the gardens and everyone looks at me . . . envious . . ."

"Jeanne! Do stop! You'll drive yourself mad with these fancies!"

"Well, I don't fancy Nicolas de La Motte," she said, her voice harsh. "He doesn't fit into my dreams at all!"

The Bishop folded his hands and stared at his shoes. "It's just that . . . you must be reasonable, my dear. In your present predicament . . ."

"I know. Beggars can't be choosers," Jeanne said testily. How in God's name had she been cornered like this? Six months pregnant and no choice but to marry a dull nobody whose only ability was sitting a horse properly. A nephew to Madame de Surmont to boot. The Bishop was so nervous that he could barely sit still. Well, he should be. After all . . . Still, she didn't blame him. How could she, when from the very first time she saw him, walking toward her across the Surmont drawing room, she had been faint with desire, when just to touch the buttons of his overcoat made her lust for him. No, she blamed her stupid, female body which hadn't let her get away with anything, not even a few wildly carnal hours in the Bishop's barouche.

"I was thinking of that distant relative of yours, the Sieur de Bonchemin," the Bishop said. "Perhaps he would be willing to sign the marriage contract as your guardian. I give up on the Marquis de Boulainvilliers. What do you think?"

Jeanne shivered and pulled the shawl up around her neck. "Do whatever you like," she said finally.

The Bishop sighed and permitted himself a slight smile. "The wedding banns will be posted immediately at the church of Fontette. You would like that, wouldn't you? And the date . . . we shall set the date of the wedding for June 6. At midnight. The traditional hour for nuptials in Champagne. What do you think?"

Jeanne sat looking at the crushed pink petals in her lap and said nothing.

"And I shall perform the ceremony myself," the Bishop said brightly.

Jeanne looked at him with a bitter smile. "Oh, lovely," she said.

8

Jubilation filled the country. Dancers mobbed the streets, dungeons released their prisoners, peasants abandoned their fields, and shops closed all over the land as old and young, rich and poor rushed into churches where *Te Deums* rang out in praise and thanksgiving. A dauphin! On the twenty-second of October, 1781, a son and heir was born to the King and Queen of France.

Of course, this was not the first royal birth. After Marie Antoinette's brother Joseph visited Versailles and refused to leave until the King allowed the royal doctor to snip away the small but disastrous piece of skin that kept Louis impotent, the Queen quickly conceived and gave birth in 1778 to a girl, Madame Royale. There was much rejoicing on this occasion, to be sure, but nothing compared with the eruption of joy following the birth of the precious Dauphin.

Immediately after the momentous event one hundred and three couriers mounted their horses to race with the glorious news to the four corners of the kingdom and all over Europe. Louis's joy rendered him foolish. Tears splashed down his fat cheeks; speechless, ecstatic, the King went from window to window of the palace holding up his newly born son for the mobs to see.

A special courier raced to the Palais-Cardinal in the Marais section of Paris to fetch Cardinal-Prince Louis de Rohan, Grand Almoner to the King. Two hours following the birth of the Dauphin, the Cardinal baptized him in the King's Chapel of the palace. Throughout the brief ceremony the King wept noisily.

For weeks a mood of hilarity reigned in the palace. Jokes

proliferated among the wags and wits of court over the name of the peasant wet nurse chosen for the Dauphin. The wife of one of the gardeners at the chateau de Sceaux, the wet nurse's name, aptly enough, was Madame Poitrine, and courtiers vied with each other in bringing their traditional gifts of finery to her in order to bring back stories of her spectacular bosom, her excellent milk, and her good health.

The King's mood could not be more propitious, Böhmer thought, as he hurried along to his appointment, the enormous red jewel case balanced awkwardly under his left arm. A group of courtiers standing near the Oeil de Boeuf looked up as Böhmer approached and broke into laughter.

In tense moments Böhmer had an unfortunate tendency to break into a profuse sweat that made his round face glow. He longed to run his nice large handkerchief over his face. The courtiers fell silent and stared at him mockingly as he passed by. Böhmer knew that he had become a figure of ridicule, forever running to the palace with the diamond necklace tucked under his arm whenever a rumor floated that the Queen might be pregnant. A desperate man always cuts a ridiculous figure, and Böhmer and his partner Bassenge were certainly desperate.

They had tried everything. Böhmer had traveled for two years with a paste copy of the diamond necklace from court to court in Europe. There had been an occasional, promising flare of interest. The King and Queen of the Two Sicilies had kept his heart beating faster for months, but nothing came of it. Later he learned that their kingdom was so poor that the monarchs were merely pipe-dreaming; never could they have afforded the princely necklace. The ambassador from Portugal strung Böhmer and Bassenge along for at least a year, haggling over a price cut that would make the necklace a wedding gift for the Infanta.

In the meantime, the jewelers' creditors were becoming more vicious and threatening by the day. Still, Bassenge would not give up his dream, his bid for artistic immortality, and now Böhmer was committed to that dream as well. Somehow, adversity had brought the two partners closer together and made them more determined not to abandon their masterpiece. Especially at a time when the King of France would have moved heaven and earth if doing so would give his queen the slightest bit of pleasure.

To his immense satisfaction Böhmer was ushered directly into the King's presence as soon as a chamberlain saw him enter the anteroom of the royal cabinet. The King, his foot resting on a low table, was bent over, busily scraping mud from his boot.

The King chuckled happily as Böhmer made a low bow.

"What have you there, Böhmer, eh?" the King said, his voice loud and jovial. "Not the famous necklace!" He laughed cheerfully and gave Böhmer a jocular wink.

"Majesty," Böhmer said with another bow, "I have the honor . . ."

"Wonderful hunting today, Böhmer," the King said. "Two boars."

"How very fine, Your Majesty!"

"I'll just make a note of it in my diary. I'll only be a moment." The King removed a brown leather notebook from his desk and thumbed through the pages. He studied the entries for a moment before dipping his pen and carefully writing *29 October 1781— two boars.* The King went hunting every day of his life, and in his private diary only the results of his kill were recorded. Pages and pages of this diary, even on the day he married his beloved Queen, even on the day his son was born, bore the single entry: *Nothing.*

Böhmer pulled out his handkerchief and mopped his brow. The King was still absorbed in his diary. He looked up with a smile and motioned to Böhmer to place the jewel case on the desk.

"Open it, Böhmer. Let's have a look at your treasure."

Böhmer fumbled with the intricate clasp to the case, and as he lifted the lid, the diamonds of the necklace flashed as if exploding with light. Instinctively, the King quickly drew back. He stood very still and stared at the necklace. Surreptitiously, Böhmer wiped his brow and placed the handkerchief back in this pocket.

"A thing of great beauty indeed," the King murmured.

Böhmer was afraid to trust his voice to say anything. He did not want to spoil the moment; he did not want to intrude on the King's entranced admiration of the necklace.

"Magnificent!" the King whispered as if to himself.

The King turned slowly toward Böhmer. "A necklace fit only for the most beautiful of women," the King said gravely, his eyes filling with tears. "And the best of wives."

9

"Where could that silly maid have gone," the Marquise said. "She knows I need her more than ever when I travel. Jeanne, dear, help me with these pins, will you? I shall faint if I can't get more air."

The Marquise de Boulainvilliers searched her reticule once again for her smelling salts. She felt weak and tremulous, and her room at the shabby little inn was damp and drafty. She was on her way to Strasbourg to consult the latest sensation, the Count Cagliostro, who was said to prophesy the future, heal the sick, and commune with the dead. The Marquis had thoroughly disapproved of her journey to Strasbourg. He thought she was demented to put up with the discomfort of dank inns and bumpy roads in the cold and rain of October just to talk with this Cagliostro, who might be just another charlatan or quack for all anyone knew. But the Marquis had no idea how desperate she was in her grief for her darling Gabrielle.

The Marquise passed the smelling salts under her nose several times.

"You mustn't fret yourself, maman," Jeanne said. "The important thing is that you are now back in your rightful place at court, the Marquis's foolishness forgiven by the King."

"Oh, the King, the King . . . who can understand the mind of a king? No, the turmoil of the past few years has been too much to bear. They've marked me. All those friends who came to eat at my table and curry my favor, then to turn their backs on us when the distillery blew up and the King sent us into exile from court. Worse yet, they mocked us with vile rhymes and songs that bill stickers plastered all over Paris. Laughed out of court. I thought I would die of shame. Then the bleak vacancy of life at Montgéron, the gentry gaping at us as if we were exotic animals, aping our clothes, our speech, our manners. It was too appalling."

Jeanne sprinkled a handkerchief with rosewater and gently patted the Marquise's brow. The Marquise noted that Jeanne was smartly dressed, which she took to be a good sign, in a high-quality silk dress, Lyon silk no doubt, with a blue and white striped petticoat. She was not wearing mourning clothes for Gabrielle, but then Jeanne was always one to ignore custom when it pleased her to do so. The Marquise fought back tears. How could anyone have foreseen the tragedy that would come out of that blissful day when the Comte de Clermont-Tonnerre, faithful to his vows, took her beloved Gabrielle as his bride in one of the most dazzling wedding spectacles the court had seen in years. Who could have foreseen that her darling Gabrielle would die in childbirth?

"I can't understand why on earth you left the convent, Jeanne. None of this . . . this business in Bar-sur-Aube would have happened. This chaotic existence . . . It breaks my heart."

The Marquise was exhausted, and all the promise and consolation of her journey had faded when Jeanne had suddenly appeared in her lodgings. The Marquise knew by the haughty look on Jeanne's face that she was in some kind of trouble. She always was. Lately. But she was prettier somehow than ever before. She had blossomed into a truly winsome creature.

"How many times do I have to tell you? The King would like nothing better than to keep Marianne and me behind convent walls. When I found out that he had offered my brother Jacques an abbey, I knew exactly what the King was up to. No more Valois descendants, that's what he's up to."

Jeanne was shocked by how much the Marquise had aged since they had last met. Her drooping jowls quivered, and thin, complicated lines spread out from her pale blue eyes. Her pert comeliness had not been able to withstand the accumulation of misfortunes of recent years. But Jeanne also noted optimistically that the Marquise was traveling in as fine a style as ever.

"My dear, my dear, you must get over this . . . what shall I call it? . . . this sensitivity about your Valois blood. You carry it too far." The Marquise's head had begun to tremble, and she looked worn and pale. "You think too much about it. You always have. It's an obsession."

"My father—wretched sod, may he rest in peace—on his death bed, begged me never to forget that I am the descendant of Henri the Second, a king!"

"And I daresay you never shall, my dear. Here, hand me that glass of orange-blossom water on the table." The Marquise drank some of the water and wiped her brow. She felt irritable and smothered with sorrow. "Well, it seems to me you haven't added much luster to your Valois heritage by your marriage to this . . ."

"Clown," Jeanne said, tossing her head. "I know what you think of Nicolas de La Motte. And you're right. He's a clown. A country bumpkin with a fondness for loud, beastly clothes. I married beneath me, I'll admit that. But the Comte . . ."

"Comte? He has a title now, does he? I hadn't heard about that."

"A Comte, yes. I added the title. Why not? As I was saying, I could have done worse. He's good-natured, he doesn't skulk about, he knows how to find his own amusements and leave me to mine. I shall make something of him. With enough money we can purchase an officer's commission for him. I don't intend to spend the rest of my days in a provincial military garrison, you can be sure of that."

The Marquise shook her head wearily. "Oh, Jeanne, will you never learn to be patient? If only you had stayed in the convent, waited until we were restored at court, then think of the match you could have made. No dowry perhaps, but with your looks, your high spirits, your title, many a man would have shrugged his shoulders about a dowry. Instead, you and Marianne leap the convent walls and go running off to Bar-sur-Aube, expecting Lord knows what kind of reception from those yokels and . . ."

"Bar is our family . . ."

"Your repeated interruptions are tiresome, my dear. Are these manners you've learned from your new husband?"

Jeanne flushed angrily and turned away.

The Marquise waited a moment, then continued. "Of course, I heard only rumors about what transpired in Bar-sur-Aube after you so injudiciously left the Abbaye. But those rumors were scarcely reassuring, as you can well imagine. It came as no surprise when one day the Bishop de Langres appeared on our doorstep in Passy begging the Marquis's consent to your marriage to this . . . I can never remember the dreadful man's name . . . this Comte whatever you call him."

Jeanne remained standing next to the fire, her back obstinately turned to the Marquise, who sighed and continued. "And this Bishop de Langres. Too handsome for his own good I would say. Tell me, what part did he play in this little drama of yours?"

Swiftly, Jeanne turned around and looked the Marquise squarely in the eyes. "I can't imagine what you could be thinking, maman," she said, in a slow, bemused way that the Marquise found very familiar. Over the years she had learned that Jeanne's displays of innocence were not always to be trusted.

"I meant only that a young woman must always be on her guard against the attractions of a handsome man of the cloth. Like the Bishop de Langres. A man known to have had his successes with . . . but what would you know of that, my dear? I only thought he pleaded the young man's . . . La Motte's case a little too urgently, and then when only a month or so after the wedding the babes were born, I thought . . . Oh, my child, don't cry!" The Marquise took her in her arms, and the two women wept together.

"I've had my losses, too," Jeanne said.

"I know, my dear. Only a mother can understand the sorrow of losing a child. To have my lovely Gabrielle snatched away from one day to the next. So young, so beautiful. I tell myself that I must be grateful that I still have Sophie and Lorraine. But it's no good." The Marquise buried her face in her hands.

"Nonetheless, what would I have done with twin baby boys at my age?" Jeanne said, briskly patting her eyes dry. "Only twenty-five. They didn't spoil my figure. I have plenty of time. It was fated to be so." Jeanne had made up her mind not to allow what had happened in Bar-sur-Aube to drag her down. And that included her marriage to Nicolas de La Motte. After more than two years in the convent, what girl would not have lost her head with so many admirers throwing themselves at her feet? At the time, they had made her feel, at last, like a real princess, especially the Bishop de Langres.

The Marquise smiled weakly. "You've always been a great believer in fate, haven't you?"

"Of course," Jeanne said. "Ever since that day I hopped up onto the step of your carriage, and you listened to my story. That was fate. You changed my life." Her smile livened the Marquise's heart. For a moment, Jeanne was once again the little beggar, hanging onto the carriage with one frail arm, dirty but irresistible.

"So? What is it you want of me now?" the Marquise asked in the mildly stern manner she sometimes used to indicate to Jeanne that she was not altogether as soft-hearted as Jeanne might suppose. "You've come a long way from your husband's garrison in Lunéville to find me here. In this dreadful weather I can't imagine that it is a pleasure jaunt for you."

The day the Marquise set out from Versailles, a light snow was falling, and then the rains came, leaving the roads rutted and slippery. Some mornings when the ruts were frozen and she was buffeted from one side of the carriage to the other, when it was impossible to keep her feet and hands warm, she thought she would lose her courage. Perhaps it was a mad quest, after all. Perhaps the Marquis was right. Still, everyone in Europe was talking about this mysterious Cagliostro, who had performed miracles in Russia and Poland, who had cured the sick, healed the lame and the blind, who could turn ordinary stones into diamonds and lead into gold, a seer, a prophet, a medium. Suddenly, he had appeared in France, in Strasbourg, where the enthralled populace lined the streets as he passed by in his black japanned carriage emblazoned with gold cabalistic symbols and swarmed about his lodgings seeking wonder-working cures and potions. Before his house in Strasbourg a veritable mountain of braces, canes, crutches testified to his healing powers. The great man took no money, not a sou, for his treatment of the poor. Could such a man be called a charlatan? Now, or so it was said in Paris, Cagliostro had captivated the Cardinal-Prince Louis de Rohan, who had invited him and his beauteous wife to stay in the Cardinal's palace in Saverne. The Cardinal, a refined man of the world whom the Marquise loved with all her heart, would not extend his famous hospitality to a quack. Certainly not. The Marquise wanted only one thing from Cagliostro. She wanted a séance. She was desperate to talk with Gabrielle once more.

Jeanne had taken a bedwarmer from the hearth and, in the absence of the Marquise's maid, stood next to the bed passing it back and forth between the sheets. The Marquise was amused. Jeanne could be wonderfully attentive when the occasion demanded.

"You haven't answered, but I hope it's not money you're wanting, my dear. This year's harvest was dreadful. Crop blight. Our steward says it's the worst harvest in thirty years."

A flash of annoyance swept over Jeanne's expressive face. "I must say, maman, I have never yet heard of a good harvest year on the Boulainvilliers estates. Each year is worse than the last. To hear your steward tell it. I can assure you that when I recover the Valois estates, I shall turn a profit or I'll know the reason why."

"Recover the Valois estates! Please, my child, no more of that nonsense. I'm far too weary tonight. Consider yourself lucky—and grateful—that the King has recognized the legitimacy of your lineage. And given you a pension from the royal purse. He was not obliged to do either, you know."

The Marquise moved slowly toward the bed. Each night on retiring, she indulged in a small pinch of snuff, just enough to soothe her nerves and send her off to sleep in a contented mood. Tonight she craved her pinch and wondered where her confounded maid, tipsy by now no doubt in the back kitchen, could have placed her *nécéssaire de voyage*, her old travel case that her godmother had given to her on her eighth birthday.

"You haven't seen my travel case, have you? The leather one with my initials?"

"Here it is under your shawl," Jeanne said, opening it for the Marquise. "Such an old thing. It's disgusting, maman. Look, there's mold here in the corner, and the strap is broken."

"Well, I'm very fond of my old things."

"I shall have only beautiful new things one day," Jeanne said, pushing the case away with distaste. "The finest, softest leather. My initials in gold. Velvet linings."

"My, my, then I shall run to you begging for money," the Marquise said.

Jeanne laughed gaily. "Perhaps," she said. "If only I can get back to Versailles and the court, I shall work wonders. You'll see. I have plans . . ."

The Marquise delicately sniffed a pinch of snuff. "Grandiose plans. Pipe dreams. Fantasies. My child, listen to an old woman who loves you like a daughter. Find yourself a country place in Bar-sur-Aube, since you have such fond memories of it and can never stop talking of your chateau de Fontette, settle down with your Nicolas, and learn to live on your pension."

Jeanne wrung her hands in exasperation. "I can't live on my pension! It's impossible."

"Why not? Some people live on far less."

"I can't . . . I don't know what happens, but the money disappears. I thought I could manage." She turned her face aside. "I've had to mortgage my pension."

"What! Mortgaged your royal pension? Have you gone mad?"

"I did what I had to do to get money," Jeanne said impatiently.

"What about your husband? This Comte-something-or-other. Surely he has some money."

Jeanne laughed scornfully. "My marriage is the union of famine with drought."

"We never gave our consent! You see, if you had only listened to me instead of to that fast-talking Bishop de Langres. But, then again, given the circumstances. He meant well. You had to marry someone. Help me into bed, will you, Jeanne? I'm feeling quite done in."

Several minutes passed, and neither spoke. They listened together as the belfry clock on the square ponderously struck ten o'clock.

"How much do you want?" the Marquise asked finally.

"Six hundred livres. Only enough to pay off the Comte's debts . . ."

The Marquise closed her eyes. "Only six hundred livres," she growled. "My dear Jeanne, you really are an extraordinary woman."

Jeanne pulled a chair up to the bed and sat down. She waited for the Marquise to say more. She did not appear to be asleep.

"You seem unwell, maman. Shall I stay beside you tonight?"

The Marquise opened her eyes and fixed them on Jeanne. "Pray, where else would you go at this hour?"

Jeanne stared at the fire and said nothing.

They were only a league from Strasbourg, and the Marquise had not stopped laughing since they left the inn. She had awakened in a surly mood, but Jeanne had coaxed her out of it before they had finished their morning coffee and jam. It was a brilliant October day with a sharp north wind that somehow could not dispel the warmth of the sunshine that fell across their lap rugs as the carriage rattled along on the icy highroad to Strasbourg. Jeanne, apparently forgetting her outrageous request for six hundred livres, was in high spirits, regaling the Marquise with lively stories of the droll provincials in Bar-sur-Aube.

"Oh, I forgot to tell you about the son of the richest bourgeois in town. Claude Beugnot," Jeanne said, her deep blue eyes bright with mischief.

"Handsome?"

"Oh, yes. Twenty-three years old. Very tall. Dapper. Dressed magnificently. Rather sober taste. Fancied himself quite the ladies' man."

"And terribly smitten with you? Or was it Marianne?" the Marquise asked.

"With me, naturally," she said, with a rich, infectious laugh that made the coachman turn around and grin. Jeanne leaned toward the Marquise. "Just between you and me, Marianne is much better off back in the convent. Though, of course, she can't stay with those frumpy Benedictines forever. I want to see her the abbess of some fashionable order closer to Paris. I have plans for her."

"Frumpy Benedictines! Oh, Jeanne, how you do go on!" On this luminous autumn day in 1783 Jeanne's grandiose talk struck the Marquise as merely a part of the girl's quirky, wayward humor. Certainly, nothing to be concerned about. "And what about your handsome young swain?"

"Well, he and his friends were the first to call on us at our ghastly little inn, the Auberge de la Tête Rouge, the only place we could afford. And we couldn't even afford that, really. We had sent out letters to all the local aristocracy calling attention to our plight. You know, two descendants of the Valois kings seeking their hospitality, their help. Anything. No responses. Then Claude persuaded Monsieur and Madame de Surmont to take us in. They were atrocious snobs, and I imagine that Claude pointed out to them that they would have a leg up on everyone else if they welcomed into their house two princesses of the blood royal."

"What was their house like?"

"Dreadful. Unspeakable. Nouveau riche. Royal blue velvet everywhere. That sort of thing."

The Marquise wrinkled her nose in distaste.

"And stingy! Lord, you never saw a woman stingier than this Madame de Surmont. Do you know what she did?"

"What?"

"Well, Madame de Surmont was enormous. And why shouldn't she be? She lay around all day long complaining of the vapors and stuffing herself with chocolates and comfits. Anyway, the first night we were in their house, Madame comes to our room with two of the most glorious dresses you'll ever see in your life. A trifle gaudy, but sumptuous nonetheless. 'Here you are, my dears,' says she, 'Two of my most expensive gowns. It would give me such pleasure to see the two of you wearing them.' And she wishes us a goodnight and trots out of the room. Marianne and I look at each other and start laughing. 'Does that old sow think we could ever wear one of her dresses?' says I, and just as I said it, I realized what Madame de Surmont was up to. Of course, she never expected us to be able to wear those dresses. That was the reason she gave them to us. Some generosity, says I to myself. I looked again at those gowns and then ran for my sewing kit. Marianne and I sat up all night long cutting and sewing and fitting—I had to keep slapping Marianne on the back to keep her awake; she loves her sleep—and by the time light came the next day we had ourselves two gorgeous gowns that would turn heads at Versailles. Perfect fits. We slept until noon, did our toilettes, and dressed for dinner at two."

"What did she say when she saw you in her gowns?"

"Nothing. I think she was so dumbstruck, she didn't say a word for two days. I laughed so hard I wet my linens."

The Marquise clapped her hands and squealed in delight.

Abruptly, the carriage swerved and bumped over ruts, pulling to the side and coming to a halt as richly liveried outriders, three abreast, galloped past. Jeanne leaned out of the window. Bearing down on them at a fast pace was a stately carriage drawn by six plumed, coal-black horses, sleek and gleaming in the sunlight.

"*Seigneur!*" she cried, "I think it must be the King himself."

"The King? Here in Alsace?" The Marquise peered down the highroad.

The approaching carriage slowed to a pace and stopped. "Why, it's the Prince! The Cardinal-Prince Louis!" the Marquise cried, bursting into tears at the sight of the familiar handsome figure striding toward her carriage. "Oh, Your Eminence, I am just now on my way to Saverne, to your palace."

"My dear Marquise, what a pleasant surprise," he said, extending his hand in greeting. "On the way to Saverne, are you? Then I am doubly pleased."

"I must consult with this miracle man, this Count Cagliostro. I have such a sorrowful burden. Like a stone pressing against my heart," she said, suddenly resenting Jeanne for charming her away from her sorrow.

"I know. I was devastated when I heard about Mademoiselle de Passy." The Cardinal took her hand in both of his and rested one foot casually on the step of her carriage. "Or I should say, the Comtesse de Clermont-Tonnerre. I still think of her as Mademoiselle de Passy, and I suppose I always shall." He leaned toward her, his eyes intense. "You are a wise woman to seek out the great Cagliostro. You will find consolation, I can assure you. Such a bright spirit, wasn't she?"

The Marquise caught her breath and sighed. "The Queen says the court will never be the same without her. They used to frolic together, the Queen and Gabrielle, on the lawns of the Petit Trianon. Like two kittens."

Jeanne leaned forward to pat the Marquise fondly on the shoulder, and as she did so, she coquettishly shook her head loose from her hood, and sunlight filled her hair.

"Ah, look at me, Your Eminence. I'm forgetting all courtesy." She waved a hand toward Jeanne. "I don't believe you have ever met my foster daughter, Mademoiselle de Valois. Or I should say the Comtesse de . . ." The Marquise whispered irritably. "Help me out, my child. The Comtesse de . . ."

"Mademoiselle de Valois?" the Cardinal said, turning to gaze at Jeanne. "Now there's a name filled with the history of France." He smiled and held out his gloved hand to Jeanne.

The Cardinal was dressed in a full-length blue fox great coat, and his supple kid gloves were a robin's egg blue. Jeanne reached out and took his hand, feeling the warmth of it, its soft weight. After an awkward moment she realized that she was supposed to kiss his ring, and as she looked up before bending to kiss it, she caught the Cardinal watching her, a mischievous look in his indigo blue eyes, a faint smile lurking at the edges of his mouth. Her lips grazed the enormous ring. The Cardinal's gloved hand smelled of perfume, something spicy, sandalwood perhaps, and as she raised her head, he gave her hand a squeeze or a slight shake, she could not tell which, that made her feel light-headed.

"Poor child," the Marquise said, "She has never had the fortune that should accompany such a glorious name. Still, I forced the King to do his duty by her. Didn't I, my dear? But I must say, Prince, you have had your own victories at court lately that I am dying to hear about. Head of the national charity fund as Grand Almoner to the King, administrator general of the Sorbonne, and what else? There was something else, something quite grand . . ."

"Abbot of St. Waast of Arras," the Cardinal said.

"The abbot of St. Waast of Arras! Imagine all that income, Your Eminence! It makes me quite giddy to think of it. Five hundred thousand francs a year! Congratulations. Well-deserved rewards, I should say, too, after all you've been through."

The Cardinal stared down at his boot resting on the carriage step. "Hollow victories, I'm afraid, Madame. Since I've fallen into disfavor with the young Queen."

"You mustn't say that, Your Eminence. Though cruel it is, to be sure, to be shunted aside and ignored by the King and the Queen. I know a bit about a sovereign's anger myself, yes, indeed. Think of your appointments as great victories for the house of Rohan. The Queen, I hear, did everything in her power to deny them to you."

The Cardinal lifted his face to the sun and smiled. "Indeed she did." He turned up the collar of his greatcoat against the wind.

"Your Eminence, we mustn't keep you standing here in the cold."

"One forgets in such pleasant company," he said, darting a bold glance at Jeanne, who sat demurely studying his every move. "You shall receive a warm welcome at Saverne, Madame. You and your charming protégée."

"Such style, Jeanne!" the Marquise sighed, as the Cardinal's carriage pulled away. "The man has such style! It's impossible not to adore him."

Jeanne sat in confused silence. Who was this prince who looked more like a king than the King himself? She remembered how disappointed she had been, seeing Louis XVI in his dusty brown ratteen suit and his hunting boots, shuffling along the grand corridors of Versailles, while courtiers in vividly colored satins and velvets strutted around him. Whereas the Cardinal had stood there, a magnificent apparition on the dull highroad, holding out his hand to her, the cold sunlight sharpening the refined features of his beautiful face, the wind lifting his silver hair, the fox fur deepening the radiant blue of his eyes. Tall and manly. She had never dreamed a man could be so handsome. And rich. Her heart began to race with excitement. This Cardinal-Prince Louis de Rohan must be one of the richest men in the kingdom. All those appointments and benefices. Didn't the Marquise say that he received five hundred thousand a year from just one of them? And his family powerful enough to tweak the Queen's nose. When everyone at Versailles knew that the King would rather hang himself than displease the Queen. Thank God, I've packed some of my best new dresses, she thought. The green with the gold lace running over the shoulders and down the back, that's what I'll wear to call on the Cardinal. Perfect. She clasped her hands contentedly in her fur muff. Why, for a man like the Cardinal six hundred livres would be nothing more than a quaint little sum.

Jeanne was not sure exactly what tack to take with the Cardinal. She was trying very hard not to gawk at the grandeur of the palace at Saverne, for she did not want to look like a country bumpkin overawed by her superiors. After all, she reminded herself, she was a Valois.

"Fourteen maîtres d'hotels and twenty-five footmen! Imagine!" the Marquise whispered as she lifted her skirts and started up the grand staircase.

It was three o'clock in the afternoon, and they met the Cardinal-Prince coming from his private chapel. He was wearing a scarlet moiré soutane and a priceless rochet of English lace, so fine that Jeanne longed to reach out and touch it.

His face brightened as he came forward to greet them and led them to an intimate corner in an imposing salon with tall windows along the west wall overlooking formal gardens that extended as far as the eye could see.

"I know you've come to see the Man of Miracles," he said, his face lively with pleasure, "But you must be satisfied with my poor company until he returns from his daily walk in the gardens. He won't be long."

Footmen in glossy black leather slippers served them a chilled white *pétillant* wine from the Cardinal's estates along the Rhine, and Jeanne waited impatiently for the badinage of courtesies between the Cardinal and the Marquise to end. She dreaded the moment when the Marquise would start in on her doleful litany of her dead daughter's charms. It was all very well to mourn someone, but the Marquise was getting carried away with her grief. Jeanne sipped the wine, keeping a polite, deliberately cool and superior smile on her face, and wondered whether she would have any opportunity to speak with the Cardinal alone.

Jeanne was so absorbed in her own thoughts that she was taken unawares when the Cardinal looked abruptly at her and said, "My dear Marquise, I long to hear the story of your protégée, Mademoiselle de Valois." He crossed his legs, settling back in his chair, and Jeanne could see the bright red silk stockings underneath his soutane.

"Of course, you do," the Marquise said. "Well, Jeanne?"

It was a story Jeanne had been telling all her life, and she was aware that she told it quite well, but all of a sudden she felt her throat tighten and her thoughts scatter.

"Tell him first of your mother, Jeanne. It's ever so touching," the Marquise said.

Jeanne's palms were sweating. She wanted with all her heart to win the Cardinal's interest. She had to begin.

"Tell him who your mother was," the Marquise prompted.

"My mother was a great hussy," Jeanne began, startling the Cardinal into a hearty laugh. With his laughter Jeanne found her rhythm and her voice, and from that point on her story smoothly unfolded with all the familiar creases and wrinkles that years of retelling had left there. Surreptitiously, she watched the Cardinal's face and knew that she had found a sympathetic listener; now and again, he frowned or indignation flashed across his face. He leaned forward, completely lost in the drama of Jeanne's life. She had just reached the point where she hopped up onto the step of the Marquise's carriage, when the double doors of the salon were flung open, and a footman in a loud, stentorian voice announced: "The Count Cagliostro!"

The Cardinal sprang to his feet and rushed down the long sweep of marble floor to Cagliostro's side. Jeanne and the Marquise watched in astonishment as the Cardinal, like a young, impressionable boy in the throes of his first infatuation, hung about Cagliostro and seemed to be pleading with him to come forward to make their acquaintance.

"I shan't rise to meet him," Jeanne whispered to the Marquise.

The two men, deep in conversation, slowly approached.

"The diamonds!" the Marquise said in a low, bemused voice. "Look at all those diamonds on his shirt front!"

A bulky man, Cagliostro was at least a head shorter than the Cardinal. He had a mincing sort of gait for such a large man and the same deep olive, swarthy complexion of the glassblowers Jeanne had seen down in the workshops off the Faubourg Saint-Honoré. He had no neck, his large head being chunked down inelegantly between his shoulders.

The Cardinal led him forward for introductions, and to Jeanne's annoyance, the Marquise looked to be on the point of falling into a faint. Cagliostro seemed delighted by his effect on the Marquise and immediately took her hand and stroked it, speaking in some kind of gibberish, a mixture of French and Italian that Jeanne could not understand. He had a braying voice, like a trumpet veiled in crepe that made her skin crawl.

"Madame's foster daughter, Mademoiselle de Valois," the Cardinal said. He looked tense and strained, as if anxious for the great Cagliostro's approval of his guests.

Cagliostro threw his large head back and fixed Jeanne with a basilisk stare. His eyes were the most arresting feature of his round face. They were, Jeanne thought, full of fire and ice, penetrating, mesmerizing. Repulsive. She turned away from him with a weak smile.

"Of course, of course, dear lady. I understand," Cagliostro was saying to the Marquise, who was now on her feet. To Jeanne's dismay, their visit with the Cardinal was clearly ending. "Tomorrow evening. One hour after the sun has set. We meet. I understand, dear lady, do not weep. Weep no more."

The Cardinal disappeared as soon as they left the salon, and it was Cagliostro himself who took the Marquise's arm and escorted her down the grand stairway to their carriage waiting in the courtyard.

Jeanne felt cheated, as if a bright, shining opportunity had been snatched from her grasp. She looked back at the majestic palace, golden in the late afternoon sun. In one of the windows on the second floor stood a man, a cleric dressed in dusty black. He stood quite still, staring glumly down at the scene in the courtyard.

Suddenly, the Cardinal, a bright blur of color, appeared, striding swiftly down the steps toward their carriage.

"My dear Marquise, forgive my manners. Something urgent in my study." He pressed the Marquise's hand and declared solemnly. "Never fear. You are in good hands now. The divine Cagliostro will dry those tears. Forever. And, Mademoiselle de Valois," he said, in a formal, cold manner that chilled Jeanne's heart, drowned her hopes. "I trust we shall meet again."

His handshake was so debonair and dismissive that Jeanne did not realize until the carriage door was closed that the Cardinal had left a note, a tiny piece of exquisite paper, in the palm of her hand. She leaned forward, hoping that he might turn and wave, might look at her again, but he had disappeared.

In the window above the courtyard the somber, glowering figure of the cleric watched the carriage depart.

Jeanne had no trouble getting rid of Agnes, the Marquise's maid, for the remainder of the evening so that the Marquise would be snug in bed and asleep before Jeanne left for her rendezvous with the Cardinal. Agnes had been overly fond of spirits since her childhood in Normandy when she would share with her father and brothers a few sips from the small crock of *calvados* her mother tucked into the lunch basket that Agnes carried to the fields every day. A few francs would keep her contentedly filling her glass with the postillions and drovers on their way to market in Strasbourg. Nonetheless, before leaving the inn, Jeanne thought it prudent to take a look in the public rooms to make sure that Agnes had settled in with a bottle for the night. Through the smoky haze she could see her near the back of the room, trying with unsteady hands to pull her shawl over her head for warmth.

"*I long to hear the rest of your story,*" the note from the Cardinal read. "*Come tonight.*" A mere scribble on a tiny scrap of paper. But it could change her life. It would change her life; she had no doubt about it. She needed money to pay off their debts, buy La Motte a commission and a regiment, and set themselves up in fashionable lodgings in Paris and Versailles. They were dead broke again, and she wondered whether she could squeeze even a few hundred livres from the Marquise. Her luck had to change. What would become of her if she simply gave up and went back to Lunéville and the garrison and the officers, flirting and sweet-talking her, trying to get her to bed? Like the Marquis d'Autichamp. The man had simply gone off his head with infatuation. Begging her to elope with him, making scenes, challenging the Comte to a duel. Thank God,

La Motte had had enough sense to decline. Well, that had taught her a lesson about yielding to a hot-headed man! Never again. A fine figure of a man, though, the Marquis, and an accomplished lover; she could have done worse. He was a lively dance partner with a cunning way about him in the quadrille. But he was almost as poor as the La Mottes—he bought her one silk dress and didn't have enough money to offer her the gloves to match—and no connections at Versailles. What was the point of being a marquis if there was no money to live at court and buy fine clothes and carriages and see the King and Queen every day?

When she arrived at Saverne, every room in the palace was lit up as if for a grand reception or ball, and her heart sank. Had she made a mistake in reading the note? Had the Cardinal forgotten? She thought of telling the driver to turn back to the inn. She sat for a moment and looked at the resplendent palace, then, without waiting for the coachman, bolted out of the carriage door.

A footman with impeccable posture led her immediately to the Cardinal's suite of private rooms on the second floor. When she entered, he was seated at a large desk with stacks of papers arranged in a half-dozen neat piles. Behind him stood a tall, gaunt priest with a gray, dingy complexion whose severe gaze fixed on her like a furious wasp as she approached the desk.

The Cardinal looked up briefly from his papers and motioned to Jeanne with a distracted nod to take a seat on a blue striped canopy next to the fireplace. Time passed and Jeanne, holding her head high, sat neglected on the canopy nursing her indignation and stared into the fire, unwilling to grant even the slightest glance of interest toward the Cardinal. The two men continued their dreary colloquy, exchanging papers, the Cardinal scraping his signature over document after document.

By and by, as evening approached, servants fanned out around the vast room lighting candles and lustres while the two at the desk droned on and on in monotonous complicity. Eventually, there was a theatrical cough, and Jeanne looked up to see the priest bowing in her direction before sidling off to the door. Still piqued, Jeanne turned back to gaze into the fire.

Suddenly, the Cardinal appeared at her side, kneeling at her feet, his gorgeous robes of scarlet silk spread about him, dazzling in the firelight. He clasped her hand against his breast and said, in a deep, seductive whisper, "Lovely Jeanne, can you ever forgive me? Keeping you waiting when all the while I have longed to take you in my arms and hold you close to my heart."

He held his head a little to one side like a winsome child, and Jeanne laughed. He smiled broadly and lifted her to her feet. When he pulled her into his arms and kissed her, she closed her eyes tightly, afraid that he would see the elation there.

Later on, when she remembered that moment, it seemed to her like being embraced by summer clouds, his fragrant silken robes soft and billowy, his manly body hard and supple beneath all the softness.

Jeanne could scarcely believe her good fortune. The Cardinal! This rich and powerful prince. And handsome and charming, into the bargain. He smelled of sandalwood and incense, and his robes rustled softly as his hands moved rapidly and expertly over her body, undoing her gown.

She was intoxicated. They were intoxicated with each other. Jeanne longed to stay in that palace the rest of her life. She would ask for nothing more than that Prince Louis never stop making love to her.

In 1783 Jeanne was twenty-seven and the Cardinal forty-nine, though he looked a much younger man. He had a full, thick head of prematurely grey hair that somehow made his noble face look remarkably young and boyish. His eyes were an indigo blue and when he turned his full gaze upon her, it fairly took her breath away.

When the time came for the Cardinal's return to Paris and his duties at Versailles, he brought out a small ebony casket filled with gold louis so that Jeanne could secure an apartment near the

Palais de Rohan on the rue Vieille-du-Temple, where their idyll was to continue.

After lingering adieux, Jeanne made her way back to the inn. She hummed to herself as she dodged wagons and carts on their way to market, elated by the prospect of setting up her own establishment in Paris. She would make it the *dernier cri* in elegance and refinement.

She could not wait to tell her great oaf of a husband of their good fortune.

10

Jeanne stood at the open window and held out her hand to the falling rain. Her nails were raw, chewed down to the quick. She looked at them in disgust. She detested women who took out their troubles on their own bodies. In a matter of days the Cardinal would be arriving in Paris and would expect to find her comfortably set up in an establishment near him in the Palais-Cardinal. Would he ask her where the money had gone? Would he rave? Would he scream? She shivered and closed the window. The broken shutters rattled and clanked aimlessly in the wind.

But would he have to find out that the money was gone? She began to walk the floor. Of course not. With a little ingenuity, and God only knows she had always had plenty of that, he would never find out that the money had vanished even before she left Lunéville and went back to Passy to the Marquise. And if he did find out, what of it? He was wild for her. She could tell by the way he had said goodbye. She still had her beautiful gowns; she hadn't pawned those. The mistake had been to split the Cardinal's money fifty-fifty with the Comte. Who went straight out and got himself rigged up in flamboyant rags that made him look more like a clown than ever. And a horse. He bought himself another horse. Can you pawn a horse, she wondered. If it came to that, the Comte would find a way. Nicolas de La Motte was a genius in juggling debts and heavy-breathing creditors. She admired him for that.

If the Cardinal finds out, she thought, I will plead distraction. I will say that I was driven to distraction with grief over the unexpected death of my foster mother. My beloved foster mother, the Marquise. Jeanne still could not believe it. The Marquise had died so suddenly, it seemed, though in truth she had lingered in the throes of smallpox fevers for a full three weeks or more. Jeanne crossed herself. Before the Marquise became totally delirious, she had yielded and given Jeanne the six hundred livres to pay off the Comte's debts. That should have helped. Perhaps it did, but Jeanne could not see how. The Comte had said, "It's your aristocratic nature, my dear, that makes you awkward with money. It's in your blood. This spending without knowing where the next sou will be coming from. All aristocrats do that." The Comte was right. Why should a Valois be forever counting money and reckoning sums like a common *serveuse* in a café?

If only she had not quarreled with the Marquis, she might not be living in this dilapidated, rat-infested Hotel de Reims, hiding out like a fugitive. Still, what would life be like at the Passy mansion with that priapic swine, the Marquis, barging into her bedroom at all hours of the day and night? The Marquise no sooner in her grave than the lecherous fool proposed that Jeanne become his mistress and share his fortune. Ha! Liar! How many times had she heard that tune before?

"What about my husband?" she had said, "You forget that I am married."

"Your husband is a wonderful convenience," he said, "an added protection for your reputation as well as mine. I will arrange a commission for Monsieur de La Motte in a regiment where he will not be near enough to Paris to bother us. Nor need you worry about what my daughters will have to say—I know how to silence them."

And then, after she had refused his offer, he turned against her, accusing her of using his house like a hotel. "Receiving your men friends at ungodly hours. My own daughters' husbands, too, going out to drive with them and who knows what other mischief you got up to. That sly Bishop de Langres mooning around. It makes me sick. And I won't have it in my house any longer, missy!"

Then to be chased out of his fine house like a stray dog, she thought angrily. If only the Marquise were still alive. But the Marquise was dead and buried these two months now. With a rush of fear, Jeanne realized that she had no idea where her next meal would be coming from. Since morning, she had eaten only a half loaf of bread and a piece of cheese. The Cardinal had written that he would be taking up residence in Paris soon after the New Year. Or was it the first week of February? She could not remember which. La Motte would be taking another month to obtain his discharge from his regiment in Lunéville. Anyway, what could she expect from her great fool of a husband? Certainly not money.

Jeanne stopped pacing the floor and looked down into the darkening street burnished with rain. A dark-haired young man in a sober costume paused under a street lantern to put his books into a large leather pouch, which he then slung over his back. He was a stranger, but something in the purposeful way he walked, the way he held his head reminded her of someone. She gazed out at the street long after the lone figure disappeared around the corner of the rue de Verrerie, and just as she was turning away from the window, the name, the face came back to her. Beugnot! Claude Beugnot from Bar-sur-Aube! Of course! She laughed and spun around giddily.

Dearest Claude, she said to herself, as she snatched up a pen, dipped it into the inkpot, and began to write.

"It's fate, Claude, admit it," Jeanne said, eyeing with satisfaction the large portion of *rollatine de veau* the waiter had set before her.

"It does look that way," Beugnot said, slightly dismayed by his keen pleasure at being with Jeanne again. He had thought, wrongly it appeared, that the intervening years, her marriage, and his dogged pursuit of his legal career had healed the old wound of losing her, his first real love. "I had no sooner opened my father's letter than my concierge handed me your note. A happy coincidence."

"Especially for me. I needed that bank note your father sent. I was desperate. You're too rich to understand. Your father is a saint, and I shan't forget him. I regard this money as a loan. I intend to repay every sou. You'll see. Another bottle of red?"

"Why not?" Beugnot said cheerfully. Jeanne was a woman of strong appetites, as it had been his delight to discover in those long summer days in Bar-sur-Aube until one of his father's tenants had spied them disporting themselves in a secluded willow grove along the banks of the river. Without further ado his father had packed him off to Paris and his law studies. When Jeanne threw herself into a hasty and imprudent marriage with Nicolas de La Motte, Albert Beugnot was so delighted to see her married off that he would gladly have defrayed all the wedding expenses. But from the moment Albert Beugnot was sure that Jeanne would never become his daughter-in-law, he, of course, fell under her spell as thoroughly as every other male in Bar. Now his father had written that he was sending along a "little something"—a thousand francs!—for the *little lass of Fontette*, as he always referred to Jeanne. He urged Claude to help her with legal advice—what better way, he said, to find out how much you have learned after all these years of study?—in her petition to the King for the restoration of the Valois properties. *But be cautious*, his father warned, *the little lass of Fontette is utterly irresistible*, a discovery that Beugnot had already made for himself far earlier.

Beugnot smiled ruefully and watched Jeanne, greedily swabbing the sauce from her plate with a piece of bread. He loved her in these unguarded moments when she forgot her imposing manners.

She looked up and caught him staring at her. "It was that long walk. I'm starved," she said. Beugnot had brought Jeanne to his favorite restaurant along the Champs Elysées, the Cadran Bleu. And it had been a long, cold trek, for few hackneys wanted to risk their horses on the icy streets. They took a ferry across the Seine to the Right Bank because the Pont Neuf had been closed since the King ordered the destruction of all the stalls and shops cluttering the bridge.

"Tell me about your husband," Beugnot said, rather plaintively.

"Oh, Claude, don't be so bourgeois," she said, and they both laughed.

"Well, what are you doing in a dump like the Hotel de Reims?" He had walked past the hotel twice, unable to believe that Jeanne could be staying in such a hangout for prostitutes and alley men. Yet when she opened the door of her room, she was resplendent in a dark blue velvet gown embroidered with seed pearls.

"I need your help," Jeanne said.

"Ah! My father thought you might."

"Dear man. I must write to thank him for his gift." Jeanne leaned back in contentment. Everything would work out splendidly, she could see that now. It had been foolish to worry. The Cardinal need never know that not a sou remained of the pile of money he had given her. Jeanne hesitated a moment. "I need to borrow your carriage and a footman."

"A footman? What on earth for? Besides, I don't have a footman. I don't need one. I live in furnished rooms."

"A lackey, then," she said.

"I don't have a lackey either."

"A servant? You must have a servant of some sort."

"Tell me first what you want to do with him," he said.

Claude's eyes were dancing, and she could tell that he was just having his fun with her before giving in. He was in love with her as much as ever. Jeanne knew that he would find her a carriage and a lackey, even if he had to hire them.

"I must call upon the Cardinal-Prince de Rohan. I can't very well walk off the streets into the Palais-Cardinal. I must present myself appropriately."

"Why must you see the Cardinal? Do you know him?"

"Of course, my dear, I know him. You talk as if you've never heard of Versailles and the court. The Prince is one of the great lords of the realm. So rich that even his maitres d'hotel go to market in a carriage. The Cardinal has promised me his patronage in regaining the Valois estates. And he intends to find a place for my husband in the King's brother's regiment. That is, the Comte d'Artois's regiment."

"Really? In exchange for what?" Beugnot said irritably, piqued by jealousy of this great man, the Cardinal, who could do so much for her, who could help her realize her dream of possessing Fontette once again. In Bar that summer she had never stopped talking of it.

Jeanne tossed her head back regally and glared at him. The Cadran Bleu had begun to empty out as the streets darkened and lamplighters hallooed to each other as they meandered down the street with their poles.

"It's getting late," Jeanne said.

As soon as he took her arm, Beugnot knew that he would do just about anything for the chance of seeing her again. He could not explain what there was about her that made her so seductive. She was not beautiful by conventional standards. Her mouth was too broad for her face, but her smile went straight to the heart. There was a radiance about her; she was alive; she was daring. Somehow or other the reticences, moral and social, of an upper-class young woman had escaped her. Her voice was sweet and insinuating, and she spoke rapidly with great assurance in a simple, direct way, full of conviction.

"I would invite you up to my room, but its shabbiness would make you suffer too much," Jeanne said sweetly.

"It's not that shabby. I shan't suffer," he said, miserable with desire for her.

"And will you lend me your carriage and your servant for tomorrow?"

He laughed, his handsome young face crinkling with pleasure. "Yes. Even if I have to hire them," he said.

11

Everyone at court knew that the Queen persisted in treating the Cardinal-Prince Louis de Rohan either as if he were invisible or afflicted with an advanced stage of leprosy. When she refused communion at Sunday's High Mass rather than receive the Host from the Cardinal's despised hands, they marveled at her treatment of this popular courtier whose family preceded in rank all the peers of the realm. Now that her formidable mother was dead, some thought perhaps Marie Antoinette would relent. It was said that the Cardinal had written letter after letter apologizing for his notorious letter mocking Empress Maria-Theresa's hypocrisy in the partitioning of Poland, letters conveyed personally to the Queen by the Cardinal's niece, the Comtesse de Guémenée, one of Her Majesty's favorite ladies-in-waiting. When the Cardinal anxiously asked his niece what became of his letters, she said, averting her eyes from his distress, "The Queen yawns and throws them into the fire."

Few realized that the Queen's stubborn hatred of him, like a festering boil underneath his calm, proud exterior, was the unending torment of the Cardinal's nights and days. Those who flocked to the glittering soirées at the sumptuous Palais-Cardinal in the snowy evenings of February 1784 saw only a handsome, witty host, a trifle arrogant perhaps, but warm and charming, solicitous, unfailingly kind and generous.

Indeed, the Cardinal's generosity was legendary. He had, for example, installed his good friends, the Count and Countess Cagliostro, in a superb mansion in the rue St. Claude. The street was clogged from early morning to late evening with the carriages of the Man of Miracles' devotees. The fashionable thronged Cagliostro's reception rooms, men fought duels over whether the Countess's beautiful eyes were brown or blue, and family fortunes were flung like rose petals in his wake. Men wore his miniature portrait in cameo rings, and women a lock of his hair enshrined in gem-encrusted lockets. Houdon's bust of Count Cagliostro was pronounced divine, and there were those who were well on their way to deifying the man himself. The encyclopedists having done such a thorough job of kicking religious faith into the cellar with other worn-out, unfashionable domestic articles, the country craved something to believe in. If not something, at least someone. Parisians wanted distractions at any price, and a general vertigo seemed to have seized every one. Both the court and the town were fatigued, worn out; something new and startling was needed. It was a time when mountebanks flourished, and of them all, Cagliostro, with his miracle cures, his predictions, his reputation as an alchemist, was the most spectacular.

Jeanne waited in vain for the Cardinal's enthusiasm for Cagliostro to wane. To her decided chagrin, the Cardinal's dependency seemed to grow apace after Cagliostro set up residence in Paris. And that dependency, as far as she could see, translated into huge sums of money being poured at regular intervals into Cagliostro's coffers. It infuriated her, and she never missed an opportunity to stick a needle into her competition for the Cardinal's largesse.

The Cardinal was overseeing the final details for a supper party when Jeanne said, in a totally innocent way, or so she assumed, "The Abbé tells me that Cagliostro and that simpering little wife of his abused your hospitality most dreadfully at Saverne."

"Really? The Abbé told you that?" Knowing that Georgel disliked Jeanne—"that insinuating creature"—perhaps even more than Cagliostro, the Prince was rather surprised that his secretary had taken her into his confidence. "Never mind the Abbé, my dear. In managing my money, he's like an old dame in her pantry, forever reckoning sums and counting the jam jars on the shelves. I told him that I had extended the *privilege* of abusing my hospitality to the Count."

"You would give away the Church silver if someone asked you for it," Jeanne said. Though she truly could never fault the Cardinal's generosity to her, she was certain that Cagliostro walked away with twice or three times as much.

The Cardinal laughed. "Oh, not the Church silver. I do draw the line somewhere, you know. You find the Countess simpering? Strange. When all of Paris is at her feet." It amused him to think that Jeanne might be jealous. "You look especially lovely tonight, *ma cocotte*," he said, caressing her hair. "That red, it suits you. Makes me feel devilish, just looking at you."

"I've invited a friend from Bar to your party tonight," Jeanne said.

"Oh?"

"The young man I told you about. The promising young barrister who's preparing my petition for the King."

"He wants me to read the petition?"

"No," Jeanne said, "he wants to lay eyes on you. He's sick with jealousy of the mighty Prince Louis de Rohan."

"So you've invited him here to still his jealousy, so that he can see what a doddering old man I am."

"I've invited him precisely to *excite* his jealousy," Jeanne said, laughing gaily and taking his hand. "Come along. We have plenty of time. I want you to show me how devilish you really feel."

Beugnot sat confounded. He *liked* the Cardinal. When Beugnot arrived at the Palais-Cardinal, exactly on the stroke of ten o'clock, the Cardinal had sailed forward to meet him, grabbing his hand in a warm clasp, chatting along with an easy informality that quite disarmed Beugnot. They briefly touched on the Comtesse's petition to the King, which the Cardinal pledged to read with all haste and to make sure that it was placed in the proper hands at Versailles.

"The Comtesse tells me that your petition is most affecting. Quite literary. What a shame that it cannot be presented in the courts of law! Your reputation would be made. But, of course, it must remain what it is, a petition to the King. Any publicity would be disrespectful to His Majesty."

Though Beugnot took due note that he was seated at table below the Cardinal's titled guests, every time the Cardinal caught his eye, he made Beugnot feel like an honored guest. Beugnot found himself almost appalled by how handsome the Cardinal was with his silver-white hair, his youthful face, full of healthy color, very fine, aristocratic features and the noblest bearing of any man he had ever seen. The Prince carried himself magnificently. At table his graceful, refined manners seemed natural and totally unstudied. Beugnot wondered how on earth this charming man could have caused him such pangs of jealousy. For not a trace of intimacy escaped from the Prince and Jeanne. It had all been the delusion of a green boy, and he vowed never to trouble himself with these unworthy feelings again.

Shortly after midnight the great double doors of the dining room were thrown open and in strode none other than the celebrated Count Cagliostro, white plumes dipping and swaying, diamonds glittering. Beugnot could feel his jaw drop. He had only half believed Jeanne when she railed against this Cagliostro with absolute familiarity. After all, the man was the talk of Paris, sought after by every salon of the elite.

But suddenly here he was, bowing over Jeanne's hand, murmuring something Beugnot could not catch, smiling into her eyes as if she were the most captivating woman in the world, casting a sparkling eye at the other guests around the supper table. The Cardinal was beaming. The guests dropped their dessert spoons and fell into a reverential hush. Servants brought forth a chair and an elaborately decorated Italian ice. Instead of eating, Cagliostro launched into what Beugnot took to be a discussion of the Egyptian goddess Isis, his remarks piling up in a kind of wild gibberish that was part Italian with a smattering of French and Arabic. Beugnot glanced around the table. All sat spellbound, convinced no doubt that they were in the presence of divine genius.

To Beugnot this Cagliostro looked more like a fantastical sideshow than a miracle maker. He laughed too much in a loud, sarcastic way, and his sonorous, metallic voice, though beguiling, was not altogether pleasant. Although Cagliostro monopolized the conversation, the Cardinal occasionally added a remark or two in a wry, unassuming way, remarks of such learning and wit that Beugnot could not help being impressed by his intelligence. The Prince had, Beugnot remembered, been elected to the Académie Française while still in his twenties.

Cagliostro's monologue skimmed twenty or so subjects, and the Cardinal's guests hung onto his every word as if his next incomprehensible pronouncement would reveal their individual and collective destinies.

In his ramblings Cagliostro began to talk of coming upon a woodcarver in the rue du Coburg who sat turning out large crucifixes with what Cagliostro considered a perfect likeness of Jesus Christ.

"I was startled," Cagliostro said—or something to that effect, "for I could not understand how this woodcarver, who had certainly never seen Christ, could create such a remarkable likeness of him."

"You knew Christ, then," Beugnot blurted out despite himself.

"We were on the most intimate terms," Cagliostro replied with a sigh. "How many times we walked together on the wet sandy shore of the lake of Tiberias. His voice was of infinite sweetness. But, you know, he would not listen to me. He loved to walk on the seashore, where he picked up a band of *lazzaroni*—of fishermen, beggars really! This and his preaching brought him to a bad end." He shook his large head dolefully.

Beugnot throttled back a laugh. So that was it! Jesus Christ simply fell in with the wrong crowd! A gang of *lazzaroni*! Around the Cardinal's table, however, it was a very solemn moment. The Cardinal's look was intense; several guests dabbed at their eyes with their napkins. Beugnot couldn't help noticing that Jeanne was less captivated by the great man than the rest of the guests at table. She ate steadily, with her usual keen appetite, and every now and again assessed Cagliostro's performance with a sly, amused smile.

Cagliostro, on the other hand, varied his lofty discourse with playful endearments addressed to her, calling her his fawn, his gazelle, his swan, and other agreeable members of the animal kingdom. Jeanne, in her *grande dame* manner, merely sniffed a little, smiled, and nodded her head. A trifle condescendingly, Beugnot thought.

If Beugnot had stopped to reflect a moment, which he did not, he would have noticed that Cagliostro treated Jeanne as if she were the Cardinal's hostess *en titre*. Instead, the demon jealousy had been entirely laid to rest, and Beugnot went away well satisfied with his evening, feeling rather privileged, if the truth be told, to have been a part of the Cardinal's high and mighty world.

The Cardinal pushed up the sleeves of his dressing gown and searched among the boxes and trunks scattered around the foyer.

"My portfolio, Schreiber. I don't see it. I thought you put it here, next to the household trunk."

Schreiber, the Cardinal's personal valet, a rosy-cheeked young man with a strapping build who had grown up in Alsace and who was never happier than when the Cardinal returned to the chateau de Saverne, pointed to a red leather portfolio and said, "Your Eminence will find it there on the commode."

"No, no," the Cardinal said irritably. "*Not* that one. The portfolio with my confidential papers. The old one with the lock."

Jeanne stood to one side and watched with alarm the Cardinal's frenzied preparations for departure. Four wagons and the Cardinal's majestic carriage stood waiting in the courtyard. Servants rushed in and out of the palace, lugging heavy trunks, their faces grim and determined. A streak of sweat slipped down the side of the Cardinal's face and locks of his thick silver hair fell untidily over his forehead.

"Your Eminence?" Jeanne said.

The Cardinal wheeled around and smiled at her, but the usual warmth that never failed to reassure her briefly flickered and died.

"Ah, my dear Jeanne, I'm neglecting you. Here, come along this way, we'll have a moment's chat before I dress for the journey."

He spoke in a breathless, distracted way as he placed his arm around her waist and steered her toward a small, dark antechamber off the ground floor library. The shutters were tightly closed though it was past ten in the morning.

"What's happened?" Jeanne said, her eyes wide in the dim light. "Why are you leaving Paris so suddenly?"

"Suddenly?" the Cardinal said, and she could tell by the way his eyes slid away from her face that he was going to lie to her. "I don't know what you mean."

"You must know what I mean! You mentioned nothing about leaving for Saverne when I last saw you two nights ago. When I was lying in your arms. Or have you forgotten that, too?" she said, her voice rising.

The Cardinal placed a finger over his lips. "Shhh. Jeanne, Jeanne. This is unlike you. Do be more reasonable. I have work to do in Alsace. Affairs of the Church. You wouldn't understand."

"But you've been in Paris only two months. We've had such a wonderful time together." She pressed against him and took his face in her hands. "So many wonderful nights together. Oh, Your Eminence, what shall I do without you?" It galled her that he had never asked her to dispense with his title, even in their most intimate moments, and suddenly she was shaken by a fear that he had taken a fancy to some other woman and was escaping to the seclusion of his Alsatian palace for a romantic interlude. It was possible. Prince Louis was a notorious womanizer.

He bent his head and kissed her with absentminded haste. "I shan't be gone long." He freed himself from her embrace and ran his hand through his hair. "I . . . well, I can't say exactly. But I shall have my secretary . . . The Abbé will be able to give you my news."

"The Abbé!" Jeanne said. She felt like slapping the Cardinal's face. Why couldn't the man wake up and understand her distress? "The Abbé loathes the very sight of me." She could feel tears of frustration welling up in her eyes. "You've been so good to me," she said. "I . . . I shall miss you with all my heart. I don't know how I shall manage without you."

The Cardinal had his hand under her elbow and was moving toward the door.

"What will I do for help . . . in times of need?" Jeanne said, feeling him slipping away from her grasp.

"Don't fret, my dear. You will do splendidly. You are a woman of spirit." He reached for the door knob.

"Could you not give me some money before you go, Your Eminence?" Jeanne said finally, her voice a mere whisper.

"What?"

"Only a little. I need just a little assistance. Gambling debts. My husband's. I'm afraid I don't know . . ."

"More money! Is this a joke? Do you forget that only last Wednesday I gave you a purse with well over two thousand francs. I believe that's what the Abbé recorded. Yes, that was it. Two thousand francs! Did you throw it into the Seine?"

His face was flushed. Jeanne had never seen him this close to anger. She bowed her head and said nothing. She fumbled for her handkerchief in her reticule, and after wiping her eyes, she squared her shoulders and hurried out of the room.

The Cardinal caught up with her and took her hand. "Ah, well, dear Jeanne, I'm quite as clumsy with money as you are. Only the Abbé keeps me from bankrupting myself. Don't cry, my dear. I shall find something for you."

They climbed the grand stairway to the Cardinal's study and library where they found Abbé Georgel, head bowed over an enormous ledger, thin shoulders lifting the antiquated black serge of his soutane. He looked up, alert as a guard dog, when he saw Jeanne at the Cardinal's side.

"Monsieur l'Abbé," the Cardinal said, "I shall be needing a sum

. . . a small sum . . . for the Comtesse . . . to tide her over some little difficulties that have arisen. Only a small sum."

Like a child begging another sweet from his mother, Jeanne thought, looking at the Abbé with distaste. He always smelled unclean, this Abbé, his hygiene suspiciously vague and incomplete. He leaned forward, his lank, unkempt hair falling like moldy noodles from yesterday's supper around his shoulders. Jeanne turned to gaze out the window, as if the small sum of money were of no concern to her.

"In addition to last week's two thousand francs?" the Abbé's voice rose and broke over *two thousand francs*.

"Only a small sum," the Cardinal said.

The Abbé stood and thrust his hands under the skirt of his soutane. He looked down at the open ledger. "I believe it would be wise, at this juncture, if the Comtesse would address herself for a loan to one of the moneylenders at the Palais-Royal. Monsieur Cerf-Beer, perhaps."

"A loan!" Jeanne cried.

"I don't see any other solution, Your Eminence," Georgel said, ignoring Jeanne and nodding toward the open ledger on the desk.

The Cardinal wiped his brow thoughtfully. "Excellent idea, Monsieur l'Abbé. I'm sure the Comtesse will agree."

"You're sending me to a moneylender! I don't believe it! I shall die of shame!"

"I shall stand guarantor for the loan, dear Comtesse," the Cardinal said in a low, exhausted voice, and Jeanne realized that further protests would be futile. She turned a baleful eye on the Abbé, who was already busy preparing a letter for the Cardinal's signature.

"Stop! Will you please for Heaven's sake stop biting your nails?" Beugnot said, slamming his book shut and getting up from his desk. Jeanne looked down at her hands and frowned. A thin smear of blood stained her upper lip.

"Let's go for a walk and have a glass of beer," Jeanne said. "It's stuffy in here. Moldy old law books. I can't breathe." It was almost four o'clock on a brisk afternoon in March, and she and Beugnot were quarreling again.

"It's going to rain. And I have work to do." Beugnot tried to sound angry. And he *was* angry. He hated to be interrupted in his work, as Jeanne knew very well.

"You always have work to do. It's a bore."

"How do you expect me to finish your petition to the King if I don't use my spare hours to work on it? You've been no help. Neither has that absurd husband of yours."

As soon as Nicolas de La Motte returned to Paris from Lunéville, Jeanne packed him off to Bar-sur-Aube to investigate land titles, while Beugnot toiled along, doing research in the Archives Office in Paris and drafting her petition for the King. Beugnot's father wrote that Comte de La Motte, out in the provinces, made a triumphal entrance into Fontette, and, for some idiotic reason, had a *Te Deum* sung in the village church, after which, apparently under some absurd delusion that he was behaving like a *grand seigneur*, tossed out handfuls of coins to the astonished villagers.

And that was the extent of his efforts on behalf of his wife's claims. When he ran out of money, he went off to stay with his sister and her husband in Bar and sent Beugnot a list of solicitors to whom he might apply for "legal trivia" surely beneath the dignity of a man of La Motte's rank and station to investigate.

To Beugnot's surprise, Jeanne's obsession with regaining the Valois lands was not entirely unrealistic, for all of the estates had reverted to the King. With one generous gesture of the royal hand those lands could be restored to her. In his petition Beugnot represented Jeanne's case as *The final insult of cruel fortune to the Valois line—the sad lot of a side branch of that ancient family tree which for so long cast its royal shadow across France and the other nations of Europe*. He beseeched the Bourbons to pay their natural debt to the Valois, who had bequeathed them so magnificent a heritage. Beugnot was given to preening himself not a little on his felicitous phrasing, and Jeanne was ecstatic, almost in awe of him and his skills until he made her understand that the process of obtaining the King's attention to the matter would be tedious and slow.

"Just a glass or two of beer. We need to talk," Jeanne said with a protracted yawn, feigning nonchalance while the crab claws of hunger gripped her stomach. Her favorite cafés would be serving hot canapés at this time of day. At Chez Florentin halfway down the rue Ste. Placide, she could always count on the waiter Hercules to slip her an extra *moules en feuilles*.

Beugnot got up from his desk. "What's the matter now, Jeanne? You're hungry, aren't you?"

Jeanne studied her bruised fingertips and would not look at him.

"And you want to go out and stuff yourself with canapés at the cafés. Don't think I haven't noticed," Beugnot said. He was suddenly weary of being dragged along in the pendulum swing of her moods. Sometimes flush with money, she would be flying so high that days would go by without a sign of life from her. Then she would appear at his door as needy as ever, beguiling, enchanting. Hungry. Whatever money she had, and she was forever borrowing petty sums from him and from her landlord at the Hotel de Reims, never stayed in her pockets very long.

"Look," he said finally as she sat stubbornly mute, "With only a little more work I can present your petition to the Cardinal."

"The Cardinal's gone," she said.

"Gone where?"

"Back to Alsace," Jeanne said, standing up and settling a fine russet cashmere shawl about her shoulders.

"When did he leave?" Beugnot said.

"A week ago. Why he left and when he'll come back, I have no idea. The Abbé tells me nothing." She knotted her shawl fiercely. "I'm sick of Paris! I'm sick of waiting. I'm taking lodgings for me and the Comte at Versailles."

"Versailles? Don't be a fool. You'll be surrounded by the worst riffraff in France, the dregs of society. The place is teeming with charlatans and swindlers and influence peddlers. You with your great ambitions, they'll latch onto you like fresh red meat."

"What would you know about Versailles?" she said, with a decidedly unattractive curl of her lip. "You weary me with your eternal bourgeois moralizing. I can't wait around forever. The Cardinal's no help. The Queen loathes him. I need a patron, and I intend to find one at Versailles."

"Do as you please," Beugnot said. "I've never pretended to be familiar with the grammar of intrigue. And I don't intend to learn it now. But don't forget this: you'll remember me and come running to me some day, when you get into real trouble. Which you most assuredly will."

She shook her head slowly and looked up at him with a roguish smile. "I doubt it. I don't think there will be much room in my life for petty solicitors after I make my mark at Versailles."

Beugnot watched her cross the street and throw her head back to catch a trace of patchy sunshine. She looked small and forlorn. For all her pretensions and her supposed worldliness, she seemed to him still the ragged little girl of Fontette forced to fend for herself in a world with scant mercy for the weak and vulnerable.

He sat back down at his desk and began to write. With any luck he could work through the night and deliver a fair copy of her petition to the Hotel de Reims by early morning.

12

Jeanne did not give a second thought to the fact that the Versailles to which she was now returning was the world of scalawags and scoundrels, of impostors and pretenders, of beggars and bribers who scrounged their way in and out of dank rooms in modest houses such as the one kept by Monsieur and Madame Gaubert on the Place Dauphine. Jeanne found them a lively bunch, and the Gauberts thought that the striking young comtesse with her grand manner added more than a little *bon ton* to their establishment. Armed with Beugnot's petition, Jeanne confided the details of her extraordinary life and name to all who would listen and began to make daily rounds in the offices of the King's ministers.

She could stroll about as arrogantly as she pleased, for Versailles was a public place open to anyone clean and well-dressed, and she had kept enough of her costly gowns out of the *mont de piété* to call attention to herself in her promenades each day along the Galérie des Glaces. Of her former companions during her brief summer of triumph as Mademoiselle de Valois, there were none who deigned to recognize her. The Comte de Blagny had been banished to his country estates in Picardy, it was said, and had taken to drink and the local peasant girls.

The court was as obsessed with the Queen as ever. Each morning Jeanne would make the booksellers installed at the foot of a ramp to one of the terraces her first stop on her way to the royal palace. There, right under the nose of the monarchs, hawkers of pornographic pamphlets and sketches of the Queen in lubricious poses found plenty of customers among the nobility strutting in and out of the palace. Some would grab up the broadsheets and stand and read them right there on the steps, giggling and tittering, winking and rolling their eyes at each other. Jeanne was not really shocked, for she was used to Paris, where the streets were filled from morning to night with strolling singers disgorging the grossest kind of filth about the King and Queen. What she missed hearing, she could always read pasted on walls and lamp-posts all over the city. It was through dirty limericks, written it was rumored by the King's brother, the Comte d'Artois, that Jeanne and all of Paris learned of the simple operation that finally, after seven long years, permitted the King to have an erection and fulfill his marital duty to his wife. Though accustomed to lewd prattle about the royal family, Jeanne wondered why the King would permit such disrespect right on his doorsteps. A Valois king would have had more sense, to be sure.

Jeanne herself would not have missed the latest gossip for the world. For a racy little pamphlet entitled *Les Amours de Charlot et Toinette* describing the supposed liaison between Marie Antoinette and her brother-in-law, the Comte d'Artois, Jeanne spent the last two francs she had filched from her husband's waistcoat pocket. Now that the Queen was a mother with a daughter and a little Dauphin, she no longer dared to frequent the theatres around Paris—where she knew she would be hissed by the audience—for no one had forgotten the Queen's antics with the King's brother, especially at the masked balls at the Opéra. Jeanne relished every word of the pamphlet, though the illustrations she found amateurish.

The Comte spent his waking hours trying his luck at games of chance at the Belle Image Inn on the other side of the Place Dauphin, and it was there, under a table, that he found a shabby copy of the scandalous *Anandria*, copiously illustrated with pictures of the Queen in lewd, lesbian embraces with the Princesse de Lamballe and Yolande de Polignac.

"It's called the 'German vice,'" the Comte said to Jeanne, as if the pictures were not sufficiently self-explanatory. "It's said that the Queen is a ferocious devotee of it."

"Ha! What would you know? You've never even seen the Queen," Jeanne said. "And I have."

But she secreted *Anandria* among her most valued possessions in a place that was sure to escape any of their hasty runs to a pawn-shop, and she read it from cover to cover. Often. Remembering with a kind of confused exaltation the Queen with Yolande de Polignac on the day of the mock naval battle on the Grand Canal, the Queen toying with a lock of the pretty young woman's hair, the Queen removing her own shawl and placing it around her friend's shoulders. *The Queen's favorite*. For Jeanne de La Motte in her bleak room up under the rafters of the Gaubert establishment no siren's song could have been more alluring. *The Queen's favorite*.

At Versailles Jeanne rose each morning as if she were committed to some sort of race. And it was a race she intended to win. From bits and pieces of gossip she inferred that the Cardinal was at the center of yet another scandal and that it was best not to mention his name as her patron. So be it. She scurried about, consulted here, displayed herself there. On days when the Comte had won some money the night before, she ate well, even extravagantly, and on days when he had lost everything, she simply starved and raced about even harder.

One afternoon as she was making her way through the Galérie des Glaces, she attracted the eye of Monsieur de Calonne, the King's Minister of Finance. They exchanged glances. After a few discreet inquiries among her shady friends at the Belle Image, Jeanne decided that de Calonne was a more than suitable target and chose the corridors just outside the minister's stately suite of offices for her stroll the very next day.

De Calonne, who owed his portfolio to the Queen's support, was a short, effusive man with oily good looks whose effect he was inclined to exaggerate. Graciously taking Jeanne's arm, he led her into his office.

"The Comtesse de La Motte-Valois, is it? Why have I never seen you at court before?"

"The injustices of fate, Monsieur," Jeanne said, her voice pleading. "I've brought you my petition to the King. If you would be so kind as to read it, you will find my entire tragic history there."

"It will be an honor to read it, dear Comtesse. An honor. But please be seated." He quickly turned and placed Jeanne's petition on his desk. "No, please, not there. Sit over here, next to the window, where I shall have a better view of your charming person."

He smiled and bustled toward her, giving a knowing nod to his assistant, who closed the door as he left the room.

"The Comtesse de Valois!" he said, gathering up his coat tails and settling his ample person into a chair directly opposite her. "The very name resonates with the illustrious heritage of France! Tell me your story. I'm sure that if it is half as intriguing as you, dear Comtesse, I shall not have wasted my afternoon."

Jeanne, who never tired of telling the story of her life, began to talk, swaying back and forth in a charming way. She had worn her most daring décolletage, a dramatically scooped blue-and-cream striped taffeta with a vivid rose petticoat, and she noted with satisfaction that Monsieur de Calonne seemed to be paying more attention to the folds around her bodice than to the fateful misadventures of her life.

When she finished her story and de Calonne reached for her hand and placed it on his knee, she knew that she had landed her fish. A fish she intended to keep gasping for breath as long as possible.

They parted most reluctantly. "I shall read your petition with . . . great tenderness," de Calonne sighed. "Until tomorrow."

But for Jeanne the many tomorrows that followed brought only promises, and she wondered bitterly if she had landed her fish after all. Fontette and its rich meadows and fragrant orchards remained as remote as ever.

She had agreed to meet de Calonne in his apartments up under the eaves of Versailles where the privileged, like the Minister of Finance, fought and betrayed each other in order to live in a rabbit warren of gloomy, stinking rooms, freezing in the winter and sweltering in the summer, simply for the honor of being near the King and the Queen, of living at court. She was in a bad temper as she toiled up the dark stairway, rank with the odor of garbage, urine, and vomit. Unless de Calonne could assure her that he had at least shown her petition to the King, she would allow him no more than some perfunctory fondling.

"My dear Comtesse," de Calonne said, drawing her into a low-ceilinged little cubicle hung with dark tapestries, a bed in one corner and a pallet on a shelf in the wall for the minister's valet. "You've made me ravenous with your delay," he said with a low chuckle.

"I'm ravenous myself," Jeanne said sharply. "I haven't eaten since yesterday morning." He was a damned fool if he thought she would tumble for any more of his gushy flattery.

De Calonne giggled appreciatively as if she had just made a fine sally of wit.

"I need to sit down," Jeanne said. "That foul stairway has made me faint."

"Of course, my dear," de Calonne said, solicitous, for he had caught a whiff of her anger. He had put on his most expensive dressing-gown and had asked his valet to give him an especially perfumed wig which had witnessed a number of his more notable amorous exploits. He had intended to wait until the end of their rendezvous to surprise Jeanne with his proposal. But, perhaps he would do well not to delay.

"Do you know Madame d'Arveley?" de Calonne asked. He was grinning slyly.

"Madame D'Arveley? No, I never heard of her."

To Jeanne's annoyance, de Calonne pulled her down on his lap. "No matter, my dear," he said. "Madame d'Arveley is my official mistress. My *current* official mistress."

He lifted her hair and blew on her neck. Jeanne wanted to strangle him. What in God's name was he running on about his mistress for? As if she cared!

"Would you be interested, dear Comtesse, in sharing with Madame d'Arveley. A comely woman though her teeth have gone bad, *la pauvre*. Too many sweets. You have excellent teeth, my dear. Your smile is quite overwhelming."

"Share what with Madame d'Arveley?"

De Calonne lowered his voice almost to a whisper. "Why, my heart, dear Comtesse, my heart and my humble self."

Jeanne bounded out of his lap. "It seems I still have a great deal to learn about Versailles," she said haughtily and started for the door.

"When shall I see you again?" de Calonne said, nonplussed. She had seemed so ardent, so willing.

"Tomorrow morning. In your office," Jeanne said drily.

The next morning, after much fumbling and evasion, Monsieur de Calonne informed her that the Fontette property, her former home and birthplace, was presently in the possession of the Duc de Vrillière, one of the King's cabinet ministers, and therefore beyond any further consideration. "The King has sold it to the Duc."

Without a word, Jeanne stood up and walked into de Calonne's antechamber where a few elderly men in court dress waited. They looked up with moist, toothless grins as she came into the room.

"Then I shall just sit down here and make your office my residence, Monsieur, until the King affords me the means to maintain one of my own."

Three days later, baffled that such a sweet, seductive young thing should have turned into a tenacious virago who had turned his ministry upside down, de Calonne brought Jeanne word that the King would increase her original pension from eight hundred to fifteen hundred francs a year.

"Pathetic!" Jeanne said. "On that measly sum the King expects me to maintain myself in the glorious Valois tradition? Ha! Just another royal dole, that's what it is. My family domains, that's what I want, and that's what I intend to get."

Nonetheless, she left de Calonne's offices and headed for the Place Dauphine, where she found the Comte still lying abed to keep warm. Since their few remaining possessions seesawed back and forth between their lodgings and the pawn shop, sometimes the Comte could not get out of their room for days because they did not have enough money to get his clothes back from the *mont de piété*.

"Pack up your things," she said to him. "We are following the court to Fontainebleau."

"You mean following Monsieur de Calonne." He yawned and stretched and settled back under the covers. He was not a jealous man, just lazy and fond of a warm bed.

"De Calonne be damned," she said. "Versailles will be completely deserted in a week or so. The court will be hunting with the King at Fontainebleau, and a good day of hunting can make a stingy man generous. You may not know what that means, but I do. Get up and get dressed."

With Jeanne in Versailles Beugnot's days yawned before him endlessly. There was no more dawdling over a meal at the Cadran Bleu until the waiters grew bored and cranky, no more days cooped up in the deeds and titles archives, fumbling his way through yellowed documents, and, especially, no more interludes on the noisy old bedstead, its mattress ropes whining and sawing, in Jeanne's dingy room at the Hotel de Reims. With a shock, Beugnot realized how much time he had given over to Jeanne and her Valois obsession.

On occasion he began to wander aimlessly in the Marais around the Palais-Cardinal, sometimes with a vague, jealous notion that Jeanne might be hidden away there in some kind of orgiastic bondage to the Cardinal. The magnificence of the palace and rumors of the sensuality of certain rooms had already brought it a certain notoriety, of which Beugnot was only too aware. Jeanne had made it a point to describe to him in excessive detail the Cardinal's "seductive" boudoir, "voluptuously intimate" she called it, with Christophe Huet wall paintings that were the talk of Paris. The paintings depicted the bawdy shenanigans of monkeys in various obscene activities.

"It's called the Salon des Singes, and there are monkeys capering all over the walls. Naughty little monkeys lifting their tails aside and snuffing out candles with their . . . you know . . . ," Jeanne laughed.

"Rather juvenile, I would say," Beugnot sniffed.

"Rather amusing, I would say," Jeanne retorted. "From the Salon des Singes there is a secret door leading to the Cardinal's bedroom. And a hidden staircase leading from his bedroom to the courtyard so that a lady may have a little privacy if she leaves the palace in the small hours of the night. The Cardinal has thought of everything!" Jeanne said with too much enthusiasm.

Beugnot willed himself into silence, but Jeanne's vivid description of the Cardinal's boudoir kept roiling to the surface of his thoughts. Just as she intended.

Late one afternoon in April Beugnot headed once again toward the rue Vieille-du-Temple, on what at the time he thought was an impulse to call in at the Palais-Cardinal and leave a copy of the petition he had prepared for Jeanne. Perhaps the Cardinal had frequent couriers to his residence in Alsace, or perhaps he would be returning to Paris soon. In any event, the Cardinal, he reasoned, had sounded genuinely sincere in his interest in the document.

As he followed a footman up a magnificent straight stairway to the Cardinal's offices, Beugnot was determined not to be intimidated by the splendors surrounding him, the Gobelins tapestries in the foyer, the Beauvais tapestries in the anterooms. And, in spite of himself, Beugnot, remembering the brilliance of the party he had attended at the Palais, wished that he had not come.

A tall, scowling priest came forward to greet him from the far side of a lofty-ceilinged room filled with leather-bound books.

"You wished to see the Cardinal?" he said in a low, weary drawl, cool and businesslike.

"I wished simply to leave off this legal document," Beugnot said, bristling under the priest's scrutiny. "The Cardinal expressed an interest in it." He held out the petition.

The priest's small, dark eyes took in the title, *Jeanne de Saint-Rémy de La Motte-Valois*, like a thirsty dog at a trough of water.

"May I introduce myself," he said. "The Abbé Georgel, His Eminence's secretary and Vicar General." He gave Beugnot a shy, plaintive smile. "Then, you are acquainted with this Comtesse de La Motte?"

"I am. We both come from Bar-sur-Aube in Champagne."

They talked inconsequentially for some time, the Abbé becoming more cordial, more eager to accommodate as the interview wore on. Though something about this dour man made Beugnot suspicious, he could not fail to respond to his affability. Perhaps the Abbé was merely lonely. They parted on the friendliest of terms, the Abbé pressing Beugnot's hand firmly between his, urging him to stop in again whenever he found himself in the neighborhood.

After that day Beugnot couldn't seem to stay away from the Palais-Cardinal. He developed a habit of stopping off from time to time to chat with the Abbé and have a glass of the Cardinal's finest *marc*, regularly sent up from his estates in Burgundy. They got on well, for Beugnot admired the Abbé's thoroughness—they were kindred spirits in that regard—in his administration of the Cardinal's affairs and his rather raw profanity. Beugnot failed to notice that, more often than not, their bibulous conversations in the lower library eventually revolved around the Comtesse de La Motte-Valois.

"Your little Comtesse has flown the coop, hasn't she?" the Abbé said, reaching for the bottle. He steadied his glass and poured himself a drink.

"What comtesse? Do you mean the Comtesse de La Motte?"

"Yes, indeed."

"I believe she has settled in Versailles for the moment. With her husband."

"For the moment, as you say. The Comtesse has her hooks in Monsieur de Calonne. The Minister of Finance," the Abbé said.

"I imagine the Comtesse is seeking his help in petitioning the King for the restitution of the Valois properties," Beugnot said.

"I wouldn't imagine anything of the sort," the Abbé said impatiently. "The Comtesse de La Motte has gone to Versailles to launch her career."

"What career?" Beugnot said uneasily, suddenly aware that he had consumed more than his usual share of the Cardinal's delicious *marc*.

"The career of dazzling men. She's very well suited for it, have you noticed? I suspect you have. That snowy bosom. A man could get lost in it! Such a pair! Such a divine pair!"

"When does the Cardinal return?" Beugnot asked, anxious to divert the Abbé, whose erotic musings he found faintly alarming.

"When his ears stop burning," the Abbé said. "He has been humiliated at court. Again. He can think of nothing else but regaining the Queen's favor. It is the unending torment of his life. Excluded from the inner circle, can you imagine it? A Rohan! This is his tragic cross, Monsieur Beugnot. His tragic cross. The Queen will have nothing to do with His Eminence."

Georgel seemed to drop into some sort of spiritual gloom. Suddenly, he looked up at Beugnot and fixed him with his small, watery eyes. "Do you want to know why the Cardinal left Paris so abruptly for Saverne? Let me tell you. Then you will understand the sorrow of the Cardinal's days and nights. The Queen planned a party and illuminations in the gardens of her Trianon palace for the Czarevitch Paul. Everyone talked of little else. Invitations went out, those precious gilt-edged cards embossed with the royal fleur de lis. As it turned out, it was an exceptionally small party, only the

Queen's pampered little band of favorites. By all accounts, it was a spectacular evening. Unusually balmy weather. Musicians strolling through the garden lanes. Huge logs set aflame in barrows dug behind the Temple of Love, illuminating its classic proportions. Lanterns in profusion. Fairyland. The Queen lives in fairyland, did you know that? The Cardinal was like a madman. Unable to sleep. Unable to work. I could do nothing with him. He would not listen to me. Finally, he put on a long black greatcoat and hied himself to Versailles. There . . . Ah, it breaks my heart. This noble soul! How could he do it, Monsieur? The Cardinal bribed the concierge of the Trianon to allow him to watch the illuminations from the concierge's lodging. He promised not to enter the gardens until the Queen's return to Versailles. Later when the concierge had to absent himself on an errand, His Eminence violated his word of honor to the concierge, slipped out of the lodging, and strolled through the garden. At the height of the festivities! The Queen caught a glimpse of red silk stockings below the hem of the black greatcoat and knew exactly who this uninvited guest was. Naturally, the Cardinal had to flee to Saverne."

Without thinking, Beugnot blurted out, "Why, he sounds the perfect fool. To get so worked up over a *party!*"

To Beugnot's surprise, the Abbé replied blandly, "You might say so, Monsieur. It does appear so. But I can assure you that you will never on this earth meet a more winsome man than His Eminence. He is everything that our nobility can take pride in. Handsome! Little wonder that there was never woman born, except the Queen, of course, who can resist him. Intelligent. Clever. Witty. So refined, so elegant in his taste that he cannot bear to use a common printed missal when he celebrates Mass. He must use instead a rare and magnificent illuminated book of devotions, a family heirloom of great antiquity. 'I must have my own beauties,' he once said to me. 'When I finger those ancient pages, the gilt, the blues, the reds of the illuminations console my spirit and speak of mysteries that only art can perceive.' For High Mass at Versailles he has a petit-point alb, so magnificent I dare not touch it—a floral design interspersed with medallions bearing the Rohan crest and device, and valued at more than 100,000 francs."

He sighed, as if exhausted by the contemplation of such magnificence. "I admire him beyond all measure."

Beugnot said, "Well, I don't understand the court, Versailles, all that ceremony. I don't see why the Cardinal can't just sit down with the Queen and have a talk with her."

The Abbé didn't laugh. The long narrow room had grown dark as the setting sun moved over to the other side of the palace. The Abbé lit a series of tall taper candles that stood in a straight line on the table that served as his desk. He smiled, showing tiny, yellowed teeth, and gestured toward the nearly empty bottle of *marc*.

"How old are you, young man? Twenty-two, twenty-three? Suffice it to say that you are young. You have time to learn that life is never simple. Especially life at Versailles. The Cardinal can't simply sit down and have a talk with the Queen because the Queen will not give him an audience.

"The Queen sounds very stubborn," Beugnot said. His entire memory of the self-assured Cardinal had slipped askew. Why should a powerful man like the Cardinal bother his head with such nonsense?

"She is. And spoiled. Spoiled rotten by her dreadful mother, the Empress Maria Theresa. *She* kicked the Prince out of Austria. Because of a letter. *The notorious letter*. What a sickening affair. To have the Cardinal's extraordinary career as an ambassador come crashing down on his head because of a single letter. Exposed by a careless, stupid woman."

The Abbé's face had gone a little slack and his accent was not as *soigné* as it had been at the beginning of the afternoon.

He put down his glass and looked at Beugnot in a disconcertingly fierce way. "Your little Comtesse, now, she's not a bit careless or stupid, is she?"

"No. On the contrary, I believe her to be rather bright."

"Indeed she is. A natural-born intriguante. She will learn a few tricks in Versailles, I dare say."

He stood up and stretched his long, thin arms over his head, exposing none-too-clean cotton stockings beneath his costly black soutane.

"Actually, they've left Versailles, the Comtesse and her loutish husband," the Abbé said. "They've taken a room in the rue Avon in Fontainebleau. The Comtesse is having a most profitable time, I hear."

A most profitable time? What was he saying? Why was he smirking as if he knew a dirty secret? "I worry about Madame de La Motte," Beugnot said. "She's young, only twenty-seven, inexperienced in the ways of the kind of scoundrels I've heard infest Versailles."

The Abbé tapped him on the shoulder and smiled. "A ravenous pack, yes. But never fear. The Comtesse will get along swimmingly, I can assure you."

They had started walking toward the entrance courtyard. Beugnot looked down and concentrated on the stair steps. "Will the Cardinal remain the Comtesse's patron after he returns to Paris?"

"Of course he will," the Abbé said, with a tight, nasty sneer. "The Comtesse is the Cardinal's latest bit of naughty."

Beugnot felt as if someone had taken him by the shoulders and shaken him.

13

In May of 1784, the Comtesse de La Motte and her husband left Fontainebleau with a sack full of money and sailed back into Paris, leasing a fine establishment in the Rue Neuve-Saint-Gilles with a stone staircase, handsome balustrades with ironwork adorned with lilies in relief, a porter's lodge, baker's oven, coach-house and stables, and richly paneled drawing rooms. Number 13, Rue Neuve-Saint-Gilles, located in the Marais, stood opposite the little gate of the monastery of the Minims.

The La Mottes were quite pleased with themselves, for they had managed to get to this impressive address only through the deftest financial jugglery. Months later they still could find no earthly way of furnishing such a grand place.

Comte de La Motte, in his flashy harlequin outfits, threw himself into the challenge of meeting their daily needs with his usual flair. For their journeys back and forth to Versailles, he hired a private carriage, for Jeanne de La Motte-Valois's name and story were becoming known at court; they must keep up appearances at all costs. In this fine carriage Jeanne would call upon one of the best mercers in the rue Saint-Honoré. After her years of apprentice-ship Jeanne knew them all as well as the quality of their goods. She would purchase a fine piece of silk, twenty-five ells at least, of a fashionable shade. On credit, of course, for a shining carriage, whether hired or not, inspired confidence in a merchant. She would then rendez-vous with her husband on the Champs-Elysées where she would turn over the silk, which he would then take to the *mont de piété* and walk away with twelve or fifteen louis in his pocket. The Comte, as Jeanne had on numerous occasions rejoiced, could work miracles in a pawnshop. It was a precarious facade of prosperity, but it worked.

"Send my carriage round for the Comtesse de La Motte" was Cardinal-Prince de Rohan's first order as soon as he returned to Paris. The notes he had received from Jeanne at Saverne drove him wild with expectation. They were hastily scribbled pieces, full of gaps and groaning with mystery, but the Cardinal kept his couriers busy on the highways bringing corroboration of Jeanne's activities at court from his niece, the Comtesse de Guémenée.

He knew that after the hunting season at Fontainebleau Jeanne had returned to Versailles and, clutching her petition, had fainted away one day in the crowded antechamber of the King's sister, Princesse Elisabeth, or Madame as she was known at court, a kind, pious soul, generous with her patronage who immediately had the ailing young woman carried away in a litter to a charming room in the Hotel de Jouy. Word of Madame's patronage of this impoverished young woman of the Valois blood spread rapidly through the court. Madame's personal chaplain, the Abbé Malet, made a collection for Jeanne that amounted to three hundred livres, Madame adding a few louis from her own purse.

The Cardinal's niece wrote of other fainting spells—or "fits" as the Comtesse de Guémenée called them—one just as the Queen was beginning her walk down the Galérie des Glaces on her way to daily Mass, another under the windows of the Queen's apartments, but Jeanne herself wrote only vaguely of these indispositions. Instead, she hinted, swearing him to silence, of a new "friend," for the term "patron" she said was far too cold to be appropriate for this particular relationship, a "friend" whose name she dare not mention, even to him, her most beloved confidant.

When he received this news, the Cardinal, pacing the finely articulated pathways of his garden at Saverne, decided he could delay no longer his return to Paris and Jeanne.

Finally, on a mild evening of late May, when Jeanne caught sight of the Cardinal's carriage waiting below, she almost wept with relief. At last! She touched scented water to her hair and glanced quickly around the bleak emptiness of her vast drawing room. Soon she would have pictures, and mirrors with thick gold leaf, and deep, silken canapés, and heavy, velvet draperies eloquently costly. She had never dreamed that she would ever need anyone as much as she needed Prince Louis.

"It's the Prince," she said, grabbing up a shawl. "He's sent for me." The Comte stood morosely at an open window, poking his hands around his empty pockets. "Don't wait supper for me."

"Do I ever?" the Comte said.

As the Cardinal watched Jeanne race up the stairs into his arms, her broad, frank smile lighting her face with joy, he thought she had never looked more beautiful.

"Ah, my devilish beauty, how I've missed you," he said. "Come. I want to hear everything."

Jeanne was alive with energy and high spirits, full of malicious gossip from the stuffy antechambers at court with now and again a delightful little anecdote about the Queen herself. The Cardinal was enthralled. He watched her closely, holding her face close to his, puzzled by her edginess, even as he caressed her.

"You bring me back to life, my dear. You're like a gale of laughter sweeping through a funeral Mass," he said.

"Am I?" she said. "I feel wretched, if the truth be told. My new friend is so demanding. She works on my nerves."

"She?" the Cardinal asked, and it seemed to him that his heart had skipped a beat. "She!"

Jeanne closed her eyes and rolled over, turning her back to him.

Prince Louis could feel his universe shifting and settling into a luminous new shape. So it was true: it was just as he had imagined, just as he had so deliriously hoped during those anxious late afternoons in Saverne. Jeanne had caught the Queen's fancy! Naturally!

She was just the sort to amuse the jaded Queen. Risqué. Daring. Why, Jeanne's humor was so earthy that even the Cardinal himself could be caught off guard and blush like a choir boy. Irresistible. Exhilarating. Jeanne was all of these. What was the pallid Yolande de Polignac beside her? An insipid beauty, nothing more.

He ran his hand gently down her back. "Jeanne," he whispered. "Tell me about this friend. Do we have secrets, you and I? Of course, we don't."

Jeanne turned to him, her eyes round and anxious. "I must not tell," she said. "Each time I see her, she swears me to silence."

"It's the Queen, isn't it, Jeanne?" He stared intently at her face, full of shadows in the dim light. "But don't you see? It's a miracle for both of us! You shall have your beloved Fontette, and I shall be reconciled with the Queen. And then all my hopes and dreams . . . I shall tell you everything, dearest, dearest Jeanne. For I have suffered so much, you would scarcely believe what I have been through. And all because the Queen despises me. I have been in torment . . . my galling thoughts turning endlessly around the void into which I am cast . . . bound like Prometheus to a rocky cliff, the awful vulture of exclusion plucking at my soul. But to have the Queen smile on me again . . . confide in me, invite me to her parties at the Petit Trianon." He took a deep breath and settled back against the pillows. "It will be just as Cagliostro has predicted," he said in a musing voice, "Cardinal Prince Louis de Rohan, Prime Minister of France . . ."

"She gives me presents," Jeanne said, hesitantly, watching him out of the corner of her eye. "Odd little things to give me pleasure. Look at this beaded reticule."

She reached out for the reticule that she had carelessly left lying beside her slippers on the floor. The Cardinal knew that everyone at court who frequented the gambling tables, and of course the Queen was notorious for her gambling habits, carried a beaded reticule just like the one Jeanne held out to him. He stared at it in astonishment.

"Take it," Jeanne said, laughing. "Don't be afraid."

Just as the Cardinal took hold of the reticule, the clasp came unfastened, and a note on small, gilt-edged paper embossed with the fleur de lis fell onto the bed. The Cardinal stared at it as if it were a magic talisman.

"It's from the Queen," Jeanne said, her voice suddenly high pitched and edgy. "Like the reticule. She's quite comical. She likes writing me these little *billets*."

Prince Louis turned the note over and studied it carefully. "*Ma chère cousine*." He looked at her in disbelief. "*Ma chère cousine!* She calls you her cousin. But naturally she would, wouldn't she? My dear cousin, why, of course you *are* her cousin!"

"I should say so! A Valois trumps a Hapsburg any day of the week," Jeanne sniffed. "Would you like to read the note?"

Prince Louis slowly turned the note as if it were a sacred object. "Oh, I dare not," he said. "I must sit and think. We have so much to do, my dear." He pushed back the bed curtains and put on a robe and slippers. "Everything is possible now, Jeanne, don't you see? I must coach you in what to do, what to say. We must proceed cautiously. You drop my name here and there, casually, indifferently, as if idly, mentioning my loyalty, my reverence for her, my yearning to see her, to talk to her, to be reconciled after all these punishing years . . ."

"She truly despises you, you know," Jeanne said.

The Cardinal raised his hands in alarm. "That's over. Forgotten. You must make her forget, my dearest. Only you can make her forget. We will rehearse everything."

Jeanne sat on the edge of the bed, shoulders slumped, her long chestnut hair falling over her face. She looked thoroughly overwhelmed. "It's such a trial, Your Eminence. Not what I had expected at all. There are so many people now, banging on my door, asking for favors, begging me to intercede with the Queen."

The Cardinal laughed. "The word is out! There will be more, my darling. Rich ones, poor ones, especially rich ones with purses full of money, ells of silk, and heavy gold bracelets which they will implore you to accept as—what shall I say, *encouragement?*—in promoting their interests."

"That's all very well and good," Jeanne said, "but I don't have a proper salon to receive them. Our lease was exorbitant . . ."

The Cardinal knelt before her and took her head in his hands. "My darling Jeanne, you mustn't worry." He was in a jocular mood, his veins humming with a renewed sense of purpose. Prime Minister of France! "But you're quite right. Money attracts money. You must set yourself up appropriately in the rue Neuve Saint-Gilles. I shall take care of everything. After all, as Grand Almoner to the King, it's my duty to dispense alms to aristocracy in distress, is it not?"

"What a good man you are," Jeanne said with a sigh, slipping into his arms. "The Queen's heart will surely soften when I tell her of your kindness to me."

14

"Sometimes I think it is a sickness, an appalling malady that keeps his mind toiling unceasingly around the idea of the Queen," the Abbé said, as he and Beugnot fairly galloped along the broad graveled pathways of the Tuileries gardens. Beugnot, reluctant to idle away his afternoons at the Palais-Cardinal now that the Cardinal was back in residence, had dragged Abbé Georgel away from their convivial bottle of *marc* and into the gardens, where in the unfashionable early afternoon they could have their usual tête-à-tête in something like the privacy of the Abbé's study.

"Sometimes I don't know what to think because I have never known anyone so possessed and bedeviled by a woman as he is. Of course, it's ambition gnawing away at him, but there's something more now. The Cardinal can spend hours, if you will let him, describing the way Marie Antoinette looked as a young bride the day in 1770 when he officially welcomed her to France. How many times have I heard him describe that catch in his throat as he came down to the bottom of the steps in front of the Cathedral of Strasbourg just as she was being handed out of her carriage, how she had given him a quick, startled look, a little awed perhaps, by the sight of him in his clerical robes, and how the glistening satin of her gown caught the morning sunlight as she bent to kiss his ring."

"All of France lost its heart to Marie Antoinette," Beugnot said, "not just the Cardinal. We French were wild with joy then. We were all delirious. She was so beautiful. I remember hearing about the scaffolding that collapsed on the Place Louis XV killing hundreds of people, and still the rejoicing went on day and night."

The two men both stopped and caught their breath. Spring had boldly declared itself, and along the Seine the young leaves of the plane trees glowed a golden green in the sunlight.

"It was bad enough before that La Motte woman started feeding him her pap. Now the Cardinal is beyond all reason." The Abbé stared gloomily at his dusty shoes.

"What pap?" Beugnot asked.

"She promises him a reconciliation with the Queen. The other night the Comtesse showed him a letter written to her from the Queen signed *your most affectionate cousin, Marie Antoinette*, and since then, he has not had a single good night's sleep. He is on fire! That letter, the proof of the Comtesse's intimacy with the Queen, has rinsed him in ecstasy. He's a sick man, I tell you. A sick man."

"I don't believe it. Where would Jeanne get a letter from the Queen?" Beugnot had not had even a glimpse of Jeanne since her return from Fontainebleau and Versailles.

"It was a note," the Abbé growled. "On terribly delicate, gilt-edged paper. Very fine quality. I saw the note, Beugnot, I didn't read it, but I saw it in the Cardinal's hand. How can I doubt what I saw with my own eyes? A letter from the Queen to the Comtesse!"

"It sounds strange to me."

"What? You mean, the Queen taking up with a little schemer like Jeanne de La Motte? What's strange about that when you think of the women the Queen has been passionate about?" He glanced down the lonely pathway. A pair of Swiss Guards made their slow and stately way toward the Palais-Royal. "The Queen has a predilection for attractive women. There was the Princesse de Lamballe, and then the Queen completely lost her head over that poor ragamuffin Yolande de Polignac. And now look what's happened. The Polignacs were riff-raff aristocrats until beauteous Yolande rescued them all with her sensual charms. Ah, they're disgusting! The smell of their self-importance lingers as they saunter out of the King's Chapel after Mass. The Queen has raised those Polignacs to such heights that the whole court is ruled by them. Why, they spy on the Queen herself! She is virtually their prisoner.

No wonder she's so infatuated with a racy little piece like the Comtesse. The La Motte woman is just the Queen's type."

"I still don't believe she has become the Queen's favorite," Beugnot said.

"How can you not believe it, Beugnot! Everyone I know has seen her on the back stairs leading to the Queen's private apartments."

"I don't know much about Versailles, but I know that I could walk up and down the back stairs leading to the Queen's private apartments if I wanted to and if I were properly dressed. Anyone can."

The gravel made a harsh, grating sound as the Abbé stopped abruptly. His lank black hair stirred in the warm breeze. "You're right, Beugnot," he said. "I hadn't thought of that."

For a long while they were silent as they turned around and made their way back to the Palais-Cardinal.

"You know, Beugnot, what worries me most is that the Cardinal has *confided* in the Comtesse!" He brought his hands up to his chest as if in severe pain. Beugnot had grown exceedingly fond of the Abbé's melodramatic gestures.

"Confided what?"

The Abbé, ever on the lookout for the importunate eaves-dropper, swept a lowering glance over both shoulders.

"The Cardinal has confided his secret ambition to the Comtesse. He has told her everything. He is too trusting, Beugnot. No one, except a faithful confidant like me, should be privy to that searing ambition in the Cardinal-Prince's breast. Now she knows why the Queen's disfavor tortures His Eminence."

"What harm can that do?"

"That's what I keep asking myself," the Abbé said. "I don't know. It gives me a bad feeling for this woman to know the Cardinal's deepest secret, his obsession with becoming prime minister of France. He sees himself in the great tradition of the cardinal prime ministers of the past. Cardinal Richelieu, Cardinal Mazarin, Cardinal Fleury. And now his consuming desire is to become Cardinal Prince Louis-René-Eduard de Rohan, Prime Minister of France. He dreams of nothing else. His ambition devours him, heart and soul. And that is why he is so obsessed with the Queen and the Queen's favor. He knows that he is nothing until the Queen smiles on him. Even with his handsome person, his great intellect, his position of power in the Church, his fabulous fortune and income, his great estates, and his illustrious family, he still cannot be happy. His income is higher than any man's in France, did you know that? I have lived with this tragedy for years now, ever since the Prince was recalled from Vienna. It is destroying him, this ambition."

"You worry too much, Monsieur l'Abbé," Beugnot said, feeling wise and all-knowing. "When a man and a woman become friends," he could not bring himself to say *lovers*, "they commonly confide their deepest secrets in each other."

"I suppose you're right. Somehow it pains me for the Cardinal's sake. It makes me feel as if it gives that adventuress some kind of power over him. Ah, but if it were true, and if she could effect a reconciliation with the Queen, what joy that would bring to my heart. You know, the Prince is an extraordinary man. You should see the papers he has drafted outlining in abundant detail the projects he proposes to undertake and carry out upon his accession to the office of prime minister of the kingdom. It is heartbreaking, Beugnot, how hard he has worked and how much he understands about the misery and poverty of this country. Albeit an aristocrat of the noblest mark, he knows the plight of the poor in Alsace, and he has *plans* to reform our system of taxation. He's a scientist. Not a charlatan like that fool Cagliostro. The Cardinal has discovered a way to extract saltpeter from sea water. A splendid way of saving millions in our manufacture of gunpowder. I wonder that a man of such nobility can fall prey to a baggage like the Comtesse. I know you keep your own counsel, Beugnot, and that in your heart of hearts you still champion the La Motte woman. Nonetheless, to my mind, she is a first-rank predator. What kind of man is she married to? I can't make him out."

"A libertine, a wastrel, without ambition, without talent."

"Compliant, however. By all appearances."

"Yes. The Comte de La Motte carries his burnt offerings to the altars of other goddesses of love," Beugnot said.

The Abbé laughed but remained preoccupied. They turned the corner of the Palais-Royal, where whores in their garish glory were just beginning their promenade, trolling for customers.

"Which calls to mind your good friend the Comtesse," the Abbé said, darting a malicious glance at the whores. "She managed to bring in a fine harvest in that drafty attic room on the Rue Avon in Fontainebleau. She came away with a pile of money. Enough to lease one of the handsomest establishments in the Marais. The Comtesse is a better *pute* than her husband is a gambler."

"What a preposterous assumption, Monsieur l'Abbé!" Beugnot said angrily. Georgel was going entirely too far.

"I don't assume anything, Beugnot. I know. I have my sources. What do you think she was doing up there in that pokey little room all day long, while respectable gentlemen, courtiers, officers, and God knows what all, called upon her, one after the other, while the Comte went off to warm himself in the reception rooms at the chateau? *Hein?*"

"The Comtesse has done what she set out to do. She has found patrons at Versailles. Calonne. The King's sister."

"Ah, yes, the Princesse Elisabeth. True enough. That good lady's patronage, *hélas*, lasted only a few weeks. Your Comtesse became a trifle greedy. The King's brother saw her in the Oeil de Boeuf and fancied her. When he sent his equerry around to solicit her for his bed, your friend leapt at the chance. Naturally, the Princesse Elisabeth found out and dropped her protégée without further ado."

They walked in silence along the arcades of the Place des Vosges. Beugnot had thought of lingering with the Abbé over a glass of *marc*, but now there would be no pleasure in it. The Abbé would only pour out more filth about Jeanne and sit there gloating over his misery.

"But you yourself say the Queen has taken her up," Beugnot said finally.

"So it seems. The Comtesse had some sort of seizure just below a window of the Queen's apartments in full view of Her Majesty. A miscarriage, or so the Comtesse alleges." Beugnot felt a sudden chill. "At any rate, the Queen was touched. So now the dreadful woman is the Queen's latest whim. It makes me wonder all the more why the La Motte woman keeps gouging the Cardinal. His Eminence has been dipping again and again into the national charity fund for indigent aristocracy."

"I see nothing wrong with that," Beugnot said, "The Comtesse is indigent, and she is an aristocrat. Of the blood royal, it appears."

"The woman has a royal pension!" the Abbé snarled. "And the Cardinal has been dropping enormous sums of money into this outrageous woman's hands! From the King's charity fund, and from *his own pockets!*" The Abbé's voice rose to a squeal, as if someone had a knife to his throat. "No amount of money can satisfy that woman!"

Beugnot could say nothing against the truth of that statement. Jeanne had it in her head that she was some sort of princess who must have all the trappings of opulence to show the world just how royal she was. She was exasperating.

"By the way, the Comtesse has added another string to her bow," the Abbé said, as the Palais-Cardinal came into view at the end of the rue Vieille-du-Temple. "He's tall, quite blond, with a sweet face I'm told. He sings and quotes verse. Quite a pair of love birds, they are. The Comtesse will be opening her salon soon. Do tell me what you think of him."

"Who is he? What's his name?" Beugnot asked, wondering how many more vales of gloom he had to cross before he could retreat to the safety of his books.

"Rétaux de Villette. A former cavalry officer from Lunéville. Now the Comtesse's personal secretary. Apparently, he writes letters for her," the Abbé said with a sardonic smile.

15

Perhaps the Comtesse de La Motte-Valois's salon was not the most exclusive in Paris, but it was by far the liveliest. There was always an amusing sideshow of some sort, usually featuring the fantastical Count Cagliostro, his massive body winking and glimmering with jewels, his wife Serafina, a slim, dark, and mysterious presence at his side. The habitués were a curious bunch: an officer or two of the guard, a gaggle of comtesses and marquises, elderly tax-collectors hovering around Jeanne with their oily compliments, and a Comte d'Olomieu who dropped in every afternoon to play a game of tric-trac with Jeanne.

There was the requisite number of fashionable abbés, and one especially unfashionable abbé. His name was Father Loth, and he was short, mule-headed, and swarthy. His worshipful eyes followed Jeanne's every move. He belonged to the order of the Minims, whose monastery was located just opposite the La Motte establishment. Shortly after making Jeanne's acquaintance, Father Loth attached himself to her household as her devoted slave. He ran errands for her, hid her silver when the bailiffs came calling, did pitched battle with her creditors, arranged appointments with her dressmakers, and, curiously enough, opened the back door of the monastery chapel every morning at ten o'clock to celebrate Mass for the Comtesse de La Motte in aristocratic solitude. For Jeanne was extremely devout.

13 rue Neuve Saint-Gilles looked for all the world like any other fashionable aristocratic residence in the Marais. Footmen in brilliant green livery with gold braid scurried around looking

important; Jeanne had a pert little maid named Sophie and a valet named Deschamps, both of whom were so loyal to their mistress that they sometimes borrowed from their own families to keep the La Motte household going. And Deschamps developed a strong back hustling the stately furniture out the backdoor to safekeeping whenever the bailiffs and creditors started pounding on the front door. Despite the Cardinal's largesse and her growing reputation as a *faiseuse d'affaires*, an influence peddler who could put in a good word with the Queen, Jeanne's imposing way of life was more than once hit by severe financial blight.

In late June of 1784, Jeanne gave a supper party, and, for the most part, her house was filled with hopefuls looking to her to intercede with the Queen. Perrin, the Cardinal's silk furnisher in Lyon, took Jeanne aside and presented her with a case of superb fabrics worth at least ten thousand francs, begging her to advance one of his projects, something to do with irrigation. She listened distractedly to the rotund silk merchant, her eye wandering expectantly toward the double doors of the drawing room, puzzled that Claude Beugnot had not yet appeared. After all, she had sent her diminutive black servant Jocqui—a fashionable gift from the Cardinal—with a special invitation.

Toward eleven o'clock she gave a short cry of delight when Beugnot stepped through the double doors and peered solemnly around the room. He was finely, even elegantly, dressed in black velvet and satin the color of freshly churned butter. There was always an air of usefulness about Beugnot that never failed to lift her heart.

"Well, what do you think?" she asked, taking him by the hand and leading him from room to room. "What would Bar-sur-Aube say about all this, *hein*? Look at the candelabra. Tessier. Yes. Truly it is." She laughed nervously and fingered her necklace. "And Madame de Surmont thought her drawing rooms *le dernier cri* of elegance! The old cow would faint if she set her eyes on my ormulu! It's all signed by Leleu. Every piece." She sighed with satisfaction and squeezed his arm. "Come. Take me into supper."

At table Beugnot had no trouble guessing the identity of Jeanne's latest admirer. By all appearances, Rétaux de Villette had taken up residence in the La Motte household, and by all appearances, he was completely besotted with its mistress. He rose jauntily to offer toast after toast to Jeanne in rhymed couplets that evoked *oohs* and *aahs* around the table. With little difficulty Jeanne persuaded him to do an imitation of Mademoiselle Contat of the Comédie Française that made everyone, including Beugnot, double up with laughter. He appeared to Beugnot to be about thirty years of age, tall, impossibly handsome, with a round, rather angelic face. Beugnot grudgingly found him entertaining, though rather too effeminate.

After supper, accompanied by Comte de La Motte at the harp, Villette sang with professional ease several melodies of Rameau and of Francoeur. Beugnot stood near the back of the assembly and watched. The three of them made quite a picture: the Comte with his big, square peasant-like hands poised delicately at the harp, his ponderous nose pulling his head forward to the strings, and Rétaux de Villette warbling away, his dreamy eyes fixed on the still dreamier eyes of Jeanne de La Motte.

Watching this cozy *ménage à trois*, Beugnot resolved yet again to stick to his work and forget about Jeanne. And this time he meant it.

"Well?" Jeanne said, breathlessly, as he bent over her hand to take his leave, "What do you think?"

"Think of what?"

"Why . . . of all this?" she said, her dark eyes sweeping over the opulent room. She found it churlish of Beugnot not to be visibly impressed by this turn in her fortunes.

"Splendid entertainment," Beugnot said, nodding toward Villette.

"You mean my talented secretary?"

Beugnot laughed. "Your secretary, is it?"

"What on earth do you mean?" Jeanne said, thrusting out her chin. "Have you lost your senses?"

For a moment Beugnot thought he had. He had never seen her look more righteously indignant. "And what does your secretary do?" he said, trying not to smile.

"He writes my letters for me. All my correspondence. Look at the invitation you received, blockhead!" Jeanne said and pushed him toward the door.

Before climbing into bed that night, Beugnot opened his desk and found Jeanne's invitation stuffed among a pile of letters and bills. The invitation had been written in a remarkably delicate, feminine hand. He brought the card closer to the light. It could have been the hand of any fashionable woman in Paris.

"Aagh! That woman gives me a headache!" he said, tossing the card to the floor.

16

The Abbé Georgel was sick with worry. For weeks Prince Louis had been consumed by his correspondence with Marie Antoinette. He could think of nothing else. He lost weight. He slept fitfully if at all. From the moment Madame de La Motte arrived with that first dainty sheet of the finest gilt-edged notepaper upon which the Queen had written, *I have read your letter and am happy that I need no longer consider you guilty. I cannot yet grant you the audience you seek; as soon as circumstances permit, I shall advise you. In the meanwhile, remember, be discreet,* this handful of words had plunged the Cardinal into inexpressible hope.

The Abbé had read the Queen's letter; indeed, he knew it by heart, for he and the Cardinal had spent hours analyzing each word, weighing each phrase. With little persuasion from the Comtesse de La Motte the Cardinal wrote a polite reply, thanking the Queen's for her gracious mercy, and the Queen, amazingly, had then responded with an exquisitely phrased note. The Cardinal was drunk with joy. He now saw the Comtesse de La Motte as his tutelary angel, opening up the paths of his future happiness and glory. This exchange of letters with the Queen had become his constant and most cherished preoccupation.

The Cardinal-Prince was obsessed by his quest to find favor with the Queen. There was no mistake about that. When the Abbé tried to reason with him, the Cardinal wasted no time putting him in his place. Georgel soon found himself excluded from the circle of the Cardinal's intimates who met each day, usually in the late afternoon, to read the Queen's latest billet and to advise the Cardinal on his reply to it. While the Count Cagliostro, Madame de La Motte, and of all people, Schreiber, the Cardinal's valet, convened in the Cardinal's study, the Abbé was forced to sit in miserable solitude in the ground floor library, occupying himself with the Prince's "lesser" affairs.

So the Abbé was obliged to fall back on other stratagems for keeping abreast of the Cardinal's activities. He began to spy on the Cardinal. Everything he learned filled him with alarm. It was as if the La Motte woman had waved an enchantress's hand across the Cardinal's eyes and shut out every ray of reason. Prince Louis's behavior struck the Abbé as nothing short of delirious. On several occasions the Cardinal had donned a disguise and taken his carriage to Versailles, where he positioned himself in just the right spot to observe the Comtesse de La Motte stopping to chat a moment with the concierge at the Petit Trianon before departing up one of the darkened pathways, presumably for a secret rendezvous with the Queen. One night, the La Motte woman seemed very well aware that the Cardinal was awaiting her departure, for she approached the palace gates escorted by a tall man who turned back before reaching the gates and re-entered the palace grounds. She then teased the Cardinal out of his hiding place and laughed and joked with him for spying on her.

"Who was that man with you?" the Cardinal asked, for the Abbé heard him quite clearly from his own hiding place.

The La Motte woman laughed and said, "Desclaux. You must have heard of him. He's the Queen's confidential messenger at the Petit Trianon."

"There was something too coy in the Comtesse's reply," the Abbé said, as he recounted the incident to Beugnot. "I can't make out what the woman is up to, but she's up to something, you can be sure of that."

Beugnot laughed. "You've been a spy too long, Monsieur l'Abbé. Everything is smoke and mirrors to you. The Cardinal is a little over-eager, that's all."

Sometimes Beugnot's youthful level-headedness drove Georgel crazy.

"Well, you'll never guess the latest," the Abbé said, flaring his nostrils in disgust. "Our divine Count Cagliostro, having communed with the Bright Angel of Light and the Dark Angel of the Shadows, has predicted that the Prince's secret correspondence with the Queen will bring him the ultimate royal favor, a position of supreme power in the government. The Prince will of course use this power to forward the noblest ideals of mankind, to the glory of the Supreme Being and to the welfare and happiness of the French nation."

"So there you are, my good man!" Beugnot said, slapping Georgel on the back. "No need to worry, is there? I think we should celebrate the Cardinal's imminent accession to power with our usual glass of *marc*."

"Splendid idea, Beugnot!" the Abbé said, his tiny eyes glinting with pleasure. "I happen to know a man who has a bottle of the finest *marc* in France."

But several days later there was little to laugh about in the ground floor library when Baron da Planta, the Cardinal's treasurer, laid before the Abbé a letter from the Cardinal ordering a sum of sixty thousand francs to be transmitted without delay to the Comtesse de La Motte. Heavily underscored at the bottom of the page was an admonition that under no circumstances must this withdrawal be mentioned to Monsieur l'Abbé Georgel.

The Abbé stared at the letter in amazement. What could this mean? His first thought was that the Cardinal must have gone mad.

"Why are you showing me this letter?" The Abbé felt cold and suddenly ill. "Since His Eminence expressly states that he wants this transaction to take place without my knowledge."

Baron da Planta, a large Swiss who tended to look ill at ease in the best of circumstances, tugged at his wig and blinked. "It's just that . . ." He smoothed his waistcoat over his round belly. "It's just that I know you have prior commitments . . . and, ah, regular disbursements that must be made, that you must guarantee as the comptroller of His Eminence's estate. And in addition to the other large sum of money already . . . I thought you should know."

"But what in God's name is the money for?"

"It's for the Queen, Monsieur l'Abbé. For a discreet charity donation Her Majesty wants to make. Secretly, so that the King will not know. With the other large sum . . ."

"What does the La Motte woman have to do with it, then? Oh, of course, how could I have forgotten." Georgel slumped back in his chair. "The Comtesse is to take the money to the Queen. Is that it?"

"Yes. Like the other sum." The Baron stared past the Abbé at the sunny tranquility of the Cardinal's garden. He never knew where to look when the Abbé threw one of his tantrums. For a tantrum was very definitely in the air.

"The other sum?" the Abbé asked quietly, as he shot out of his chair.

"Yes. The other sum. The other sixty thousand francs. Which the Queen requested a fortnight ago. Which the Cardinal borrowed from Cerf-Beer. Who was most obliging to His Eminence."

"One hundred and twenty thousand francs!" A clenched fist pressed against his lips, his eyes wide, the Abbé stared at de Planta in disbelief. "One hundred and twenty thousand francs!" he murmured again, then fell silent. He sat down and rested his head in his hands. "You have done well, Monsieur le Baron, to inform me of this . . . this . . . I shall not forget it. As you say, I am in a sense guarantor of the estate and with this impossible . . . impossible . . . fortune doled out in this way. You must excuse me, Monsieur, I am quite at a loss. I am not myself. Will the Cardinal be returning from Versailles this afternoon?"

"His Eminence is not at Versailles. He has withdrawn to Saverne. At the Queen's request."

"He has left Paris? Without advising me?"

Georgel felt faint, as if his world had suddenly turned upside down leaving no solid ground beneath his feet. After all these years of loyal service, of being the Prince's confidant and support, now to be left behind in ignorance, told nothing, while huge sums of money were being plucked from the treasury, his authority as comptroller undermined, and . . .

Baron da Planta cleared his throat. "I believe, that is, I understand His Eminence has retreated to Alsace while the Queen prepares his triumphant return to Versailles. To the court."

"What! So soon?" It seemed only yesterday that he and Beugnot were laughing their heads off over Cagliostro's silly prediction. *Silly!* So the La Motte woman had triumphed after all. In so short a time! The Abbé's head reeled. He held out his hand weakly to the Baron. "Forgive me if I do not stand. I am in your debt . . ." He knew that he should say more but could not.

As soon as da Planta closed the door, the Abbé's first thought was that he would hand in his resignation as soon as the Cardinal returned to Paris. Georgel would crawl back, ingloriously, to Auvergne, to La Chaise-Dieu. He would stand waiting for the Cardinal at the top of the staircase and coldly hand him his letter of resignation. The Cardinal would look up at him apprehensively, would open the letter, run his eyes over it, then bring his hand to his forehead as if wounded beyond all measure.

The Abbé could not push his imagination further. It was too painful. On the wall opposite his table an immense portrait of the Cardinal as a young man in his late twenties, soon after his election to the Académie Française, stared benignly down at him. All the familiar odors of this room—the stale smell of old leather, the lingering scent of sandalwood that the Cardinal always used after his morning bath, the perfume of the Cardinal's yellow roses in the eastern parterre, even a pungent whiff from his own socks— soothed the Abbé's spirits. An aimless summer breeze stirred the papers in front of him. This was his world. This was where he belonged. In this palace four cardinals de Rohan had succeeded each other, prince-bishops of Strasbourg, and the last, Prince Louis, the most brilliant of them all. When the Cardinal-Prince chose him to join his retinue, the rejoicing of the Abbé's family resounded throughout the province. His mother, sitting at her window looking out upon a gloomy, wind-scoured square, wept tears of joy, warm flooding tears that coursed over the puffy wen on her neck and crumpled the starch of her collar. How bountiful the

Prince had been to all the Abbé's kin! His smile was golden, the kindly sparkle in his deep blue eyes a wellspring of benefices and appointments. What would Georgel's family think of him when he was only a humble curé in La Chaise-Dieu?

Leave the Cardinal? Impossible. The Abbé lifted his eyes to the Cardinal's portrait. The summer light played over the handsome young man with his head of incongruous silver gray hair. The Abbé could not stop staring at the portrait. The young man radiated confidence, trust, goodness, as if he had only to bend a little at the waist to scoop up the rewards of this world.

The Abbé bowed his head and began to pray.

17

Beugnot had given up any hope of having Jeanne, as in the old days, turn up hungry and frolicsome at his door. What further need had she of him and his heavy, dry, legal talk, now that she was supposedly the Queen's favorite? With a charming male secretary to take care of her correspondence and God knows what else. There were no more invitations to her bright and glittering salon. What news he had of her came from the bilious Abbé, and even that source dried up when the Abbé himself disappeared without a word at the end of June.

Before Beugnot left Paris for his usual vacation in Bar-sur-Aube, he tried every trick he knew to get Jeanne to meet him privately. Even the prospect of a *boeuf en daube* at the Cadran Bleu, her favorite dish and one of the more reliable ploys in his seduction repertoire, failed to arouse more than a few effusive—and patently hasty—lines of regret. After several attempts Beugnot made up his mind that Jeanne and her dubious shenanigans at Versailles were a lost cause.

On Beugnot's first night at home, when he and his father were having a cup of coffee after dinner in the library, the house-keeper brought in an elaborately sealed letter addressed to Claude Beugnot.

"It's from Jeanne," he said to his father. "Jeanne de La Motte."

"The little lass of Fontette? Poor child. What does she say?"

"Well, I can make neither head nor tail of it. She says she has a few days free and is coming to spend them with her friends here in Bar-sur-Aube."

Jeanne wrote in a breezy, offhand style, as if she and Beugnot had just parted, mentioning as if it were the most natural thing in the world that she had sent her household furnishings and saddle horses on ahead and she herself would follow two days later. What in God's name was she up to now, Beugnot wondered as he folded the letter carefully and put it into his pocket.

"I'm afraid you may be disappointed in your protégée, father."

"The little lass? Why so?"

"Suffice it to say that for some months now Madame de La Motte has been engaging in activities of a questionable nature. I won't elaborate. Despite the exalted society now frequenting her drawing rooms, a self-respecting man like yourself, father, would do well to keep your distance from her."

"Surely you are too harsh, Claude."

"Not harsh enough, I'm afraid," Beugnot said.

The tone of the letter nettled him: Jeanne, in the offhand manner of the grand lady, the chatelaine, giving orders to her *vileine sujet*, instructed him to find suitable accommodations for her and her staff.

After giving the letter some thought, Beugnot decided to ignore it, putting her extraordinary demands down to another one of her flights of Valois fancy. He was not in the mood to humor her.

Two days later, Nicolas de La Motte's sister, Madame de Latour, a pale, dutiful female who had in the past shouldered more than her fair share in keeping a roof over the heads of the La Mottes, came running to Beugnot with a letter of her own with identical instructions indicating that the La Mottes would be arriving in town in two days with an entourage that seemed likely to tax the amenities of a modest chateau.

"She wants the house of the Carnavallets, near the river. Because it has commodious stables," Madame de Latour said, her eyes bulging with the enormity of the idea. "She and Nicolas will be bringing their saddle horses! What can it all mean, Monsieur Beugnot? Saddle horses! And carriages! Surely my sister-in-law can't be serious, Monsieur."

"Surely not," Beugnot said. "A prank more than likely, Madame de Latour. To stir up country folk like us."

"Paris has gone to her head, Monsieur Beugnot. We all knew it would, didn't we? I shall think no more of it then."

"Nor shall I, Madame," he said. "Saddle horses!" And they both laughed heartily at the impertinent idea.

Beugnot had no sooner dismissed the idea of Jeanne's regal arrival in town than it began to happen. He awoke one morning to the sound of a heavily-laden wagon drawn by a team of horses groaning along the high road. And behind the wagon followed a pair of unmistakably valuable saddle horses.

A maitre d'hotel and his assistants arrived first, accompanying wagon-loads of silver, china, linens, and other household effects, and helped Madame de Latour quickly bundle the Carnavallet family out of the way before setting to work making their mansion suitable for the installation of the La Mottes. The maître d'hotel then proceeded to order enough provisions to supply the best-stocked larder in Bar-sur-Aube for six months. It was a vision from a fairy tale that had the whole town gawking out of windows and hanging around the streets. People stopped one another outside shops, exclaiming over the latest developments, reeling down the streets in disbelief as one wagon-load after another of provisions and finery labored into town. Not since Julius Caesar passed through Bar-sur-Aube to hang a few of his miscreant magistrates had the town seen such a parade of opulence.

As it turned out, that was merely the three strokes of the cane before the curtain rose on the real spectacle: the entrance in all their glory of the Comtesse de La Motte and her husband in an enameled and gilded carriage with brilliantly liveried coachmen and outriders.

Beugnot, standing on the garden terrace with his father, gaped in amazement as Jeanne gave him and his father a regal flourish of the hand as her carriage passed by.

"My son, you've fallen into the dreadful habit of making snap judgments," Albert Beugnot said to his son. The old man was purring with delight at the sight of his "little lass of Fontette" returning for a visit in all her glory. "That poor child! How many times I used to give a handful of coins to the curé of Fontette to help clothe the little creature!"

Beugnot stood on the terrace, dazzled into silence, and watched Jeanne's carriage slowly circle the square before turning left toward the Carnavallet house and the river. At least, Beugnot thought, she has spared me the grinning face of her bonny secretary.

"An honest man admits the error of his judgments, Claude. You've put Madame de La Motte down as a woman of no consequence. Or worse, if I am to understand your remarks correctly. No doubt because she failed to show proper appreciation of your briefs and petitions on her behalf. Never mind. As you can see with your very own eyes, Madame de La Motte is a woman about to recover possession of the family properties belonging to her noble name. I may not be as well versed as you on the subject of royal-domain, but I do have absolutely reliable sources who inform me that the Queen herself is taking a personal interest in this poor child's fate."

With that, he gave his son a nudge of the elbow as if to say that it was rather a pity that a great oaf like Beugnot could reside in Paris and yet remain ignorant of this sort of information.

"I do hope that you will come to your senses and show our little Madame de La Motte that you have never ceased to be her devoted and respectful friend."

The day following her arrival in Bar-sur-Aube, Jeanne rose early and dressed for a round of formal visits to the local nobility. Though there were those who found her air of familiarity rather impertinent, they were one and all charmed by her grand manner, the Valois name, and her rumored intimacy with the Queen. When they returned her call, Jeanne exulted that it had been just as easy as she had predicted to win them over. She saw herself one day taking her place as the head of this charming little society with great and small coming to pay her court. However, when she tried to organize a series of small dinner parties, the respectable ladies of the town under a variety of pretexts sent their regrets.

Baffled but defiant, Jeanne fell back on the only resources she had: her husband's family, including the much-despised Surmonts. Even so they were only eight at table: her husband's sister and brother-in-law, Monsieur and Madame de Latour; her husband's uncle and aunt, Monsieur and Madame de Surmont; the ever faithful Claude Beugnot and Mademoiselle Suzanne Colson, an orphan cousin of Nicolas de La Motte whom Jeanne, ever mindful of the necessities of fashion, intended to take back to Paris as her reader and *dame de compagnie*.

Jeanne, who loved food and knew her wines, coaxed from her chef a feast that would have done honor to the King himself. "I want an *homard farci à l'estragon* that will bring them to their knees, André," she said.

"Of course, Madame la Comtesse. An *homard farci* that will bring them to their knees and make them weep. I understand."

Her guests assembled around the table at two thirty in the afternoon, somewhat late for provincials, but Jeanne assumed this was a small price for them to pay for being fashionable. When she swept into the dining room and surveyed the sumptuous beauty of the table, it was all she could do not to gasp with pleasure. The crystal shimmered, the linens gleamed a stiff, bright white, the china had the beautiful allure of newly minted money. So this is it, she said to herself as she slipped into her chair, and she knew for a certainty that she was happy.

Yet right away, as soon as she picked up her fork, she realized that something was amiss. For one thing, the guests kept up their chattering as they took their seats, dipped their heads and started to eat with the relish of farmhands, without a word of comment, as if such exquisite food were their daily fare. Jeanne watched them with disgust. They might as well be feeding at a slop house for all they noticed the elegance of the table.

At the other end of the table, her husband cleared his throat and swept his large, gleaming nose right and left. "Such a happy choice of silver, my dear," he said, lifting a knife as if he had just noticed it. "The very last word in style and craftsmanship. Your taste is excellent, as always." He laid it back down carefully and smiled around the table.

Monsieur de Latour, his brother-in-law, picked up his knife, scrutinized it, then put it down dismissively. "The very last word? I should say not. This is a very old style. Discarded for its impracticality, I believe."

Mademoiselle Colson looked up with a startled face, as if she had just swallowed a giggle. The other guests kept their heads down, but Jeanne was sure that she saw Beugnot and Latour exchange amused glances. Her husband was a fool, she had no quarrel with that, but those two, Beugnot and Latour, were deliberately maneuvering the conversation, heading off any compliments, setting a tone of appearing unimpressed by the dinner, no matter how splendid it was.

She was outraged. And certain that she had judged correctly. Immediately after dinner, she invited Beugnot to follow her into the study.

"The insolence of my brother-in-law!" she burst out as soon as she had closed the door. "You were both odious! The two of you, sitting there at my superb table, smirking at the footmen, squashing compliments about the table and dishes."

"Perhaps we were all overwhelmed," Beugnot said.

"Overwhelmed by what?"

"Why, by the display of such affluence. Such sudden and mysterious affluence."

Jeanne drew herself up and stood for a moment considering him, as if he were a shoulder of meat that she was reluctant to purchase. "You must surely by now be aware of my—how shall I say this without being offensive?—of my lofty connections at Versailles." She gave a sharp, brittle laugh. "Yes, I suppose *lofty* would be the correct word for the very top of the heap." She relaxed her shoulders and touched her hair. She was dressed in a peach silk gown embroidered with tiny amethysts. "There has been a profound change in my fortunes, Claude. And there's a favor I must ask of you. I hope I can count on you, dear friend."

"Of course you can. If it's something reasonable," Beugnot said.

"*Reasonable!* You make me laugh. You and your bourgeois scruples. It's really a very small request. I meant only that you're always so diplomatic. And sensible. You would do me the greatest possible favor if you would let it be known here in Bar among my husband's family and friends that they would be well advised to adopt a new tone with me. In future I shall insist on being approached with the respect that is my due. I wish you to make that perfectly clear to everyone, especially my brother-in-law."

This brother-in-law was a curious character, a fine example of the vagaries of provincial marriages. Monsieur de Latour's proper milieu should have been the most fashionable café or salon in Paris. He was a ruthless wit, with a sharp eye for the ridiculous, the pretentious, the absurd. In Paris he would have been the most actively detested man in the capital—and the most sought after.

"Ah, well, as far as Monsieur de Latour is concerned, I can promise you nothing. I shall do my best, however."

Beugnot was still smarting over the chill of her addressing him as *dear friend*. She seemed to have no recollection whatsoever of their lusty afternoons in the willow groves along the river in Bar or in her dilapidated room at the Hotel de Reims.

Jeanne shrugged her shoulders impatiently and walked over to the large windows giving out onto the garden. "Ah, Claude, you can't possibly understand. This husband of mine and his family are a millstone around my neck. If only I had married a man of title and position at court as I so easily could have done! Instead, I'm stuck with a man whose name means nothing, whose connections are vile and provincial. Nicolas de La Motte is a dead weight. To get myself this far, I've had to use my name above his. This violation of etiquette revolts me. Even here, in my birthplace, I've been shunned. Look around that table tonight. Not a true aristocrat among them."

"I should think you would have known what to expect in Bar."

"I had every reason to expect a better reception," she said haughtily. She gazed out at the garden where lackeys were raking fanciful patterns into the gravel paths. "Dear Fontette . . . Today I stopped to walk around the old chateau. There were chickens nesting where the ballroom used to be. The roof is gone. The moat is a stinking rut filled with heaps of stones. It breaks my heart. I dream of restoring it and coming back here to live, you know."

"A pretty dream," Beugnot said, "but like all dreams, not at all sensible."

"I expected you to say that," Jeanne said with a melancholy smile.

"Just tell me where the money came from, Beugnot, that's all I want to know."

Latour, a dainty little man with bright auburn sideburns, was in high spirits, playfully skipping along the path bordering the discreet little Aube river. "Did you hear? The most high and mighty Comte and Comtesse de La Motte have bought a house on the edge of town, paid twice what it was worth—all cash, too, mind you—and have hired architects to proceed with every structural folly money can buy."

"Bought a house?" Beugnot said. "She told me she was going to restore the old chateau."

"Oh, that, too. She'll use the house as a modest residence while the chateau is being restored."

After Jeanne's departure her brother-in-law had pursued Beugnot day after day with salty speculations about the La Mottes' sudden wealth. "*Diable!*" he said, "You Parisians think you're so sophisticated. Oh, Paris! Holy Mecca of fools and rascals. You're the most gullible people on earth! Where else but in Paris could this little hussy and her great gawk of a husband have made off with a bundle like that? Why, no one in Bar-sur-Aube, with the exception of your good father, of course, would have lent them a sou! And the Queen! Ho, Ho, Ho! the Queen! An imprudent lady by all reports, but even so! even so! She can't be wild enough to get involved with a little rogue like Jeanne de La Motte! *Ergo*, where did the money come from? *Hein*? You know as well as I do. Though you won't admit it. Therein lies a tale, I suspect. No pun intended, *mon cher! Passons!* You know that of all our lady Jeanne's acquaintances, only the Cardinal de Rohan would have pockets deep enough to put on this show. Only the Cardinal! Am I right? Then tell me this: how could a two-bit provincial wench like Jeanne seduce a prince, a prelate, a *bon à rien* who happens to head one of the greatest families in France?"

"That's enough!" Beugnot said.

He liked Latour and would have been bored senseless in Bar without his company, but the man's unceasing banter, like the Abbé's venomous comments, turned him inside out. He immediately leapt to Jeanne's defense; he could not help himself. "You don't know the titled company Jeanne associates with now. She has financiers like Darcy and Lecoulteux de La Noraye, the Comte d'Estaing, and the governor of Champagne falling all over each other in her salon. You're buried in the country. You don't have any idea of the figure she cuts in the very best of Paris society. The Cardinal is only one of her many acquaintances."

Beugnot almost said "admirers," but stopped himself. He had already arrived at Latour's conclusion about Jeanne's change in fortune. But the more he stared at it, the more he shied away from it. He could not bear to think about it because he knew the situation at the Palais-Cardinal well enough to know that Abbé Georgel would not willingly allow the Cardinal to part with such an enormous amount of money. That being so, Jeanne—foolish, headstrong, proud Jeanne—must be wading into deep, turbulent waters.

Monsieur de Latour stood twisting the ends of his mustache as he studied Beugnot closely. "Ah, well, you may be right, I daresay. Still, the Cardinal's liberality is legendary. Even among us country folk."

"Yes, his generosity is legendary," Beugnot replied uneasily, thinking that not even the Cardinal would *give* a fortune away.

18

"Don't worry about me, Monsieur l'Abbé," the Cardinal said. "I'm quite all right."

In truth, the Cardinal had never felt worse in his life. He was depressed. His head ached constantly, and his dry hands trembled with anxiety. His retreat to Saverne had resulted in naught. Those endless, hot summer days of pacing the rose garden paths, waiting for a signal, waiting for the enchanted words that would send him back to Versailles in triumph brought only more empty promises from the Queen. He came to dread the sight of his footman slowly approaching with yet another pale blue envelope embossed with fleurs de lis resting on a silver platter.

"Perhaps Your Eminence could go hunting. A bracing sport, I'm told," the Abbé said.

The Cardinal looked dreadful. He had lost even more weight, and his hands trembled like an old man's. He had a stricken look. What had happened in Saverne to send him back to Paris looking like this? As soon as he saw the Cardinal alight from his carriage, the Abbé knew that something was wrong. The Cardinal's step was always springy and supple, like that of a young boy, not careful and slow. The Abbé felt guilty for his shameful moment of weakness when he had thought of resigning his post, of quitting the Cardinal's service. It had been good to return to La Chaise-Dieu and its eternal grayness to realize how foolish it would be to leave the Cardinal.

"It's not the hunting season, I fear." The Cardinal smiled at him indulgently. "This August heat. When will it break? I can't breathe."

Prince Louis was still dressed in the light silk dressing gown he wore in the mornings. It was late afternoon, and he had not yet called Schreiber to shave him.

The Abbé saw his chance and leapt in. "May I speak freely, Your Eminence?"

It was the moment the Cardinal had been dreading. The Abbé was about to go off into one of his rants, lashing out at him with prophecies of financial doom. The Cardinal nodded his head listlessly.

The Abbé clasped his hands and brought them to his chest as if beginning to pray. "I'm afraid for you, Your Eminence. To see you sunk so far in your hopes and plans for the future. Forever talking about the Queen and court intrigue, it's undermining your health, your strength. I was saying to myself only yesterday, if only you could spend less time reading and discussing the Queen's letters with the Comtesse de La Motte and even I daresay the Count Cagliostro, what if you could go about more, see more of your old friends, perhaps the Marquise de Marigny, who I understand . . ."

The Cardinal burst out laughing. "The Marquise de Marigny! My little choirboy of the Vienna days! Oh, dear, Monsieur l'Abbé, whatever are you thinking?"

The Cardinal leaned back in his chair and laughed until tears swam in his eyes. What a relief! He felt decidedly better. The Abbé had not once referred to the huge chunk of money gone missing.

The Abbé covered his mouth and giggled. A fine thing it was to see the Cardinal in good spirits! He ought to talk to him about the crisis in the estate's treasury, but how could he, when the Cardinal already looked so wretched and dispirited? The Abbé's stomach churned. But the debts! The debts! It was as if the floodgates had been opened and even the Prince's stupendous income could not hold back the deluge. Soon they would be obliged to go begging Cerf-Beer for loans. And Cerf-Beer would quite obviously play the highway bandit in setting his interest.

"You are a good man, Georgel. I mean that. Your loyalty

humbles me, indeed it does. Come, I must bestir myself. The day is almost done. Let's see now. The first order of business. You must send for the Comtesse de La Motte. The usual time. I'll have Schreiber send up some supper."

"But, Your Eminence . . ."

"Don't worry, Monsieur l'Abbé. It's not what you're thinking. I'm not making any progress in my . . . affairs. As a matter of fact, I seem to be getting nowhere. There are certain matters I must explain to the Comtesse. Urgently."

"I've had enough, Jeanne," the Cardinal said as soon as he had closed the door behind her. "I'm sick of this constant *va-et-vient* of letters that brings me not one step closer to the prime minister's portfolio!"

His voice had almost reached a shout. Jeanne stood with a hand fondling her necklace and looked at him with wide eyes. "I'm depressed. Who wouldn't be? Her Majesty sends me away to Saverne promising to lay Versailles at my feet when I return. But, God knows, if I had waited for the magic word from Her Majesty, I would still be holed up at Saverne."

"You've grown querulous and distrustful," Jeanne said, stroking his arm. "So unlike you. Remember Cagliostro's prediction. Have you forgotten so soon? You're too impatient, that's what."

The Cardinal laughed scornfully and pushed her hand away. "Impatient, yes. Naturally. But certainly not distrustful. Why should I be? The fact of the matter is that I'm bored. Bored senseless with sweating over every stroke of my pen, every word and shape of each phrase, trying with all my intellect to maneuver the Queen into a full and public reconciliation. And what have I received? Nothing! Nothing!" The Cardinal paused for a deep breath, then turned his angry deep-blue eyes to Jeanne. "And that stupendous . . . that extraordinary loan of one hundred twenty thousand francs!"

"What about it?" Jeanne said, watching him carefully.

The Cardinal screwed up his face and whined in a mocking, high-pitched, syrupy voice, "Oh, Your Eminence, can I ever thank you enough! Ta, ta, ti and ta, ta, ta. How sweet!"

"She's been very busy lately, I don't know why she can never sit still a minute, not even with . . ."

"Busy!" the Cardinal roared.

Jeanne covered her ears with her hands. "Please, Your Eminence. Control yourself. What is it you want me to tell the Queen?"

The Cardinal sat down and rubbed his forehead. "Tell her that I want a sign of our reconciliation, a concrete sign," he said sternly. "Not another of those mewling letters! I want her to make clear to me that I enjoy her favor, now and henceforward."

Father Loth had just finished the *Agnus Dei* and ordinarily that was the moment when Jeanne could count on having her entire being stilled in quiet peace. She remained kneeling and watched the candles flickering beneath the statue of the Virgin Mary. The barefoot Virgin was clothed in a bright blue robe lined with gilt, her head bowed attentively to the lamb nestling at her feet. What must it be like to feel so serene? Father Loth lifted the chalice and drained it, then slowly unfolded a clean white cloth and rubbed and rubbed the chalice inside and out, then round and round the rim, until Jeanne thought he had lost his mind. She shifted her weight and crossed herself and tried to concentrate on hurrying Father Loth through the Mass. She was not a worrier, what a waste of time that was, but she was exasperated at not being able to sit back and enjoy the fruits of all her efforts. Without a doubt, the Cardinal was a difficult man, demanding, impatient, and as she had seen recently, rather hot-tempered when he wanted to be. Life was like a tormenting fly on a slow, hot summer afternoon, forever buzzing about, when all one craved was a nice, deep nap.

Startled, Jeanne looked up and saw Father Loth with his hands raised for the benediction. By the time she had scrambled to her feet, he was at her side. They walked together to the back of the little chapel.

"You seem distracted, Madame la Comtesse. I do hope nothing is wrong. Were you disappointed with the foie gras I sent over yesterday?"

"Disappointed! Even the gods on Mount Olympus would have regaled themselves."

"Good. I'm glad you liked it. Our brothers in our monastery in the Southwest make it."

Father Loth thought the world of the Comtesse. She was the cleverest woman he had ever known, and the most spirited. Why, she could skin the hide of a delinquent maid or valet with the tartness of her tongue. And when she cut her dark eyes at you, what man wouldn't believe that he was the luckiest man alive?

"Everything's going well, thanks to all you've done. I don't know what I would do without you, dear Father Loth. I never seem to see the end of my problems."

"Is it your husband, dear Comtesse? Come, do sit down and tell me all."

Jeanne laughed scornfully. "Oh, that clown. If he buys himself another striped waistcoat, I shall poison his wine. The man has hopeless taste. But you're right, I am distracted this morning. I have a problem that must be solved and solved very soon. I'm at my wit's end thinking about it. You know, my Versailles friend . . . well, she has such impossible caprices. And it's my job to satisfy them."

"You mean, Her Majesty?"

"Really, Father Loth! Of course, I mean the Queen! You're exasperating this morning. Go back to bed!" Jeanne said and headed out the door.

Father Loth raced out into the monastery's kitchen garden and stopped in front of her. "Do forgive me, Madame la Comtesse. I only wanted to be clear."

"Well, here is the problem," Jeanne said, lowering her voice almost to a whisper. "The other night, completely out of the blue, the Queen says to me, *You know, you're constantly pestering me to grant an audience to your friend, the Prince de Rohan,*—she lay propped up on an elbow, twisting a lock of my hair around her finger, just imagine it—*well, I have had an inspiration. Somehow or other I can't bring myself to trust the Cardinal yet. I need to put him to a test. I will agree to meet him without actually meeting him, if you know what I mean.* Of course, I didn't. Then she says, *I want to set up a situation where I can see how he acts and hear what he says when he meets someone he is led to believe is me. Don't you think that is a clever idea?* 'Very clever, Your Majesty,' says I, for you can never flatter her enough, 'but I don't see how this can be done without the Prince catching on.' *Why, it's easy,* says she. *Under cover of darkness the Prince would meet my substitute, someone so like me that the Prince would never for a moment suspect that he is being fooled, and I, in the shadows, for I want to be able to watch everything, can observe the decorum of his behavior and his manner of addressing himself to His Sovereign. Then, depending on the way he behaves, I can decide whether or not to grant him an interview.* You can imagine how flabbergasted I was that a royal princess would indulge in such an extravagant charade. The trouble is, she's a bored woman, shackled to a fat, sluggish worm of a husband, forced to furtive amusements of this sort. That's the whole labor of court, keeping this flighty woman entertained. It's the hardest job I ever had, I can tell you that."

"A whimsical, antic woman, indeed!" Father Loth said, sucking a lone front tooth in dismay. "She's wearing you out, dear Comtesse. What does Her Majesty expect you to do?"

"She expects me to do the impossible. Here's what she says to me as I'm rushing to get into my clothes. *Do you think that you or your husband could find such a person to perform this harmless little scene for me?* Harmless little scene! What is she talking about? I've spent days trying to figure out how to stage this silly business. I've made some progress. I've got a fairly good idea of where I want it to take place. But what good is all that if I don't have someone to double for the Queen?"

They stood staring down at their shoes. It was a cool morning and the sun had not yet burned away the mist that hung over the garden.

"It won't be easy, Madame. Finding a tall woman with pale blond hair and a perfect complexion. Ample in the bosom . . . I'm saying only what I've heard so often."

Father Loth tried to look sheepish but was too worldly to manage it.

"Yes. A swelling bosom and the tiniest waist imaginable."

"Voluptuous and tall. Not a French combination," Father Loth said, shaking his head ruefully.

"I thought perhaps with all the work you and the brothers do in the parish, you might recall a young woman I could do something with. An orphan, say, a young person without family who's keen to earn a little money. For there'll be money in it, I can tell you. I intend to make the Queen pay dearly for her stupid game."

Father Loth scratched the scraggly beard along his jaw. "Let me see now. The parish, no. I wish I could help. It's a wicked business finding the likes of the Queen."

"I won't give up," Jeanne said fiercely.

"What I'm thinking is, perhaps your husband . . ." he ducked his head and grinned, "In your husband's, hmmm, *parish*, might you not find a double for the Queen there?"

"My husband's parish? What on earth are you talking about?"

Father Loth pursed his lips into a smile and slyly sucked his front tooth. "Why, the Palais-Royal, Madame. In the late afternoon and evening."

"Ah, you cunning rascal!" Jeanne laughed gaily and punched his arm. "Why didn't I think of that? The Comte spends two or three hours there every afternoon with all the other idlers who have more time than money on their hands. He goes there to leer and ogle and covet and show himself off in those hideous clothes he insists on wearing. I never have time for that kind of nonsense myself. Idling is my husband's business, not mine."

"I must confess I rather like to go there myself. The Orleans palace has always been such a lovely spot, and now that the Duc has rented out all of the spaces on the lower level of the palace, all of the fashionable world take their promenade there. It's a sight to see. There's a little shop on the east side where I buy your beauty patches. At quite the best bargain in town, I might add."

"You can be sure the Comte doesn't go to the Palais-Royal to buy beauty patches," Jeanne said.

She knew that hanging around the great stone stairway leading up to the Duc's private collection of paintings and watching the ladies swish up and down in their finery had become a favorite pastime among court society. It was to the staircase that prostitutes flocked to pick up their assignations for the evening.

"Lord, lord! You've saved the day for me, Father. The Comte may be a fool, but sometimes I think I couldn't get along without his vices."

Father Loth pulled his lips together tightly and smiled broadly. Such an angel, the Comtesse!

Nicolas de La Motte hurried along the rue de Richelieu. For the past five days he had loitered around the Palais-Royal for hours with no success. This day he was determined that his luck would change. Today he would not allow himself to get waylaid by the gambling tables on the south side. He would take up his post at the Duc's staircase, and if nothing came of that, he would take a seat at one of the sidewalk cafés skirting the arcades of the Palais-Royal, where ladies of easy virtue who had not yet found a customer came to rest their feet and enjoy a cheap glass of red wine.

As La Motte turned into the arcades and walked past the Café Procope, he spotted a slim young woman with long blond hair piled up in a simple fashion on the top of her head. Great God, he said to himself, is this a joke? Is this some kind of delusion afflicting my weary brain? For the young woman was Marie Antoinette's exact double. At least from a distance. La Motte slowly walked on, then circled back even more slowly, and finally took a seat at a table close enough for an unhampered view of the young woman. She was seated at a table with a little boy not more than four years old. She was laughing and listening to the child's prattle; yet all the while her eyes sought out the glances of the men strolling past.

La Motte ordered a glass of red wine and a plate of hot canapés and set to work studying the young woman carefully. He had to take his time. Jeanne would tear him apart if he came home and falsely raised her hopes. But he could scarcely contain his elation. The young woman was tall and slim with a fresh, fair complexion, and decidedly billowy curves. Moreover, and La Motte considered this a particular bit of luck, she was very young and quite clearly a lady of the evening, for why else would she be wearing a deeply ruffled red petticoat, and why else would she appear as interested in the men passing by as they were in her? She had no doubt positioned herself in this strategic spot with the child as a pretty accessory to call attention to herself.

A half hour had passed before La Motte crossed glances with the young woman, and they exchanged smiles, a clear enough invitation, or so it seemed to La Motte, to join her at her table.

As he took a seat, La Motte assumed the grave air of a seriously smitten suitor. "Your little boy is most handsome," La Motte said, anxious to strike exactly the right tone. This girl was perfect. He mustn't lose her.

"Oh, he's not mine. Pierre belongs to a neighbor. I take care of him when his mother can't."

She had a quick bright smile with fine teeth, but, unfortunately, without a swelling pout of her lower lip. It would be perversely like Jeanne to cavil about this detail and insist on searching for a more Hapsburg lookalike. The Comte was fed up with searching up and down for the Queen's twin. He had a hankering to make a fast killing at the gaming tables and forget about Jeanne's elaborate schemes.

Quite smoothly, without revealing his own identity, La Motte learned that the young woman was called Nicole Leguay and that she lived alone in a small apartment on the rue du Jour in the

Sainte Eustache section close by the Palais-Royal. He reckoned that Jeanne could not have done better herself.

They chatted amiably over a second round of drinks, the Comte noting happily that Mademoiselle Leguay was not inclined to ask questions. When he took his leave and asked whether he could come calling that very evening at her room, she gave him a wink and a nod, which pleased La Motte mightily.

He walked away so satisfied with his afternoon's work that he could not resist the pleasure of stopping in at his favorite shop and ordering a set of pea green plumes with gloves dyed to match.

21

It was no accident that Jeanne chose the gardens at Versailles for her little entertainment for the Queen. The latest twist in Marie Antoinette's foul reputation came from her fondness for evening strolls during the fine summer months in the garden groves of the lower palace grounds just below the Great Terrace, in the shadow of the Hundred Steps. Until two or three in the morning the Versailles townspeople crowded the palace grounds, and gossip flew that many a fine lady, including the Queen, ventured to stray down into the dark gardens for assignations of a dubious nature. Called the Queen's Grove because of the Queen's fondness for it, or the Grove of Venus because of the statue adorning the space, Marie Antoinette thought of it as her "summer salon."

"We'll have our 'Queen' stand just opposite the statue," Jeanne said.

She and Rétaux de Villette were on their way to the rue du Jour to meet the Comte's discovery. "The only access is through the labyrinth. I'll have to lead the Cardinal. The Queen keeps adding layer after layer of *charmilles* so that it is the devil's own work to get through the maze."

"I've looked at the calendar," Villette said. "We'll make the rendezvous tomorrow night, August 10th. Just in case."

"Just in case what?"

"Just in case the Comte's lady is not as much a duplicate as he thinks she is. We can't take any chances. The night of the tenth should be pitch black. Not a trace of a moon."

"Perfect. How clever you are, my darling. Lord knows what

kind of baggage the Comte has turned up. You know how he is. Anything to get out of a job and get on with his whoring and gambling."

St. Eustache being a modest, working-class quartier, Jeanne had taken the precaution of hiring a plain carriage to keep from drawing attention to herself. Mademoiselle Nicole Leguay herself opened the door to them, and from the smug look on the Comte's face, the two had gone a long way in getting to know each other.

"This is the highly placed lady I've told you about. And her personal secretary," La Motte said to the girl, who appeared struck dumb by Jeanne's grand appearance and superior manner. The girl dropped a quick curtsey, then rushed to a dark corner of the small room and brought forth a chair.

"Actually, I'm attached to the court of Versailles." Jeanne drew an envelope from her pocket and said, "I have here with me several letters from the Queen."

Mademoiselle Leguay shrank back as Jeanne drew out the letters and held them out to her. "I don't read, milady," she said, bowing her head.

"Ah, well, no matter," Jeanne said. "Then listen carefully, my sweet, to what I am about to tell you. I am the Queen's confidante. She and I are just like this!" Smiling broadly, Jeanne held up two fingers intertwined. "You may trust me, dear child, in what I am about to tell you. Her Majesty has commissioned me to find for her a person to render her a service, and it is you I have chosen. How old are you, dear heart?"

"Twenty-three, this February past," Mademoiselle Leguay said.

"Perfect!" Jeanne said. She was fairly beaming. She gave Villette a reckless wink. "If you agree to perform this service for the Queen—don't worry about the details now; you shall be told in good time—I will make you a gift of fifteen hundred francs. What you will receive later from the Queen will be worth even more. Many times more, I can assure you. What say you?"

"Well . . . ," Mademoiselle Leguay said, rubbing her nose. "I can't say. The Queen! I just don't know . . ."

"If you don't care to take my word for it," Jeanne said haughtily, gathering up her things, "we will go together to a notary's office. I have plenty of guarantees, if that's what's bothering you."

"Oh, no! no! I'm only too flattered to be able to render a service pleasing to Her Majesty. I cannot refuse my Sovereign."

"Good. Sensible girl. The Comte will come to fetch you in a carriage tomorrow night as soon as it's dark to drive you to Versailles. See that the necessary arrangement are made," she said, nodding her head toward the Comte as she closed the door behind her and Villette.

As the carriage rolled away, Jeanne and Villette fell laughing into each other's arms.

"Astonishing!" Villette said. "Would you ever have believed that there could be anyone walking around on this earth who looks exactly like the Queen? And that Nicolas de La Motte of all people could find her?"

"Incredible! I can't believe she's real. And a perfect ninny! With such a likeness to the Queen, any other woman with an ounce of wit and gumption could have made herself a fortune. I know I could have. Ah, it never fails. Just when you start to think that Nicolas de La Motte is as worthless as the day is long, he turns up and does something enormous like this! Oh, my dear, we must celebrate."

"Not yet," Rétaux de Villette said. He was a feckless man content to follow wherever Jeanne decided to lead him. Though he was still awed by the heady society into which Jeanne had introduced him, Rétaux de Villette feared that her impulsiveness could spoil their adventure. "Tomorrow night. We still have work to do."

Indeed there was plenty of work to do. With notes containing ever changing instructions, Father Loth, his robes flying, his sandals flapping against the paving stones, scurried back and forth between the rue Neuve Saint-Gilles and the Palais-Cardinal, where Prince Louis waited in a state of nervous anxiety and called repeatedly, but vainly, for Jeanne's presence to soothe his nerves. It was decided that he would dress himself as a great lord in formal black with a full-length black cape. Jeanne herself shopped for the proper costume for Mademoiselle Leguay.

"Her name!" Jeanne cried, in the middle of their frenzied preparations.

"What's wrong with it? No one will ever know it!" the Comte said.

"*I* will know it. And I can't bear this breach of etiquette! This little wench must have a title. A commoner cannot impersonate the Queen and receive one of the grandest noblemen of the country. No, it's quite impossible. I won't have it! I'm a perfectionist at heart."

"Nothing simpler," Rétaux de Villette drawled in his prissy, plummy accent. "We'll call her the Baroness d'Olisva!"

Jeanne thought for a moment. "Oh, you darling droll! How clever! The Baroness d'Olisva, it is."

The Comte, who did not seize the play on *Valois*, said irritably, "Shouldn't we get on with what she is going to do tonight in the grove?"

"In due time. Don't presume to tell me what to do, Monsieur," Jeanne said. "I'm off to call on the Cardinal. Bring our trollop to me at Versailles well before eleven o'clock. She has to be dressed and coached in what to do."

Darkness had fallen when the Comte de La Motte arrived with the "Baroness d'Olisva" at the hotel on the Place Dauphine where the Comte and Comtesse de La Motte had maintained a stylish suite of rooms for several weeks.

"Don't you know what watches and clocks are for?" Jeanne snapped, as the Comte, luminous in red and vivid blue, ushered the Baroness d'Olisva into the room. "And get out of those beastly clothes!" she rasped as she closed the door behind him.

"Come along, dear heart. Let's have a look at you." Jeanne led the young woman over to an assortment of gowns and hats and accessories laid out over chair backs. "Her Majesty is much pleased. She can't wait to see how all this will come off."

"What shall I do, milady?"

"We'll start with the clothes. You must look exactly right."

Jeanne began to get nervous as dress after dress failed to fit the very tall and willowy young woman. "Ah, *mon dieu*, too short, too short. *Merde!*" Finally, she found the gown she wanted in a very fine white chemise of *linon moucheté*. "Lawn cloth! Hmph! Why on earth everyone has gone dotty over this plain and simple fashion I'll never know," she grumbled. "It's the Queen and Mademoiselle Bertin, that arrogant dressmaker of hers. I myself never cared for the *en gaule* look. The attractions of simplicity are completely lost on me, I fear."

She stepped back to study her creation. Stunning! What a resemblance! There was no need after all to be afraid of exposing the little impostor to the light of the moon. "And now a coiffure *en demi-bonnet*. We haven't much time left. I want you stationed in the grove before eleven o'clock."

"I do look grand," Mademoiselle Leguay said wistfully, gazing into the mirror. "But what am I supposed to do for the Queen?"

"It's very simple." Jeanne stood very straight and walked toward the door. "Notice how I move and hold myself. You must walk like a court lady, as if your feet were caressing the ground. You will be escorted to a position in the palace garden. You must simply stand there until you are led away."

Jeanne removed a rose from a fresh bouquet on the center table. "Here are a red rose and a letter," she said to the young woman. "A great nobleman will enter the grove. After the great lord approaches and does his courtesies to you, you must hand him the rose and the letter and say only this: *You know what this means.* Only that one sentence, is that understood? Nothing more. You give him the rose and the letter and you say to him, *You know what this means.* Stay exactly where you're placed, and don't move. Is everything clear?"

Mademoiselle Leguay nodded her head nervously and formed the words silently on her lips. "Milady, this seigneur, will he expect to embrace me?"

Jeanne tried not to smile. Clearly, the Baroness d'Olisva was expecting some great romantic adventure. "Oh, undoubtedly," Jeanne said.

"What . . . what if he should expect something more?"

"Oh, I hardly think that likely," Jeanne said, laughing merrily. "I must leave you now. The Comte will escort you to your station. And remember," she lowered her voice to a vehement whisper, "the Queen will be watching your every move!"

濞

"What time is it now, Monsieur l'Abbé?" the Cardinal said.

"Twenty past eleven, Your Eminence," Georgel said. "It can't be long now."

Though he had terrible misgivings, he was trying to be cheerful for the Cardinal's sake. Besides, he knew that it was a mark of the highest trust when the Cardinal, aware of the Abbé's deep distrust of the Comtesse de La Motte, had asked him to accompany him to Versailles for this rendezvous with the Queen.

The two men held themselves at some distance from the flow of promenaders on the Great Terrace of the palace directly below the Queen's suite. On the Green Carpet lawn the royal-chapel musicians played the kind of light comic opera tunes favored by the Queen. The night was hot and still; beyond the terrace the vast gardens disappeared into darkness.

The Cardinal paced back and forth, scanning the crowd for the sight of the black moiré domino by which he was to recognize Jeanne. This was the moment he had been waiting for, praying for, the moment when all those years of cold exclusion would fall away and he would stand within the charmed circle, the earthly paradise of the intimates of the Queen, from whom all blessings flowed.

Standing shivering in the warm night air, he felt bruised by elation. The assignation had come about so suddenly: Jeanne arriving breathless in the deep of night with such a tender, piquant note from Her Majesty that the Cardinal had despised himself for his doubts, his irritation, his impatience. And, yes, his arrogance. Those weeks of sulking in Saverne, resenting being shunted aside like a naughty schoolboy after having performed such an extraordinary service for the Queen by lending her a colossal sum of money, what was that but his confounded Rohan pride rearing its ugly head?

Somehow or other over the past few days there had been a subtle shift in the tone of their correspondence—oh, God, he hoped he wasn't reading too much into her words. No, there was definitely a tenderness, a warmth—dare he say it?—an intimacy, a flow of feeling that seemed to bind the two of them together with loving manacles. In her letters he could detect a certain loneliness in her life, an expectation thwarted, a pleasure postponed . . . And God alone knew, the Cardinal himself did not dare cast a plumb line into the depths of his own loneliness. Yet when the note requesting a meeting came so abruptly, his hopes and dreams had pitched him into a tumult of emotions. From the moment he set out for Versailles with the Abbé, he had the sensation of plunging, of being pushed like some blinded animal, into a bottomless trap. How to account for these queer misgivings?

The Cardinal wiped his brow. "Why don't I go ahead on my own and search the gardens for the Queen? You know the Comtesse has no sense of time. I feel like a fool hanging around like this."

The Abbé rushed forward and grabbed the Cardinal's arm. "Please, Your Eminence, do nothing rash! You must be patient! Have you forgotten your humiliation the night of the garden party for Czar Paul? You must wait until you are summoned by Her Majesty."

The Abbé's words were enough to freeze the Cardinal to his place on the terrace. "You're quite right, Georgel. I must not run the risk. A Rohan does not suffer humiliation lightly."

As he turned away, he glimpsed Jeanne's black moiré domino pushing through the crowd on the steps.

"Quickly, your Eminence," she said, taking his elbow. "I have just left the Queen on her way to the Grove of Venus. Quickly. The Queen almost decided against keeping the rendezvous at all because her lady-in-waiting brought her word that Madame Elisabeth and the Comtesse d'Artois have decided to join her for a stroll around the gardens this evening."

The Cardinal was aghast. "Then we shall have no time. Would Her Majesty agree to a meeting tomorrow? Or perhaps even later? I have so much to say. We must have time to talk, Jeanne. Otherwise—"

Jeanne tugged at his elbow. "Have no fear. Her Majesty will find a way to escape the princesses. Come along. She's waiting. You'll have only a few minutes, but time enough for Her Majesty to give you unmistakable proof of her favor. Hurry!"

They rushed down the broad staircase and out into the paths leading into the evergreen maze. The Cardinal concentrated on his footing. Towering topiary animals full of darkness crowded around them, and hurrying onward, the Cardinal had a fleeting thought that the earth smelled like freshly sliced cucumbers. Suddenly, Jeanne stopped, dropped his arm, and pushed him forward into the grove.

Then, he saw her standing little more than an arm's length away. A blurred vision in white, her head held a little uncertainly in his direction, she wore a white cape around her shoulders and a lace thérèse over her hair. The Cardinal, full of apprehension, stumbled his way toward her.

Later he could not recall precisely what happened next. He remembered that he fell to his knees and lifted the hem of her skirt—or was it her tiny satin slipper?—to kiss. She was slimmer than he remembered, and she was trembling from head to foot. His heart flooded with tenderness for her.

"Your Majesty," he sighed as he got to his feet.

A hand awkwardly nudged him. "You know what this means," she whispered, her voice shaking, as she held out a rose for him to take.

Just at that moment, Jeanne swooped out of the thick darkness. "Quickly! The Comtesse d'Artois and Madame Elisabeth are approaching. *Dame!*" she said. She grabbed the Cardinal's arm and hurried him through a shortcut out of the maze.

As the Cardinal turned to look back at the figure in white, he heard voices and heavy footsteps on the gravel path.

↝

More than he cared to admit to himself, Claude Beugnot, on his return to Paris, missed Jeanne and the excitement she always trailed in her wake and the mellowness of lingering with her over a good meal at the Cadran Bleu. Being, however, an emotionally thrifty person, he quickly made up his mind not to spend the small change of his sentimental life in pining for his lost intimacy with the Comtesse de La Motte. He started to go about more, especially to fashionable balls, where he found that his situation as a promising young magistrate entitled him to the attention of as many attractive young ladies as his busy life could reasonably accommodate. He was in fact quite a success, and he was sorry that he was not able to boast to Jeanne about it.

One oppressively warm night in August, feeling somewhat ill, he left one of these balls early, around ten o'clock or so. He headed for the carriage stand on the rue Saint Louis, but when he reached the corner of the rue Neuve Saint-Gilles where Jeanne lived, he found himself turning the corner, and before he knew it, he was standing at her door.

Her young swarthy porter, who habitually smelled of garlic, poked his head out of the porter's lodge.

"Would Madame be at home this evening?" Beugnot asked.

"Sorry, sir. The Comte and the Comtesse are abroad tonight. Versailles, most like."

"And Monsieur de Villette?" he persisted, though why he would ever want to spend five minutes of his time with this pretty fop he hadn't the slightest idea.

"*Non plus.*" The porter said, pushing at his forehead with a sooty handkerchief. "He went along with the Comtesse early in the day. Only Mademoiselle Colson is in the house this evening."

Beugnot was delighted. This Mademoiselle Colson, Jeanne's *dame de compagnie*, the latest evidence of the La Motte household's change of fortune, could always make him laugh. Like Monsieur de Latour, Jeanne's brother-in-law, Suzanne Colson was an irreverent wag. She was bright and opinionated, nobody's fool, least of all Jeanne de La Motte's. Mademoiselle Colson needed a roof over her head, to be sure, but she had established her limits as to how far she would go to keep her employment with the La Mottes. Subservience and obsequiousness did not fall within those limits.

"Something enormous and enormously complicated afoot tonight, Claude," she said as soon as Beugnot walked into the little sitting room off the grand salon. Her nutmeg brown eyes glittered with mockery. "Something grandiose and secret. The Great Ones have been to-ing and fro-ing to the Cardinal's palace, secret messages, furtive glances, tight lips. Our pretty face Villette spending more than his allotted time in Her Highness's boudoir. His Reverence Father Loth reduced to listening at keyholes; sent running time after time to the Palais-Cardinal without being able to make out a damned word of the confidential messages he has been sent to deliver. The poor little monk is beside himself. He's as curious as an old nun, you know."

"And where are the Great Ones this evening, dear lady?"

He bowed ceremoniously over her hand and settled himself into a comfortable chair for an hour or two of choice gossip at the expense of the La Mottes.

Mademoiselle Colson drew a small cameo watch from her skirt pocket and pretended to study it carefully. "Let me see . . . The *mont de piété* has been closed for hours, I would say. No more pawning until the morrow then. The Palais-Royal has settled down to its more serious vices. The Male Great One could be chasing around there, of course. Most likely, though, they're all together, our cozy little threesome. Sniffing around Versailles and the royals, I've no doubt."

Beugnot laughed. Suzanne Colson was a spunky girl with a nimble wit who had not taken long to see through the pretentiousness of the La Motte establishment. Toward one o'clock in the morning Beugnot finally took some notice of the hour and reckoned that he should find his way home.

"You'll never find a carriage for hire at this hour," Suzanne said. "Stay on until The Great Ones return. The Female Great One would never allow her promising young magistrate to walk all the way across the river to his humble Left Bank lodgings. She'll send you home in fine style in her carriage. She still wants to impress you, you know."

A few minutes later they heard the sound of wheels on the courtyard cobblestones; then the La Motte threesome reeled into the room on a wave of boisterous hilarity. On Comte de La Motte's arm was a young woman, pale, blonde, and remarkably well built.

"The Baroness d'Oliva," the Comte said with an extravagant flourish and bow.

"D'Olisva," Jeanne corrected, and Villette burst into peals of girlish giggles. "Well, Claude, what have you two been noodling on about? Hmmm? At this late hour?" Jeanne clapped her hands for supper to be served. "With the best champagne."

"Ah, nothing but the best!" Villette said, cutting his eyes toward Jeanne.

At table Beugnot found himself gazing at the beautiful stranger the entire evening. He was puzzled. He was sure that he had seen her somewhere before. He could not account for the feeling. The face and figure were as familiar as his concierge's; yet he could not put a name to the face.

Throughout the supper the La Mottes and Villette babbled and giggled and rolled their eyes as if they were privy to a tremendously amusing joke, while the beautiful stranger appeared intimidated by finding herself in such a magnificent setting. She said little, smiled bravely in response to the foolishness of the La Mottes and Villette, but otherwise seemed more interested in casting her eyes around the apartment.

Beugnot and Mademoiselle Colson exchanged quizzical glances, wondering when and if they were going to be let in on the reason for the general high spirits.

As the raucous mood of celebration, of triumph, continued unabated with a great deal of nudging with elbows, shushing, and suppressed laughter, the stranger appeared almost as mystified as Suzanne and Beugnot.

As they grew rowdier, Beugnot heard La Motte whisper to Villette, "What do you think? Can we tell Beugnot about the letter forgotten in the pocket?"

"The better part of discretion is valor," Villette said, and began to hum an idiotic street tune.

Jeanne, seated beside Villette, slapped her fingers across his lips and said, almost angrily, "Hush! Claude is too honest a man to be interested in sharing our confidences."

Beugnot was not terribly flattered. He knew Jeanne's vocabulary well enough to know that in her eyes an honest man inevitably meant a fool.

All of a sudden Jeanne seemed eager to get the meal over with and get on with whatever secret matter the three of them found so hilarious.

"Claude, will you be good enough to accompany the Baroness in my carriage?" she said, as they all rose from the table.

"With pleasure."

Actually, he could not wait to be alone with the beautiful young woman who might possibly, among other things, be able to explain what the boisterous tomfoolery of the evening had been about.

"And continue on to your own lodgings, of course," Jeanne added imperiously.

"Of course," he said, lifting her hand for a formal kiss, to show her that he was quite used to his new status as a family friend.

In the carriage, with the beautiful stranger demurely arranging her skirts opposite him, Beugnot was struck once again by the familiarity of her face. Not only of her face, but of her entire aspect.

"Surely we have met before, Mademoiselle," Beugnot said.

"I think not, Monsieur," she said, and turned her maddeningly familiar profile toward the window, though the streets were deserted except for the occasional cat concluding a nocturnal prowl.

As they clopped along through the quiet of early morning, Beugnot asked her question after question about her friendship with the La Mottes, about their activities that evening, about her circle of acquaintances. He could dredge nothing out of her. Was she simply too refined, Beugnot wondered, to converse with a stranger assigned to see her to her door? Perhaps that was it; perhaps she simply regarded him as a pushy boor treating her with undue familiarity. Her language, however, when she did utter a word or two definitely bespoke an ambiguous milieu. Moreover, he remembered her roving glances around the La Motte apartment, and the way she sat forward slightly in her chair, as if she were not quite sure that she had the right to sit down amid such luxury.

It was all very strange, Beugnot said to himself, as he dropped her off at a dark doorway in the rue du Jour.

Beugnot fell into bed that night and completely forgot about the beautiful stranger until, several weeks later, he caught a glimpse of her turning into the rue de Richelieu near the Palais-Royal and, suddenly, like a flash, had the bedeviling illusion that he had just seen the Queen, incognito, strolling along like an ordinary citizen in the streets of Paris. The Queen! Precisely! He stood there stock still staring after her.

At the time, he thought that, by some miracle, he had just been given a precious clue to an enormous puzzle, but on reflection, he could not determine what to do with it. What did it mean? So what if this mysterious Baroness d'Oliva—or d'Olisva—did bear a breathtaking resemblance to the Queen? What possible significance could that have?

20

"He's in love with her! Stark, raving mad in love with her!" the Abbé wailed, as soon as Beugnot came in.

The Abbé, clutching at his stringy hair and flapping his bony arms, paced back and forth in front of his cluttered desk, his heavy old shoes scuffing the fine Persian carpet.

Beugnot settled back contentedly in his chair and waited for the Abbé's storm to subside. He could not believe how contented he was to be back in the Abbé's cavernous den at the Palais-Cardinal.

"What? In love with the Comtesse de La Motte?" Beugnot said, alert for any twinges of jealousy.

"The Comtesse! That little baggage!"

The Abbé wheeled around and looked at Beugnot in disgust. "Of course not! It's the Queen! The Queen! The Cardinal is mad with love for the Queen!"

"What makes you say that?"

The Abbé cuffed his clenched fists to his ears. *"Bon sang!* If you had seen what I have seen, Beugnot, and if you knew what I know, you wouldn't just sit there looking so calm and reasonable. This is a serious matter, my good man." The Abbé raised his eyes imploringly to the ceiling.

"Has the Cardinal done something terrible?"

"Oh, dear Lord, no, not yet! But he will, mark my words, if this madness does not stop. Listen, Beugnot, I have to admit that I am only partially in the Cardinal-Prince's confidence. But he did grant me the honor recently of . . . I'm afraid I cannot tell you more. Suffice it to say that Her Majesty gave His Eminence a rose and . . ."

The Abbé stopped abruptly, alarmed that he had gone too far. He had no right to discuss the Cardinal's private business in this way with a stranger, relatively speaking. But who would not trust Beugnot? There wasn't a devious bone in his body, the Abbé could tell that; he was an earnest young bourgeois, hard-working, reliable, as straight as an arrow. Besides, he could prove very useful.

"A rose? A rose?" Beugnot said, clearly intrigued. "Now that *is* strange."

"Exactly," the Abbé said. "And His Eminence has gone wild. He has commissioned Grouine to fashion an expensive coffer in which to place the rose. *Something small and refined*, the Cardinal says to me, *that will set my standard of taste before her. Something to strike a sympathetic chord, for we are both lovers of beautiful objects.* That's the way he talks now: *we are both lovers of beautiful objects.* For the sake of poring over her letters and writing answers to them, he neglects everything. Here's what I think: there must have been a change in those letters because he no longer shares them with the Comtesse and that oaf Cagliostro. He sits by himself in a kind of ecstasy brooding over the letters and happily spinning out his replies. Like an infatuated madman. He will listen to no reason. When I try to discuss business or church matters with him, he looks up at me with an idiotic smile and says something like, *What think you, Georgel, I've renamed my favorite walk at Saverne the 'Rose of Happiness!'* Just think of it! A man of the Cardinal's intellect pouring his energy into confecting a name for a garden path! I'm afraid, Beugnot, I'm terribly afraid."

The beads of his rosary banged noisily as he collapsed melo-dramatically into his chair.

"Come, Monsieur l'Abbé, let's look at the situation dispassion-ately. I agree, the Cardinal does sound carried away by some sort of . . . of . . . enthusiasm. But he's done nothing foolish. If the Queen has taken note of him and given him this rose, nothing more than a token of her esteem, no doubt, why shouldn't he have his moment of euphoria? I thought you were both trying hard to get the Cardinal back into the Queen's good graces."

"Of course. You're quite right, Beugnot. It's what the Cardinal, and I his faithful servant, have hoped and prayed for."

"Then there's nothing to be afraid of."

"Ah, there you're wrong!" the Abbé jerked his head forward. "What I fear, Beugnot," he said, lowering his voice, "is the Cardinal's passionate nature. He's an emotional man. You know what *lèse-majesté* means, don't you?"

"Doesn't every Frenchman?" Beugnot said.

The Abbé Georgel's condescension was annoying and uncalled for. Beugnot was, after all, no country hick. "It means an offense to royalty in showing a lack of proper respect to the King or to the Queen. And it's a capital crime, by the way."

"Precisely," the Abbé said, staring glumly at the Cardinal's portrait. "He's going away again, you know. To Saverne. He hates being shut away in Alsace. But the Queen's asked him to absent himself from Paris for a while, so off he goes next week. At least, his departure will mean that I won't have to put up with the sight of that La Motte woman flitting in and out of here with the Queen's letters."

At the mention of Jeanne de La Motte the Abbé sat up straight and turned to Beugnot. His voice became grave and businesslike. "My friend Beugnot, I hope you don't mind my calling you *my friend* for that's the way I have come to think of you, my good friend Beugnot. I would like to ask of you a small favor. Just something to ease my mind."

"By all means," Beugnot said.

Whether it was his chronic awkwardness, his histrionics, or even his casual hygiene, Beugnot had to admit to himself that he found something strangely endearing about the Abbé.

"To tell you the truth, I'm puzzled. There's something afoot at your friend the Comtesse's, and I can't make it out. For instance, most of the time she refuses to have His Eminence call on her at the rue Neuve Saint-Gilles; instead she prefers to come here. On the one or two occasions when His Eminence has called on her, she has received him in some cramped, dingy little rooms at the top of the house. I find that passing strange, don't you?"

"Indeed it is."

As far as Beugnot could tell, Jeanne took a childish delight in showing off her newly acquired riches. Then why would she not receive her good friend the Cardinal in her sumptuous rooms below? Why would she be reluctant to give him a glimpse of her prosperity?

"Even the Cardinal, who has come to look upon her every word, her every look as a precious oracle, has commented on this peculiar behavior—he hasn't set foot in her drawing rooms for over two months. I can't tell you what a hold that woman has over the Cardinal after recent events. It terrifies me. He bends to her will like a sapling in a gale wind."

"Would you like me to ask her what she's up to?"

"Oh, no! Nothing like that!" the Abbé said, fluttering his hands anxiously. "As one of her familiars, you must go there rather often. I would like you simply to have a look about on the evenings you frequent her salon. Keep your eyes open. Tell me of anything or anyone unusual you find there. Let me know who comes to her suppers—I understand that she has started to entertain in a lavish way. Especially what court society you see there, in particular from the Queen's entourage."

"I'll do what I can," Beugnot said.

He was amused. The Abbé always had some bee in his bonnet that afforded an excuse for a little espionage. Beugnot would do what he asked, though he did not intend to report anything that could possibly cause Jeanne any trouble. Beugnot was a young man who prided himself on knowing exactly where his loyalties lay.

Böhmer had let himself go. He had aged dramatically, and he had grown fat and no longer cared whether his gloves were clean or of the latest fashion. Of the two jewelers Böhmer had been the popular one, urbane, loquacious, always with a sparkle in his eye. No more.

In the late fall of 1784 Bassenge welcomed his partner back from yet another unsuccessful trip. Böhmer had shopped the celebrated necklace around the crowned heads of Europe, all nine of them, but there were no takers. Even kings blanched and turned their heads away after hearing the asking price.

As the financial crisis of the two jewelers mounted, they clung even more tenaciously to their obsession with their place in the history of their craft: under no circumstances must the magnificent necklace be disassembled, its stones sold hither and yon; the necklace must remain intact as the most breath-taking piece of jewelry ever designed and executed. Each refusal of the necklace convinced the crown jewelers that their only remaining hope for the necklace was the frivolous, spendthrift Queen of France, so notorious for her appetite for diamonds.

Bassenge ran his handkerchief around the bruised and somewhat battered edges of the huge red leather jewel case. "The King was only a step away from purchasing the necklace as a gift of *relevailles* to the Queen at the birth of their first child. Only a step away. We must remember and keep up our courage!"

"And when the Dauphin was born, he was crazy to buy it for the Queen. He said that he would gladly cancel a ship of the line for the Navy, and then he could afford to make her a gift of it," Böhmer said.

They had had this same conversation many times. Sometimes they switched parts, but always the words were the same.

"Look," Bassenge said. "We know the Queen admires the necklace. After the Dauphin was born, she kept it with her for a month. Just for the pleasure of looking at it."

"That's right. She wants it, I'm convinced," Böhmer said. "What's holding her back is the price. And what the court would say. And what the public would say. She's afraid to buy it. But she wants it with all her heart. That's the important thing."

"You can point out to Her Majesty that we are perfectly willing to work out payment by installments. We can make the same kind of arrangements she used for the purchase of her pair of diamond bracelets. The King need never know."

"The King need never know," Böhmer said, squaring his shoulders. "We can work out something for the Queen. Where there's a will, there's a way. If it comes right down to it, I will throw myself on the Queen's mercy."

"They say that at heart she is a kind person," Bassenge said, without much conviction.

Böhmer had been hanging around the Queen's apartments for four days, hoping to gain an audience. One gloomy November day Madame Campan, Marie Antoinette's trusted lady-in-waiting, took pity on the rotund little jeweler with his untidy wig and squeaking boots and led him directly into the Queen's boudoir.

It was late afternoon, and the Queen sat at a low table slowly turning the pages of a thick book filled with swatches of fabric and sketches of gowns. From time to time she paused and plucked a pin from a small bowl on her right. She was selecting her wardrobe for the coming week, designating the gowns for her tiring woman by sticking a pin into the swatch of fabric alongside each sketch. Picking out her gowns was such pleasure after a dull day spent in her stale, airless apartments. She glanced up irritably as Böhmer was ushered into the room.

"What is it, Böhmer?" she snapped without raising her head from the sketchbook. "Did I send for you? If I did, I don't recall it."

Böhmer blinked and stared. So it was true: the Queen was pregnant again. Marie Antoinette, still in the early months of her third pregnancy, had gained weight. The candlelight threw soft shadows around the small rolls of flesh under her chin, and her gown bulged prettily over her stomach. Though she sounded in a foul humor, surely her delicate state would dispose her to be kind.

"I have come to throw myself on your mercy, Your Majesty," Böhmer said in a rush.

"My *mercy?*" She drew her head back and fixed him with such an icy stare that Böhmer fell to his knees.

He joined his hands at his breast as if in prayer and wept. "Your Majesty, I am ruined, bankrupt, dishonored, if you persist in refusing my necklace. I beg of you, reconsider. You are looking at a desperate man. If you do not answer my prayers, I shall go direct from here to throw myself into the river!"

Böhmer began to weep noisily, snuffling and wheezing. The Queen watched him in disgust for a moment.

"Stand up, Böhmer!" she said sharply. "An honest man never gets down on his knees to plead. Such nonsense! Ah, *fichtre!* Look what you've done! I've gone and pricked my finger. Madame, another handkerchief . . . I've been none too happy with the terms of my last purchase. After all, three of those diamonds were my own—a gift from my mother when I was a child—that you reset in the new bracelets. You and Bassenge, you're forever full of promises."

"If Your Majesty will only give us a chance! I beg you! We are open to your terms. We insist: *your* terms, whatever they may be . . ."

In the winter of 1784 Jeanne de La Motte had never looked lovelier; her splendid chestnut hair glistened, her eyes sparkled with high spirits, she smiled, she laughed, she fairly crowed with pleasure. Her stunning gowns bespoke an undeniable affluence as did the rather Roman decadence of her dining table. Her drawing rooms were resplendent in furnishings from the most expensive carriage-trade shops: carpets and draperies from Tessier, bronze statues from Chevalier, marble accoutrements from Adam, and crystal glassware from Sikes. Jeanne moved like a queen amid all this luxury, tickling her vanity as often as possible by summoning her old friend Beugnot to her parties to witness her ascension into the headier realms of Paris society.

Although he found his new status as "family friend" galling, Beugnot was more than happy to oblige. There was always a nip of intrigue in the air at Jeanne's soirées. Naturally, the usual irritants were there every evening, namely the very blond and devoted Rétaux de Villette and the feckless husband in his appalling costumes. The man obviously mistook himself for a signal flag and dressed accordingly. Most evenings Cagliostro swept in for a bite of supper and a word with Jeanne and a chance to dispense his macaronic claptrap.

The Cardinal's absence, however, was unsettling. Having fallen into the habit of jealously scrutinizing the handsome Cardinal's every move, his every glance and gesture while he was in Jeanne's company, Beugnot felt like a child without his rattle. And there was something feverish, not to say, frantic about the luxury and gaiety in the rue Neuve Saint-Gilles that Beugnot could not help associating with the Cardinal's absence from Paris.

"I've done it, Claude," Jeanne said to him one miserably cold night in December. "Look at all this! I have my perfect house being remodeled in the latest style in dearest Bar-sur-Aube—wait until my in-laws have a look at it! They'll curl up in a ball with envy. I have friends and courtiers swooning around my salon day and night, clamoring for invitations to this and that, never a moment's peace. I love it! I love every minute of it."

She squeezed his arm and glanced toward the double doors of the drawing room where a short, spindly-legged man was obviously trying to catch her eye.

"Who's that man staring this way, the odd-looking fellow sporting a Louis XIV perruque?" Beugnot asked.

Jeanne laughed good-naturedly. "His name's Laporte. He's a lawyer. Spends all his money on clothes that would have suited well enough in the court of Louis XIV. You can't help but stare at the creature, can you? *Passé!* The man must have invented the word!"

"How do you know him?"

"Oh, I've done him a favor or two in the past—some business about toll collection at the locks on the Canal du Midi—and he thinks that I could fetch him the moon and the stars if I set my mind to it. I wouldn't exactly call him a decorative ornament in my salon, but the man has his finger in every savory pie around Versailles and therefore is not to be ignored. So, I'm off. Find yourself another beauty to keep you company."

"I have a 'situation,' *mon trésor*," Laporte said, as soon as Jeanne reached his side.

"What situation is that?"

"The crown jewelers, Bassenge and Böhmer. They're desperate to sell their incomparable diamond necklace, and we need your help."

"*We?* My help? Why would I want to get mixed up with losers like Bassenge and Böhmer? For that's what they are: a couple of losers. You can smell it all over them."

"They are friends. Old and loyal friends," Laporte said. "I have promised to help them." His small eyes grew dark and beady. Jeanne knew a crafty look when she saw one. She bent her head closer and smiled encouragingly. "We are aware that your dear friend covets the necklace, and we need your nimble wits to find a way for her to purchase it."

"Well, I know she kept it with her for a spell. A month or so, some time back. She's mentioned it."

"Precisely," Laporte said, his dark eyes moving greedily over Jeanne's rich gown.

"The problem is those two jewelers have created something that not even a sovereign king can afford. You see what I mean? A couple of losers! What's their asking price?"

"One million eight hundred thousand francs."

"Go on!" Jeanne guffawed. "How much did you say?"

"One million eight hundred thousand francs," Laporte repeated.

"Your eyes bulge when you say the price, did you know that? What's the matter? Does it make your hernia act up?" Jeanne held her sides and laughed like a schoolgirl.

"This is an important matter, Madame," Laporte said, clearing his throat disapprovingly. "Bassenge and Böhmer are prepared to offer a tempting commission to anyone who can persuade the Queen to purchase the necklace."

"How much?"

"Two hundred thousand francs."

"Hmmn, that *is* tempting," Jeanne said.

22

As his sleigh whipped down the snow-filled rue Vieille-du-Temple and turned into the courtyard of the Palais-Cardinal, the Cardinal-Prince Louis de Rohan could think only, I live again! At last! At long last! After the painful loneliness of months at Saverne, the agony of nights pacing, sleepless, back and forth, the tedium of days spent doling out his attention to matters that concerned him not at all. The time was too long, waking in the morning with one devouring thought: to push the hands of the clock around again to darkness and sleep. Or worse horror: sleeplessness.

He sprang from the carriage, sinking up to his knees in snow as his servants flailed about with brooms clearing his way up the great staircase.

The Abbé Georgel appeared like a sleepwalker at the top of the stairs, a candle shaking in his hand. "Your Eminence! Past three in the morning! And the snow falling as thick as sin since twilight!" He looked like a resentful owl startled from a peaceful slumber.

The Abbé turned slightly aside to allow the Cardinal to pass. "You look radiant, Your Eminence," he said, his lugubrious voice solicitous, as if he had just announced that the Cardinal had a mortal disease.

"Do I?" The Abbé's remark caught him off guard. The Cardinal tried to sound astonished. "It must be the cold night air."

The Cardinal hurried into his dressing room, where his valet Schreiber had already started a blaze in the grate. Standing before the fire, his hands extended toward the flames, the Cardinal could bear it no longer. He turned to Georgel exultantly and said, "She has summoned me to her side!"

"Who?" the Abbé said.

"The Queen, my good fellow! Her Majesty the Queen of France! Here. Read this." He withdrew a small blue envelope from his pocket and held it out to the Abbé.

The Cardinal sat down and watched the Abbé's face. Only two days before, as the Cardinal was sitting in his study on a hollow January afternoon, feeling his bones ache as an icy branch scraped against a frozen window pane, Schreiber appeared before him patiently offering him another envelope. The Cardinal had looked down at it like a child facing a punishing dose of salts. And then, the envelope reluctantly opened, the words leapt out at him. The Queen had stopped shilly-shallying: she was taking him into her circle. She was giving him a mission.

Georgel stood quite still, his head bent over the small sheet of paper.

"Read it aloud, Monsieur l'Abbé," the Cardinal said.

The Abbé stammered. "It says . . . I'm afraid I'm very nervous. It says, *The time is not yet ripe for your public triumph, but I urge you to hasten to Paris for a secret negotiation of great personal interest to me, one which I would entrust to none but you. The Comtesse de La Motte will speak for me to supply you the key to the enigma.*

"She has summoned me to her side! My Queen sees me as her protector, Georgel. She calls upon me to help her in a matter requiring my absolute discretion."

"This 'key to the enigma,'" the Abbé said, his face sour and pinched, "You'll be wanting to see the Comtesse de La Motte right away."

"Of course!" the Cardinal said jovially. "But the 'key to the enigma,' you and I don't need the Comtesse to tell us what that means, do we? You and I have the key already! *A secret negotiation of great personal interest.* What does that bring to mind, Georgel?"

"Something to do with Austria?" the Abbé said hesitantly. "Is that what you mean?"

"*Mais oui!* Austria! What else could it be? A matter of great delicacy, something concerning her beloved country. And, I am uniquely qualified. Of course, of course! Finally, my Queen has come to recognize what an invaluable diplomat I am. How respected and idolized by her mother's court. If not, alas, by her mother. May she rest in peace. A secret negotiation, that does appeal to me. I am the very soul of discretion."

"And you know all the key players at the Austrian court! You know them all." The Abbé began to pace back and forth excitedly. "Her brother Joseph wept to see you leave Austria in disgrace, chased back to France by his ruthless mother." He stopped suddenly and faced the Cardinal. "So they must be true, then, the rumors that the Queen carries on shadow diplomacy in the interest of Austria. Doubtless also true that the court is infested with Austrian spies and agents."

"Mere mischief-making rumors by the Queen's enemies. I believe none of it," the Cardinal said.

"But these rumors must have some validity if the Queen is asking you take part in some secret negotiations on her behalf and . . ."

"Perhaps," the Cardinal said. "Perhaps. But I will not believe ill of her. She has only the best interests of France at heart. And what could serve France more than the certainty of peace with Austria?"

"Quite right, Your Eminence."

"Secret negotiations, a mission that she would entrust to none but me! Look at me, Georgel, I feel as if I have been embraced by history! *Public triumph!* At last! The time is not yet ripe for my public triumph. How wise she is! My heart is afire! My two great loves, France and the Queen, I will now be able to serve them both."

"And the great diplomatic skills of the Cardinal-Prince Louis de Rohan will resound throughout the courts of Europe," Georgel said, his head wagging ecstatically. "Peace, prosperity, an end to these ravaging wars. This moment is everything you've always deserved, Your Eminence."

"Yes, after years of being shunted aside like a leprous pariah, I must savor those words: *Public triumph!* I must nurse them in my bosom like a healing balm. Public triumph, the eyes of the court fixed on me."

The next day, despite the deep snow along the paths and the biting chill in the night air, the Cardinal, his thoughts in dismal confusion, left his palace for a walk in the garden. Peace muffled the street beyond the garden walls. The Cardinal's feet thundered along the ice-encrusted pathway, sinking into the snow. For a while, he floundered around like a noisy drunk, then stopped and laughed out loud. What a fool I am, he said to himself, to allow my heart to slap me around like an unruly child! He took a deep breath and tried to clear his thoughts. He had to laugh at himself. *Bon sang!* What a clown he had become! Getting so worked up that his thoughts chased around and around in his head like a dog trying to bite the fleas tormenting his tail. He took another deep breath. How beneficent the crisp, unforgiving air of winter. Despite his heavy cloak he could feel the hair on his head stiffening with frost.

He wished he could be more like Jeanne—cool, controlled, yet vivacious, gay, full of wild, animal spirits. She was irresistible. He could not believe the ferocity of their coupling today. All those months of separation. Sometimes it frightened him to need her so much.

"I've come here to seduce you all over again," she had said after he kissed her, lifting her little chin like a naughty actress. And, *mon dieu*, she had succeeded in doing just that. Looking back, he could not remember when she had been in a more lubricious mood. *Diable!* It was wonderful!

He stuffed his hands up the sleeves of his cloak. Oh, God, he said to himself, here comes my heart again, battering me with recriminations.

But, no, it was only the acid of bitterness seeping into his heart, poisoning drop by drop his innocent adoration of the Queen. Like a novice acrobat he kept falling from the impossible heights he set for himself. Or, rather he was forever being pushed from them, he thought miserably.

He pulled himself up straight and began to walk again. Enough of such self-pitying nonsense. Jeanne was good for him. A stiff dose of reality. Thank God, he had been wise enough not to confide in her what he had assumed the Queen would ask of him. Jeanne would have laughed herself silly. Covert diplomacy, international intrigue, he and the Queen in fetching disguises engaging in nocturnal negotiations with a Viennese courier in some deserted farmhouse near the Trianon, or in a moldering cellar in Paris somewhere near the Opéra. Ah, what a melodrama of intrigue and erotic longing his wretched heart had woven . . .

He should have suspected something less than grand from the boisterous way Jeanne disported herself when she came to him that morning.

"Her Majesty informs me that you, my child, will provide the key to the enigma. You know, this secret negotiation, this delicate mission that she wishes to entrust to my care," he had said to her as soon as they had dispensed with the formalities of greeting each other after such a long absence.

"Not now," Jeanne had said, breathlessly, and soon her flushed face and urgent caresses had enflamed him beyond reason.

Hours later, it was Jeanne, who had to remind him of what had called her forth into the fretful wintry day. He thought she spoke with some reluctance.

She said, "We ought to talk about the business you must do for the Queen."

Suddenly she grew quite solemn. She began to pace around the room in a distracted, aimless way, never once looking in his direction, talking in the air as if musing to herself. It was so unlike Jeanne that he could feel the excitement building inside him. What could it be, to turn his savage little Jeanne into such a serious mood?

"Business?" he said, his heart in his throat. How much had the Queen told her about the Austrian problem?

"An affair," Jeanne said, "That will require your sharpest, keenest negotiating skills. An affair, the Queen begs me to inform you, that will earn you her undying devotion."

The Cardinal placed his hand on the back of a chair to steady himself.

"If you are successful," Jeanne said, abruptly turning to look him in the eyes. And then she described to him the *glorious* mission that the Queen could entrust to none other than the Cardinal.

And so he was commissioned to acquire a necklace for the Queen! The unique diplomatic skills of the Cardinal de Rohan were to be put to use haggling with Bassenge and Böhmer. Damn it to hell! For the notorious diamond necklace those two had been hawking around the courts of Europe for years.

What a laugh! He, Prince Louis-René-Edouard de Rohan, must hang about in the perfumed antechambers of Messieurs Bassenge and Böhmer. Such a noble quest! Ha! A quest for a diamond necklace fit only for a queen. A quest that will forever leave his mark on the history of his beloved France! Ha, Ha, Ha!

Ah, he groaned, was there ever a lackey more miserable than I tonight?

23

Being essentially of a sanguine nature, the Prince soon resigned himself to what he considered the demeaning task of negotiating for the diamond necklace. But he decided to set about it in his own good time. Moreover, he would not be writing any more *billets doux* to the one he called, in his heart of hearts, *Toinette*, the fond nickname given her by her mother as the Cardinal knew from the old days of intercepting the Empress's letters. He evoked less and less frequently his cherished memory of the Queen, quivering with passionate emotion, in the Grove of Venus, and the slight brush of her trembling hand against his. He now consigned her letters, unopened, to a lower drawer in his desk and sometimes left them there for days before he got around to reading them. He decided that his spirits needed a bit of healing, and he was in the mood to warm himself in Jeanne's capacious bosom until the snows melted and the cold grip of disappointment loosened its hold on his heart.

As days passed, he was surprised by how easy it was to slip into the warm, sensual pleasures of the Palais-Cardinal and his daily assignations with Jeanne. Perhaps it was only a case of winter sloth, but he was enjoying himself. Jeanne, however, appeared to be falling into a dither of female nerves. His cool, collected little vixen was behaving quite unlike herself.

One day, after handing over the latest blue envelope from the Queen and watching as he tossed it into his desk drawer, she stood staring into space for a moment, then, her face stony, said, "Aren't you going to read Her Majesty's letter?"

"In due course, my love, when the mood strikes me."

Clearly, she was mystified by his indifference to the Queen's "mission." The Cardinal wondered just how much the Queen had told her of the deep intimacy of their correspondence.

"And what price are the royal jewelers asking for the diamond necklace?" Jeanne said.

"I'm sure I wouldn't know."

"You don't know?" she queried, biting her lower lip.

"I haven't asked."

She mulled over his reply for a moment or two. Though she made an effort to appear unconcerned, she looked nonplussed by his brazenness.

"You are aware that Böhmer has sent a sketch of the necklace to the Princess of Asturias?"

"Truly? No, I didn't know. On the other hand, why should I care? If the Princess of Asturias buys the necklace, then I shall be spared the humiliation of haggling with those confounded jewelers."

"If they send the jewel to Spain for her inspection, the purchase may be delayed for months. The Queen will be sorely vexed if she loses this masterpiece to some paltry Spanish royal."

The Cardinal said nothing. Jeanne suddenly became preoccupied with rearranging a lock of hair, but he could see that her hands trembled and that she was close to tears. He looked at her and cursed himself for the callous mood that had taken possession of him. His darling was caught in the middle between him and the Queen, who would surely make Jeanne's life miserable until the necklace rested securely in the royal boudoir.

"Poor darling. Ah, now, don't fret, the Queen shan't lose her precious necklace," he said, taking her in his arms.

She gave him that dazzling, broad smile that never failed to melt his heart. He would always remember that night as the happiest they ever spent together.

The Cardinal had to work fast. It was already the twenty-fourth of January, and according to Jeanne, the Queen proposed to wear the necklace on the second of February at the Cordon Bleu investiture, a state occasion and one of the grandest ceremonies at court for which protocol called for the wearing of pearls and diamonds.

After long reflection the Cardinal decided not to divulge any details of his negotiations for the necklace to the Abbé Georgel. Thus far, he had managed to evade the Abbé's questions about the Queen's secret mission, and he gathered from several of the Abbé's remarks that he was still excited by the idea of clandestine diplomacy. The Cardinal did not have the heart to disillusion him.

It was a sparkling clear January day when the Cardinal in his carriage drew up at the elegant shop at number 11 rue Vendôme to keep his appointment with the royal jewelers. Tall, erect, his scarlet robes swinging in rhythm with his broad strides, the Cardinal-Prince was ushered along a path of low susurration of *Your Eminence* to the private office of the two jewelers.

They chatted amiably of the dreadful weather and conjectured at length about its end. Finally, the Cardinal, sensing the mounting excitement of the two jewelers, said, "I have been authorized to purchase the diamond necklace of some renown created by your establishment. I cannot at this time disclose any names."

"We understand, Your Eminence," Bassenge said, exchanging a blissful glance with Böhmer. "No names."

"I wonder if you would care to tell me your lowest possible asking price. The price is important. Extremely important."

"Ah, yes, Your Eminence, we agree, the lowest possible asking price, that's exactly what we wish to propose, but you must understand that it is not easy for us, after all these years, and the mounting interest on the money we have been forced to borrow to pay for the precious diamonds that we have been obliged to collect from all over the world. All seventeen stones for the choker, for instance, were taken from mines in South America, at great expense, purchased for us by our buyers in Amsterdam at terrible risk both personal and financial. And let us say that we forget about the exorbitant interest we are paying for the loans for this incomparable necklace, what can we do about the labor costs . . .

and the time, the time we have both spent in bringing this precious necklace to completion, and none of our labor costs, our time and energy can ever be compensated . . ."

"How much?" the Cardinal said, coldly.

Böhmer, his face glistening with eagerness, said, "We never intended to make a profit on the necklace, did we?" He glanced quickly at his partner. "It was conceived as a tribute to royalty. Yes, that's it. In concept and execution, a tribute to royalty."

The Cardinal said nothing. He folded his hands and stared into space. This whole business was far more degrading than he had anticipated. At the count of ten, he would bolt out of there and have done with the whole affair.

"One million six hundred thousand francs. Our lowest possible price, Your Eminence," Bassenge whined in a low voice.

"What?"

"One million six hundred thousand francs. For a priceless piece of jewelry."

The Cardinal felt a dull pain start up at the back of his head. What kind of nonsense were these two talking?

"Would you care to see the necklace, Your Eminence?"

"What? Yes. By all means." With some difficulty he rose and followed them to the vault in a back room.

There, Böhmer withdrew a case so large that the Cardinal thought he must be up to some silly prank when he came forward to set it on the table. His eyes bright with pride, Böhmer opened the lid with a flourish and stood aside so that the Cardinal could come forward for a closer look.

The Cardinal took one long look, then tightly shut his eyes as if he had had a seizure. He rubbed his forehead. He was sweating profusely.

"Go ahead, Your Eminence," Bassenge said, with a chuckle. "You may pick it up."

The Cardinal opened his eyes and looked at the necklace. Great God, he thought, it is so ugly! Bassenge caressed the necklace with his fat, shiny fingers and asked the Cardinal again if he would like to pick it up. The awful thing sprawled, in all its grotesque glory, on purple velvet cloth. Purple! The Cardinal stretched out his hand, but his fingers curled away from the necklace, as from a slimy, revolting thing. He could not bear to touch it.

He turned to Böhmer and said, with almost desperate urgency, "I must go now." He hurried out of the shop and threw himself into his carriage as if he had just escaped from a collapsing building.

With dismay Bassenge and Böhmer watched his departure.

"He was overwhelmed by the price," Böhmer said.

"Did you see his face when he looked at the necklace? He's never dreamed of anything so stupendous," Bassenge said.

"He's never dreamed of anything so expensive," Böhmer said.

"What does it matter? He's the richest man in the kingdom."

"Besides, he's been authorized to make the purchase for someone else. And we know who that someone else is," Böhmer said with a contented sigh.

The Cardinal sat before the fireplace in the Salon des Singes and waited for Jeanne. He could not get the hideous necklace out of his mind. He could not bear to think of that heavy, deformed thing disfiguring the Queen's slender neck and tender bosom with its blowsy vulgarity. He remembered how charmingly she looked up at him that day in Strasbourg, she was only fifteen and already breath-takingly beautiful! How fair she was! Her golden-ash hair aglow in the morning sun. Impossible that she should choose to mar that beauty with this ghastly necklace. A whorish thing, winking obscenely on its velvet cloth. He hated it! He felt as if the ugly sight of it would haunt him for the rest of his days.

He was in a foul mood when Jeanne arrived, as usual bright and playful. "I have grave misgivings about the necklace, Jeanne," he said.

"Misgivings? What kind of misgivings?"

"Quite frankly, I'm shocked. I can't believe the Queen would be in the slightest way interested in such vulgar display. The diamond necklace is a blowsy, tarty abomination."

"You don't know women," she said with a flirtatious smile.

"Perhaps not. But I think I do know the Queen. And her taste for the beautiful." He was determined not to let her jolly him out of his low mood.

"You don't know how passionate women can be about jewelry."

The Cardinal said nothing. Her presence annoyed him. He missed Cagliostro terribly and had on his return from the jewelers' shop sent a messenger to Lyon with an urgent request for his return to Paris. He needed his mentor's help now as never before.

"Then shall I tell the Queen that you are reluctant to carry out her commission because you don't find the diamond necklace to your taste?"

She sensed that he wanted to be alone. She glared at him until he finally looked away.

"You will tell the Queen nothing," he said. "The diamond necklace is none of your affair."

"Indeed," she said.

24

Cagliostro sensed immediately that something held the Cardinal as tightly in its grip as the icy snows that continued unrelentingly over the land. As they sat by the fire, the Cardinal laid before him the entire concatenation of events beginning with his return from Saverne at the request of Queen.

"Now here's my Queen's letter, dear friend."

Cagliostro took the pale blue envelope and held it to his broad brow. "I must take it away with me. I must subject it to the test of my occult powers."

The Cardinal waited by the fire, relieved that his ever reliable guide and friend had come to his aid. When Cagliostro returned to the Cardinal's study, he looked both grave and elated.

"For a certainty, Your Eminence's hour of public triumph as prime minister approaches. Confounding all your enemies." He slapped the letter three times. "It's here in the secret negotiations!"

"Can you elaborate?"

Cagliostro placed his right hand to his forehead as if in sudden, acute pain, and the Cardinal's heart clouded with dismay.

"You must, however, proceed with extreme caution in this affair," Cagliostro said. "This is no mean sum. These jewelers are asking a sum that could bankrupt a nation. The Queen is quite right to keep this acquisition secret from the King and the court, which would surely cry out in alarm. On the other hand," and here his voice took on a resounding heartiness, "The very fact that the purchase is on such a colossal scale and the negotiations of such delicacy and secrecy, why, then, the Queen's gratitude will necessarily be all the greater."

Right away, the Cardinal saw the logic of his friend's argument. Clearly, this was no mean assignment within the reach of any courtier. Only someone like the Cardinal-Prince de Rohan with a name resounding throughout the history of France and with a fortune to match could even attempt to negotiate for this . . . this . . . The Cardinal's spirits drooped and withered at the memory of that unnamable thing, those great blobs of diamonds serving no purpose.

"Yes. Proceed with caution! Convey your anxieties about this purchase to Her Majesty," Cagliostro whispered.

The Cardinal worked through the night drafting a contract for the purchase of the necklace, and at first light, he summoned Bassenge and Böhmer to the Palais-Cardinal. He presented to them a contract outlining not only the terms of the purchase and but also a schedule for payments which he sought to make as lenient as possible for the Queen's sake:

> 1) *The price of said necklace to be 1,600,000, subject to appraisal by Messieurs Doigny and Maillard. A reduction in price of the necklace would obtain, should they so indicate.*
> 2) *The first payment of 400,000 francs would not fall due for six months, i.e. the first of August 1785; successive payments of this amount to be payable every six months thereafter.*
> 3) *The said necklace must be ready for delivery on Tuesday, 1 February, 1785.*

The jubilant Bassenge and Böhmer duly signed the contract, to which the Cardinal affixed the date, *This Day of Our Lord, Saturday, 29 January 1785*, and unctuously made their departure. The Cardinal then sent his carriage to 13 rue Neuve Saint-Gilles to fetch the Comtesse de La Motte.

"Listen, my child," he said to her. "You will take this contract to the Queen. I want it read by her, each item approved, and the whole of it signed and returned to me."

"She won't do it. She has no patience for this sort of thing," Jeanne said, throwing the contract back down on the desk.

The Cardinal, however, was prepared for her anger and determined not to be dissuaded by it.

"You mean, you have no patience for this sort of thing, my dear."

This he knew to be only too true. The Cardinal had on more than one occasion concluded that Jeanne, for all her charm, was a poor flibbertigibbet, her head full of grandiose schemes never to be realized, unfortunately, because her mind seemed incapable of settling down to the task at hand.

To his great surprise, Jeanne was back, contract in hand, before the deepening of twilight. The Cardinal quickly read through the document, *"lu et apprové"* (*read and approved*) appropriately inscribed next to each item.

"No signature," he said, handing the contract back to her.

"What?" Her eyes blazed at him.

"No signature. The Queen has failed to sign the contract."

Without a word she snatched the paper from his hand and was gone. He felt a pang of guilt as he watched her clamber into the carriage and whirl out of the courtyard. Poor girl, he and the Queen were driving her too hard.

"I know that I should feel honored, being selected by the Queen to perform this service for her, my dear Count, but I am plagued by doubts. Unaccountable doubts. I can't even describe them to you. They're vague, confused, the stuff of nightmares. I must be slipping into my dotage." The Cardinal pushed aside his dessert and rose from the dinner table. "For one thing, with the contract I have drawn up for the jewelers, I shall be forced to reveal the Queen as the purchaser of the necklace."

"Enjoin them to silence. Gratitude will keep them quiet," Cagliostro said.

The Cardinal felt weary in every limb. What if the Queen refused to sign the contract? What would he do then? "Please excuse me, dear friend, but I must retire for the evening. I must sleep if I can. Tomorrow is the fateful day."

Cagliostro rose and bowed deeply from the waist. "Do not take your cares to your bed, I beg of you."

The Cardinal smiled weakly and left the room.

Shortly before midnight Cagliostro, dressed entirely in black, knocked on the door of the Cardinal's bedchamber. He wore no jewelry, no wig, no adornments of any kind. His austere appearance, his stern yet distant look startled the Cardinal.

"I have come to plumb more mysteries of the occult," Cagliostro said. He stared across the dimly lit room and pointed to a Chinese silk screen in the corner opposite the Cardinal's bed.

"You must stand there," he said. "Behind that screen. Make no noise. Merely observe the scene which will unfold before you."

No sooner had he left the room than he reappeared with what the Cardinal at first thought must surely be an apparition from the Invisible World: a ravishing young creature shimmering in a white and silver dress with an enormous golden sun covering her breast, a cerulean blue sash at her waist.

The Count Cagliostro led her to a table on which he carefully placed a carafe of water and a constellation of paper stars alongside papier-maché figures of the goddess Isis and Apis, sacred bull of the ancient Egyptians.

The Count then stepped back into the shadows of the candlelit room.

Behind the screen the Cardinal, trying with all his might to follow Cagliostro's every move and gesture, felt dizzy.

Slowly, Cagliostro lifted his sword and held it aloft over the carafe of water.

"What do you see in the water, my dove?" he asked the young girl. "Do you see there a woman in white?"

"Yes," the girl said in a clarion-clear voice. "I see there a woman in white."

The Cardinal strained to see the water himself.

"Does she look like the Queen?" asked the Count.

"Yes," the girl answered.

The Cardinal's head was pounding. His eyes misted over. He was so overcome with emotion that he could not tell what happened next. He thought he heard the young girl invoke the Great Cophta and the angel Gabriel, but he could not be sure.

Time passed, or seemed to pass, and then the Count Cagliostro said, "Look into the water, my dove. Do you not see there the Cardinal on his knees, holding a snuff-box in which there is a coin?"

The Cardinal held his breath as the girl moved closer to the carafe. She stared and stared into the clear water of the carafe.

"Yes," she finally said.

The Cardinal cried aloud and fell to his knees, overwhelmed with the certainty of his glorious destiny: Cardinal-Prince Louis de Rohan, Prime Minister of France!

The Cardinal sat dozing by the fire. It was half past ten in the morning on the last day of January.

"Wake up!" Jeanne said. "This is no time to sit around in a trance. Here's your damned piece of paper. Signed."

She laid the contract in the Cardinal's hands. He studied it curiously for a moment as if he could not remember what it was, then shivered as if he felt a cold draft cross the room.

"I shall send my valet to fetch the necklace right away."

"And none too soon," Jeanne said. "Tomorrow is the first of February, you know."

She touched his cheek with the back of her hand. "What on earth is wrong with you? Your speech is thick. You're pale, as if you'd just seen a ghost."

"Not a ghost. A dove," the Cardinal said, smiling to himself.

"You've been playing games with Cagliostro again. Take a nap. I shall expect you in my rooms at Versailles at twilight."

In the late afternoon the Cardinal decided that it would be more prudent to call on Bassenge and Böhmer and collect the necklace himself. After the Night of Glorious Revelations, as he now thought of the previous night in his room, he had reached a deep peace within himself. The wondrous memory of the Queen trembling with emotion as he approached her in the Grove of Venus came back to him in full force, crowding out any lingering uncertainties. He was almost nonchalant as he showed the jewelers the contract. When they saw the Queen's signature on the contract, Bassenge and Böhmer exchanged a complicitous look, then turned to oil before the Cardinal's very eyes.

All the way to Versailles the Cardinal held the impossibly large case on his knees and never once thought of opening it to take another look at the most famous diamond necklace ever created. He could not help thinking of it as a reprehensible thing, a lewd gewgaw unfit for the lovely apparition in white in the Grove of Venus. A tribute to majesty indeed! Rather, a tribute to vulgarity!

As he passed the Petit Trianon, he asked his driver to slow the carriage. His heart full of yearning, he gazed at the palace, imagining behind its charming facade the preparations for a delicious evening of intimate revelry with the Queen. Soon, he, too, would take his rightful place among the fortunate few. Soon, very soon.

With little difficulty the Cardinal's man found the La Motte lodgings, for the Comtesse seemed to be something of a celebrity on the Place Dauphine.

"Is this your idea of punctuality?" Jeanne shouted down to the Cardinal as he alighted from his carriage.

"It's my idea of twilight," he shouted back, suddenly full of good cheer.

"Quickly, quickly," she said, hurrying him along like a slow, slightly awkward pupil. "Shush. Not another word. Here, put the case on this table, and take a seat over there in the alcove. The

Queen's messenger is on his way. Thank God, he didn't get here before you. I've been frantic."

She was in truth breathless, and despite the chill in the air, beads of sweat stood out on her upper lip.

In spite of the general obscurity of the rooms the Cardinal was taken aback at their obvious luxury. He had never stopped to think about the material rewards of Jeanne's intimacy with the Queen. All the objects around him spoke of money, a great deal of money.

Utterly relaxed, the Cardinal sat down in the alcove, folded his hands over his knees, and waited. Almost immediately, a rather tall, slender man with an elegant step appeared from a door on the far side of the sitting room and swiftly approached the center table where the necklace case waited.

"In the name of the Queen," he said, as he took up the case and disappeared into the shadows.

This mysterious figure seemed familiar. The Cardinal searched his memory in vain. Where had he seen the fellow before? Then, it came back to him: the Queen's man who accompanied Jeanne along the garden paths almost to her carriage that night when she caught the Cardinal spying on her as she emerged from a rendez-vous with the Queen. Of course! No mystery man at all but the Queen's man. What did she say his name was? Desclaux? Was that it?

Jeanne was at his side, urging him to his feet. "I must join the Queen at once. She will have more instructions for you tomorrow."

"Instructions?" the Cardinal asked, perplexed.

"You have done well," Jeanne said hastily. "You can go back to the Palais-Cardinal and sleep deeply this night, knowing that the diamond necklace is in good hands."

And knowing that, thanks to me, dear Toinette has her heart's desire, the Cardinal added to himself.

25

Just when Suzanne Colson thought that the commotion and hullabaloo in the La Motte establishment was about to calm down,
it got worse. These days she had few duties as the Comtesse's
dame de compagnie because her mistress had thrown herself into
another of her buying frenzies and seemed intent on emptying
out the exclusive shops in the Faubourg Saint-Antoine: statues and
bronzes arrived by the dozen from Chevalier's on the rue des Petits-
Champs, marbles from Adam's on the rue de Popincourt, more
crystal from Sike's and clocks of every size from Furet's. Furnishers
of every kind streamed in and out with their wares, their fabrics,
their measuring sticks, and their oily spiels.

"What in God's name is that supposed to be?" Suzanne asked
Father Loth as he stood swaying back and forth, admiring a
gilded cage.

"Why, it's a pair of automatic singing birds. Watch. I turn this
key here . . . it's still a bit stiff . . . and we wait a minute or two . . .
and . . . *voilà*" He giggled and stroked his scraggly beard in disbelief
as the tiny gold beaks of the two birds moved back and forth, chirp-
ing and cooing. "The Comtesse says they remind her of the lovely
songbirds in the orchards of her beloved Fontette. Ah, it makes me
weep to think of how hard she has worked to get where she is this
fine day. Here, I'll just wind it up again. Such a wonder, isn't it?"

Father Loth had every reason to feel cheerful and full of pride:
the Comtesse had placed him in command of the disposition and
packing of the new goods that would accompany her and the
Comte on their trip to their new residence in Bar-sur-Aube.

"It's a wonder all right," Suzanne said. "How in the world are you going to manage to cart all this stuff to Bar?"

She had made up her mind that she would abandon the La Motte household as soon as she got back to her hometown. She couldn't really complain about her treatment under their roof. For whatever reason she had thus far been spared the rough side of the Comtesse de La Motte's tongue. But she was no longer amused by the Comtesse's obsession with her bluer than blue blood and the pendulum swings in the La Motte fortunes. She longed to find herself a humble place with humble folk whose feverish desires had long been extinguished.

"I've hired wagons. Lots of wagons. Guess how many," Father Loth said, his small, weasel eyes gleeful.

"Too many. You'll need an army to haul away everything that's been pouring into the storerooms here this past month."

"Forty-two!" Father Loth said triumphantly.

"Good Lord," Suzanne said.

Father Loth was disappointed. She could at least have the good grace to show more enthusiasm for the spectacular wealth of her employers. Though a pretty girl in a plain kind of way, Mademoiselle Colson had too many opinions for Father Loth's taste. She read the Encyclopedists and Voltaire and her attitudes were altogether suspicious. She missed Mass as if it were the most natural thing in the world. And rarely confessed herself. But in spite of himself he liked Mademoiselle Colson.

"The Comtesse has ordered a new carriage. A pearl-gray berline. Its doors are enamelled with the Valois coat of arms and the *devise: From my forebear the King I possess the blood, the name and the lilies.* Just think of her rolling into Bar-sur-Aube like a true princess!"

"Oh, yes," Suzanne said. "She's a true princess all right. One is not likely to forget that in this house."

Father Loth was busily arching his brows mysteriously and jerking his head in the general direction of the Comtesse's boudoir. "I've seen them. She showed them to me. She has a whole bagful."

"A bagful of what?" Suzanne said, putting down her embroidery.

"Diamonds."

"Diamonds! What are you talking about, Father?"

"Ssssh, sssh! I shouldn't be telling you this. But it's been so exciting! I can barely contain myself. This is what happened. The Queen has broken up an old diamond necklace and is having the master craftsman of the palace refashion it for her in the latest style. She had some stones left over that won't fit the new design, and she's given them to the Comtesse. As proof of her affection! A whole bagful! I've seen them."

"Well, I suppose that would explain some of the excitement around here lately," Suzanne said.

"And I suppose you've noticed that Monsieur Pretty Face has disappeared. The Comtesse is angry with him. I know that for a fact. She told me so herself."

Father Loth despised Rétaux de Villette with all his heart. If pushed to explain why, he would probably say that Rétaux de Villette was unworthy of a splendid woman like the Comtesse, totally unworthy. A mincing braggart, weak, feckless, without ambition, forced to hang onto the Comtesse's petticoats to make his way in life. What the Comtesse saw in him, he could not imagine.

"What did he do?"

"He got himself arrested. On the fifteenth of February. He was picked up by the police tipped off by a jeweler named Adan in the Palais-Royal. I know the shop well. Adan deals in only the choicest pieces. I understand even the Queen has bought several of his designs."

Father Loth was in his element. He was an insider in the La Motte household and Mademoiselle Colson was not, and though she obviously prided herself on her lack of curiosity about the La Mottes, he could tell that she could be impressed by how much he knew.

"Did Villette steal something from this jeweler?"

"Worse than that. He was peddling diamonds that the Comtesse gave to him as a personal gift. Can you imagine the gall of that young coxcomb? He sold a rather large quantity of diamonds—the Comtesse didn't tell me how many—to this Adan at an unusually low price and the jeweler became suspicious and notified the police."

"So he's in jail?"

"No, not that slippery eel! He was brought in for questioning and asked where he got so many diamonds. He told them that they were a gift from the Comtesse de La Motte-Valois, and since no costly piece of jewelry had been reported missing or stolen, the authorities had no reason to detain him. They had to release him."

"Then why isn't he here demonstrating his lovely penmanship for the Comtesse?"

"He's gone off to pursue his studies in Italy. His studies! At the Comtesse's expense, I might add. That wonderful woman! How can she be the dupe of that young scoundrel?"

"One wonders," Suzanne said, with her usual ambiguous smile.

❧❧❧

The Cardinal was growing dizzy with celebratory dinners almost every night of the week. He found that he had lost taste for any society other than his small coterie conversant with his relationship with the Queen. When he was not actively avoiding the Abbé Georgel, he was doing everything in his power to evade any further questions from him about the "Queen's mission," letting the matter drop entirely and treating it as if he had other matters far too pressing to give it any more of his attention at the present moment. At any rate, it would be hopeless to try to explain to Georgel the strategic advantages of the diamond necklace purchase.

Each evening the Cardinal escaped from his own palace and the Abbé's dark, scrutinizing stares and supped with the Count and Countess Cagliostro in their mansion on the rue St. Claude, often bringing with him one of his own chef's celebrated *entrées* to satisfy his gourmet tastes. At the Cagliostro table he joined his treasurer, the Baron da Planta, Jeanne, and her raffishly dressed husband, who usually managed to excuse himself on some pretext before the gaming tables at the Palais-Royal closed down for the night. Jeanne was the blithe spirit of these nightly revels where toast after toast was offered to the future prime minister of France, the Cardinal-Prince Louis de Rohan, who sat in great dignity at the head of the table, a modest smile playing over his thoughtful face.

His head busy with schemes of all that he would do once he laid claim to the prime minister's portfolio, the Cardinal scarcely found time to sleep. He sorely regretted the years lost in exclusion from the inner circle of power, especially the dreary months of exile at the Queen's behest in Saverne. Yet the time had not been wasted, the Cardinal consoled himself. He had listened to the country, observed the soundless, seething rage. Once out of the shadows he intended to bring the court and the Parlement together. Well, perhaps not together, that would be impossible at this stage. But certainly a *rapprochement*. The King clearly failed to see the isolation of the court at Versailles, while the Cardinal, shunted aside, excluded, could see that separation all too well. Don't you see, he would say to the King, the people *will* have a voice, and that Parlement *is* the voice of the people? It must be heeded, Sire.

The day after his delivery of the diamond necklace, the day of the Cordon Bleu investiture, the Cardinal sent his valet Schreiber to the palace to observe the Queen at the dinner hour, where all decently attired citizens were admitted to the spectacle of the royal family dining together, and to take careful note of her attire and her jewelry.

That evening the Cardinal drew Jeanne aside. "Schreiber tells me that the Queen was not wearing the diamond necklace today," he said.

"Really?" She seemed genuinely puzzled. "After all that hurry and fuss! She'll be the death of me, that woman! It's Jeanne do this, and Jeanne do that. And for what? I ask you. I don't mean to complain, Your Eminence, but the Queen will break my spirit yet." Her underlip trembled, and she quickly dashed away a tear before averting her eyes.

"There, there. Don't trouble yourself, my dear. It does strike me as odd, though. In her letters the Queen was extremely precise about the date."

It seemed logical to the Cardinal that there could be any number of reasons why the Queen had failed to wear the necklace to the court ceremonies, and he was swiftly drawn into the evening's merriment as Jeanne's deep, infectious laughter rang out again and again.

What worried the Cardinal most was the Queen's silence: her almost daily letters had ceased. When he questioned Jeanne, she spoke vaguely of the Queen's preoccupation with her pregnancy, pointing out that Her Majesty was due to be delivered of her third child in mid-March.

Thus, for a month or two the Cardinal drifted along from day to day, by turns gay, nervous, carried away with excitement about the magnificent future unfolding before him. His moods, however, became increasingly changeful, sometimes fiery, as if he could not quite settle into his newfound happiness. Despite his cheerful nature, he was beset with anxiety as days and weeks passed and still the Queen did not appear in public wearing the diamond necklace.

Then, near the beginning of April the Cardinal received a letter from the Queen that fairly took his breath away: *Your absence is indicated*, it read, *in order to afford me the opportunity to make my final preparations for your appointment to that high post to which you rightfully aspire.*

What a fool he had been to worry!

❧

No sooner had the Cardinal's carriage and outriders swung out of the gates and onto the rue Vieille-du-Temple than the Abbé Georgel set out in pursuit of Claude Beugnot. He found him studying the menu in front of a tidy little restaurant on the corner of the Boulevard Saint-Michel.

"Menus, my favorite reading material," Beugnot said with a laugh as they shook hands. "How have you been?"

They fell into step and headed toward the quays along the river. There was a chill in the air, as the sun dabbed inconsequentially at the damp streets.

As soon as they reached the river, the Abbé, his small eyes fiercely bright, turned to Beugnot and said, "Where is that La Motte woman?"

"I believe she's left for her residence in Bar-sur-Aube." Or her "country seat," as Jeanne had put it when she told him, watching his face carefully to make sure that he was duly impressed by the term. "She left this morning."

"Really?" They sat down on a bench as far as possible from the noisy ferry landing. "I'm thinking about coincidences, Beugnot," the Abbé said after a long silence.

"Are you? What kind of coincidences?"

"Strange coincidences. The kind that make me wonder about many things. I'm noticing for instance that the last time the Queen asked the Cardinal to absent himself from Paris, the La Motte woman took off for the country. And now it's happened again. The Cardinal left for Saverne this morning. At the Queen's request, of course."

"I wouldn't get too excited about your coincidences, if I were you, Monsieur l'Abbé. There's nothing strange or sinister about what Jeanne de La Motte does when she's in Bar."

"Then, what exactly does she do there?"

The Abbé was sure that he was on the track of some crucial revelation, and he refused to be dissuaded by Beugnot's reasonableness, really only a faintly disguised defense of the Comtesse, as far as the Abbé was concerned.

"The usual things. She makes the social rounds. She entertains."

Beugnot was acutely aware of what he was not saying: that the sole purpose of these visits to her hometown appeared to be Jeanne's childish efforts to show off her prodigious new wealth to the people who had known her as just another starving offspring of a dissolute poacher.

"What's become of her husband?"

"He's back in Paris," Beugnot said.

"Where has he been?"

"Apparently he took a trip to London. I saw him a few nights ago at the Café Procope."

Beugnot had caught sight of him, his cerise pantaloons with matching vest flashing like a beacon in storm-tossed seas, in the midst of a half-dozen ladies of the evening gathered around his table. Beugnot determined to pass him by with only a slight nod of recognition, but La Motte would have none of it.

"He invited me to sit down at his table and have a glass of champagne."

La Motte had fixed him with a bright, slightly drunken look, as if he were about to share with Beugnot a stupendous joke. *I'm celebrating,* he said. *I'm just back from England. Bit of luck at the Newmarket races. Bit of luck! Tonnerre de Dieu! I'm the richest man in Paris tonight!*

Beugnot had a sudden, desolate feeling as he remembered La Motte lording it in front of his whores at the Café Procope. "The Comte was celebrating a lucky day at the races," he said, half-heartedly.

"A lucky day at the races," the Abbé muttered. He leaned over and hung his head in his hands. "Now let's just think, Beugnot. Think. Reason it through. There is some pattern here. The Comtesse's heartthrob, Villette, goes off to Italy. What was that all about, I wonder? Then he comes back. The husband goes off to England. Then he comes back. Then the Cardinal receives a letter sending him off to Alsace. What's going on, Beugnot?"

"Not much is my guess."

"Ah, there you're wrong, young man!" The Abbé turned and glared at Beugnot. "I shall keep my counsel for the time being. But I intend to get to the bottom of this infernal Circe's sorcery."

26

"It's now the end of June, and the Queen has not once worn the diamond necklace!" the Cardinal said, his dark eyes full of fire.

He had not slept through a single night since he received the Abbé's letter, which sent him bolting back to Paris and confirmed all the suspicions that came roiling, willy-nilly, to the surface of his consciousness throughout the wretched days at Saverne. Only the Queen's wonderfully straightforward note asking him to leave Paris so that she could prepare his imminent return as prime minister kept his spirits alive, like a lone candle at the end of a long corridor. And now that candle had begun to flicker, threatening to plunge him into darkness.

Jeanne stood her ground. "And why should she?" she asked. "Her Royal Highness feels the necklace is overpriced and demands that the price be reduced by 200,000 francs. Subject of course to an appraisal by Messieurs Doigny and Maillard. If they find the necklace to be worth the additional 200,000 francs, then naturally the Queen will pay. Not until the price is reduced will the Queen wear the necklace. I should think you, of all people, would understand her delicacy in this matter."

"Then I must go to Böhmer and Bassenge right away. Why wasn't I told this before? More haggling, confound it!" He turned on his heels. "And how do you know these are the Queen's wishes? You've just come back to Paris from the country."

"You aren't the only one to get letters from her, you know," Jeanne said, not a little annoyed.

"What about our creditors, Your Eminence?" Bassenge pleaded. "A reduction in price of two hundred thousand francs! A fortune! You're asking us to toss away a fortune. We shall be ruined."

"You *are* ruined, I should think, if the Queen returns the necklace and leaves you with that millstone around your neck," the Cardinal said peevishly.

Normally a sunny, happy man, the Cardinal was dismayed by his own bad temper, as if it were a foul taste in his mouth from a dish he had not particularly enjoyed.

"But our creditors," Böhmer said. "What are we to . . ."

"We all know what creditors are all about," the Cardinal snapped. "Do I have your assent, yes or no?"

The two jewelers looked at each other and spread wide their palms in a gesture of helplessness.

"Very well. I shall report to Her Majesty your agreement to waive the two hundred thousand francs," the Cardinal said. "And have you expressed your gratitude to the Queen for taking this confounded necklace off your hands? It should have been done, as I suggested, as soon as the necklace was delivered."

Bassenge and Böhmer looked at each other again and wrung their hands.

The Cardinal sighed and beckoned toward Böhmer's desk. "Please be seated, Monsieur Böhmer. A humble note of thanks is all that is required," he said. "Common courtesy. Nothing more."

At length, Böhmer held out the letter for the Cardinal's approval:

Madame, Böhmer wrote,
We have attained to the pinnacle of happiness in presuming to think that we have expressed our respect and devotion to Your Majesty's orders by our submission to he latest terms which have been proposed to us, and we find vast satisfaction in the thought that the most beautiful jewel in the world is to grace the greatest and the best of Queens.

Though the Cardinal's stomach rose a little at the monstrous falsehood of *the most beautiful jewel in the world*, he politely corrected the spelling and returned it to Böhmer, who assured him that he would deliver it personally to the Queen the following day.

27

By mid-July the full blast of summer set in over the hazy skies of Paris, and the Cardinal, brooding by his bedroom window, watched the heavy summer rains drown his garden paths. He had fallen into the habit of rising late, attending to a little business with Georgel, and then retreating to the solitude of his own chambers. His small band of admirers no longer beckoned to him. He preferred the company of his own troubled thoughts. In his letters to the Queen, he pleaded with desperate passion for her help in giving him patience until the day when he could step forward from the shadows into the glory of her favor. He went to Versailles only when strictly necessary, dreading as he did any glimpse of the Queen, tightly hemmed round by her favorites, her lovely neck bare.

The world seemed to have lost its gaiety. The Cardinal could not remember the last time he had laughed effortlessly. He missed Jeanne sorely and kept hoping that she would soon deliver him from his uncertainties. Instead, more often than not, they fell to quarreling as soon as they saw each other.

"I bring very bad news indeed," Jeanne said, late one night in July.

Jeanne herself looked signally untroubled, or so it seemed to the Cardinal. She was dressed in a fashionably pale lawn gown with deep green ribbons and announced that she had just come from the theatre.

"The Queen tells me that she will be unable to meet the first payment to the jewelers at the end of this month. She's in a mess again. Is it any wonder, the way she throws money out the window with both hands, day and night, hanging over the gaming tables night after night and—"

"I believe, on the contrary, Her Majesty has confined herself a great deal since the birth of the child," the Cardinal said, trying not to give way to anger. "Do you mean there will be no 400,000 francs for Böhmer and Bassenge on the thirty-first? Why, they won't stand for it! Those poor devils will be fit to be tied!"

"Now stop working yourself up into a lather," Jeanne said. "Someone will come along to pay for the Queen."

She gave him a meaningful stare, but he was too overwrought to notice it. The Cardinal gave a nasty laugh. A snort.

"Someone with 400,000 he doesn't know what to do with? Is that what you mean?"

"Exactly. Someone like Cagliostro's friend, Boudard de Saint-James. I figure that anyone who can bankroll the French Navy might have enough spare change to lend a hand to the Queen."

The Cardinal stopped pacing the floor. "Saint-James?" He said nothing for a moment. "Brilliant. Absolutely brilliant. Saint-James, of course. The man is such a pushing social climber that he will be enchanted, honored to help the Queen through this bad patch. Excellent idea!"

"You see?" Jeanne said, but he was already headed for the door, on his way to Cagliostro in the rue St. Claude.

Count Cagliostro assured the Cardinal that the banker, one of the Count's most enthusiastic proselytes, would be flattered by the Cardinal's attention in this matter. The Cardinal therefore decided to invite Boudard de Saint-James to an intimate tête-à-tête the very next day, for with the scheduled first payment fast approaching, the Cardinal wanted above all else to avoid any more mewling and whining about money from the crown jewelers.

The Cardinal believed Saint-James, like all bankers, to be a most consummate parvenu. After a cordial or two in the *Salon des Singes* the two men retired to the intimacy of the Cardinal's study. There, the Cardinal divulged the entire necklace transaction to Saint-James and showed him the contract with the Queen's signature.

"I can assure you, Monsieur," the Cardinal said, "Financial assistance in this matter is the surest way into royal favor."

"400,000 francs," Saint-James said.

He walked toward the windows giving onto the street. The banker was a tall man, bulging in a rather unseemly way around the middle. His heavy tread made the parquet squeak most painfully to the Cardinal's sensitive nerves.

"I will not conceal from you, Your Eminence, that I have long aspired to some government appointment." He gesticulated vaguely toward the street below. "A decoration. The Cordon Rouge, perhaps." He turned and looked at the Cardinal hopefully.

"A coveted honor," the Cardinal said, "But, speaking in the name of the Queen, I believe that I can promise you the Cordon Rouge as a reward for this service to Her Majesty."

Saint-James's great round face grew lurid in the sunlight.

"Then, I would deem it a privilege to offer Her Majesty this proof of my devotion," he said, with a kind of rapture. "If Her Majesty will but honor me with her order to that effect I will relieve her of all anxiety on the score of these 400,000 francs."

The two men shook hands and parted most cordially. Why should I ever doubt Jeanne's insight into the human heart, the Cardinal wondered as he watched his burly guest hurry down the stairs. The woman is brilliant! Absolutely brilliant!

Two days passed and still no letter came from the Queen confirming for Saint-James her desires. Normally, Jeanne procured an answer within the day. In a matter of such urgency, for with the month's end, Bassenge and Böhmer would certainly set up a great howl if their 400,000 francs were not forthcoming, the Cardinal was bewildered by the Queen's silence. If the truth be told, he was also nettled that Saint-James had turned out to be such a stickler for detail. Why should he not take the Cardinal's word, as a nobleman, that he had truthfully conveyed to him the Queen's wishes in this matter?

On the twenty-eighth, with Jeanne nowhere to be found and still no letter from the Queen, the Cardinal, worried to distraction about the approaching payment to be made, went to supper at the Count Cagliotro's, where he was certain to find Saint-James. The Cardinal, accustomed to the banker's fawning and flattery, perceived immediately that Saint-James acknowledged him with some reluctance. In truth, Saint-James behaved toward him in a most peculiar fashion.

"I had thought," the Cardinal began boldly, for his pride rankled, "that you would have been considerably more prompt, Saint-James, in coming forward to relieve the Queen of her embarrassment."

The banker murmured vaguely and kept casting his eye about apprehensively, though he and the Cardinal stood at some remove from the guests who were heading toward the Count's gaming tables.

"Forgive me, Your Eminence," he said finally, bringing his hand to his mouth. "I had a rather nasty tooth extraction yesterday, and I am still not quite myself."

"Ah, my dear fellow," the Cardinal was quick to add, "you must have no vanity with me, you know."

"Of course not, of course not," Saint-James mumbled, though he looked upon the point of breaking for the door.

"I won't detain you further," the Cardinal said. "Clearly you need the sympathetic ministrations of a mistress." He gave Saint-James a jocular wink. "But about the Queen's embarrassment," he persisted.

"Afraid not, Your Eminence."

"Afraid not? You mean, you cannot advance the funds?" the Cardinal said, unable to disguise his irritation.

"Unforeseen circumstances," the banker murmured. He nervously glanced about the now empty room. "Are you quite certain, Your Eminence, that you have correctly understood the Queen's orders in this affair? Is it not possible that you are mistaken, or that you have been deceived?" Saint-James kept ducking his head in a flustered manner.

"If you are at all uneasy in this matter, I can give you my own personal note," the Cardinal said, a trifle arrogantly.

"That won't be necessary, Your Eminence. Unforeseen circumstances," he mumbled again before bowing and taking his leave.

Good Lord! the Cardinal said to himself, staring after Saint-James in disbelief. What an impertinent fellow! If I have any say in the matter, and as prime minister I most certainly will, he shall go to his grave panting after that Cordon Rouge!

The next morning, dreaming that a slimy-fisted demon held him by the throat, the Cardinal awoke in a cold fright. Saint-James's refusal of the money alarmed him because it made no sense. Why, he asked himself, should such a one as Boudard de Saint-James, who would lap his way in spittle to the royal throne, not come forward to lend the Queen these 400,000 francs? Ambition such as his knew no impediment. Unforeseen circumstances indeed! With Schreiber's help the Cardinal dressed hastily and rushed to confer with the Count Cagliostro, whom he found still in his nightshirt, attending to his morning affairs.

"Agreed. Most extraordinary, Your Eminence," Cagliostro said when the Cardinal acquainted him with Saint-James's refusal.

"There was, how shall I say, an element of distrust in his manner when he refused me," the Cardinal said, feeling his anger rise. "Not me, of course! He did not refuse me, but Her Majesty the Queen."

"Have you any word from Her Majesty?" Cagliostro asked, his lofty brow thick with concentration.

"Not a word. Though I expect that the birth of the little prince in March, you know, other distractions . . ." He could feel his spirit falter. He felt suddenly alone in the dreadful necklace business, hounded by greasy jewelers. "I have written the Queen this morning," the Cardinal said, feeling somewhat better, "apprising her of Saint-James's refusal. She will not be pleased. Saint-James, by the way, asked me if I were entirely certain of the Queen's wishes in this matter of the loan. He seemed to think that I might be deceived. Queer fellow, Saint-James."

"I feel strange currents in the air, Your Eminence!" Cagliostro said, making calming motions in the air with his large hands, his eyes whelmed in a prophetic glow. "Strange currents! Remember only this! The snuff box, Prince. Your destiny as the King's minister, your hand guiding this frail craft of a nation in stormy times to a fair harbor!"

Despite his low humor, the Cardinal thrilled to his words, though feebly, to be sure.

"However. We must summon the Comtesse de La Motte!" Cagliostro said, suddenly fixing his gaze on the door.

Toward noon Jeanne arrived, looking exquisite, the Cardinal thought, in rose satin with deep Alençon laces about the bosom and sleeves. She bantered a moment with Cagliostro, and when she turned to the Cardinal, he fairly shouted at her, "Woman! You have cruelly deceived me!"

The Cardinal looked stunned, as if this outburst, so unlike him, had taken him unawares. Jeanne recoiled not at all, but looked at him as if in deepest pity, and with a voice vibrant with self-assurance said, "Your Eminence, you insult me at the very moment I have succeeded in determining the Queen to rip aside the veil of secrecy which has hitherto shrouded her real sentiments for you. You will soon have reason to be ashamed of your suspicions."

And ashamed he was, for, scarcely had he cleared the entrance steps of the Palais-Cardinal when a footman came forward with an envelope of delicate blue, gilt-edged, with the familiar handwriting of the Queen. It was a most tender, loving note, with sad reflections on the Saint-James business. The Cardinal reminded himself of the scene in the Grove of Venus when the Queen, almost overcome with emotion, had leaned forward, offering him the rose and whispering to him, *You know what this means!* He need look no further for proof of the Queen's devotion to him. What is more, if he required any additional reassurance in this vexing necklace affair, he had only to look in the top right drawer of his desk where the contract authorizing the purchase lay securely enclosed in a bright red-leather portfolio.

The Cardinal despised himself for having for one moment doubted his good and true Jeanne. He was such an impulsive, passionate creature, he feared his nerves were ill-fitted for the life of court intrigue.

28

The Cardinal's handsome carriage whirred along the hot, dusty streets, pulling finally into the courtyard of number eleven rue Vendôme, the elegant establishment of the crown jewelers.

To the Cardinal's great joy, Jeanne had arrived that very morning, the 30th of July, bearing 30,000 francs on the part of the Queen.

"Her Majesty accepts your reduction of the price of the necklace and begs me to remit to you this sum of 30,000 francs." He placed the bag on Böhmer's desk. "At the moment Her Majesty is unable to raise more than this sum."

"Only 30,000 francs," Bassenge wailed. "But, Your . . ."

"Please wait, Monsieur Bassenge," the Cardinal said. "Hear me through. Her Majesty, as I have said, cannot give you more than this sum at the present time. However, the Queen can now confidently promise to pay the entire purchase price of the necklace, the full 1,400,000 francs, by the end of August."

"Payment in full!" Böhmer said.

"Indeed," the Cardinal said. "And, in view of these 30,000 francs in hand, the Queen begs me to request in her name a month's delay in the payment."

"Oh, no, no, no, Your Eminence. Out of the question," Bassenge said. "No postponement."

"I agree. The first installment of 400,000 francs we must have. No month's delay. No postponement," Böhmer said, making fists of his small hands as he talked.

"Our creditors!" Bassenge said.

"My dear gentlemen, I'm afraid you haven't entirely grasped what I am saying. The Queen will *complete* the payment of the necklace at the end of August," the Cardinal said, baffled by their stubbornness.

"Believe me, Your Eminence, we do understand," Bassenge said.

"But we will not agree to the postponement of the payment of 400,000 francs, which falls due tomorrow," Böhmer said.

"Tomorrow we must have 400,000 francs. Without fail," Bassenge said.

"Oh, well, no, 370,000 francs will be due," Böhmer said, pointing toward the bag of money on his desk.

"Yes, of course. We will apply this 30,000 to the principal," Bassenge said with a tentative smile.

"Are these your final words?" the Cardinal asked, motioning for the door to be opened.

"Final, yes, Your Eminence," Bassenge said in a small voice.

"Then, they shall be conveyed to the Queen," the Cardinal said as he hurried from the room.

Toward noon on the second of August, Father Loth arrived at the crown jewelers' shop with an urgent message from the Comtesse de La Motte requesting that Messieurs Bassenge and Böhmer come at once to her house on the rue Neuve St. Gilles.

Bassenge's optimism rose as soon as he stepped into the Comtesse's luxurious carriage, smart and elegant in every detail. And the unstinting opulence of the Comtesse's residence could not have been more satisfying to a debt-ridden jeweler staring at his financial ruin. The Comtesse, as everyone knew, was the Queen's favorite, Bassenge said to himself as he passed through the Comtesse's magnificent reception rooms.

Father Loth walked jauntily ahead of Bassenge, nodding his head condescendingly to the footmen as he ushered Bassenge to the Comtesse's boudoir.

"Böhmer is away in the country with his lady, Comtesse,"

Bassenge said, bowing over Jeanne's hand. "What pleasure to see you so handsomely installed!"

"I shall get directly to the point," Jeanne said. "You may close the door behind you, Father." She waited until Father Loth shuffled from the room. "Have you seen the Cardinal recently?"

"As recently as this morning, Comtesse. I was at the Cardinal's bedside at six this morning. Böhmer and I are on the rack, dear lady."

"Did the Cardinal give you any news from the Queen?"

"Indeed he did not." Bassenge began to sweat.

Jeanne tapped her lips thoughtfully with her handkerchief and began pacing about. "I must tell you, dear Monsieur Bassenge, that the Cardinal presently finds himself in a dreadful dilemma."

Bassenge could hear himself panting in short jerky breaths.

"Yes, you see, he's in a terrible fix. Do you remember the contract you signed and that was subsequently signed by the Queen?"

"The contract authorizing the purchase of our necklace? Of course, I remember."

"Well, the Queen's signature on the contract," Jeanne said drily, "It's proven to be a forgery."

"What?"

"A forgery. The Queen did not sign it."

Bassenge tried to say something, but his mouth was bone dry. He swallowed hard. "A forgery you say?"

Jeanne smiled brightly and led him to a chair. "I haven't the slightest idea how the Cardinal plans to extricate himself from his predicament. But my advice to you, dear Monsieur Bassenge, and I feel it my duty to advise you in this matter since you've been ever so kind to me, well, my advice is that you must avoid further risk. Who knows what this affair is all about, eh? I advise you, without delay, to fall back on the guarantees given you by Cardinal Prince de Rohan and call upon him to fulfill his pledges."

"You mean, force the Prince to pay for the necklace?"

"Of course."

Bassenge stiffly shook his head. "I don't believe I could do that.

There must be some other way . . ." His voice drifted off. He stared dully at the floor.

"What other way?" Jeanne snapped. "Have you any idea what a vast personal fortune the Cardinal enjoys? Tell me who else in France is in a position to pay you in full for your necklace?"

"The Prince, too, has debts they say . . ." Bassenge murmured.

He felt as if he were trapped in a smothering thicket. He had to get out; he had to call for help. And only one person was capable of answering that call: the Queen.

29

Bassenge and Böhmer, fearing that they would never be able to obtain an audience with the Queen, decided that they would open their plea with Madame Campan, the Queen's trusted confidant and lady-in-waiting. Since it was generally known that Madame Campan and her father-in-law were accustomed to inviting friends out from Paris to their country place at Crespy on Sundays, the jewelers decided that Böhmer would present himself there on the third of August just as the guests were rising from table.

"May we have a word in private, Madame?" Böhmer asked as Madame Campan followed her guests to the drawing rooms.

"Certainly, Monsieur Böhmer. As soon as our guests take their departure for Paris. Which shan't be long, I'm afraid, with those black clouds up above threatening a mighty downpour."

An earnest young woman with a kind heart, Madame Campan felt sorry for the plump little jeweler whom the Queen delighted in abusing. Toward evening, as the wind rose and the dark skies lowered, Madame Campan led Böhmer for a walk in the garden.

"Have you any message for me from the Queen, Madame?" Böhmer asked.

"None. Why on earth should I?"

"We were expecting some response to our letter. The one we gave Her Majesty after Mass on July 12."

"Oh, *that* letter. Why, I'm afraid the Queen could make no sense of it."

"What?"

"I must confess I could not understand it either. I read it myself," Madame Campan said, alarmed by the terrified look in Böhmer's eyes.

"You were not expected to understand it since *you* are not in on the secret," Böhmer said, his voice pitched high with impatience. "I must see the Queen! I must have a reply to the letter I handed the Queen!"

"Please calm yourself, Monsieur. It does no good to become so agitated. I can tell you that there will be no reply. The Queen promptly set fire to your letter. She held it to the flames of the candle for sealing wax on her writing table. Her Majesty was completely bewildered by your letter."

Overhead, thunder crashed melodramatically, lightning flashed, and a driving rain poured down upon the two gesticulating figures so transfixed by the ominous revelations of their conversation that they made no move to seek shelter.

"Oh, Madame," Böhmer cried, "that isn't possible! The Queen knows very well what that letter was about. She knows she owes me money!"

"Money? What do you mean? I know for a fact that we settled the Queen's account with you in full a long time ago."

A bitter smile twisted Böhmer's face. "Obviously, you are not in Her Majesty's confidence. A man can hardly be said to have been paid in full to whom one million four hundred thousand francs are owing—a man who is being ruined because he cannot collect!"

The wild look in the jeweler's eye frightened Madame Campan.

"Monsieur, Monsieur, have you lost your mind? For what jewel could Her Majesty owe you such an exorbitant sum?"

"For my treasure, Madame. For my incomparable diamond necklace," Böhmer said coldly.

"*What?* You told me yourself some time ago that you had sold it to the Sultan in Constantinople for his favorite."

"It was the Queen who sent orders to make that reply to any question on the subject. The Queen has wanted my necklace since the first time she saw it but thought it unwise to buy it in a public way, with the King's knowledge and so forth. That's why she discreetly asked Cardinal Prince de Rohan to handle the transaction for her."

"My good man, you are raving!" Madame Campan cried. Her gown was soaked through and pulled like a dead weight from her shoulders. She was beyond all patience with Böhmer, who was talking like an imbecile. "The Queen has not addressed a single word to the Cardinal since his return from Vienna ten years ago. No man at court is in such disfavor."

"It is you who are mistaken, Madame," Böhmer said desperately. "The Cardinal is so much in her good graces that she receives him in private. I've been told that by someone extremely close to the Queen. Just the other day the Queen entrusted to His Eminence the thirty thousand francs which were delivered to us as first payment for the necklace."

Madame Campan clasped her hands tightly and groaned. "Oh, *Mon Dieu!* I do not know what dreadful intrigue is afoot, but I do fear that you have been robbed, Monsieur Böhmer!"

Böhmer's head slumped forward. "I begin to be frightened myself. His Eminence assured me that the Queen would wear the necklace on Pentecost, but I have not yet seen her with it on. No one has. Oh, dear lady, tell me what to do!"

"Just let me think a moment," Madame Campan said.

Böhmer must not try to approach the Queen. She would be furious. His having acted in so important a matter without direct orders from the King or the Queen constituted a betrayal of his oath of fidelity to the monarchs taken at the time of his appointment as crown jeweler. "You must go to Versailles at once and seek an audience with the Baron de Breteuil, the Minister of the King's Household and Governor of Paris. Tell him everything you have told me, then be governed by the Baron de Breteuil's advice."

The Queen must be protected at all costs in this mysterious affair, and the Baron de Breteuil, the Cardinal's enemy since Breteuil had taken over the embassy in Vienna, was just the man to keep the Queen out of harm's way.

❧

That same evening, as rain lashed at the windows and wind shook loose roofing tiles into the streets, the Cardinal, his whole house asleep, was awakened near three in the morning by Jeanne with her little maid.

"Save me, Your Eminence!" Jeanne cried, throwing herself into his arms.

"Calm yourself, my darling," he said, while her little maid assisted her with smelling salts. "What is the matter now? The Count? Has he abused you?"

Her wonderful eyes were red with fatigue.

"Oh, no, it is the Queen. That damned Queen of Cruelty. I have just come from her. You cannot imagine what she has done to me. She has treated me like a piece of trash, Your Eminence. Casting me from her embrace, refusing even to look at me."

She closed her eyes and took a deep breath. "Heartless creature! She assures me that she will deny ever having loved me in the slightest, ever having known me at all!"

"Surely you are mistaken, dearest."

How many more worries would arrive on his doorstep like this? Poor Jeanne was no doubt about to follow in the footsteps of many another favorite, a victim of the Queen's boredom.

"Mistaken? Mistaken? Ha!" she fairly snarled at him. She lowered her voice, "And that's not all: she will deny that she ever received the necklace or that she ever gave you authorization to act for her with Bassenge and Böhmer! This diamond necklace affair is simply another of her dirty tricks, a means of encompassing your ruin! She vows that she will bring you . . . and all the haughty house of Rohan down on its knees before her."

"Mere melodrama, my darling. It would take more than the Queen of France to bring down the house of Rohan," the Cardinal said, striving with all his might to disguise his growing anxiety. Why would Toinette even think such a thing? Was Jeanne simply inventing it all, testing him? But why? What did it all mean?

"Well, she will have me arrested, I'm sure of it. My house, even at this hour, must be surrounded by police. You must, you must, if ever you had any tenderness for me, give me asylum here until my husband and I can work out secret arrangements for our departure. Don't abandon me!"

She clutched his robe and sobbed against his shoulder.

"Here, here," he said. "I shall never abandon you, dearest Jeanne. Of course you shall stay here as long as you like. Flee Paris if you must. I have estates across the Rhine where you will be quite safe. Only say the word, and I will send you on your way."

He kissed her face and caressed her hair. Jeanne was trembling in his arms like a convulsive.

"No. I shall go only to Bar. I'll find the Count, and we will set out for Bar-sur-Aube tomorrow. Only let me stay the night."

"Of course. As you will, my darling Jeanne."

He sent her away with her little maid to the upper floor apartments and spent the remainder of the dark hours studying his entire collection of letters from the Queen, searching for clues that his loving sovereign might in a fit of caprice turn against him as well. At four in the morning he called up his bodyguards and sent them to Jeanne's house to look for signs of the police. Shortly after dawn they returned, reporting that they had seen nothing. The Cardinal concluded that Jeanne's melodramatic imagination was playing tricks on her.

Despite his anxieties, and they were appalling, the Cardinal considered himself a very lucky man, having as he did in a secret compartment of his desk unassailable proof of the Queen's wishes in the diamond necklace affair. He clung to that contract to chase his demons away, congratulating himself for having been astute enough to get it signed, despite Jeanne's ill humor, by the Queen.

After Jeanne's departure for Bar-sur-Aube a disturbing silence rested like a shroud over the Palais-Cardinal. Böhmer and Bassenge, who in previous days, like bloodhounds after their prey, had left him no peace about their 400,000 francs, no longer appeared at his bedside at six in the morning, the sun still shy of the front windows of his apartments. Perhaps they had resigned themselves to a postponement of the Queen's payment until the end of the month after all.

Strangely enough, the Cardinal's servants reported that the Comtesse de La Motte's residence had been entirely stripped of its furnishings. Everything cleared out. Gone.

No one came near the Cardinal. Abbé Georgel would be away on diocese business in Strasbourg for another ten days. Even the streets around the Palais seemed unusually deserted to the Cardinal.

He worried. And then called himself an idiot for worrying. Why would the Queen send along 30,000 francs, no negligible sum, if she had not received the necklace, and if she did not fully intend to pay for it? Why? And why would Jeanne, if she, as Cagliostro now proposed in no uncertain terms, was playing him false, come to his house and deliver herself into his hands? To have her arrested or detained or whatever he wished.

And especially why should the Queen deny her authorization when the Cardinal had the contract for the purchase lying securely in his desk? Of course, Jeanne could be powerfully swayed by her emotions. After her scene with the Queen, she no doubt persuaded herself that she heard all manner of outrageous things.

But why, for pity's sake, had that ungodly pair of jewelers disappeared from his bedside and antechambers?

30

Even before dawn the highway to Versailles teemed with rickety *pots de chambre*, battered old coaches in which those with modest means could for a few sous travel to the royal palace. August 15, Assumption Day and the Queen's official birthday, her saint's day, was the occasion of great ceremony at Versailles. On this day the halls of the palace would be thronged with the populace from Paris and the provinces enchanted by the pomp and color of the royal procession. On Assumption Day of 1785, the smothering heat stretched out indolently over the dusty roads, shortening tempers and drenching brows in sweat.

The Cardinal Prince de Rohan rose early and took a refreshing bath before leaving for the palace. He was filled with energy and hope that morning as he dressed for High Mass in the King's Chapel. This was his favorite holy day because it was the Queen's *jour de fête*. As Grand Almoner to the King, the Cardinal would take his place at the head of the royal procession—the King and Queen, the royal children of France, the King's brothers the Comte of Artois and the Comte of Provence, the King's three spinster aunts, and all the princes of the blood would follow as they solemnly made their way down the Galérie des Glaces, past the Oeil de Boeuf, to the King's Chapel. The Cardinal thought with a thrill that he would be so close to the Queen that he could reach out and touch her, as close as that dark night in the Garden of Venus when she handed him the rose.

Schreiber had just helped the Cardinal into his Roman purple vestments when a court chamberlain appeared at the door.

"In the name of the King, Your Eminence. You are summoned to His Majesty's study," he said.

The Cardinal, though somewhat startled by this unusual request, detected nothing in the chamberlain's voice or manner that could prepare him for what he was about to behold.

Quickly donning his square red cardinal's hat, he followed the chamberlain to the King's study. When the doors were thrown open, the Cardinal very nearly cried out in alarm.

There, standing to face him, were the King and Queen and three of the King's key ministers—the Baron de Breteuil, Monsieur de Miromesnil, the Keeper of the Seals, and the Foreign Affairs Minister, the Count de Vergennes. Breteuil was beaming. Vergennes and Miromesnil shifted their weight and looked at the King. The Queen stepped swiftly forward with her eyes fixed on the Cardinal.

The Cardinal had time to notice only that she retained much of the plumpness of her recent maternity and that her face was quite flushed.

"Read these," said the King, thrusting a sheaf of papers toward him without so much as a nod of greeting.

The Baron de Breteuil broke into a moist grin. The Cardinal had to force his eyes away from him and onto the papers. He skimmed them hastily: a memorandum dictated by Messieurs Böhmer and Bassenge and a very long statement by Boudard de Saint-James insinuating that the Cardinal had attempted to extort money from him in a scheme that used the Queen's name in the purchase of a diamond necklace.

The Cardinal handed the papers back to the King. The room was filled with hot silence. The King rustled the papers noisily.

"These are grave charges, Prince," said the King. "What say you in your defense?"

"The jewelers state the facts correctly, Sire," the Cardinal said, trying to recall Saint-James's words more precisely. He was aware that he was being closely watched. "Monsieur Saint-James misstates the situation. I purchased the necklace for the Queen, Sire."

No sooner had the words left his mouth than the Queen shrilled, "And who commissioned you to do so?"

"Why, you, Madame," the Cardinal said. He tried to look her straight in the eyes, but she was staring wildly at Breteuil. The King, watching her, looked ill at ease.

"I? I? I who have ignored you, who have refused again and again to give you audience despite your mulish persistence, I who have made my disdain, my contempt for you obvious to everyone at court, why would anyone suppose that I would ever stoop to ask a favor of you?"

She tossed her head and swept her eyes around the group. Vergennes and Miromesnil stared at the floor. Her red, congested face made her pale blue eyes look like ice.

The Cardinal felt weak, the heat in the room perhaps, but quite calm. "Your Majesty signed a contract authorizing me to purchase the necklace."

"And where is this contract?" the King asked sharply.

"In a desk at my Paris residence, Sire," the Cardinal said.

"A forgery!" the Queen shouted. The King reached out and touched her arm, pulling her back a little toward his side. "That contract is a forgery!"

The Cardinal looked at her apprehensively and, in his confusion, tried with a knowing glance to force her to acknowledge all that had passed between them. The King must have understood the significance of the Cardinal's glance, for he suddenly snapped imperiously, "Go now!"

The Cardinal heard the doors of the study being closed behind him. A debilitating peace enshrouded him; he felt unable to think, incapable of finding his way out of the maze of emotions in which he wandered. Mechanically, he walked forward into the crowd thronging the Galérie des Glaces, expecting at any moment the King and his retinue to fall in behind him on the way to the King's chapel.

The crowd thickened around him as he made his way down the long hallway toward the chapel. Suddenly, the Baron de Breteuil's unmistakable, booming voice, like a knife slashing down the Cardinal's back, rang out, "*Arrêtez le Cardinal!*"

The Cardinal kept walking, certain that he had not heard correctly, unwilling to believe the outrage of what was happening to him.

Behind him, he heard the sound of footsteps rushing forward, a silence fell over the crowd, and he could feel all eyes turning toward him. In an instant, the captain of the guards, the Duc de Villeroi, touched his robes and the lieutenant of the Royal Bodyguards, the Comte d'Agout, appeared to his left. Out of the corner of his eye the Cardinal could see Breteuil's fat, gloating face.

"The King has issued an order for your arrest, Your Eminence," Villeroi said to him in a low voice. He said it in a kindly way, as if he were embarrassed for the Cardinal, who wanted to acknowledge his kindness in some way, but could not. He could think only of Toinette, of the Queen rather, and her honor. The compromising letters. The Cardinal could think only of Breteuil's vulgar, prying eyes reading Toinette's tender, loving letters to the Cardinal, pouring out her soul to him in letter after letter. He could think only of that fierce look the King gave him when he sought the Queen's eyes.

The Cardinal was in the thick of the crowd; he could feel their hot breath upon him. He was desperate. The Queen's reputation was at stake. He felt helpless, but as a man of honor he had to do something. Suddenly, he turned a little to one side and bent over, pretending to adjust his garter. Shielding his hand with his cardinal's hat, he quickly scribbled on a scrap of paper orders in German to his valet to destroy all the letters inside the red leather portfolio in his study in Paris. He straightened up, and they continued on their way, down the stairs and out into the summer morning sunshine.

At the Cardinal's residence in Versailles, by some miracle, when they arrived there, his servants stood in double file before the door, as if welcoming him back from a long absence. He hastily removed his cardinal's hat, and as he passed by his valet Schreiber, the

Cardinal surreptitiously slipped the scrap of paper into his hand. Nothing could have been simpler, and the Cardinal felt tremendous relief at that moment.

With all his might the Cardinal was trying to hold on. He kept pushing aside from his consciousness the one word that he knew would break his heart: *Betrayal. I have been betrayed*, he thought, I must look at my world in a new and ugly light. *I have been betrayed. I have been betrayed.* He felt like a schoolboy whose punishment is to write one sentence on his slate until his hands, his brain, his being go numb with the pain of it. *I have been betrayed.*

Only the Comte d'Agout was to accompany the Cardinal in his carriage to the Palais-Cardinal. The Baron de Breteuil announced in his loud, peasant's voice brimming with glee, "The Duc de Villeroi and I will follow momentarily to affix the royal seals to the Cardinal's papers and effects. You must not leave his side, Agout; he is allowed to speak with no one."

The Cardinal, the sunlight playing over his silver hair, took great pains to lift his head and stare Breteuil full in the face. He refused to cower before his old enemy.

"What is it, Schreiber? For God's sake, what's happened?" Abbé Georgel cried.

He came rushing out of the library as soon as he heard the explosive clap of horse's hooves in the courtyard. From the stables he heard lackeys shouting and crying out mournfully, and then he saw Schreiber reeling toward him as if he could not control his legs and feet.

As soon as the cool air of the foyer hit him, Schreiber sank to his knees before collapsing on the floor. "Dead. He's dead," he whispered weakly.

"Oh, my God! Not the Prince!"

"No. God be praised. My horse. My fine horse." He was struggling to remove a piece of paper from his pocket as he got to his feet.

"Oh, for God's sake, Schreiber, never mind! The Prince will buy you a dozen fine horses. What's happened? What's that?" He took the scrap of paper from Schreiber's hand but could not read it. It was a ragged blur of two or three words.

"It says *Burn the papers!*" Schreiber croaked. He held onto the Abbé's arm as they headed toward the stairs. "In the Cardinal's study. Hurry!"

The Abbé dragged Schreiber up the stairs and into the Cardinal's study, where Schreiber fell into a chair and began to weep. "All is lost, Monsieur l'Abbé. The Cardinal has been arrested! Arrested by the King's men at Versailles."

"Holy Mother of God!" the Abbé wailed.

He stared incredulously at the meticulously beautiful study where he had spent so many hours of each day, writing, discussing, planning with the Cardinal. How was it possible that everything should continue to look utterly familiar when nothing could ever be the same again? "*Burn the papers! Burn the papers!* Is that what he said? We must do it quickly! But what papers, Schreiber?"

"The letters from the Queen. And everything to do with the diamond necklace negotiations," Schreiber said.

"What diamond necklace?"

"The necklace for the Queen," Schreiber said.

As the Abbé searched the desk, Schreiber told him the story of the fabulous diamond necklace purchased by the Cardinal at the Queen's request. The Abbé said nothing, but, like a frenzied animal, he tore through files of papers, black with rage that the Cardinal should have taken his valet into his confidence while excluding his trusted secretary of more than twenty years.

"There's nothing here," the Abbé said finally, and as he pronounced the words, he remembered the secret compartment on the right side, which, to his knowledge, the Cardinal had never used. He removed a small brass bolt underneath the long drawer on the right and pulled the drawer out to its full length.

There he found a large red-leather portfolio.

❧

At around three in the afternoon, the Cardinal, escorted by the Comte d'Agout, arrived in the courtyard of the Palais-Cardinal. As they alighted from the carriage, the Comte d'Agout turned to the Cardinal and said, "If you will excuse me for a moment, Prince, I have some small business that I must attend to, now that we are here in Paris. I shall only be a moment."

Remembering Breteuil's admonition not to leave the prisoner alone, the Cardinal looked at the Comte in some surprise, until it occurred to him that this was a mere pretext invented by the Comte to allow the Cardinal the liberty of some privacy in his house.

Even before he reached the *Salon des Singes*, the Cardinal detected the lingering smell of burnt paper, and he knew that the Queen's honor was forever safe. As soon as he opened the door of his study, the Abbé rushed forward to meet him.

"It is as you wished, Your Eminence. The letters are destroyed," the Abbé said, judging it unnecessary to mention that he had saved two of the Queen's *billets doux* from the fire for reasons that were unclear even to himself.

The Cardinal's eyes filled with tears. "Ah, my good and faithful Georgel, can you find it in your heart to forgive me?"

"Never doubt it, Your Eminence," the Abbé said as the two men embraced.

He was reassured by the Cardinal's calm dignity, his peaceful mien, as if he hadn't a care in the world. "I see the heavy hand of Breteuil. He's settling old scores, grinding his own corn."

"The Queen's authorization, you saved that?"

"Yes, it's still in the secret compartment."

Schreiber came into the study through a secret door leading off the Cardinal's bedroom. "The Comte d'Agout has returned, Your Eminence."

"Then I must go to him immediately, my dear friends. I mustn't abuse his kindness."

At four in the afternoon there was a great commotion at the gates to the courtyard as the Baron de Breteuil bellowed, "Open these gates, by order of the King!"

"There will be no denying him his grand moment," the Cardinal said with a tired smile.

Breteuil brought with him Monsieur de Crosne, the lieutenant general of police, and the two of them stalked through the Cardinal's apartments affixing the royal seal to his papers and to the Abbé's as well.

As they were about to withdraw, Breteuil turned to the Abbé and with a swelling of his chest said, "As you can see, Monsieur l'Abbé, we are no longer in Vienna, are we?"

The Abbé did not reply. He had turned his back and stood at a window, gazing down into the courtyard that was now filled with gawkers and minor officers.

The Cardinal said, "I trust I shall be allowed to receive my family and household staff this evening."

Breteuil ignored him. The Comte d'Agout and Monsieur de Crosne stared angrily at Breteuil. Breteuil then said, "The Cardinal may receive his kin. By order of the King," and he strode importantly out of the room.

Almost as soon as Breteuil left the Palais-Cardinal, the Cardinal's numerous relatives began to arrive from Versailles, filling up the courtyard and neighboring streets with their carriages and attendants. That a prince of the Rohan family, not to mention a prince of the Church, should be arrested in full view of the hoi polloi had staggered the entire court.

They assembled in the large drawing room near the celebrated staircase. The Cardinal spoke little, and he was grateful when his uncle the Prince de Soubise asked for quiet.

"I shall have a private audience with the King this evening. This very evening! I shall speak for the entire house of Rohan. We as Rohans cannot and will not tolerate this insult."

Before he took his leave, Soubise asked the Cardinal for a

detailed description of the steps leading up to the purchase of the diamond necklace, exactly when the purchase had been proposed and when he had approached Böhmer and Bassenge. It was at this point that the Cardinal went over to his desk and withdrew the contract with the Queen's signature from the secret compartment.

Prince Soubise took the contract and held it close to the candelabrum on the desk. For a long time he perused it in silence, and all that while the Cardinal was thinking of how this single sheet of paper would rescue him from the abyss into which he had fallen.

Finally, Soubise raised his eyes from the contract.

"What is it, Soubise? What is the matter?" the Cardinal said.

"The signature, nephew! The signature!" The Prince de Soubise looked appalled.

"What about the signature? What's wrong?" The Cardinal reached for the paper.

"*Marie Antoinette de France*. No queen would ever sign her name in that way. The Queen would use only her Christian name," he said, his voice drowned in despair. "What shall we do?"

"Oh, God," the Cardinal said. "Jeanne! Jeanne!"

"What?" he asked. Soubise looked at the Cardinal, his earnest face defeated.

"Nothing," the Cardinal muttered.

He turned away, ashamed of the anguish Soubise must surely see in his face. My warm and loving Jeanne, he thought. Betray me! Mock me with a forged contract! A mere piece of paper, worse than worthless. Jeanne, Jeanne! Why did you do this to me!

"You did not notice?" Soubise persisted.

"No," the Cardinal said. "I don't know, I think I must simply have glanced at the signature and paid it no mind."

"But you know the difference?"

"Of course, of course!" the Cardinal cried, beside himself with vexation.

"Because that will be their first point of attack."

"I know," the Cardinal said.

"They will all wonder how a nobleman of your rank and familiarity with the throne, a diplomat, too, would be ignorant of this royal custom," Soubise said. "So you must play the fool. Maintain that you did not know. That you believed it to be the bonafide signature of Her Majesty."

"I shan't have to pretend that I believed it to be the signature of the Queen. I did believe it. I never for moment questioned it. And I shall have no problem playing the fool, uncle." He tried to smile to reassure his uncle but could not.

"I shall speak with the King tonight," Soubise said as he took his leave of the Cardinal.

As soon as the Prince de Soubise left the room, misery caught hold of the Cardinal's limbs, so that it was agony dragging himself to the supper table where Abbé Georgel and the Comte d'Agout waited for him. Images of Jeanne, playful sorceress, affectionate, gay, humoring his every mood, his every whim, darted at him like vengeful wasps.

"I fear I am very poor company tonight, Comte," the Cardinal said finally.

"Please, Your Eminence," d'Agout said, "You mustn't be distressed. All will come right again."

The Cardinal nodded. But in his heart he knew that nothing in his world would ever come right again.

The Cardinal scarcely noticed when at around eleven o'clock the Abbé retired for the night.

"Your Eminence, now that the Abbé has left us to ourselves," the Comte said, reluctantly drawing from a small leather portfolio a folded letter with the King's seal. He placed the letter next to his wine glass.

The Cardinal stared at it in horror. Was it possible?

"What is it, Comte?" he asked, though he knew only too well.

"A *lettre de cachet*. The governor of the Bastille will arrive at midnight to escort you to prison."

"I see. I had thought, rather I had assumed, that I would be placed under house arrest," the Cardinal said, wondering how many more blows were yet to rain down on his head.

"So did we all, Your Eminence," the Comte said.

A few minutes after the stroke of midnight the Marquis de Launay arrived in his carriage to escort the Cardinal to the Bastille.

"You have been most courteous," the Cardinal said to Comte d'Agout, as he took his leave of him. To the Cardinal's surprise the Comte leaned forward and gave him an affectionate farewell *accolade*. The young man's cheeks were cool and smelled of lilies of the valley.

Afterwards the Cardinal remembered little of the drive to Saint-Antoine and the Bastille except that, accustomed to his own carriages, he rapped his head soundly as he climbed into Launay's small *berline*. He startled himself, being rarely caught out in a moment of animal clumsiness.

Launay, awed by the extraordinary circumstances of taking a Rohan and a cardinal to his prison, was extremely solicitous. "Your rooms have been prepared for your entire comfort, Your Eminence."

"It is no matter," the Cardinal said.

"And I have taken the liberty to instruct your majordomo to bring tomorrow your crystal and linens and china. We want you to be entirely at ease," he said. "You may want to do some little entertaining."

To escape Launay's pitying chatter, the Cardinal turned his face to the darkened streets so that he could grasp exactly where he was and where he was going. How had he come to such loneliness? The trajectory seemed clear enough now. He thought of that day on the highroad to Strasbourg when he stopped his carriage to greet the Marquise de Boulainvilliers, that dear, wall-eyed lady, and there sat Jeanne beside her, hair aglow in the autumn sunlight, eyes bright, daring, fearless. He could not wait to possess her.

"Jeanne," he murmured to himself, and his heart rose. "Jeanne, Jeanne . . . How could I have known that I loved you with all my heart?"

31

By the time Claude Beugnot arrived in Bar-sur-Aube for his summer vacation, the La Mottes were already lavishly installed in their showy new mansion with their entire staff from the rue Neuve St. Gilles. Only Rétaux de Villette, Beugnot noted with satisfaction, had been left behind in Paris.

Bar, which had been dazzled by the La Mottes' previous display of splendor, met this fresh exhibition of riches with indignation. Everyone believed that the La Mottes had become Cardinal-Prince de Rohan's favorite charity and that funds from the Grand Almoner treasury were financing these latest extravagances.

There was much sniffing and shrugging and rolling of eyes among the town folk. Beugnot did his share. Why not? All the foolish gimcrackery, the silver, the porcelain, the clothes, the crystal, the carriages custom-built in England, were, in the long run, exasperating.

The Comtesse de La Motte discreetly let it be known that her collection of diamond jewelry alone was valued at more than 200,000 francs! This did not include, needless to say, the ambulatory collection of diamond jewelry worn by the gem-bedecked Comte and Comtesse de La Motte themselves.

With her usual impudence Jeanne settled into Bar like a queen bee with a steady round of entertaining calculated to attract the best society in the town and the neighboring chateaux. She could not have been happier, swanning about town and countryside in her regal little *berline*.

Much to his regret, Beugnot let himself get involved with the
La Mottes' ardent social climbing. Beugnot had a weakness for the
theatre, one that he shared with Jeanne, whom he had escorted to
many a costly first night. For years amateur theatricals had been
the height of fashion in every chateau across the kingdom. When
the Comte de La Motte one day announced that he had been
invited to a performance of Molière's *Tartuffe* at the chateau de
Brienne, where some of the wittiest and most intellectual Parisians
had gathered to pay court to the Comte and Comtesse, Beugnot
naturally accepted his invitation to go along with him.

As soon as Beugnot stepped into the Comte's flashy English-
made carriage, he knew that he had made a mistake. There were four
magnificent horses in harness, three lackeys riding behind, and to
cap it all, a tiny blackamoor, Jeanne's *jocqui*, dressed in silver cloth
from head to toe. It was an outlandish sight. And when the Comte
himself strolled out of the house wearing a cerulean coat over a white
vest trimmed in gold braid, and a pair of canary-yellow taffeta pantaloons, Beugnot considered taking to his heels and running away.

Later Beugnot wished that he had, for once at the chateau, he
realized that the Comte had not been invited at all, and the entire
evening, as far as Beugnot could tell, was spent in making fun of
the Comte and his nouveau riche bad taste. While Beugnot turned
as red as a poppy in the face of all the nodding and elbowing and
laughter that spread among the other guests as soon as La Motte
appeared, the Comte appeared totally at his ease.

Later, at the supper table practical jokers had the time of their
lives keeping very tempting dishes from ever reaching La Motte.
That was the last straw. Finally, even La Motte had had enough
and called for his carriage and attendants. To Beugnot's intense
mortification, as they got into the carriage, Beugnot looked out
and saw that the Comtesse de Brienne and all her guests had
flocked to the windows of the grand salon to watch the splendor
of their departure, and as the horses started, the assembly clapped
and broke into gales of laughter.

Several days later Jeanne begged Beugnot to accompany her on a visit to the Duc de Penthièvre, who had taken up summer residence at his nearby estate of Châteauvilain.

"Accompany you to Châteauvilain? Don't be ridiculous. I've had enough of your sallies into high society," Beugnot said. "Let me at least get over the wounds to my pride from that excursion to Brienne."

"Oh, *those* people, the Comte and Comtesse de Brienne, they are hardly the first cream, are they? But the Duc de Penthièvre is of the blood royal, like me. Besides, he adores me. We will be royally received."

"Why? Because you were both born on the wrong side of the blanket?" The Duc de Penthièvre's father, the Comte de Toulouse, was the son of Louis XIV and his mistress the Marquise de Montespan. Like Jeanne's ancestor, the Comte de Toulouse was a "legitimized" as opposed to "legitimate" son.

Jeanne laughed gaily. "What would you know about the wrong side of the blanket?" she said, stroking back a stray lock from his forehead. "Come along to keep me company."

"No. The Duc carries royal etiquette to an absurd degree. I went there once to petition him on behalf of a relative, and all of us commoners had to eat supper with his First Gentleman while the nobility supped with the Duc. Afterwards, when we were allowed the grace of the Duc's presence at coffee, the nobs smirked and looked us up and down as we came into the room. I should have smirked at them, silly fools, strutting around with an old family sword or a hunting knife buckled around their waists to show off that they were nobles."

"Well, they have to wear something. You wouldn't want anyone to confuse them with a good bourgeois like you, would you? Don't be stubborn. Come with me. We can have a nice talk in the carriage," she said.

"Only as far as the Abbaye de Clairvaux," he said, feeling himself weakening. He had no doubt that in a minute or two he would hear himself agreeing to accompany her to India if she asked him.

They set out at eight o'clock in the morning on August 17, 1785, a day neither of them was ever likely to forget.

Jeanne dropped Beugnot off at Clairvaux and continued on her way to Châteauvilain. Beugnot had been a frequent visitor to Clairvaux, where the abbot had become something of a friend of his family. He was invited to stay on for the Saint Bernard's Day festival, a celebration of the abbey's patron saint when alms were distributed to the poor at the abbey gates, and a festive meal was held in the refectory to which the bourgeoisie from Bar-sur-Aube were invited. This particular year the celebrated Abbé Maury was to drive in from Paris that evening to deliver the saint's official eulogy.

At about eight o'clock Jeanne's carriage returned to the abbey. The abbot, a handsome figure of a man and a notorious gallant with the ladies, made a fool of himself bowing and scraping to her. Everyone in the religious community was well aware of Monseigneur Cardinal Prince de Rohan's admiration for the Comtesse de La Motte, and the abbot was intent upon paying her the full honors of a "princess of the church," so to speak.

Jeanne agreed to stay for supper, which was scheduled at nine o'clock. Beugnot and Jeanne strolled about the garden waiting for the distinguished guest speaker from Paris to arrive. Jeanne looked beautiful in the waning summer light. She was like a happy child, telling Beugnot of how the Duc de Penthièvre had astonished all the courtiers there with his welcome of her: His Highness had personally escorted her as far as the door of the second salon, to the top of the grand staircase. This was an honor he reserved solely for princesses of the blood.

"I felt such a princess!" she said, "A true Valois. A king's daughter."

At nine-thirty when the Abbé Maury had still not arrived, the abbot decided that they should delay no longer. No sooner had the guests sat down to table, however, than they heard the sound of carriage wheels in the gravel courtyard. The abbot darted out to welcome the guest of honor, persuading him to come immediately to the table without changing his travel clothes.

As they were settling into their supper, the abbot said, "And what news from Paris, Monsieur l'Abbé?"

"What news of Paris? Why, you must be joking! Are you living in darkest Africa that you haven't heard what has happened? You mean you know nothing about Cardinal de Rohan? Why, the day before yesterday, on Assumption Day, Prince Cardinal Louis de Rohan was arrested in the Galérie des Glaces. In his pontifical garments, on his way to say Mass in the King's Chapel! Prince Cardinal de Rohan thrown into the Bastille! Paris is reeling with the shock of it!"

"Arrested in his pontifical garments! But why?"

"It's all a puzzle," the Abbé said, "Some say that he was supposed to buy a diamond necklace for the Queen, but didn't. What no one can understand is why the King should have seized a powerful nobleman like the Prince de Rohan for such a trifle. They say the Queen is very angry."

The table had grown completely silent. Beugnot looked at Jeanne. Her face frozen in wide-eyed shock, she held her dinner napkin to her lips. Suddenly, she dropped the napkin to her plate and ran out of the room. Mumbling a few apologies to the abbot, Beugnot set off after her.

In the carriage, she said, "I shouldn't have bolted like that, should I? I should have mumbled some sort of excuse to the abbot."

"It was obvious that you were very upset," Beugnot said.

"They will think it quite odd. They will all remember it, won't they? Won't they, Claude?"

"Probably."

Beugnot was afraid that she would see how terrified he was. He had sense enough to know that the King would not dare arrest the Prince de Rohan unless a crime of major proportions were involved.

"Listen," he said, "I have a close friend in the village of Bayet along the way to Bar. He will take you in for the night; I will go along in your carriage to Bar, where I'll alert your husband to gather up what he can and come to collect you at Bayet. From there you can get to the Normandy coast and a boat to England."

"England! What are you talking about? What on earth would I do in England? No one eats well there. I shall go straight to Bar and go to bed," she said. She had entirely regained her composure and was so relaxed that she had begun to yawn from time to time.

"If the Cardinal has already been arrested, the police will certainly be after you," Beugnot said.

"Why should they?"

"Don't play the innocent with me, Jeanne," Beugnot said.

"Worry, worry, worry, that's all you know how to do. What? Why are you looking at me like that? This is none of my affair."

"Then whose is it? Certainly not the Cardinal's."

"It's some of Cagliostro's deviltry, that's what. You have no idea what influence he has over the Cardinal. Cagliostro has led the Cardinal into some kind of tomfoolery, mark my words."

She closed her eyes, feigning sleep to put an end to the conversation. It was almost ten o'clock. Soon they would be in Bar, where Beugnot feared that they would be met by police armed with a *lettre de cachet* from the King.

"Jeanne," Beugnot said, "Be reasonable. How many times have you told me yourself that you wished you had listened to my advice? If you won't go to England, then you must take all the precautions you can."

She sat bolt upright. "What precautions?"

"For one thing, you must destroy any letters or papers that might be compromising in any way."

"You're right. You can help me do that."

Once in Bar, they streaked up the stairs to her bedroom suite. Comte de La Motte was away on a hunting trip. Jeanne dragged out a large chest full of documents and letters. Beugnot built up the fire, and they got down to work, Beugnot merely running an eye over each document, Jeanne more deliberately studying each piece.

The fire crackled briskly, and the perfume from dozens and dozens of wax seals filled the room with a slightly nauseating sweetness. Beugnot came across a complicated array of bills, notes, and receipts from Böhmer and Bassenge, packets of pawn slips and papers, even a love letter or two that he had written Jeanne that first year when he began his studies in Paris, and she was still collecting admirers in Bar.

Suddenly, his heart fell as he fished out from the bottom of the chest a large bundle of letters on paper of the very finest quality tied up in silk ribbons embroidered with gold thread. He immediately recognized the seal of Prince Louis de Rohan. There were hundreds of letters. Hundreds. He tried to heave them all into the fire, but he couldn't. He glanced at Jeanne. She was absorbed in sorting through heaps of bills. Beugnot began to read the Cardinal's letters.

Beugnot was only twenty-five years old, and the language of passion in the Cardinal's letters was totally unfamiliar to him. The Cardinal wrote like a man in the grips of a raging disease.

"You have destroyed the Cardinal. He has been destroyed by a fatal combination of love and ambition," he said. The blaze from the fire burnished Jeanne's face. "You had an affair with the Cardinal. You were his mistress."

Jeanne looked up at him. "What?" she said. "An affair with the Cardinal? *Si tu veux.*" She shrugged her shoulders in a bored gamine way she had.

"What do you mean? If I like. It's all here. He's wild about you!"

"Don't shout! You'll wake my maids. Don't be so bourgeois, Claude, there's nothing to shout about. Throw them into the fire."

His hands shaking, he threw the love letters into the fire and watched them burn. "I want you to leave for England tonight. Don't let them arrest you. Leave the country. For my sake, Jeanne, do it for me." he pleaded. "It's three o'clock. It's not too late."

"It's not too late to get some sleep," she said, yawning and stretching indolently. "Stir up that fire and go home. I'm off to bed."

At the door he turned and said, "You and the Cardinal are both doomed. I'm certain of it."

"Oh, we'll see about that," Jeanne said gaily.

At six the next morning Nicolas de La Motte came round to Beugnot's house to inform him that Jeanne had been arrested and taken away to Paris.

"I had just got home from hunting when two men showed up at the door and warned me not to make an outcry. They said they had orders from the King to seize all our papers. There was a stench in the house to knock you off your feet. I myself swept a heap of scorched papers and ashes back into the fireplace."

"Did they say why they were taking Jeanne away?"

"Well, they took all my papers and affixed the King's seal. The Comtesse they took along with them to be present at the breaking of the seals. No reason for alarm. She's gone to give the Baron de Breteuil some information he needs. I figure she should be back by Wednesday or Thursday. How about coming along with me to meet her along the road and give her a triumphal homecoming?"

Though he suspected that La Motte's nonchalance was merely a pose in the hope that Beugnot would spread a benign version of Jeanne's arrest throughout the town, he was nonetheless infuriated.

"Look here, La Motte, you're either a moron or a lunatic if you don't do what I advised Jeanne to do last night: take the shortest route to England you can find before the ports are on the lookout for you. Don't hang around here cultivating your own exotic illusions and pawning them off on others."

"My, aren't you the high and mighty one this morning! What in the world could my wife have told you to put you up on your high horse?"

"She told me nothing. I'm sufficiently acquainted with your situation to tell you to stop wasting your time playing the *grand seigneur*. Harness your horses and get out of town."

La Motte shrugged his shoulders and went off, whistling jauntily. Later that night of 18 August, as soon as darkness fell, Nicolas de La Motte, after unlocking a secret compartment in his desk and taking out a plump packet of letters tied with royal blue silk ribbons, hopped into one of his fine carriages and headed for the Channel coast and England.

On August 22 the police arrived in Bar-sur-Aube with orders for his arrest.

32

News of the diamond necklace affair traveled rapidly from Versailles and Paris to the provinces and across all Europe. The sudden arrest of a mighty figure such as the Cardinal Prince de Rohan suggested that no one was safe from the thundering wrath of royal despotism. To most people, in France and in the courts of Europe, the affair was a complete enigma. Whereas in Paris rumors grew that the Cardinal had mounted an elaborate scheme of theft in order to pay off his massive debts, at the court in Versailles those hostile to the Queen, and they were increasingly numerous, believed her guilty of leading the Cardinal into a trap which the Baron de Bretueil was only too happy to spring. Theories of exactly what had happened abounded as the scandal spread, new arrests were made, and the diamond necklace affair became the consuming interest of the day.

Jeanne de La Motte had truly believed that the King's men who took her away from her home in the small hours of the morning were escorting her to an interview with the Baron de Breteuil. She slept most of the way to Paris, awakening with a shock as the carriage stopped at the gate of Saint-Antoine.

"You bastards!" she cried. "You're taking me to the Bastille!"

Like everyone else, she was terrified of the grim fortress huddled behind a moat and massive stone walls where stories were told of people being flung into lightless, airless dungeon tombs on the whim of the King.

"I won't be deceived like this, you cowards!" Jeanne shouted, as the drawbridge lifted behind the carriage and the heavy iron gates clanged shut.

Beyond the inner gate the carriage stopped at the door of the governor's residence, and the Marquis de Launay himself, hastily tying the sash of his dressing gown, sprinted down the steps to help her down from the carriage.

"My apologies, Madame la Comtesse, greeting you like this in *déshabillé*. I'm no worshipper of Aurora as you can see. Some coffee? A cordial perhaps?"

"They tell me the Baron de Breteuil wishes to see me," Jeanne said.

She spoke so faintly that the Marquis had to bend down closer to her face to hear her. In the faint, coral glow of dawn he thought she looked like some mysterious, exotic flower pitched up in a sea of gray stone.

"Yes. That's likewise my understanding, Madame. Do take some refreshment after your journey," he said, reluctant to send her away to her quarters.

"I shall wait until the Baron's visit, thank you all the same."

"The King's lieutenant general of police will show you to the Comtée Tower. It has nice light and air. You'll find it most suitable, I'm sure."

Monsieur de Crosne, the King's Lieutenant General, came forward out of the shadows and took her arm. As they made their way in the semi-darkness to the tower, Jeanne appeared to have regained her serenity, taking fright only at the guards in their dark blue capes and hoods concealing almost the entire face, who whirled away, turning their backs, the moment de Crosne and his prisoner came near.

The next day the Baron de Breteuil did not appear for an interview with the prisoner in the Comtée Tower. Instead Jeanne was taken before the King's lieutenant general and Monsieur Chesnon, commissioner of the Châtelet Court, in his robes of office, and given a crucifix and asked to swear to speak the entire truth in answer to their questions.

"You are accused, Madame, of having taken flight from the kingdom with a diamond necklace which you appropriated illegally," Monsieur de Crosne said to her.

Jeanne burst out laughing. "How patently absurd! What sort of joke is this anyway? Let's be reasonable. Would I have sat quietly at home, going about my usual affairs in Bar-sur-Aube without a care in the world, my jewels in an upstairs coffer? If you thought I had stolen a necklace, why didn't your men search my residence when they came to arrest me? Why not send someone there immediately? I beseech you, Monsieur de Crosne! Send someone to Bar-sur-Aube to clear my name once and for all."

"Calm yourself, Madame."

"Why should I?" Jeanne said petulantly.

"Come now, you will tire yourself. The interrogation has only just begun," Monsieur de Crosne said with a warm smile. The Comtesse de La Motte was decidedly a dashing sort of creature with a certain *ton*. He could well understand why the Cardinal had been reluctant to name her in his statement. Only the direst threats had pulled her name out of him.

Jeanne's first interrogation lasted three hours; the second continued until one in the morning at which time the Comtesse de La Motte confessed that there was a certain necromancer, a Rosicrucian in the Cardinal's entourage who exerted tremendous power over the Prince.

"He's a foreigner. For all I know he's a spy. I know for sure that he's a Freemason plotting the overthrow of the monarchy. Not just here in France but all over Europe. That's where his vast fortune comes from. He's the Grand Coptha. If anyone has stolen a diamond necklace, it's this quack. The Count Cagliostro on the rue St. Claude."

On Wednesday morning, August 23, Monsieur de Chesnon and nine policemen appeared at Count Cagliostro's door. They did not treat the Count gently. After all, as the Comtesse de La Motte had said, he was a foreigner, and most probably a spy into the bargain. They pillaged Cagliostro's wardrobes, chests, and desks, confiscating rolls of Venetian, Roman, and Spanish gold coins and bank notes of France worth thousands of francs. They tossed about the Count's precious elixirs, potions, and balms with indifference.

When the time came to take him away to the Bastille, Monsieur de Chesnon refused to allow him to be driven there in his carriage. Count Cagliostro was manacled and dragged through the streets on foot, until there were so many protests from citizens along the way that they finally allowed him to hire a fiacre for the remainder of the journey.

As the terrible drawbridge was lowered across the moat of the Bastille, Count Cagliostro abandoned any further notion that he had been dwelling among a witty, amiable, and generous people. In the late afternoon Police Lieutenant General de Crosne began questioning Cagliostro.

"Of what crime can I possibly be accused?" Cagliostro asked, his fleshy jowls quivering with indignation.

"We'll come to that. If you'll only be a little patient," de Crosne said.

"I can think of no misdeed that could account for this rude arrest. Perhaps you are thinking of the assassination of Pompey? That antique crime? Don't waste your time! I might as well tell you that I was merely acting under strict orders from the Pharoah!"

Monsieur de Crosne calmly shook out the laces at his wrist. "I prefer not to discuss criminal matters that transpired under my predecessors in office," he said, and Cagliostro nodded sagely.

At the end of Monsieur de Crosne's extensive interrogation of the Count Cagliostro, he had nothing to report. The Baron de Breteuil was very well pleased: the burden of proving his innocence lay entirely with the Cardinal, since neither the jewelers' statement nor Boudard de Saint-James's implicated anyone other than the Cardinal in the theft of the diamond necklace.

33

In Bar-sur-Aube when he learned of the arrest of the Count Cagliostro, and the following day, of the Count's wife Serafina, Claude Beugnot was certain that it would soon be his turn to be awakened in the middle of the night and carted off to the Bastille. He dared not leave Bar-sur-Aube for fear of raising suspicions; yet he was tormented with the prospect of being shamefully dragged away from the parental roof in full view of the entire town.

It so happened that Bar-sur-Aube was in the throes of a lawsuit that was just on the point of being judged before the Council of State. The town voted unanimously to send young Beugnot to Paris to prepare their brief for the Council.

As soon as he reached the capital, Beugnot sought out the Abbé Georgel, judging him to be his best source of information about the progress of the necklace affair. The gangly priest looked dingier and more distraught than ever.

"The Baron de Breteuil issued an order yesterday for my arrest," Georgel said as he shifted papers around his broad work table. "It was rescinded, of course. By the King. His Majesty has gone too far, and he knows it. But, let them arrest me. I know nothing. Now, you, young man, I'd not sleep deeply at night if I were you. You were as thick as thieves with that Jezebel, and don't tell me that you weren't."

"Don't worry, Monsieur l'Abbé. My Bastille overnight case is already packed, waiting at the foot of my bed like a friendly sentinel ready to accompany me to prison at a moment's notice," Beugnot said, and they both laughed.

But it was true. Since the night Jeanne was taken away, the dread of imminent arrest hung over him. The Bastille filled him with such secret horror that he had deliberately set out to come to terms with the idea of incarceration. He packed his kit with a set of small paperbound classics referred to as "Cazins" from the name of the publisher. To these he added a mathematics text, an atlas, paper and pens and ink, and a supply of body linen. And he did not stop there. Several times he walked to the Faubourg Saint-Antoine and studied the Bastille from a distance, picking out one of the narrow slits that served the fortress as windows, and tried to imagine himself inside a cell with a shard of light filtering through from that particular window.

"They took away the Cardinal's treasurer, the Baron da Planta, last night," the Abbé said. "Denounced by that La Motte woman. Brazen hussy! If only the Cardinal had listened to me! But he didn't, and now I must fight her tooth and nail to get to the truth and free the Cardinal. And I know nothing, Beugnot! You must help me. His Eminence never once took me into his confidence. This diamond necklace business is all a mystery. I can't make head nor tail of it. But I'm sure that sorceress is at the bottom of it."

On that score Beugnot had not one single doubt. Even before he went through Jeanne's papers the night of her arrest, he knew that she was playing for very high stakes.

"Beugnot, you must tell me the name of everyone who was a regular in that household. Someone must have witnessed enough to help us unravel the mystery."

"Well, there was the Comtesse's *dame de compagnie*. Her name is Suzanne Colson. She did not exactly approve of the Comtesse, who most certainly did not confide in her. What about Villette?"

"Fled to Switzerland. I'm trying to locate him now. Bring him back to Paris to be questioned. The husband fled to England. Now, doesn't that set your mind wandering? Why all these sudden disappearances?"

"Why didn't the Baron de Breteuil get his arrest orders out

more promptly is what I would ask," Beugnot said. "As far as I can see, the Baron has already bungled the investigation."

"He intends to pin the theft on the Cardinal. Send him to the scaffold, if he can. You have no idea how much the Baron loathes the Cardinal. Villette and the husband would have the key to the mystery. I'm not going to rest until I find that pretty boy secretary. Wasn't there anyone else, a maid, a servant, whom this woman would have taken into her confidence?"

"No one that I can think of. There was a priest always hanging around. Running errands. He took himself quite seriously. He thought the sun rose and set with the Comtesse. I think he worshipped her more than the Good Lord. He kept the keys to the rue Neuve Saint-Gilles apartments when the La Mottes went into the country or stayed in Versailles. His name was Father Loth."

"A priest? What priest? I mean, what was his order?"

"I don't know. He belonged to the monastery just opposite the Comtesse's apartments."

"The Minims. He would be one of the Minims. Near the Place Royale. I'll find him, wherever he is, I'll find him."

"You look exhausted, Monsieur l'Abbé," Beugnot said.

He suddenly felt sorry for this grimy, homely man who burned with such passionate loyalty to the Cardinal.

"I don't get enough sleep. I can't. There's no time. I've had to take on the spiritual and the temporal administration of the Grand Almonership and the Quinze-Vingts—that's the hospital for blind *gentilshommes* with three hundred patients here in Paris —the bishopric of Strasbourg and the abbeys of St. Waast and Chaise-Dieu. Besides that, I have to manage the Prince's personal affairs and the daily correspondence with the government ministers, the judges, the lawyers, and the Prince's family. I confer with the Prince twice daily. Most days I dine with him. It takes me six or seven horses just to get through the average day."

"Is there no one to help?"

"My two secretaries. The Cardinal counts on me, Beugnot. He

has for over twenty years. I can't fail him now. His very life depends on my efforts to unravel this affair. And the efforts of Maître Target. The other lawyers I don't count. Target is the master mind."

"The best that money can buy," Beugnot said.

"The Rohan family can do no less. Whatever the cost. Target is a giant of a man and a giant in his profession. He may be the ugliest man in God's creation, but he can charm the birds out of the trees when he pleads before the courts. His Eminence is to be tried by the regular judicial processes. The diamond necklace case will be judged by the Parlement of Paris," the Abbé said.

"What? You mean the Cardinal isn't throwing himself on the mercy of the King! That means the King is relinquishing his sovereign power. He's climbing down to struggle in the judicial arena with one of his own subjects. It's going to be a royal circus."

"I know. The scandal of a public trial will crucify the Cardinal. But there's no avoiding it. Think of the danger of entrusting himself to the mercy of a king led around by the nose by an enraged wife and a vindictive minister."

"The King is making a dreadful blunder," Beugnot said.

At Versailles the Cardinal's partisans, ever more numerous, stubbornly flaunted their opposition to the King's rash action. The great ladies of the court rose vehemently to the Cardinal's defense and created a fashion furor, a high-style straw bonnet in the shape of a cardinal's hat trimmed with cardinal-red ribbons. The hat was called "The Cardinal in the Straw," referring to the heap of straw used as a bed on the floor of the Bastille prison cells. To add piquancy to this fashion, the court ladies made a point of wearing the hat in the Queen's presence, an act of considerable bravado, for it was becoming increasingly unwise to allude to the case in public, several arrests having taken place for indiscreet comments, oral as well as written.

Despite royal disapproval streams of noble guests visiting the Cardinal continued to flow over the Bastille drawbridge, which was left down over the moat throughout the day, something never known to happen before. As autumn wore on, the Cardinal gave a few dinner parties, inviting twenty guests to join him for champagne and oysters.

The Comtesse, too, had her admirers. Not a month had gone by before the governor of the Bastille began to visit the Comtesse de La Motte daily. The Governor would send for his tapestry loom and sit stitching at it for an hour or two while the two of them chatted and gossiped. Jeanne's self-assurance, her boisterous spirits, even in prison, even faced with the gravest charges, enchanted the tall, handsome Governor de Launay. She knew at least sixty arias by heart and had a great flair for the street songs of the day.

Bobbing and winking at de Launay, Jeanne sang merrily:

> *Prince de Rohan, clad in his cloak of red,*
> *Was called to the Vatican for a chat.*
> *Asked the Pope, "Monseigneur, if you lose your head,*
> *Where will you wear your cardinal's hat?"*

"And where did you learn that?" de Launay asked, twisting with laughter.

"From the turnkey. He's my friend."

"Well, for God's sake, don't sing it while His Eminence is taking his daily walk in my garden."

"You mean, the Cardinal is allowed to walk in your garden, while I sit here and stare at these gloomy walls?"

"You may have your walk in the garden, dear lady. But only if you allow me to give you my arm," de Launay said with a gallant swagger.

From that day forward Jeanne had her daily stroll with the governor in his garden where he tried with no success to dispel her notions of the horrors and mysteries of the Bastille, of subterranean cells filled with prisoners who would never again see the light of day.

Governor de Launay, she soon discovered, was quick to provide her with anything she required. Her pewter service was replaced by dishes of the finest porcelain with silver covers, and she was given a menu appropriate to the table appointments. When she complained that her bed smelled musty, it was removed and replaced by a fine feather bed with tapestry curtains.

Governor de Launay was not the only highly placed officer to succumb to the charms of the prisoner in the Comtée Tower. Monsieur de Crosne, the Police Lieutenant General, took Jeanne's plight so much to heart that he could not sleep at night. He worried about who would defend her, who would write her *mémoire*, or defense plea. The practice of the time called for the printing and publication of a legal trial brief that formed a crucial part of the defendant's dossier at the trial. These defense pleas, copies of which were sold or distributed free of charge to the public months before the beginning of the trial proper, were enormously influential in forming public opinion and influencing the judges.

Monsieur de Crosne believed that only the flintiest heart would be unmoved by the pitiful story of the Comtesse de La Motte. If properly told. And Monsieur de Crosne also believed that the Comtesse's story could be properly told only if any reference to the Queen were stringently kept from entering the Comtesse's account of the diamond necklace affair.

⌒⚜⌒

At ten o'clock on a rainy November night as Claude Beugnot sat at his desk carefully applying a wax seal to a letter to his parents in Bar-sur-Aube, a note came to him from Monsieur de Crosne, inviting Beugnot to present himself without delay at his offices.

Beugnot looked at his Bastille overnight case and was seized with panic. A call to the Bastille at ten o'clock at night! What else could it mean other than disaster? With shaking hands he changed his shirt and tied on a fresh cravate and went directly to the police lieutenant general's office.

"It is on the subject of Madame de La Motte that I wish to speak to you," Monsieur de Crosne said, and Beugnot felt as if his face must have told the entire story of his guilt. "I regret having disturbed you at this hour of the night. But I had to see you. I couldn't sleep. I've just left the Comtesse. Poor, poor lady is in such a state tonight. She has chosen you as her defense counsel."

"What?" Beugnot said.

"The Comtesse has convinced me, we've talked about the matter again and again, and I had my doubts, but the Comtesse has persuaded me that you would best represent her cause. Dear woman, it would raise her spirits no end if you could visit her no later than tomorrow morning between nine and ten, as soon as the gates open."

"But this . . . this I take to be a capital case . . . why, I have no doubt that Madame de La Motte is headed for the death penalty. I'm flattered, of course, but I am young, too inexperienced for this kind of . . ."

"Young, yes. But a brilliant writer I'm told. The point is the Comtesse believes you have her interests at heart. Here, this is your pass for entry tomorrow morning and subsequently. Visit her as often as you like, as often as possible. She must be reassured. What a spirit she has, Monsieur, but the Bastille, well, you know, the Bastille can break the noblest spirit in the world."

"I must decline, Monsieur. Honor obliges me to say that I have neither the necessary experience nor the talent for this defense. I must decline. Please understand. It would be presumptuous on my part to undertake it."

"Presumptuous? Never, if the lady wishes it, and I know that she does. Why, this affair is already so highly publicized that your reputation will be made. You will be celebrated throughout the entire kingdom. Go ahead and take this pass."

"Truly I cannot be of assistance to Madame de La Motte in this affair," Beugnot said.

"Ah, I believe I know what's bothering you, young man. Would you not be afraid of the danger inherent in the proposed role of lawyer for the defense? If that's what's holding you back, think no more of it. Go discuss the matter with the Baron de Breteuil. He will make the entire situation clear. Go and have a little talk with the Minister."

"You mean, the Baron de Breteuil will take a hand in the Comtesse's defense?"

"In a manner of speaking. I can't help thinking that your compliance in this matter will be extremely helpful in forwarding your political and legal career. Poor, dear lady, she has not seen a friendly face in over two months now. She will be immensely cheered to see you. I have promised her that tomorrow morning without fail you will be there at her orders."

34

The silence of the Bastille unsettled Beugnot as he moved through the twisting corridors with the turnkey. It was like walking through a tomb in which the sounds of misery had only recently been stilled.

When the door of her cell was opened, Jeanne threw herself into Beugnot's arms and began to weep.

"You *did* come! I was afraid you wouldn't. I swore to de Crosne that you would drop me like a dead rat once I landed in the Bastille. *Caution* is Beugnot's middle name, I said to him."

She was shaking with excitement, her eyes brilliant, her voice a high whine. Beugnot had never seen her in such an agitated state.

"The Police Lieutenant General tells me that you have chosen me as your defense counsel. I've come to tell you that's impossible, and you of all people should know why, Jeanne."

"Impossible? I don't see why! You mean you don't want to defend me. You mean you want to see me mount the scaffold. That's what you want, isn't it, Mr. Holier-than-Thou!"

"Please don't get hysterical! Listen to me. You know yourself that I sat with you for hours the night of your arrest and burned as much evidence as we could lay our hands on. I've kept an eye on you ever since you came to Paris, and I don't have many doubts left about how you came so suddenly into more money than even you and the Comte can throw out the window."

"My money! The Queen gave me a fat purse every time I left her and the prince and the princesses of the blood set up a fund to supplement my pension. They couldn't stand to see a Valois princess destitute! You can't imagine how the Queen doted on me! She said she had never known such pleasure before me! She'd have given me the crown jewels if I had asked for them."

"Would she, now? Well, I don't believe that you've ever been within twenty-five feet of the Queen. I never have believed all that poppycock!"

Beugnot was relieved to find himself getting angry with her. He couldn't wait to get rid of the terrible aching tenderness he had felt when she fell into his arms. With no maids to assist her in prison, Jeanne was more simply coiffed and dressed. Her dark chestnut hair was pinned loosely at the crown of her head and fell in soft swirls around her face. She looked wanly beautiful in the thin light from the narrow window high above her head.

"*Not know the Queen!*" Jeanne laughed shrilly, throwing her hands up into the air. She turned her back to him and was silent for a long time. When she looked at him again, her eyes were haunted with fear. "Claude, I've got to tell you what they're doing to me here!" She lowered her voice and began to pace about the room. "You've got to hear me out. They've got me in a vice. The Queen and the house of Rohan, between them they are going to crush me. The Baron de Breteuil assures me that the Queen will spread her wings and protect me if only I suppress any reference to her at all. I must deny that the Queen ever knew me in any way, that she ever gave me presents. I must lay the guilt solely on the Cardinal. They're at me day and night. Everyone. From Breteuil down to the turnkey who brings me my supper."

Monsieur de Crosne's constant refrain, *Go and have a word with the Minister*, passed fleetingly through Beugnot's mind.

Jeanne bit her lower lip. "I'm going to tell you everything," she said, in a low, confiding voice. "Come over here. We'll stand next to the far wall. Oh, God, I hate this place!" She took a deep breath and held him with a steady gaze. "This is what happened. The Queen and the Cardinal were *lovers!* They used me. I was their go-between. I carried letters, I led the Cardinal to his assignations with her, I did all their little errands. He always wore a disguise of some sort when he went to her. Usually part of the disguise was a package he carried under his arm. Way up under the arm like this." She put a hand under her armpit. "Their meeting place was a small octagonal pavilion on a hillock behind the Trianon. The Pavillon de Venus, I think it is. The Cardinal and I had to walk over a barrow on a narrow plank to get to the pavilion. I saw the inside of the pavilion only once, maybe twice. Really voluptuous. Soft draperies. Silk, I think. A few couches. A chair or two, and lots of statues of Venus. That was the mood. Venus, love. But . . ." Jeanne pulled him closer and whispered. "You know what they were doing? Besides rutting like a couple of dogs in heat, I mean. Well, they were plotting against France. No, I guess that's too strong. That's not the way it was. The Queen was using the Cardinal as some kind of emissary or something like that. The Cardinal was carrying messages and papers from the Queen to couriers in Paris. My God, I think there were these Austrian couriers just about everywhere because afterwards we would go in the Cardinal's carriage and leave off these things with men with strange accents all over the city."

Jeanne sighed and shook her head as if remembering these things pained her. "And then, guess what? The Queen gets tired of the Cardinal. The same way she got tired of me. The woman's insatiable, I can vouch for that. She used up the Cardinal, wore him out, and now she wants to throw him away. Towards the end the Cardinal was having a terrible time with his . . . with . . . with his ardor. There's a place he keeps in the Bois de Boulogne filled with nubile young girls from the country, from Alsace, from the farms around Saverne. I don't believe a one of them is over twelve years old. He took me there one time to see. It's disgusting, but what else could the man do? I felt sorry for him. She dreamed up this diamond necklace business so that she could have the necklace— she's always wanted it because it was the most expensive necklace ever made—and get rid of the Cardinal at the same time. Damned clever, you have to admit that. The Queen exhausted him with her demands and with her constant . . ."

"Jeanne, I have to go now," Beugnot said. He knew that at any minute now he was going to burst into tears.

"I haven't finished yet," Jeanne said.

"Is there a lot more to tell?"

Jeanne pushed back her hair and stared into space. "No. I suppose not. Are you going to take my case?"

"I told you. I can't."

"Why not?"

"I'm too young. I'm too inexperienced. This case is way over my head."

"De Crosne says that you can hire as many assistants as you like. They're ready to help you in any way."

"Jeanne, your lawyer must write a defense plea that comes straight from his heart. It must throb and flow with his own heart's blood. I know I can't do that."

"The Cardinal read the petition you wrote to the King for me. He said it was brilliant. He said that you're going to be a formidable lawyer. One of the best lawyers in the land."

Beugnot's spirit quickened with pride. "I'm sorry, Jeanne. Please forgive me."

"But what am I going to do, Claude? The Queen . . . I live under constant threats. How can I turn against the Cardinal, who has been so good to me? Tell me what to do, Claude. You always know what to do."

"Just try to be as honest as you can, and pray for mercy."

Jeanne's lips twisted and trembled, but her eyes were wide and dry. "I've never been very good at being honest," she said wistfully.

35

Police Lieutenant General de Crosne, after Beugnot's defection, recommended his own family lawyer, Maître Doillot, a sage old gentleman deep into his sixties, to serve as the Comtesse's defense lawyer. On December 4, 1785, the Comtesse de La Motte's first defense plea was published, creating a furor, and the tide of public sympathy turned against the Cardinal.

The dashing Comtesse of much vaunted charms completely turned the venerable lawyer's head. Doillot's trial brief swelled with delirious emotion as he portrayed his client as the innocent victim of intrigue and cupidity, denying in every particular the Cardinal's deposition. Who in his right mind could believe the Cardinal's story that this simple, unassuming woman who had never even been presented at court could have engineered an entire series of diabolic hoaxes to ensnare the powerful Prince? Arrange a rendez-vous with the Queen in the gardens of Versailles? What kind of deluded madman would believe that this young person without a single court connection could promise such a thing?

The defense plea enjoyed a sensational success. Police had to be called in to control the crowds clamoring for copies around Doillot's house. In the first week alone he passed out ten thousand copies gratis and was obliged to issue three thousand more in response to demand, in addition to five thousand copies sold at very high prices by the printers.

The success of the Comtesse's trial brief, her extraordinary self-assurance and gaiety in her prison cell, put the Cardinal's counselors and defenders in a state of high anxiety. The assistant prosecutor openly told the Rohan family to resign themselves to the fact that their kinsman's case was all but lost. Rumors swarmed that the Queen had personally intervened with a number of the most influential judges and that she had promised immunity to the Comtesse de La Motte for her cooperation in bringing about the Cardinal's ruin.

Abbé Georgel's frantic efforts had so far left him stranded in dead ends. He had a hunch that this Father Loth mentioned by Beugnot could prove a useful witness, but as far as he could learn, the monk had taken a false name and buried himself in a provincial monastery. Moreover, the British authorities adamantly refused the extradition of the Comte de La Motte, who had fled London after several abortive attempts, originated by the Queen's faction according to current rumors, to assassinate him. La Motte remained safely ensconced in Dublin, enjoying local society and apparently not overly concerned about his wife's welfare. And while Georgel had succeeded in locating Rétaux de Villette in Switzerland and was keeping him under surveillance there, the Abbé had not the faintest idea of how to fit Madame de La Motte's social secretary into the tortuous twists and turns of the diamond necklace affair.

The Abbé Georgel was therefore forced to concentrate on issues closer at hand. There were two matters that weighed heavily on the Cardinal's spirits. He could not rest easy until some sort of settlement had been reached with the crown jewelers. Much as he had chafed under their constant niggling, he felt duty-bound to make sure that Böhmer and Bassenge did not suffer from his own bad judgment.

The Cardinal's legal staff and the Abbé agreed. It would be impossible to mount a defense strategy for the Cardinal until the threat of a civil suit from the crown jewelers, or worse, their hostile testimony, had been removed. With great difficulty the Abbé persuaded Böhmer and Bassenge to accept an assignment of 300,000 francs annually on the revenues from the Abbaye de St. Waast until the capital debt and the interest had been paid in full.† Granted extensive powers by the Cardinal and acting in concert with the princes of the house of Rohan, the Abbé effected great reforms in the Cardinal's various establishments, reducing the household expenses in both Paris and Alsace to the barest minimum and making arrangements with creditors for the gradual liquidation of the Prince's debts, which at that time amounted to over two million francs.

The Abbé could do nothing to help the Cardinal with his other dread concern: his letters to the Queen. The Cardinal had nightmares of having these letters fall into the hands of his enemies, of hearing himself accused of the heinous crime of *lèse-majesté*, an affront to majesty. Encouraged by the tone and sentiments of the Queen's letters, the Cardinal had responded in kind with a freedom of thought and emotion which would most certainly lead him to the scaffold, should these letters come to light.

As preliminary hearings continued and depositions were taken, the Cardinal's legal team struggled to piece together any scraps of evidence that would link the Comtesse to the diamond necklace affair.

And then, one glacial December day when obstacles seemed at their most insurmountable, a certain Abbé Juncker arrived in the early morning hours at the Palais-Cardinal and asked with some urgency to speak to the Abbé Georgel.

Georgel slowly came forward to meet him. Wintry mornings were painful for Georgel, and this morning especially, his arthritic limbs were stiff with aches.

"A monk has come to me, his name is Father Loth, and he claims to have important revelations to make concerning the diamond necklace affair," the Abbé Juncker said.

---

† The descendants of the house of Rohan completed the reimbursement of the debt to the descendants of the crown jewelers in 1881, four years short of a century after the theft.

"Where is he?"

"At my residence. He is following the dictates of his conscience."

"I'll go to him immediately," the Abbé said, breathless at this stroke of good fortune. "No. Wait. Should he have revelations that would fit him to be a witness in the trial, we must not risk any suspicion of collaboration. Listen carefully. He must come to me here, in disguise, tonight. As late as possible. Around midnight."

"He is not a bad man, Monsieur. Only somewhat witless. And most susceptible to the female sex," the Abbé Juncker said as he climbed into his carriage.

That evening at midnight in the disguise of a liveried servant, Father Loth was shown into the ground floor library at the Palais-Cardinal.

"I want to hold back nothing, Monsieur, as God is my witness, and I shall take an oath on my mother's crucifix that everything I tell you is true, and though I am loath to be a traitor, especially to betray that lovely woman who was my friend, a kind and generous friend indeed, it breaks my heart, but I must tell you all, for my conscience puts me on the rack, and the Cardinal, that fine noble man has ever befriended me, too, when I would bring him messages and such and he was always courtesy itself, though I am as nothing compared with the Prince de Rohan . . ."

Georgel stared amazed at this outlandish apparition, dark and swarthy in brilliant blue velvet and gold livery, and on his feet his battered old monk's sandals.

"How did you come to know the La Motte woman?" Georgel asked.

"We were neighbors, so to speak. She confided in me. I heard her confessions, for she is a devout believer, may God have mercy on her, and in the early days she was a lady often in distress, and I made some small contributions to help her out, and she took to me after that, and I was soon admitted to the utmost intimate familiarity of the household." Father Loth nervously twisted his tongue around his front tooth.

"But what do you know about the diamond necklace affair?"

The Abbé was driven almost to distraction by Father Loth's nervous tics and twitches.

Father Loth cast his eyes about the immense room filled with shadows. "I was beguiled by the Comtesse," he said slowly. "She had such a hold on me that even now, even now, I fear I cannot . . ." He broke off and stood for a moment sucking his tooth thoughtfully. "I heard her talk about . . . she let things slip sometimes when she was gay . . . she talked about some handsome presents the court jewelers were going to give her if she found a buyer for their expensive necklace, and after she did, they gave a big party for her, for her and the lawyer Laporte, too, the one who dresses like Louis XIV in funny wigs and bows . . ."

"Was Laporte a friend?"

"The Comtesse did business with Laporte. They got 200,000 francs from the jewelers as a commission for the sale of the necklace and then the jewelers sent assistants around to the rue Neuve St. Gilles to measure everyone's fingers for rings—the Comte, the Comtesse, and her premier maid, and that . . . that parasite who preyed on the Comtesse, battening on her like a louse. Rétaux de Villette, worthless scum. He got two rings," Father Loth said glumly. "He wrote all her letters. And more, too. He was Madame de La Motte's stud bull, that's what he said to me one day, taunting me, leering like a mad satyr. He turned my stomach, that coxcomb. In her boudoir all the time, writing those little letters that she said were from the Queen to the Cardinal, but what kind of fool did they take me for, I looked at those blue envelopes and the hand-writing was just the same as Monsieur Pretty Face's, and I saw the Cardinal's letters to the Queen, too, because the Comtesse . . ."

"Where are those letters now? The Cardinal's letters to the Queen?" the Abbé asked as calmly as he could. His heart was thudding in his throat. He was numbed by the treasures tumbling about in Father Loth's nervous narrative.

"The letters? She burned them all before she set out for Bar-sur-Aube, while she was stripping down the apartment and sending everything to the country."

"She burned all of them? You're certain of that?"

"Certain. I saw her do it. Villette helped her."

"Do you have any specimens of this Rétaux de Villette's handwriting?"

Georgel's stomach knotted with excitement: he had only to open his shabby old leather pouch to lay his hands on the letters from the "Queen" he had prudently held back from the flames.

Father Loth pulled at the stiff hairs along his jaw. "I believe I may. I should have, he was forever sending me lists of things to do, lock up this, and go buy that, and look for another cook, and fire that maid. He ran me up and down. Mind you, the husband was no better. A wastrel chasing after his whores around the Palais-Royal, that's all he amounted to. Poor Comtesse, she was the strong one. They would be nothing without her, and they knew it. All the Comte ever did was to supply the whore to play the Queen in the gardens of Versailles and even then . . ."

"A whore to play the Queen?"

"Oh, it was something the Queen dreamed up to amuse herself. The Baroness d'Olisva, or d'Oliva, mainly was the way they wrote it, that was the name they gave to the whore, a tall beauty, blond like the Queen, and the Comtesse thought she played her part to perfection. She was mighty pleased with her." Father Loth twisted and untwisted the lace cuffs of his livery. "I knew about the whole scheme," he said finally, "from the very beginning."

"The scheme?"

"The scheme to get the diamond necklace. And break it up, and have a fortune, she beguiled me into it, Monsieur l'Abbé! I could not resist her, I swear to Blessed Mary, Ever Virgin, and she urged me to flee Paris with her and her husband, join them in Bar-sur-Aube, but I couldn't do it, weak as I am, I had to withdraw, find my brothers in solitude, and then, it was there, in that quiet, that I knew I had sinned enough, I must sin no more by keeping secrets. Even though I know that . . . that the dearest woman who ever walked the face of this earth will call me a Judas and spit in my face."

"You mustn't worry about that woman now," the Abbé said. "You must think about yourself."

"I'm to be charged as an accomplice, is that it? That's what I feared, that's why I didn't come forward sooner, I could have stayed in Figéac forever and no one would . . ."

"You must look to your conscience, Father Loth, you must set yourself right with your Lord and Saviour Jesus Christ," the Abbé said with severity.

ॐ

"I refuse to believe it," the Cardinal said in a weak, discouraged voice. "It's impossible. The Comtesse is incapable of carrying out a plot so wicked, so daring. You don't know her, Georgel. I do. Why, she's . . . she's a flibbertigibbet, flying off in a thousand directions at once. Impulsive. Impatient. What you have described is a calculated, cold-blooded plot."

"Of course it is, Your Eminence, and that La Motte woman not only conceived it, but carried it out with her henchmen—her worthless husband and Rétaux de Villette, the latter, one of her numerous lovers, by the way," the Abbé added.

The Cardinal winced. "I tell you, Georgel, I cannot be more positive that I saw and spoke with the Queen in the gardens of Versailles that night. My own eyes and ears did not deceive me. That incident alone contradicts the idea that the correspondence with Her Majesty was a diabolic invention of the Comtesse to lead me on."

"The 'Queen' in the Garden of Venus was a Palais-Royal prostitute named Mademoiselle Leguay d'Oliva, now apprehended in Brussels with her lover. I have located the coachman hired to drive the Comte de La Motte and the young woman to her rendezvous with Your Eminence. I have the testimony of the coachman, as well as witnesses to the visits paid and the presents given to this Oliva by the La Mottes. As for the so-called letters from the Queen, I have compared samples of Rétaux de Villette's handwriting with that of the two little letters I preserved from the flames for just such an emergency as this. The match is perfect."

The Cardinal had turned ashen. He slumped forward and cradled his head in his hands.

"I am moving heaven and earth to bring the Oliva woman and Rétaux de Villette back to France. The Comte de Vergennes is determined to help me, though he must proceed carefully. He is the Minister of Foreign Affairs, after all, and he must keep away from the searching eyes of the Queen. She's become a termagant, suspicious of everyone at court. But I count on Vergennes absolutely. He despises the Queen for never allowing his Greek wife to be presented at court."

The Abbé rose and came forward to put his hand on the Cardinal's shoulder. "Steel yourself, Your Eminence, the confrontations begin tomorrow."

36

After weeks and months of receiving depositions from an elaborate array of witnesses at the Palais de Justice, the examining magistrates—Monsieur Titon de Villotran, Monsieur de Marcé, and the court clerk, de Frémyn—removed to the Bastille to conduct further interrogations and the all-important confrontations, the face-to-face encounter of accuser and accused.

The Comtesse showed no signs of flagging energies as she tilted swords with one witness after another. Near the end of January, 1786, she sat gaily chatting with Monsieur Titon de Villotran when the Baron da Planta was brought into the room.

"Ah, ha! The Cardinal's surly Swiss lackey!" Jeanne cried with a gleeful laugh.

Without deigning to look at her or to take note of her taunt, the Baron da Planta took his seat and began his testimony. "I swear in the name of justice that I have often heard the Comtesse de La Motte say that she enjoyed the honor of meetings with Her Majesty, and that Her Majesty desired the Cardinal to purchase the diamond necklace for her."

Jeanne slapped her thighs and roared with laughter. "I? I never laid eyes on the Queen except once. At the Opera. She was so far away, she could have been my mother for all I could tell. The man's a fool."

Baron da Planta worked his jaw and stared straight ahead at the examining magistrate.

"To continue, I take oath upon my head and honor that I brought, in two installments, the sum of one hundred twenty thousand francs to the Comtesse de La Motte, who had requested that sum of the Cardinal in the name of the Queen. As a loan for one of her charities."

"He's mad, I tell you!" Jeanne shrieked. She was shaking with indignation. "Tell them what happened, you swine!" She caught her breath, glaring at da Planta, who refused to look at her. "Well, then, I'll tell them. This man here is a creature of lust!" She threw back her head and slowly looked at the two examining magistrates. "Over a year ago, in October of 1784, this Baron da Planta came to me in my Paris residence and cornered me in a small room off my boudoir. He pushed himself against me and insisted that I yield to his filthy desires, saying that he had ever lusted for me, promising me that he would make my fortune if I would only let him have his way with me. Which, of course, I would not. What woman in her right mind would? Look at him, Messieurs, is that a man any woman would want creeping up her skirts? I tried to call for help, but there was no bellpull in this little room. My maid used it for her afternoon naps and a little sewing. I resisted, pushing him away, whereupon he exposed himself, making all manner of lewd and menacing gestures. I went screaming with all my might into the salon where I found the Comte d'Olomieu, an exceedingly strong man who adored playing tric-trac with me in the late afternoon, and several other visitors whose names I no longer remember. I was pale and trembling and almost fainting."

Jeanne bowed her head and began to sob quietly.

"If the court clerk has finished his report, we shall adjourn for the day," Monsieur Titon de Villotran said gently, rising to his feet with an amiable bow to Jeanne.

The confrontation on Monday, January 30, between the Count Cagliostro and the Comtesse, arch enemies in the struggle for the Cardinal's bounty, predictably turned into a spirited session in which the Count, despite a constant volley of invectives by the Comtesse, remained unshakable in his story of the confidences the Comtesse had made him about her situation as the Queen's favorite. In prison, lonely for his wife and his adoring multitudes, Cagliostro had grown increasingly morose. The injustice of having his precious Serafina thrust into a dank cell led him into such deep melancholy that Governor de Launay ordered a sympathetic officer to remain with the Count at night, lest he do himself harm.

"There was no question about the Queen's wish to acquire the necklace," Cagliostro said lethargically. "When the Cardinal delayed in making the purchase, it was this La Motte woman who pushed him to the task. I warned His Eminence again and again against this woman."

"And was it Madame de La Motte, who delivered thirty thousand francs to the Cardinal in the Queen's name," asked Monsieur de Marcé.

"Indeed, as a payment on account for the necklace," Cagliostro said.

"Ha! Listen to the charlatan! Tell me, Grand Cophta," Jeanne said sweetly, turning to him with a smile, "among all your amulets, charms, and incantations is there not an abracadabra to whisk us both up over the Bastille walls? And, if so, pray tell us why you have not used it to get yourself out of here!"

At that, Cagliostro's face grew beet red with rage, his great, thick neck bulging with ropy veins. "Hear me well, harlot! This is my prophecy. Someone else will be here soon—your Villette! He's on his way from Switzerland now. And when he gets here, he'll talk, that pretty fellow. Mark my words, he's the one who will tell all!"

Soon after the beginning of the confrontations the Prosecutor General for the crown imposed a strict isolation of all the defendants imprisoned in the Bastille. From that point on until the day of judgment there must be no further communication with defense lawyers, friends, or family members.

Two exceptions were made for the Cardinal: he was permitted to continue receiving communications from the Abbé Georgel concerning diocesan business and the affairs of the Cardinal's various estates. In this way, using a secret code of names of persons and places they had used during the Vienna embassy days, the Abbé was able to pass along the counsel of the Cardinal's legal advisers without arousing the slightest suspicion. And because the Cardinal, always a hearty, athletic individual, began to suffer visibly from his confinement, his personal physician was allowed to visit him daily. With a supply of invisible ink carefully hidden at the back of his black leather *nécessaire de voyage*, the Cardinal communicated freely with Maître Target and the Abbé.

"That wicked woman went quite mad today in her confrontation with the Count Cagliostro," the Cardinal wrote to Georgel. "My turnkey tells me that she hurled a heavy candelabrum at him when he called her a 'damned cheat.' I am quite depleted with fatigue. Governor de Launay claims that he is so alarmed by my greensickness that he will order an inquiry. Does he suspect a *Versailles bouillon*, I wonder?"

The Cardinal put down his pen and rubbed his forehead. Tomorrow or perhaps the next day he would be confronted with Jeanne. What would she look like in this raw, new light? *That wicked woman* he had written, but he did not really believe it. He remembered her softness, her waywardness, the joy he had had in making love to her. *That wicked woman* . . . He said the words out loud and had a sudden image of Jeanne tossing back her head and exploding with laughter. Had she, lying in the circle of Villette's warm arms, mocked his stupid gullibility? He saw himself, cloaked in scarlet, his cardinal's hat askew, a comic figure in a grotesque *grand guignol*, prancing about, wringing his hands in despair over the Queen's disdain of him, pining for the prime minister's portfolio and a place in the history of France. The very idea of worldly ambition sickened him now.

He sighed and picked up his pen again. "I understand that the title *Count* has been struck from all legal documents referring to the Count Cagliostro. Though I realize that you cannot abide the man, I beg of you, for my sake, to see that everything possible is done to rectify this slight. He is still my dear friend, you know, and very touchy on this subject of title."

Down below the Cardinal's tower a dog howled plaintively, and it seemed to the Cardinal that none of God's creatures would have any respite from misery that night. He was suddenly weary. He was writing his letter between the lines of the letter he had received that day from the Abbé. The next day his physician, Monsieur Portal, would take it away and deliver it to the Palais-Cardinal.

The Cardinal commended the Abbé to God's grace and was about to sign the letter. Instead, he dipped his pen in the small container of invisible ink and wrote, "Have you had any recent news of the Q? Please tell me if it is true that she still appears so sad."

37

Cagliostro's fiery prophecy languished without fulfillment as the French foreign minister worked behind the scenes for Rétaux de Villette's extradition to France and the Abbé Georgel sent his own agents to Brussels to bring back Mademoiselle d'Oliva, now big with child, and her lover to the dungeon cells of the Bastille.

In the meantime, Maître Target, the Cardinal's chief counsel, felt confident enough to publish the Cardinal's first defense plea, which produced a sensation. The defense plea described in great detail the entire intrigue, offering the public for the first time persuasive evidence, such as the Cardinal's repeated efforts to get the crown jewelers to write a word of thanks to the Queen, of the Cardinal's good faith.

All of France and Europe were obsessed with the diamond necklace trial. No one cared a fig any more what might be happening in the rest of the world. Crowds milled around the streets surrounding the Bastille, hoping for a glimpse of the Cardinal or the comely Comtesse de La Motte or the celebrated Cagliostro taking a stroll on the parapets of the prison. Foreign journalists poured into the capital, setting themselves up in popular cafés around the Palais-Royal, ears open for the latest scrap of gossip and rumor.

Gradually, the public and journalists picked their favorites and their villains from the cast of characters, whose portraits, selling briskly at very steep prices, proliferated in the shops around the arcades. At court and in the capital, hateful sentiment came to revolve more and more around the one person whose name must under no circumstances be mentioned: the Queen. Most believed that the entire affair was all an intrigue between the Cardinal and the Queen that had blown up in her face when the Baron de Breteuil caught wind of the diamond necklace purchase and confronted the Queen, who, of course, had to deny as strenuously as possible any knowledge of the purchase. Once denied, she must perforce continue to protest any involvement. The Queen's putative disdain of the Cardinal was nothing more than a ploy to conceal their little game; in actual fact, he was very much in her good graces—and bed—and she did commission him to arrange the purchase of the long-coveted necklace. By the year 1786, the public had settled its opinion of Marie Antoinette. She was "Madame Déficit," as her brother-in-law called her, and she and her perverse, profligate ways were the source not only of the deficit but also of France's crop failures and mounting ills.

Though the Queen made an occasional pathetic, symbolic gesture to show her concern for the people and the future of the country—when, for example, Parmentier was trying to introduce the cultivation of potatoes to guard the country from famine, the Queen wore potato flowers instead of her usual corsage—few found her gesture as significant as she obviously did.

Playing the dairymaid at her dainty little farm installed at the Trianon, the Queen took up the simplicities of rural life and dress. It was in this spirit that Madame Vigée-Lebrun portrayed the Queen in her 1785 portrait for the annual Salon exhibit. The Queen, her hair unpowdered and flowing, appeared in a plain shift-like dress and a rustic hat. The public was outraged. They looked at the unregal dress, the fancy imitation of peasant garb, and condemned her for arrogantly flouting the proprieties of her station. They accused her of being more the Queen of Fashion than Queen of France, more a reigning belle than a reigning queen.

But it was Marie Antoinette's foul reputation that pulled her down into the brawling pits of the diamond necklace affair. Public opinion was fast reaching the conclusion that the whole disastrous affair would never have transpired had the Queen's good name not already been dragged down into the mucky obscenity of the streets. By the time the diamond necklace affair burst upon the scene with the Cardinal Prince Louis de Rohan's spectacular arrest in the halls of Versailles, people could believe any foul rubbish about the Queen. And they did.

⟨ᴇᴥᴈ⟩

Giving his age as thirty-two, Louis Marc Antoine Rétaux de Villette signed the ledger at the Bastille on March 26, 1786. Confident that Jeanne de La Motte would never mention his name and believing that there was no direct evidence linking him with the crime, Rétaux de Villette, at his first interrogation in the Bastille on Friday, April 7, persistently denied any involvement with the diamond necklace affair and any association with the La Mottes beyond the simple boundaries of friendship.

"And you never served the Comtesse in any capacity? As her personal secretary perhaps?" Titon asked.

"Never. La Motte was a fellow cavalry officer, a friend. And his wife, the Comtesse, well . . . I loved that woman to distraction." Villette's head drooped to one side as if inviting the magistrates' pity of his lovelorn condition.

"She never gave you money?"

"Why would she?" Villette stared at his muddy boots in dismay. Prison life appeared to leave no time for the niceties of life, such as a valet. And every time he looked up and caught the eye of the court clerk de Frémyn, he could not help shuddering. The man was impossibly ugly, repulsively so, his stub nose flattened against an oily, round face pitted with scars.

Monsieur Titon de Villotran sighed and shuffled a stack of papers on the desk. It was a bright, sunny spring day, and the cheerful sound of bird calls echoed within the inner walls of the prison. Titon was bored and restless. Nonetheless, after the King's recent generosity in assisting him to a coveted position in the civil courts, he must put on at least a show of zeal. "Tell us what you know of a certain Demoiselle Leguay, also known as the Baroness d'Oliva."

Villette noticeably paled. He sat up straight and ran his hand over his hair. "Nothing. I know nothing." Thoroughly disconcerted, Villette imagined that de Frémyn looked up and gave him a salacious wink. "I don't believe I have the honor of being acquainted with this lady," Villette said, adding a polite smile.

"And a certain Father Loth?"

"A monk?" Villette asked.

"I believe so, yes."

"Not too tall? Dark hair? Bad teeth? Is that the man?" Villette's right leg started to quiver.

"I take it you know the man?" Titon said.

"I may very well," Villette hesitated. "I wouldn't say categorically 'no.' There were a great many people in and out of the La Motte establishment, you see. It was a large household."

Monsieur Titon yawned and scratched behind his ear. "Then, I believe Monsieur Dupuy de Marcé has a document for you to examine."

Villette was instantly alert, alarmed by the smile exchanged by the two magistrates. De Marcé came forward and held out for Villette's inspection the diamond necklace contract as if it were a particularly delicious bonbon.

"Do you recognize any of the handwriting on this document?" de Marcé asked with unexpected severity.

Villette was trembling so much that he dared not reach out to take the contract. He drew back from it and clasped his hands firmly over his knees. "It's not my handwriting," he stammered. "I mean, I don't recognize this contract. I've never seen it before. That is, I don't know who wrote it."

"Do you recognize the handwriting of the signature *Marie Antoinette de France?*"

"The Queen," Villette murmured. "No, I don't believe I do."

"And the notations *lu et apprové*, read and approved, alongside each item? Do you recognize the handwriting there?"

Villette cleared his throat. "Not at all. No, I would say definitely, no."

"Then we will give you a little time behind the bars of your prison cell to search your memory. But don't take too long, young man. Monsieur Sanson the executioner hasn't much patience, I fear," Monsieur de Marcé said, holding the precious paper daintily between two fingers.

Even before the handwriting experts, Messieurs Harger and Blin, returned the opinion that the signature and the marginal notations on the diamond necklace contract and specimens of Rétaux de Villette's handwriting revealed clear similarities, Villette had reached the conclusion that only a full-throated confession could save his neck.

At his next interrogation, Villette, as Count Cagliostro had predicted, told everything he knew. Which was a great deal too much as far as Jeanne de La Motte was concerned.

With Villette's confession in hand the examining magistrates proceeded to a confrontation of Villette, Jeanne de La Motte, and the beauteous young Mademoiselle d'Oliva, whose naiveté and demure grace had already won the hearts of her jailers and the examining magistrates.

Those days of early spring Jeanne could feel a chill wind following her in the twisting corridors of the Bastille as she made her daily round from interrogation to confrontation. The whole climate around her had changed. Monsieur Titon de Villotran's eyes failed to sparkle seductively when she walked into the examining room. Monsieur de Crosne seemed to have lost all interest in her, and Governor de Launay no longer called to chat over his tapestry work or to take her for a walk in his garden. Even the turnkey, Saint-Jean, addressed her coldly and found excuses not to linger for a conversation. The special little favors to which she had grown accustomed gradually ceased.

Villette swiftly turned his head away when Jeanne, with her familiar self-assurance, walked in and took her seat. A few seconds later, the turnkey brought in Mademoiselle d'Oliva, walking slowly, cradling the weight of her bulging stomach. If Jeanne felt any astonishment at seeing both Villette and d'Oliva, she revealed nothing. She stared at the magistrates, steadfastly hoping that today Titon would look at her with his former interest.

The Court Clerk began the session by reading Villette's full confession describing the Garden of Venus episode in which Mademoiselle d'Oliva had played such an important part. As for Villette, he confessed that he had performed no role at all, being obliged by a painful blister on his heel to wait on a garden bench until the others returned. Madame de La Motte had assured him that the whole scene, inspired by Beaumarchais's popular *Mariage de Figaro*, had been staged to gratify a whim of the Queen. Letters to the Cardinal, purportedly from the Queen, he confessed to have written at Madame de La Motte's behest and solely at her dictation.

At this point, Jeanne could contain herself no longer. "You treacherous dog!" she shouted. "You cur! You viper!"

"But you always knew I was spineless!" Villette said, unable to raise his eyes.

Jeanne began to weep. "Oh, my dear, I know. They've made you tell these lies! The devils, they've coerced you."

"Are they lies, Monsieur de Villette?" Titon's large, baggy eyes sagged with displeasure. He was in a dreadful fix. It would be fool-hardy to turn up his nose at the patronage of the King, so warm and generous of late, but pinning this diamond necklace affair on the Cardinal was no easy matter. "Speak up, young man!"

Rétaux de Villette stared at the floor. "No," he said quietly. "They are not lies." He looked on the point of tears.

Titon turned to Jeanne. "Be so good as to tell us how you came to know this young woman, the Demoiselle Marie Nicole Leguay d'Oliva, aged twenty-four."

Jeanne shrugged her shoulders and peered down her nose at Mademoiselle d'Oliva, who had taken a seat as far from Jeanne as possible. "This little baggage? How should I remember? I scarcely know her. I met her quite accidentally. Somewhere around the Palais-Royal."

Mademoiselle d'Oliva looked at the magistrates in alarm. "Well, now, I just don't see how the Lady de La Motte can just sit there and say that she barely knows me when the way it was was that the Comte de La Motte came to me in my apartment in the Rue du Jour and then he brought his lady with him and she showed me letters to her from the Queen, Her Majesty, and then . . ."

"Bravo!" Jeanne crowed. "I never heard such bald-faced lies in my life. This is what happened. My husband and I felt sorry for this dumb-ox girl, and when she begged us to take her to Versailles to show her the palace, we took her along and . . ."

"And dressed me in a fine white gown with a fine white veil!"

"Only because your old bonnet was hideously soiled. You can't walk about with someone dressed from a garbage heap. She looked so awful, I dumped her with my husband and Villette while I went off for a stroll with the Cardinal. As far as the Trianon. We sat down and rested ourselves under the colonnade of the gallery and started back around midnight."

"She gave me a rose and a letter," Mademoiselle d'Oliva said, looking beseechingly at the magistrates.

"Give it up, Jeanne," Villette said in a low voice. "It's no use."

The two examining magistrates and the court clerk sat staring coldly at her. Jeanne tossed her head. "It was a practical joke! Can't you understand that? *Tiens!* It was the Cardinal himself who gave me the idea for the prank. He and the Queen were at odds over something he had done, one of his foolish indiscretions I've no doubt. I can tell you a word or two about those . . ."

"Give it up, Jeanne," Villette pleaded.

"The Cardinal wanted a rendezvous in the Grove of Venus to

patch things up. To get things going again with the Queen. It was a joke. A prank."

Though the room was still and utterly silent, they could barely hear her. De Frémyn strained forward toward her over his desk. Jeanne's voice sank to a whisper before she fell silent, staring fixedly into space, swaying slightly in her chair. Suddenly she pitched forward out of her chair, her legs and arms twitching convulsively.

For a moment, no one stirred, as if transfixed by the spectacle of Jeanne de La Motte's raging emotions.

"Help her, for God's sake!" Villette cried.

Titon sent his attendant flying to fetch smelling salts, while de Frémyn himself went in search of Saint-Jean, the turnkey in the Comtesse's tower.

Jeanne's eyes were rolled back in her head. Villette bent over her, tears flooding down his face.

"Here," the burly Saint-Jean said, dipping one knee to the floor. "I'll just carry the Comtesse back to her cell." As he rose to his feet with Jeanne in his arms, she opened her eyes and with a piercing shriek sank her teeth into his shoulder. The turnkey let out a howl and dropped her to the floor.

"Vicious bitch!" he said, clutching his bleeding shoulder.

The confrontation between the Cardinal Prince Louis de Rohan and Jeanne de La Motte was set for four o'clock in the afternoon to continue until midnight. In their interrogations of the Cardinal the examining magistrates observed the strictest etiquette, taking elaborate precautions not to violate any protocol. On the appointed examination days, the Cardinal dressed himself in his ceremonial regalia, his scarlet robes, scarlet calotte, scarlet hose and all the attributes of his position. Governor de Launay himself appeared at the Cardinal's prison door to escort him to the council chamber of the Bastille, and at the end of each session escorted the Cardinal back to his apartments.

For days the Cardinal had been mentally preparing himself for his confrontation with Jeanne. How much would she dare, he wondered. He had glimpsed enough wildness in her nature to realize that she would not yield easily. If at all. What he now saw as her shrewdness shook him to the core. How astutely she had calculated that once the plot unraveled, he would willingly settle the colossal debt, never mind the financial consequences, to avoid scandal and humiliation. Only the crown jewelers' hysteria about their money, their frantic rush to the Queen and the Baron de Breteuil, had spoiled her scheme and led to this disaster.

The Cardinal nervously smoothed his soft leather gloves. In the distance he could see the tender green of new leaves coloring the trees, but inside the prison a cold dampness clung to the walls. The Cardinal shuddered as he coughed. He was feeling stronger now that the mystery of his greensickness had been solved. The verdigris of the copper pots used in the preparation of his daily whey had sickened him for months.

"Remember, be firm!" Maître Target had exhorted in yesterday's encoded letter of counsel. "Don't let that La Motte woman trip you up and pull you into the toils of her charm!"

The Cardinal coughed again and felt a nudge of misery like a chilling draught at his back, reminding him that in a few minutes he would see for the first time in months the woman he had loved more than any other, the woman who had taken his life, his reputation, his fortune, and ripped them to shreds.

The Cardinal, his tensions eased, stood chatting amiably with the examining magistrates, decidedly more deferential for the past few months. They inquired about the Cardinal's health and gossiped about the court. The Cardinal listened absentmindedly, as if they were speaking a foreign language he could no longer understand.

Abruptly their chatter ceased, and the doors of the interrogation room were swung open. Jeanne, dressed in a heavy green woolen gown and a hooded cape, her thick chestnut brown hair tied with a velvet ribbon at the nape of her neck, walked slowly into the room.

The Cardinal turned and looked at her, his heart capsizing in a deep well of tenderness. "Oh, my dear," he said in a low voice as he hurried toward her, "what have they done to you?"

The examining magistrates and the court clerk watched in amazement as the Cardinal gently enfolded the Comtesse in his arms.

"Jeanne! Jeanne!" he whispered, "What a wretched pair we are! To have come to this!"

Pale, visibly unsteady on her feet, Jeanne de La Motte looked as if she had just risen from her sickbed. She rested for a moment in the Cardinal's arms before shaking her head and pushing back from him.

"Come," the Cardinal said, "Warm yourself by the fire." He took her hand and led her to the fireplace at the other end of the long room. "Here, hold out your hands. That's it. A chair, Monsieur de Marcé. Perhaps the Comtesse could sit here by the fire while you ask your questions."

De Frémyn, his flat, ugly face smeared with derision, clucked disapprovingly and took up his pen. The two examining magistrates, not bothering to conceal their bafflement, went to their customary places and began their questions.

For over two hours they concentrated their interrogation on the crown jewelers' affidavit which made no reference whatsoever to Madame de La Motte, asserting that the Cardinal spoke to them as if he had been commissioned directly from the Queen. Next, they took up the banker Boudard de Saint-James's affidavit, which presented the same difficulty for the Cardinal. No mention was made of Madame de La Motte. Saint-James declared that the Cardinal requested a loan of four hundred thousand francs in the Queen's name, and when the banker had asked for a written request to that effect, the Cardinal had assured him that a letter would be forthcoming.

"And did you indeed receive a letter of confirmation from Her Majesty?" asked Titon de Villotran.

The Cardinal stared moodily at de Frémyn's pen, moving in

steady, implacable rhythm from inkpot to paper. He sat mantled in confusion. In his cell it had been easy enough to rail at Jeanne, to call her a vicious slut, a wicked woman. Where had his anger gone? "No. I did not," he said finally. The Cardinal gave his answers mechanically, as if by rote, for he had been rehearsing endlessly, scrupulously obedient to Maître Target's advice.

"Your Eminence, the prisoner Louis Marc Antoine Rétaux de Villette alleges that you received more than two hundred missives of a personal nature from Her Majesty, the Queen," Monsieur de Marcé began.

"I received none," the Cardinal said, his voice high and tense.

"None?" Titon asked.

"And you wrote how many letters to Her Majesty, the Queen?" Monsieur de Marce said.

"I wrote none," the Cardinal said.

Jeanne stared into the fire as if indifferent to the proceedings.

"And you, Madame, did you ever see any of these alleged letters from the Queen to the Cardinal?" Titon asked.

"What?" Jeanne lifted her head and looked at him. "Letters from the Queen? Of course, I did. His Eminence was careless; he left them lying around for all the world to see. I saw a few, one or two, I can't remember. But there was one . . . I remember it well because it shocked me."

"Shocked you?"

Jeanne rubbed her brow. She spoke in a low voice, utterly calm and composed. "Yes. Because the Queen addressed His Eminence with the familiar *tu* instead of *vous*, which I myself always used with His Eminence. I have never called him *thee*. The Queen did so in this letter I saw."

The examining magistrates and the court clerk gasped.

"Dear God!" the Cardinal groaned.

Jeanne reached out and took his hand. "Shh, shh. What does it matter now? You know as well as I do that neither of us has spoken a word of truth since we came over that moat into the Bastille. If we dare not talk about the Queen, how can either one of us tell the truth?" Jeanne threw back her hood and stroked her hair into place. "Versailles has made up its mind that someone must take the fall in this wretched business. That role they've assigned to me." She looked around the room and gave the examining magistrates a broad, glowing smile. "Come, Monsieur de Frémyn, you're being remiss again. I notice you haven't written down a word I've said."

38

The interrogations and confrontations completed, the examining magistrates began their summation for presentation before the joint session of the Parlement on May 22, 1786. The Bastille had already begun to clean house, ridding itself of extraneous prisoners who had been caught up in the scandal's net. Among the first to be released, after eight eloquent petitions from her husband to the Parlement, was the Countess Cagliostro, set free after a vote of thirty-two to twenty-six. The newspapers were quick to report that it was now all the rage to call at the mansion in the rue St. Claude, where more than three hundred visitors a day stopped by to pay their respects to Madame Cagliostro, whose "velvety orbs," it was said, "had been well-nigh washed away by the flood of tears shed during her confinement at the Bastille." Much to the government's discontent, whenever Madame Cagliostro made a public appearance on the streets, her path was strewn with flowers.

The sister of the fugitive Comte de La Motte, Madame de Latour, who had gone to the Bastille to deliver a letter to Jeanne only to be locked up and held a prisoner for six months, was likewise released, as was the Baron da Planta, and Mademoiselle d'Oliva's lover, Toussaint de Beausire.

The report of Titon de Villotran and Dupuy de Marcé would be presented to the King's Prosecutor General, Joly de Fleury, who in turn would prepare his conclusions and make his recommendations to the Parlement. These recommendations were to remain in a sealed envelope to be opened only after the conclusion of the reading of the examining magistrates' report before the assembled judges and the final interrogation of the accused.

A few days before the opening day of the trial the Queen summoned Titon, de Marcé, de Fleury and the president of the Parlement, the Marquis d'Aligre, to a conference at the Tuileries.

The Queen, looking slim and youthful again a year after the birth of another son, met them with a face pinched with bitterness and anxiety.

"I should like a list of the various judges of the Parlement with a clear indication of their opinion regarding the Necklace Case," she said, her ice blue eyes imperious.

Titon, who had the most to lose, should the sovereigns' wishes be thwarted, spoke up first. "I feel quite sure that we can accommodate Your Majesty with a memorandum to that effect."

"Very well. I shall ask you to see to it, then, Monsieur Titon. Now, I should like to see Monsieur de Fleury's recommendations to the judges."

De Fleury, a tall, bilious man, his brusque manners worn smooth by years of sycophancy, quickly sprang forward with two portfolio pages bearing his seal of office.

"Thank you, de Fleury," the Queen said, turning her back to them. She walked over to the open window and stood reading the pages in the sunlight of the warm spring day.

The four men hung back awkwardly, trying not to stare as the Queen slowly studied the papers. From time to time she raised her eyes and gazed at the dozens of workmen in blue smocks kneeling among the moist, elaborate parterres of the garden.

"It won't do," Marie Antoinette said finally, moving toward them out of the sunlight. "It simply won't do." She sat down at a desk and picked up a pen. Her lower lip thrust forward, she slashed through paragraph after paragraph.

"At the trial I want no mention whatsoever of the midnight

rendezvous in the Grove of Venus. I can't go into my reasons, but I am determined, and it is essential, de Fleury, that these paragraphs be struck from your report. Is that entirely clear, Monsieur?"

"Of course, Majesty," de Fleury said, smiling as he walked toward her. "Is there anything else you would care to amend, Majesty?"

The Queen did not hesitate. "I find it unconscionable, Messieurs, that you have managed to wash this dissolute, arrogant Cardinal as clean as a lamb." Her hands trembled with anger. "What he has done to me, what he has done to foul my sacred honor, warrants the severest penalty!"

"But, Majesty," Fleury pleaded, "The Cardinal-Prince has been foolish indeed, but all the evidence indicates that the La Motte woman has taken advantage of his good faith by . . ."

"So! You believe that twaddle, do you? A man of the Cardinal's intellect? My good man, no one has ever taken advantage of a Rohan."

"Then what would you have me recommend?" de Fleury asked, still smiling sweetly. Titon and de Marcé glared at him accusingly.

"How should I know? Exile . . . the loss of all his offices . . . public dishonor! He must be punished! He must be humbled!" She rose wearily and held out her hand for de Fleury to kiss. "I take it that I can count on you, de Fleury."

"Absolutely, Majesty."

"The entire Rohan clan must be humbled. They've been cabaling and intriguing furiously for months, buying off honorary councilors of the Parlement with money and women. Subornation of justice! It's shocking and mustn't be allowed. I insist on justice, Fleury! Just remember that when you rewrite your recommendations!"

⟨⟩

Beugnot sat having his second glass of beer at a sidewalk café near the Palais-Royal. Appalled by the carnival spirit pervading the Necklace Case, he had not come near the Palais-Royal in months, for the shops along the arcades disgorged ever proliferating trinkets, trial briefs, cartoons, engravings, pornographic prints of the Queen and Jeanne de La Motte in lewd poses, etchings of the Comte de La Motte paying a call on Mademoiselle d'Oliva in her bedroom, the coverlet suggestively turned down. Beugnot's friends from Bar-sur-Aube, and even his father, wrote imploring him for the latest jingle about the trial. The public obsession with the trial had reached such a fevered pitch that any little memento immediately became a family treasure or a rare gift suitable for the most august occasion.

A barefoot boy in a sparkling new red jacket and ragged breeches passed by Beugnot's table waving a newspaper. "*Dernières nouvelles! Du nouveau dans l'affaire du collier!* Read the latest news in the Necklace Case!"

Reluctantly, Beugnot dug into his pockets and pulled out ten sous for the yellow sheet. He laid the paper on the table and took another sip of beer. Beugnot was unhappy with himself despite his recent success in winning a unanimous verdict from the council in favor of Bar-sur-Aube's case. As a reward he had been elected the youngest representative in the town's history. He could take some pride in that distinction, but he didn't. He felt guilty because he had let Jeanne down by refusing her case. While the other lawyers involved in the trial had become overnight celebrities, their futures assured, just as Monsieur de Crosne had predicted, only Jeanne's attorney, Maître Doillot, continued to cover himself with ridicule. Doillot had published three trial briefs for Jeanne, each one filled with outrageous contradictions in her story.

All the more reason to have shied away from the case, Beugnot said to himself, but not with any satisfaction. He was lonely. Lonely for Jeanne, shut away now for months, and for Georgel, who had been suddenly served with a *lettre de cachet* from the King and sent into exile thirty-six leagues from Paris.

"It's another of the Baron de Breteuil's tricks," Georgel had said, his gaunt shoulders working restlessly under his dingy soutane. "He wants me out of the way to do his dirty work. I was just on the point of exposing him, and he knew it."

"So you did talk with Bassenge and Böhmer?" Beugnot said.

"Of course, I did. I smelled a rat there, and I went after it. I kept going back to talk with them, until last week, in a burst of confidence, Bassenge told me that the Baron de Breteuil had been hounding them for months and had even sent his secretary to them to promise full payment of the necklace if, during the confrontations, they would go beyond what they had said in their depositions!"

"I think I can guess what Breteuil wanted them to say." Beugnot did not doubt for a moment that the Abbé was telling the truth, and it made Beugnot's blood boil to think of Breteuil's callous tampering with justice. Not that Beugnot would count himself among the Cardinal's partisans. The man had caused Beugnot many a jealous pang, and he was not grateful. Still, he had no use for the government's blatant interference in the case, its brutal effort to suppress clandestine publications, its despotic *lettres de cachet*.

"Of course you can. It's all too obvious. Breteuil wanted them to say that the Cardinal had given them absolute assurance that he had seen the Queen, had talked with her, and received her direct orders for the purchase of the necklace. Naturally, Bassenge and Böhmer refused. Such a lie would destroy the Prince. A man cruelly deceived who had acted in good faith toward them."

"When do you leave?" Beugnot asked.

"Tonight. They've given me barely twenty-four hours to prepare my departure. I worked through the night. All is in place. The Abbé Juncker will take charge here. I trust him. He proved his worth in bringing Father Loth to us. His testimony before the examiners has been priceless."

"I doubt that the Abbé Juncker will be able to do what you've done. Encoding instructions to the Cardinal, carrying on the Cardinal's duties."

"Don't worry. We're ready. The Baron de Breteuil is in for a surprise." Georgel gave Beugnot a vicious wink. "You see, my young friend, we're cleverer than the Queen's men."

Beugnot picked up the newspaper and read an epigram that

made him smile in spite of his low mood. Frederick, the King of Prussia, was quoted saying that Cardinal de Rohan will be obliged to call upon all the resources of his not inconsiderable intellect to convince his judges that he is basically a stupid man. This unprecedented scandal of a case, with its web of intrigue and counter intrigue, the newspaper said, held all Europe spellbound, breathless, waiting for the denouement.

Beugnot folded the flimsy newspaper carefully and tucked it into his pocket. He for one was not eager to see the unfolding drama play itself out. As the afternoon shadows filled with crisp breezes, Beugnot got to his feet. Before going on to his lodgings, he intended to drop off a note to the Abbé, to be forwarded from the Palais-Cardinal.

As he walked along the narrow streets to the Marais section, he noticed that the quarter, normally quiet and sedate, was growing noisier and busier. Turning the corner into the rue Francs-Bourgeois, he saw the whole street explode in front of him. A mob surged toward the handsome palace of the Prince de Soubise, the Cardinal de Rohan's uncle. In their midst the King's mounted guard flailed about with whips and the backs of their swords raining down blows on the shouting, cursing crowd. Two splendid carriages with ducal coats of arms on their enameled sides were stranded at opposite ends of the street, hordes of people pushing and shoving around them, trying to make their way to the palace. Two boys clutching packets of paper broke free from the mob and rushed toward him, nearly knocking Beugnot against a wall.

"Want to buy it?" asked one of them, waving his packet at Beugnot.

"What is it?" Beugnot said.

"Maître Target's latest defense brief for the Cardinal. I'll sell it to you."

"How much?" Beugnot said.

"Thirty francs," the boy said.

"That's ridiculous."

The boy shrugged. "Go and get your own, then. They're

giving them away free of charge in the Prince's courtyard," he said good-naturedly and took off at a trot around the corner.

The noise in the street had become deafening; the turmoil a writhing, tormented roar. Poor, poor Jeanne, Beugnot thought, his heart full of sorrow and love, as more and more people tore past him, clutching their precious packet.

☙❧

Titon de Villotran began reading the summary of the preliminary interrogations before the Parlement in joint session at six in the morning on the twenty-second of May in the Palais de Justice. The notoriety of the case had drawn an extraordinary assembly of judges, some of whom had never bothered to sit in Parlement before. Their number totaled sixty-two, the princes of the blood and the peers of the realm having voluntarily surrendered their privileges. The reading of the summation continued uninterrupted until the afternoon of the twenty-ninth of May, at which time all prisoners were to be transferred from the Bastille to the Conciergerie prison at the Palais de Justice.

At eight o'clock that evening Saint-Jean, the turnkey, brought Jeanne her supper.

"What do you think, Saint-Jean? How do you like my new hat?" The governor of the prison had yielded to Jeanne's request for fresh clothes for the trial.

"My, aren't you the gay one tonight, Madame! Hasn't Maître Doillot told you what's in store for you tomorrow morning?"

"He told me that I'm to go before the Parlement. I'm glad of it." Jeanne unfolded her napkin and placed it fastidiously across her knees.

"Hmph! You're a queer one! Upon my word, things don't look too good for you, Madame. It wouldn't surprise me at all to see this business send you up the scaffold in the Place de Grèves."

"Bring me some decent wine, Saint-Jean," Jeanne said coolly. "This stuff is abominable, not fit for vinegar. Then hurry along and ask Monsieur de Launay whether I'm to be taken to the Conciergerie tonight. If not, I should like to make ready for bed, if you please."

At ten o'clock Saint-Jean returned.

"The transfer is set for eleven o'clock; so make ready. You're to be the first to leave."

At precisely eleven o'clock Jeanne was taken down to the council chambers of the Bastille, where Governor de Launay and two officers searched her pockets.

"It's an ancient custom, Madame. Please don't take offense." Monsieur de Launay smiled and deftly extracted a packet of letters from her left pocket. "I shall personally escort Madame to the carriage," he said, offering her his arm.

On the way to the Conciergerie prison Jeanne's hungry, darting eyes followed every gleam of light, every figure, every hackney cab that emerged from the shadows as the carriage sped down the boulevard and across the Seine to the Ile de la Cité. The carriage pulled into the great Cour du Mai of the Palais de Justice, where the faded flowers of a maypole drooped amid fluttering flags and ribbons.

Stepping out of the carriage, Jeanne looked up at the Palais de Justice, ablaze with light from every window of every floor. Swarms of people milled around the Cour du Mai and the broad stairway of the Palais de Justice. Monsieur Hubert, the keeper of the Conciergerie prison, and his wife emerged from the crowd and came forward to meet the new prisoner.

"If you'll just come this way, Madame; we've kept some refreshments for you. A drop of calvados perhaps and some cheese," said Madame Hubert, a dark, birdlike woman with shallow eyes.

As Jeanne turned into the vast Salle des Gens d'Armes of the Conciergerie, the enormous crowd of onlookers fell back to make way for her. Admiring smiles and murmurs followed her along way.

"*Qu'elle est belle!*" one man said, nudging his neighbor.

"As pretty as they make them," another said.

People were everywhere, in the embrasures of the windows,

jamming every room, every corridor. Some clamored up on tables to get a better look at her.

"*Bonne chance, ma belle!* Good luck, my beauty!" a woman shouted as Jeanne and Madame Hubert reached the corner of the room where a few fruits and cheeses waited on a long table. When Jeanne turned and gave the woman a broad smile, the crowd clapped and whistled cheerily.

"It's close to midnight. What have these people come for?" Jeanne whispered to the keeper's wife.

"Why, they've come to have a look at you, Madame. That's the Parisian way, you know. And they want to give you a little encouragement for going before your judges, come tomorrow. Show you their sympathy and all that."

As she nibbled at Madame Hubert's cheese and coarse bread, Jeanne smiled and addressed appreciative nods to the crowd. Soon a well-dressed man, a draper or a milliner perhaps, came forward hesitantly.

"Would you remember me, Madame? Head milliner at Dupré et Fils? I made your hats for the summer of 1776, just before the Marquise de Boulainvilliers and her family went into . . . well, left for the country and you and your sister were sent into the convent. The Abbaye de Longchamps I believe it was."

"Of course!" Jeanne laughed gaily. "One hat was a dear confection of pink tulle. Yes, yes, I remember." She warmed herself in his admiring eyes and felt happier than she had in months.

"Well, now," he said, holding out a rather large etching for her to take. The subject purported to be the Comtesse de La Motte dressing Mademoiselle d'Oliva for her appearance in the Grove of Venus.

"Lord, what's this?" Jeanne said, turning to show the etching to Madame Hubert. "Why, it's no likeness at all!" She hooted with laughter. "Look at those fat eyes. And chins! Look at all those chins. Do I have chins like that?" She looked at those crowding around her and stroked her small, pert chin. She looked like a child enjoying a peculiar kind of game.

"I was wondering if you might sign the etching. It's a gift for my wife. Our tenth anniversary. I wanted something special for her."

"Certainly, Monsieur," Jeanne said, giving him a radiant smile. Madame Hubert produced a pen, and Jeanne cheerfully signed next to the title at the bottom, Jeanne de Saint-Rémy de Valois de France, adding an intricate paraph to her signature.

Gradually, dozens more took courage and came forward with their newspapers, their broadsheets, pamphlets, and other scraps of paper relating to the Necklace Case.

Near two o'clock in the morning Madame Hubert pulled at Jeanne's arm and said. "You'll be weary in the morning if you don't get some sleep now, Madame."

"Ah, is it so late?" Jeanne said. "I had no idea."

39

The Cardinal rose early so that he could pray before the clatter and noise of prison life began. He remained for a long time on his knees beside his bed, mainly telling over his blessings, which appeared to him more astonishingly numerous now that he spent more of his time in prayer. He prayed for the Abbé Georgel, tireless, loyal, smelly in his exhausted old shoes and boots and his grimy soutanes, and the Abbé's ancient mother, now blind and bedridden, in Auvergne, where winter winds would still be licking and hissing greedily around the Abbey. Even in May. He lifted his head and watched a piece of lacy cloud linger for a moment before coiling away into the blue sky. He bowed his head again and prayed for Jeanne. Holy Mother of God, keep her safe, he said. Keep her safe. She was still so young. Only twenty-nine. Too young surely for the cruelty which must be her lot.

He crossed himself and rose to his feet. Monsieur Hubert had pressed and laid out his clothes for his appearance before Parlement. The Cardinal slowly began to dress himself. Though he had made a great deal of progress, he was still somewhat clumsy without his valet Schreiber. He had chosen for that day of judgment long violet robes, the official color of mourning for cardinals. When he made the choice, he meant to call up the humiliating path he had followed after a young, despotic king had hurled his thunderbolt at him, arresting him in spectacular fashion before the feast day crowds at Versailles. He wanted to suggest mourning for his sacred robes, his rank, his powerful family that had ever figured in the greatness of France. He was deeply satisfied with his mourning clothes for other reasons now: in his heart he knew that he would forever grieve for a lifetime lost in frivolity, dissolution, and the vanity of ambition.

With a long sweep of his pale hands the Cardinal smoothed the mantelletta of violet cloth lined in red satin and straightened the Cordon Bleu, the blue ribbon of the royal Order of the Holy Ghost across his chest. About his neck he placed the bishop's cross on a gold chain.

He heard footsteps in the corridor and then a short, sharp rap on this cell door and the rattling of keys.

"They are ready for you now, Your Eminence," Monsieur Hubert said.

⚜

Rétaux de Villette, dressed in black silk, was the first of the accused to be brought before the Parlement. Though he could not stop crying, Villette answered the questions put to him in a strong, confident voice, all the while dabbing nervously at his flowing tears with a soggy handkerchief.

After Rétaux de Villette was taken away, Jeanne de La Motte made her appearance, wearing an exquisitely cut gown of blue-gray satin trimmed with black velvet piping, a black velvet belt embellished with steel beads, a black hat trimmed with black lace and ribbon, and an embroidered muslin cape edged with net.

She looked magnificent, a picture of absolute self-confidence, until she stepped forward and saw the *sellette*, a humiliatingly low, three-legged stool used in the courts of France since medieval times. Jeanne looked at the stool and quickly turned her head away, her face and neck flushed scarlet. The sergeant-at-arms took her by the arm and pushed her toward the stool. Courage, Madame, someone whispered. Jeanne tossed her head defiantly, pulled her skirts aside gracefully, and then settled herself onto the stool, taking time to arrange the folds of her satin skirt.

The hearing lasted over three hours, the Comtesse de La Motte impressing everyone, *The Leyden Gazette* reported, with "her fetching appearance, her grace and her beautiful figure, her air of breeding and distinction."

By turns truculent and sweetly charming, Jeanne frequently refused to answer questions put to her. "I cannot answer that question," she said when asked about a certain letter sent to the Cardinal by the Queen. "Should I answer that question I would most certainly offend . . . the Queen. Why should I compromise my sovereign?" Indeed, Jeanne, showing amazing presence of mind in inventing circumlocutions, appeared reluctant to refer to the Queen at all.

At the end of the hearing she bowed respectfully to the judges and withdrew on the arm of Monsieur Hubert, who escorted her back to the Huberts' apartment with a huge crowd of spectators and journalists thronging in their wake.

As soon as the Comtesse de La Motte left the courtroom the sergeant-at-arms, looking neither right nor left to his superiors, stepped forward and quickly removed the *sellette* before the Cardinal was ushered into the room.

As the Cardinal, looking infinitely weary and full of sorrow, stepped forward, every voice was stilled. It had been months since anyone except the keepers of the Bastille had seen the Cardinal, and the great room bristled with curiosity. Through long months of inactivity the Cardinal had lost the healthy color of his cheeks but not the athletic spring of his step. He stepped forward purposefully toward the bar. Throughout the two-hour long hearing he remained standing, though the President of the Parlement repeatedly invited him to take a seat.

The Cardinal had eaten nothing at all since the night before, and as the hearing wore on, he could feel his strength waning as well as his will to extricate himself from his humiliating position. He barely perceived that the questions of the judges had become intensely personal in nature. He answered as best he knew how, ever mindful of Target's admonitions.

"But how came it, Your Eminence," the Prosecutor General asked finally, "that you of all people, one of this kingdom's mightiest figures, a Rohan, an ambassador, and Grand Almoner of the King should not have recognized the enormous falsity of the signature Marie Antoinette de France?"

The Cardinal dropped his hands to his side in a despairing gesture of hopelessness. "I was utterly blinded, don't you see, by my overwhelming desire to regain the Queen's good graces!" the Cardinal cried out as if exasperated by his own credulity.

A murmur of sympathy spread up and down the rows of judges. Monsieur Joly de Fleury, looking pale and discomfited, searched for faces sympathetic to the Queen. Suddenly, as one, the judges solemnly rose to their feet and bowed to the Cardinal, the High Bench in quick order standing as well to salute him. Completely spent, only vaguely aware of the extraordinary distinction being paid to him by the court, and resigned to whatever fate might have in store for him, the Cardinal bowed to his judges and withdrew.

The next morning at half past four o'clock when the streets around the Palais de Justice were still muffled in darkness and sleep, nineteen members of Cardinal-Prince Louis de Rohan's family, dressed in mourning clothes, quietly took their places in a row on each side of the entrance to the Great Hall of Parlement.

Shortly after five o'clock the magistrates began to arrive. The Cardinal's relatives from the distinguished houses of Rohan, Soubise, Guéménée, and Lorraine spoke not a word, only bowing gravely as the magistrates filed past.

Outside the Palais de Justice fights and brawls began to break out among spectators and journalists, who had camped there for days. Around the Palais de Justice all the streets and bridges were clogged with mobs wild with curiosity and excitement over the impending sentencing. At six o'clock the government called out the foot guard and mounted guard to patrol the area and to keep order.

Inside the Great Hall, Prosecutor General Joly de Fleury rose to his feet and with a studied display of deliberation slowly opened a sealed envelope with his recommendations to the court.

The first and longest recommendation ordered that the forged signature Marie Antoinette de France be struck out and expunged from the contract with the jewelers Bassenge and Böhmer.

Monsieur de Fleury preened himself in the general ripple of assent. He was a vain man with a strutting step and a pompous, stentorian voice. He next recommended that Rétaux de Villette be banished for life from the kingdom of France. Nicole Leguay d'Oliva and Alexander Cagliostro were to be acquitted, the former with a reprimand from the court for criminal presumption in impersonation of the sovereign, the latter to be totally exonerated. Again, Fleury raised his eyes and smiled as a murmur of approval worked its way through the audience.

Marc Antoine Nicolas de La Motte he condemned in absentia to be flogged and beaten, naked, with rods and the letters G.A.L. for the galleys branded with a hot iron on his right shoulder by the public executioner before being conducted to servitude in the galleys for life.

In the Prosecutor General's sixth recommendation he urged the sentencing of Jeanne de La Motte to be flogged and beaten, naked; to be branded upon both shoulders with a hot iron with the letter V, for *voleuse*, thief, and taken to La Salpêtrière, the female house of correction, to be imprisoned for life.

A shuffle of excitement spread through the assembly. The Prosecutor General had laid down for Jeanne de La Motte the severest penalties short of the death sentence. The Cardinal would be next. Everyone strained forward as Fleury picked up a separate sheet of paper and began to read:

> I hereby recommend that the Cardinal-Prince de Rohan be sentenced to appear eight days hence in the Great Hall of the Palais de Justice to make public statement to the effect that he has been guilty of *lèse-majesté*, of disrespect to the sacred persons of the sovereigns. That the said Cardinal-Prince de Rohan be sentenced to express his repentance publicly, and publicly to seek the pardon of the King and

Queen. That he be condemned to divest himself of all his offices. That he make a special contribution of alms to the poor. That he be exiled for life from all the royal residences and be held in prison until the execution of said sentence.

Shouts and oaths broke out from every corner and soon the Great Room was in an uproar beyond Fleury's control. The Advocate General, Monsieur de Séguier, was the first on his feet.

"How dare you, you miserable old fool!" de Séguier shouted, pulling down on his wig with both hands. "Close as you are to the tomb, how can you have agreed to dishonor your ashes? How can you have agreed to try to involve this court in your habitual venality?"

Fleury snorted derisively. "So! You will stick with a fellow libertine, will you?" he cried, wagging his finger at de Séguier. "Well, I'm not surprised. You disgust me with your debauches. A worthy partisan, indeed, the Cardinal de Rohan has found in you, Monsieur."

"Occasionally I visit ladies of the evening, I don't deny it. And I don't care who sees my carriage waiting before their door. But no one will ever see me stoop to sell my vote for power and fortune! The Cardinal should be completely exonerated. Have you heard nothing? Have you seen nothing during the testimony here? Or are you such a toady that your ears and lips are sealed?" Around de Séguier other judges barked their raucous encouragement.

Titon de Villotran rose to his feet. "I urge the assembly to accept the Prosecutor General's recommendations, given the . . ."

"The point is, where do these recommendations come from?" Robert de Saint-Vincent, a magistrate well-known for his high principles and his persuasive argumentative skills, shouted. "Certainly not from these chambers! Why should the Cardinal suffer further humiliation from Versailles? Enough, I say. His Majesty has been poorly served by his counselors from the very beginning of this loathsome affair. Arresting a man of the Prince's stature in broad daylight in the Galérie des Glaces! What lame-brained minister could sanction such an abomination! The King is young, and his advisers are foolish, petty men. Carelessly undermining the sanctity of the Church, jeopardizing the dignity of the throne, and painting His Majesty as a tyrant. The government has handled this whole affair in a scandalous manner, creating sensation upon sensation. And now they are asking us to throw the Cardinal-Prince Louis de Rohan to the wolves! I for one won't have it!"

The debate raged for eighteen hours until finally at nine o'clock in the evening, a verdict was reached.

40

Alone in his cell the Cardinal sat staring numbly at the small patch of gray light in a window high up in the stone wall. The moon would be very nearly full tonight, he reckoned, and the ferries would still be working their way, back and forth, across the river. But in his cell it seemed as if the whole world had slipped away into the soft maws of silence. Alert but peaceful, he felt as if he could drift along on the serene tide of his thoughts for an eternity.

Suddenly as the clock of the Conciergerie struck nine o'clock, there came a tremendous swell of jubilation from the Cour de Mai of the Palais de Justice. It rolled over him in wave after wave, an explosive roar of joy. He stood up and listened. From the tumult of sound he could hear the word *Bravo!* repeated over and over. Bravo! Bravo! Bravo! He could not imagine what had happened.

Within minutes the sound of racing footsteps reverberated down the long corridor outside his cell. Apprehensive, the Cardinal backed against a wall and waited. The riot of exultation from the courtyard swelled. Bravo! Bravo! *Vive le Parlement!*

"My dear Prince," de Séquier said, rushing into the cell. "You are free! Free!"

Red-faced and breathless, Monsieur Hubert, following closely behind the Advocate General, threw himself to his knees before the Cardinal.

"Free?" the Cardinal said, overwhelmed by the sudden tumult of sound after months of silence.

"Listen!" de Séquier said, cocking his head toward the great courtyard.

"Ah, Your Eminence, the crowd is ecstatic!" Monsieur Hubert said, getting to his feet and gathering up the Cardinal's cape.

"All of Paris it seems is here to acclaim you," de Séquier said.

"Am I then completely exonerated of the charges?" the Cardinal asked, thinking of Jeanne, fear spreading through his heart like a wet stain.

"Completely. There will be no rejoicing in Versailles this night, I can warrant you that! Come, Your Eminence. You are expected in the courtyard."

As soon as Madame Campan heard the Parlement's verdict, she ran as fast as she could to find the Queen. Alone in a dimly lit room opposite the children's nursery, Marie Antoinette sat weeping, clenching and unclenching her small hands nervously.

"Come and weep with your sovereign, dear Madame Campan," she whispered. "Ah, Madame, I am so afraid!"

"Please, Majesty, you mustn't cry. It pains me to see you so distressed."

The King came quietly into the room and took the Queen's hand and held it in his. "No, no, stay, Madame Campan. Don't get up for me. The Queen needs sincere friends like you around her now. She doesn't have many, I'm afraid." His large round face was paler than usual, and his full lips seemed swollen with indignation.

The Queen looked at him, her eyes fierce. "It is a slap in the face of the monarchy, you know that, don't you? That dreadful Rohan acquitted without so much as a reprimand! It's open defiance of your authority. The Parlement knows exactly what it's doing."

"Outrageous. That's all I can think of. Inconceivably outrageous. Cardinal de Rohan is nothing more nor less than a cheap swindler, and this diamond necklace business was nothing more than a shady, disreputable scheme of his to hoodwink the jewelers out of the necklace—only to be hoodwinked out of it himself in the end, as it turned out. Miserable fool!" the King said.

"Parlement has taken its vengeance against you, against the

throne." Marie Antoinette shook her head wearily. "And I'm the victim!" Her voice choked with tears. "Police Lieutenant General de Crosne has so much as told me that I am never to visit the capital again."

"You mean, not go to Paris?" Madame Campan asked.

The palace was unusually quiet. No one waited in the ante-rooms; no evening revelers strolled in the gardens beneath the Queen's windows.

"The imbecile went on at such length, hemming and hawing, pulling at his sleeves, toying with his gloves. In the end he gave me to understand that my presence in Paris might occasion some unpleasantness on the part of the citizenry."

"Public demonstrations?" The King colored.

"Where is their respect? Their reverence for the sacred person of royalty?" the Queen said.

The King stood bulkily at her side, deep in thought. "Never mind, my dear," he said finally. "His Eminence has not heard the last from me."

The morning after the verdicts were delivered, Charles-Henri Sanson rose early and dressed himself in the traditional uniform of executioners: blue breeches with a red jacket embroidered in black with the symbols of his trade, the gibbet and the ladder, and a pink, two-cornered hat. At the Conciergerie he was admitted through a low, cellar-door entry by the Hubert's fourteen-year-old son, Gustave, who carefully wiped the door handles and crossed himself twice after letting Monsieur de Paris, as the executioner was popularly called, pass through.

Sanson went directly to collect Rétaux de Villette from his cell. On seeing the executioner, Villette leapt to his feet and instinctively joined his hands together as if in prayer.

"What do you mean to do with that rope!" he cried.

Sanson moved forward and swiftly turned Villette around to face the wall. "It's but a halter," Sanson said, and gravely proceeded to adjust the rope around Villette's neck as if following some ancient ritual that only an executioner would know and appreciate.

Just as dawn began to fleck the sky with shards of light, Sanson led Villette, already weary and footsore, to the Porte de Vincennes. It was not long before a hooting and jeering crowd, in the process of setting up the day's market, fell in behind the pair. At the gate Sanson removed the halter from Villette's neck and read out his sentence, banishing him to perpetual exile. The reading finished, Sanson turned Villette's back to the city, handed him a loaf of bread, stepped back, and with great solemnity kicked Villette sharply in the breeches, sending him stumbling forward through the gates.

"Never show thy face in the kingdom of France again," Sanson said, as the crowd of onlookers cheered.

That evening the Cardinal finished a small supper in his study. He had been too agitated during the day to eat at all. And he had rarely been alone. So many well-wishers spilled into his salons that he had been carried along by their affection.

"Without you, Soubise, and the family, I would never have had the courage to bear the Bastille. I was very close, during those long months in prison, to breaking down altogether. Thank God, the family name is vindicated." The Cardinal and his uncle had escaped to a secluded corner bench in the garden.

"It's over now, Louis. The King's knuckles have been soundly rapped, and let us hope that the Queen has learned her lesson." The Prince de Soubise stretched his legs and yawned lazily. He was a handsome man with a strong, cleanly shaped nose and thick silver hair like the Cardinal's. "His Majesty will think twice before he tangles with the Rohan family again."

"I wonder . . ." the Cardinal said, hesitantly, "what has become of the others?"

"Well, Cagliostro was borne home in triumph last night on the shoulders of his admirers. To the arms of his luscious wife. A happy man tonight, I daresay. That charming little coquette Oliva is the latest fashion at the Palais-Royal. She really is quite dear, you know. And the forger . . . what was his name?"

"Villette," the Cardinal said.

"The executioner kicked him out of the city this morning," Soubise said.

The Cardinal fiddled with his ring. "And the Comtesse . . . ?"

Soubise, his dark brown eyes bulging angrily, stared at the Cardinal. "How should I know, and why should you care?" Soubise snatched up his gloves and got to his feet.

"Ah, must you go now, uncle? I must confess I've enjoyed our quiet corner."

Actually, the Cardinal was not unhappy to be left alone. He had much that he wanted to think about, and many letters to write, the first of which would be a long letter of appreciation to the Abbé Georgel, still in exile in Mortagne.

Near six o'clock Schreiber brought a tray of soup and cheese to the study. "Your appetite is failing you, Your Eminence. It's that greensickness, I expect. You'll be months getting over it."

The Cardinal drank off his wine and listened contentedly to the familiar sounds of his household. His thoughts drifted back to the day before and the terrible ordeal of standing, accused, before the Parlement. Suddenly, he heard a fierce racket break out in the courtyard.

He had not quite reached the head of the great staircase when he heard the Baron de Breteuil bellowing with all his might, *In the name of the King! Open these doors!*

The Cardinal peered down into the courtyard, still filled with friends and relatives come to pay their respects and leave their calling cards. He saw Baron de Breteuil being carried forward in a sedan chair, his swarthy face dark and twisted with pain.

"What is it, Breteuil?" the Cardinal asked, hurrying down the steps. "Have you had an accident?"

"No! No accident. It's the gout!" Breteuil roared, then lost his breath.

"You're in pain. Come this way. Schreiber! Bring some cooling towels and cold water."

"In the name of the King!" Breteuil wheezed, his face contorted in agony as he tried to find relief in rearranging his legs. The crowd had grown still and quiet. Breteuil's bearers carefully lowered the sedan chair into place just in front of the Cardinal, who stood at the bottom of the grand staircase, his silver hair stirring slightly in the evening breeze.

"In the name of the King!" Breteuil shouted again. "You, Cardinal Prince Louis de Rohan, are ordered to surrender all offices and decorations which have come to you from the hand of your sovereign!" Breteuil fought for breath. "The Grand Almonership, the Cordon Bleu. You are stripped of them. And here . . ." Breteuil reached forward with shaking hands and handed a letter to the Cardinal, who betrayed no emotion whatsoever, observing his old enemy with calm interest. "A *lettre de cachet* from the King!" Breteuil barked triumphantly. "His Majesty orders you to depart his city of Paris within three days. Exile! You are to go into exile!"

"Where?" the Cardinal asked quietly.

"Why, your Abbaye de la Chaise-Dieu!" Breteuil gloated, his pain all but forgotten.

The seat of God! The Cardinal could feel a humiliating sweat break on his brow. The *danse macabre* for companionship, an eternity of loneliness and loss. Why not the sweet solace of Saverne, green and golden, laden with beauty? Exiled to Auvergne, leaden, austere, unforgiving. The Cardinal shivered. He reached out and took the *lettre de cachet*.

He turned it over in his hand, studying the King's seal for a moment, then said, his voice cool with contempt, "Are you quite sure, then, that you won't have some refreshing cider? Or a glass of lime water, perhaps?"

41

On that same day, June 1, 1786, another *lettre de cachet* from the King was delivered to the Count Cagliostro, ordering him to be out of His Majesty's city of Paris in eight days' time, and out of His Majesty's kingdom of France within three weeks. Murmurs of tyranny and despotism grew louder as word spread of the King's harsh banishment of the Cardinal and his friend Cagliostro. When Cagliostro and his wife sailed for England from Boulogne, crowds of citizens from every walk of life lined the shores to bid them farewell. Hostility to the Queen was rife. Tradesmen in Paris openly spat and called her the Austrian whore.

As the early days of June passed, predictions and rumors proliferated about the fate of Jeanne de La Motte, who alone of the accused remained incarcerated in the Conciergerie. There were days when Jeanne entirely forgot that she was in prison. Monsieur and Madame Hubert were enchanted with their frolicsome charge, insisting that she dine with them in their apartment every night. They loved her high spirits, her raw jokes, her audacious combination of princess and adventuress. A constant parade of visitors from the highest society of Paris and the court came calling and went away claiming that they found the singular Comtesse de La Motte even more exotic and alluring in her present situation.

In the evening, after Monsieur and Madame Hubert retired for the evening, young, lovesick Gustave Hubert stayed to keep Jeanne company, joining her in the window seat for a game of piquet or a cozy chat. Sometime after midnight Gustave would gallantly escort her back to her quarters, stopping on the way at the foot of the central staircase in the courtyard to feed the rabbits he kept there in a little hutch.

And then there was the priest from the Sainte Chapelle just beyond the courtyard of the Palais de Justice. A witty, sophisticated man, cultured and highly educated, he sat enthralled as Jeanne told her stories, weeping with her over the cruelties of fate.

"It's the Valois curse, Father," she said many times, and always to great effect.

"So it would seem, my dear," the priest, a tender-hearted listener, would answer. He overwhelmed her with gifts and little attentions. When he found out that Jeanne was fond of cider, he begged his family in Brittany to send him cases of the best cider in their cellars.

Since the custom of French courts dictated that only those sentenced to death be apprised of their sentence, Jeanne remained ignorant of the punishment meted out to her by the Parlement. Nonetheless, in the small hours of the night, she would awaken with a start and wonder why her attorney, Maître Doillot, previously so attentive, should now neglect her despite her many letters pleading her need to see him.

"I suspect that Maître Doillot will soon publish another brief for you to clear you completely in the eyes of the King. Rumors are that the King may send you into exile," Monsieur Hubert said one night at the supper table when the conversation veered, as it tended to do, to the trial and the Comtesse's sentence.

"Exile? Then I shall go to England," Jeanne said brightly. "Sweet land of liberty. My rapscallion of a husband is there. I shall join him." She did not altogether trust the Huberts. Appreciating as they did her jokes and her wild spirits, they were inclined to lie to her about what they heard in the streets for fear of upsetting her and sending her into a low mood that would spoil the fun around the supper table.

"Some people are predicting," Madame Hubert said, dipping a piece of bread in her soup, "that is, I've heard it said that the King will issue a *lettre de cachet* in your name, sending you to a convent."

Jeanne shot up from her chair and let out a horrendous shriek.

"A *lettre de cachet!* No! No! Better death than smothered in a convent!" With flailing arms and hands, she sent her plate smashing to the floor, jerked off the tablecloth and sent glasses, plates, knives and forks flying out in every direction.

"Madame! No! Please!" the priest shouted, as Jeanne grabbed up a large porcelain vase from a sideboard and, with both hands, struck herself in the head with it until it shattered into pieces.

Gustave Hubert, weeping, and the priest both struggled to pry loose from Jeanne's fingers a jagged fragment of the vase that she was trying to plunge into her throat. Her white arms and her face bled profusely. With a prolonged shudder she sank to the floor unconscious, her body twisting with convulsions.

"Never fear, *ma petite*," the priest crooned, "the Queen will not desert you. Her Majesty will never allow the sentence to be carried out."

✒

"The end of June is well nigh," Henri Sanson said to his father, the executioner, as they sat down to their breakfast. "And still no word of when we're to do our work on the La Motte woman."

"It's to be soon. I received the orders yesterday. She's to be dealt with tomorrow morning well before dawn in the courtyard of the Palais. I'm sending for your uncle Charlemagne in Provins to help us out. Everything must be done as quietly as possible. Those are our orders."

Monsieur de Paris was worried. Meticulous in everything to do with his profession, he was ill at ease punishing women, especially a woman of noble birth. Not just noble birth either, but a descendant of the Valois kings. The executioner was superstitious, and to lift his rod over the back of a Valois princess queered his universe, as if the noonday sun had decided to shine at midnight. And he would have to administer the beating himself instead of delegating it to one of his assistants as was his custom. It would be an insult to the woman to be whipped by an underling.

"There must be no disturbance," the executioner said. "We've got to despatch the business as neatly as possible and keep the crowds down."

"I don't see much chance of that," Henri said, "with that pack of foreign journalists camped out around the Ile de la Cité just waiting like vultures for some fresh meat."

"We've got to be careful. The Huberts say that the La Motte woman is a real hellcat with a red-hot temper. There's no telling what she will say or do when she's under the rod. Versailles doesn't want anything ugly to happen."

Henri laughed. "It's going to be hard to make what we have to do to her look pretty."

The executioner chewed his bread in silence. Henri was the only one of his sons who took real pride in helping his father with his work and who looked forward to taking his place one day. Henri had never shown any shame about his family's ostracism because of their profession.

The executioner was deeply uneasy and longed to confide in his son why the sentence worried him: Monsieur de Paris had never before branded anyone.

Well after midnight, the executioner and his assistants, careful not to make unnecessary noise, set up a scaffold in the great courtyard of the Palais de Justice.

On the morning of June 21, 1786, all was ready for the execution of Jeanne de La Motte's sentence. The executioner, in his usual methodical way, had learned as much as he could about her habits in prison and her friendship with the jailer and his wife. Shortly after four o'clock, the sky still heavy with darkness, Sanson sent Madame Hubert to Jeanne's cell with instructions to tell her that she was wanted in the corridor.

When Madame Hubert entered the cell, Jeanne lay sound asleep on her back, her arms draped gracefully on the pillow above her head.

"Comtesse," Madame Hubert whispered, touching Jeanne's shoulder, "someone is expecting you just outside the door."

"What?" Jeanne said, making a face. "It's dark, I'm sleepy, it's too early to get up, dear heart." She rolled over and turned her face to the wall.

"But you must get up, Madame, indeed you must. It's Maître Doillot, the one you've been begging to come to see you, who's outside waiting."

"Doillot!" Jeanne said, springing out of bed. "Well, Heaven be praised! Here, help me get dressed, dear heart."

"Oh, there's no time for that, I'm afraid. Maître Doillot is on his way to his country house. His carriage is standing down in the courtyard. You look splendid, dear Comtesse, just as you are."

Jeanne snatched up a silk déshabillé of brown and white stripes covered with small nosegays of roses. On her head she wore an embroidered cap.

"I'm sure I look a fright. But, no matter, the old fool dotes on me."

As soon as the door closed behind her, the executioner and his son leapt forward and seized her arms. Struggling like a nimble, wild animal with extraordinary strength, cursing, shrieking at the top of her lungs, Jeanne very nearly made Sanson fall. At the end of the corridor, four police guards came running forward to assist the executioner and his son.

"We wish you to listen to your sentence, Madame," Sanson said. On hearing this, Jeanne seemed to grow slack in their arms. She shuddered, looked down and clenched her hands. The executioner and Henri lifted her slight body and carried her along between them to the main hall where the Court Clerk, de Fermyn, awaited them.

At the first words proclaiming her guilty, Jeanne's rage burst out with renewed strength. "I call upon that hussy the Queen!" she bellowed then fell backwards so suddenly that she would have fractured her head on the stones, had not the executioner caught her in his arms.

Despite Jeanne's kicking and screaming de Fermyn kept his eyes on his document and continued to read the sentence. Feeling weak and breathless, unable to keep up with Jeanne's demonic twisting and turning, young Henri, who had always prided himself on having the strength of a stallion, cried out to his father, "Tie her up, for God's sake. The rope! The rope!"

The executioner's assistants crowded around, and after a protracted struggle they tied her up and placed a halter around her neck. Jeanne's screams continued unabated, broken from time to time by a stream of coarse obscenity.

"What's the use?" de Frémyn said, throwing up his hands in disgust. "Get on with it, Sanson."

They led Jeanne out into the courtyard by the halter around her neck and tied her to a cart.

"Oh, dear God!" Sanson said. "Look at that!" The scaffold had been erected opposite the gate of the Cour de Mai, and someone had left the gate open. It was not quite daybreak, yet hundreds of people had crowded into the great courtyard. Looking up, Sanson could see spectators hanging out of windows overlooking the courtyard, perched on rooftops and atop walls.

Sanson, nervous, full of misgivings, surveyed the scaffold quickly to make sure that the cauldron with the coals for the branding irons was ready. He led Jeanne up onto the scaffold and motioned to his attendants to come and loosen her bonds. All the while he spoke to her in a low, soothing voice, like a doctor with a fearful patient. Jeanne stopped screaming, gasping for breath in loud, harsh gulps.

On the scaffold, when the assistants began to strip her of her clothing, Jeanne again fought them off, wailing like a banshee. "Where are you now, you Austrian whore!" she screamed. "Now that you've satisfied your lusts with me! You want no more of me! I'll get you yet! Oh, citizens of Paris," she said, suddenly aware of the mob of spectators surrounding the scaffold, "Save me! Save this daughter of a Valois king from the vengeance of that damned trollop who calls herself the Queen of France."

"Enough!" Sanson said under his breath. He ripped off a strip of cloth from Jeanne's silk déshabillé and gagged her.

"Put her face down over the bench," Sanson said, taking up the rod.

The crowd fell into a stunned silence as Sanson's assistants lifted Jeanne's naked body and forced her down on the bench. At the sight of her superb body, exquisitely white and beautifully proportioned, the crowd growled with delight, whistling and yelling obscenities.

The hullabaloo suited Sanson well enough. He turned his back to the crowd and caned Jeanne with a touch so light that he barely left a trace on her delicate white skin.

Every now and again Sanson felt the hot air of the cauldron on his face, and his will faltered. The crowd had grown quiet and watchful again.

As Sanson went to the cauldron to pick up the branding iron, his assistants were not quick enough in pinioning Jeanne, who worked herself free of their grasp and ran off the scaffolding, her white thighs and breasts flashing in the morning light. Sanson leapt off the scaffolding in pursuit, the red-hot branding iron held high over his head. Just as he was drawing near, Jeanne suddenly slipped and fell on the paving stones, slick with morning dew. Sanson quickly plunged the branding iron against her right shoulder. There was a loud, sizzling noise, and a bluish vapor floated upward over her loosened hair. The crowd groaned.

Jeanne's tortured body pulled itself away from the executioner, writhing and rolling across the paving stones of the courtyard to the very foot of the grand staircase.

Sanson, unable to move, the putrid odor of burnt flesh filling his nostrils, stood looking at her. He had to pursue her; he had to brand the left shoulder. She was quiet except for a low, guttural moan; her small hand reached upward and clutched the stone step as she tried to lift herself and get away from him. Just as he was raising the branding iron for the second letter v, she turned her head and looked up at him. At that moment her entire body was seized with a convulsion so violent that the iron came down, not on her shoulder, but on the tender flesh of her left breast. Before falling unconscious, Jeanne let out a weak, forlorn cry, her body turning and buckling in a prolonged convulsive paroxysm.

Panting, Sanson, weary and ashamed, stood over Jeanne's lifeless body. The spectators did not stir. Henri came forward with a blanket and quickly covered Jeanne's nakedness.

"What are we going to do, father? She'll never be able to walk to the Salpêtrière prison."

"She's paid her debt. Tell de Frémyn I want a coach."

"A coach! He'll never consent."

"I mean for her to be spared any further suffering by my hand," Sanson said.

The executioner had his way, and much as he detested any deviation from custom, he watched with satisfaction as Jeanne's limp, mutilated body was gathered up and taken away in a coach to the Salpêtrière.

Mother Superior Victoire was afraid that the notorious new inmate would expire before she and the other sisters could get her inside the prison. Young Henri Sanson carried her in his arms directly into the registry office where the women prisoners were signed in. Jeanne remained unconscious for well over an hour, her face so covered with cuts and bruises that she was barely recognizable.

Like everyone else in Paris, Mother Superior had her doubts about the Diamond Necklace trial and felt great compassion for this dirty, disheveled young woman wrapped up in a foul, rat-chewed blanket. At that moment, Jeanne de La Motte looked very much like the pathetic victim of ruthless power and privilege.

"I doubt that she'll survive if we have to put her in one of the communal beds for six," Mother Superior said, swabbing Jeanne's face with rosewater.

"We won't have to. One of the prisoners has come forward to offer her bed for the poor creature," Sister Agnès said.

"Well, thank God for that," Mother Superior said.

Toward the end of the day Jeanne regained consciousness.

"Is there anything more we can do for you, *ma petite?*" Mother Superior Victoire asked.

Jeanne lay speechless, her eyes fastened on the small brass crucifix at the foot of the bed. She slowly raised her hands and folded them in an attitude of prayer. She opened her mouth as if to speak, but her lips and tongue were so swollen that she could not make a sound.

"Poor, poor child. Don't worry. We shall all pray for you," Mother Superior said.

42

In London on June 26, 1786, Cagliostro published an open letter to the people of France. Cagliostro's letter, charged with the spirit of revolt, quickly found its way into France, where newspaper vendors sold copies for unspeakably high prices. In the letter Cagliostro inveighed against tyranny, injustice, the arbitrary exercise of power by means of the despotic *lettre de cachet*, and predicted that one fine day the Bastille would be razed to the ground and a public promenade erected on its ruins.

❦

A few days after Jeanne had recovered sufficiently to take some weak gruel and bread, Sister Agnès led her to a prodigiously vast space which would be her dormitory by night and a workhouse by day. At first, when the grated doors of the room were dragged open, Jeanne thought that the creatures she saw bending over a long table in the middle of the room were a gathering of scarecrows. But they were her fellow inmates, skeletally thin, wearing coarse gray dresses with gray stockings, brown wool petticoats, round gray hats and wooden sabots.

"Must I wear those dresses?" Jeanne asked meekly.

"You must, yes," Sister Agnès said. Young and still impressionable and something of a beauty, Sister Agnès, before her father gambled away his chateau and lands, had dreamed of going to court and making a fashionable marriage. With the new prisoner she was diffident and awestruck, for she had heard the rumors that the Comtesse de La Motte had been the Queen's favorite.

Listlessly, Jeanne looked around the bleak room where far above their heads were windows open to rain, snow, and wind with neither glass panes nor shutters but only iron bars. Spaced out along the walls were pine boards where the prisoners placed their daily allotment of bread and other pitiful possessions.

"You'll receive a weekly allowance of a pound and a quarter of bread," Sister Agnès said, trying to sound comforting, "Three ounces of meat thrice a week, cheese and soup on alternating days."

"A Valois princess . . ." Jeanne murmured.

Sister Agnès looked discomfited. "Some of the inmates . . . some can be kind. They aren't all bad. *Tiens!* There's Angélique, the one who gave up her bed for you when you came to the Salpêtrière. Come along, she wants so much to make your acquaintance."

"Where will I sleep now?" Jeanne asked dully.

"Why . . . at night there are beds here, six beds . . . ."

"For all these people? For a hundred people?" Jeanne could not take her eyes off the scarecrow women hunched over the table, sewing and mending.

"For a hundred-odd, yes. The beds are wide."

"Covered with straw," Jeanne said. Prison straw. The idea was humiliating, like bedding down an animal.

"Would you like to meet Angélique?"

"No," Jeanne said. "I will make my own way."

Sister Agnès had not yet reached the fourth courtyard when she heard alarm bells tolling from the innermost prison. Mother Superior and four guards rushed by her. When Sister Agnès opened the doors to the workroom, she saw one of the guards lifting the lifeless body of the Comtesse de La Motte onto a litter. Her swollen face was blue; her pale arms dangled alongside the litter.

"*Mon dieu!* What's happened, Mother?" she asked.

"Madame de La Motte tried to choke herself by stuffing the corner of an old coverlet down her throat. Send for the chaplain."

Father Tillet cracked the narrow door of the confessional and looked out over the empty pews of the small chapel. Near the front there were four or five inmates kneeling in prayer, waiting their turn to confess. Behind them he saw Jeanne, her pale face downcast, her fingers working feverishly over her rosary. "You've worked wonders with her, Father," Mother Superior told him, and it was true. They had almost lost her the day she tried to choke herself, and only Father Tillet's boundless devotion had pulled her back from the abyss and reconciled her to her grim lot.

With absent-minded impatience Father Tillet listened to confessions and doled out penance until the grate was pushed back, and he heard Jeanne say, "Forgive me, Father, for I have sinned."

"Ah, Comtesse, it is you," Father Tillet said, giddy with happiness. A beautiful young man from the poorest section of the St. Antoine quarter, Father Tillet saw the Comtesse as a figure of high romance, a tragic heroine straight out of the romances that he pored over in his lonely hours. Tall, thin, his lungs rotten with consumption, Father Tillet was determined to do everything in his power to help the Comtesse bear the sordid conditions of the Salpêtrière.

"I want to thank you for the engraving. Sister Agnès put it on my wall yesterday," Jeanne said.

"At the foot of the bed? I told her to place the repentant Magdalen just so. To give you comfort as soon as you open your eyes each morning. The Magdalen's eyes are just your color of blue. Darker than most."

The nuns at the Salpêtrière thought the world of Father Tillet and could deny him nothing. He nagged Mother Superior until she gave Jeanne a cell to herself with a decent bed. And he made sure that she had a new rosary, a nice one with onyx beads, and an ivory crucifix to adorn the headboard of her bed.

"The Magdalen does give comfort. But she makes me weep," Jeanne said. Beyond the chapel doors they could hear the inmates sweeping down the courtyard with their coarse stick brooms. Soon the worktables would be taken down and beds made up for the night.

"You must always remember, Comtesse, that our Lord and Saviour Jesus Christ forgave Mary Magdalen her sins. Which were many. Look at your friend, little Angélique, entombed here for life, a mere child accused of murdering her illegitimate baby. God forgives. Can you doubt it when you see with what sacrifice little Angélique serves you. Her devotion to you has made her the talk of Paris."

Jeanne's eyes brightened. "Does Paris still talk of me?"

"With winter coming on they talk of little else. Last week the *Leyden Gazette* put out a special issue devoted to you. They called you the unhappy Valois and said that you were showing the true spirit of Christian humility by resigning yourself to your dire fate. You see? Mother Superior and I talked for hours about that particular article. They described Angélique and all the little things she does to make your life here less miserable. I think it must have been Mother Superior who told the journalists that you spend the better part of your waking hours in reading and in meditation upon *The Imitation of Christ.*"

"Oh, father, I've read little lately. I fear for my eyes. They have bothered me . . . now and again."

"But you've meditated. That's the important thing. No one expects you to be an ascetic, dear Comtesse. Mother Superior tells me that the *Gazette de Hollande* has interviewed her many times. They're preparing another special issue. She told them how the other inmates have been so touched by your virtue and resignation that they have pooled their meager resources in order to give you some relief from the appalling food here. Remember last week? The special treat of peas and bacon?"

"I know. But I couldn't eat it."

"You must eat, Comtesse! You must force yourself. You have to build back your strength." Father Tillet lowered his voice to a whisper and pressed his lips against the grate of the confessional. "You must have enough strength to make a long journey."

Jeanne's heart was racing. Her attention had wandered, for Father Tillet was forever scolding her to eat more, to get more rest. "A long journey?" Her ears began to ring.

He waited a moment, then said, "If need be. There is reason to believe that those in high places are not happy with your imprisonment here in Paris. The newspapers are full of your story; they will never tire of it so long as you remain here behind these gray walls. I happen to know that the Lieutenant General of the Police . . ."

"Monsieur de Crosne? He was once so nice to me. In the Bastille. Then he turned against me like all the rest," Jeanne said sourly.

"He's been here to the prison. Asking questions of the wardens. There have been some reports that you have been talking too much. Naming individuals at court."

"And what if I have?" Jeanne said angrily. "It's my right. After all that's been done to me."

"Of course you have every right, dear Comtesse. My worry is that it would be very simple to silence you. Why would Lieutenant General de Crosne be sent here if they didn't intend to imprison you in some remote convent in the provinces where they hope that no one will even know your name?"

"A convent in the provinces! Bloody hell!" Jeanne cried.

"Shhh! Shhh! But if you eat your food and get back your strength—you're young, Comtesse, why we're the same age, you and I—then you will be able to make that long journey I mentioned. Do you understand what I mean?"

Jeanne stared hard at his face on the other side of the grate. "I don't know. I'm not sure," she mumbled.

"Then, put your trust in me, Comtesse," Father Tillet said.

43

Contrary to Versailles's hopes and expectations the foreign journalists who had flocked to Paris as soon as the news of the arrest of Cardinal de Rohan rumbled through Europe remained in the capital. Scarcely had the gates of the Salpêtrière closed behind Jeanne de La Motte when the tide of popular opinion, avidly reported in the newspapers, turned in her favor. Much was made of Jeanne's imprecations against the Queen before being stifled by the executioner's gag. The Paris correspondent of Russia's Catherine the Great reported that "In Paris everyone's heart melts with pity at the thought of the brutal punishment suffered by Madame de La Motte."

In November of 1786, Madame Vigée-Lebrun's latest portrait of Marie Antoinette had to be withdrawn from the Salon for fear that an angry public might slash it to shreds. The Queen, it was said, had retreated into haughty disdain for the people.

For whatever reason—curiosity, compassion, a desire to thumb their noses at the King and the Queen—it became a fashion craze to make a pilgrimage to the immense gray stone prison flanking the river in search of a glimpse of its famous prisoner. Journalists from all over Europe and France waited at the gates, taking due note of the glittering array of sleek carriages and the prominent personages coming to call.

One day in November a tall, superbly dressed woman wearing a black mask, only a hint of blond hair showing beneath her hood, swept into Mother Superior Victoire's sitting room. The visitor seemed nervous as she signed the prison registry.

Mother Superior Victoire shook her head in wonder when she saw the name. "Ah, the Princesse de Lamballe. We're honored, truly we are." The Princesse de Lamballe, as everyone knew, especially in the gossip mills of the convents, had been the Queen's beloved favorite before Marie Antoinette took up with the notorious Duchesse de Polignac. "Though I don't know why in the world I'm so surprised to see you here. Lord knows, I've just sent a list to the police of no fewer than fifteen hundred persons of the greatest distinction in the kingdom. Fifteen hundred! There have probably been more who have slipped in and out who've not been made to sign the book. Even though I tell these visitors as soon as they step down from their carriages that the Comtesse will see no one at all, neither friend nor relative."

"But I must see her, Mother. It's imperative. Today," the Princesse said, quickly removing her mask and her hood. Her voice was gentle but insistent, agitated. Her hands fluttered nervously about her face. "You see, my visit is . . . different."

"Different? How? They all say that. They all think they have a special reason." Mother Superior, the daughter of the *petite noblesse* in the provinces, her father a hardworking farmer without the means to dower all three of his daughters, had little patience for the high-and-mighty manners of the court aristocracy.

"Mother, listen to me. I'm here on a mission of such importance to the Comtesse . . ."

"Very well, then, I shall see whether the Comtesse will make an exception." Mother Superior Victoire sent a young novice with the Princesse de Lamballe's card to Jeanne in the prison workhouse.

The Princesse walked around the small sitting room, politely feigning interest in the religious objects on exhibit there. She appeared too edgy, too distracted, to indulge in small talk.

"It took a great while to find a pencil," the young novice said breathlessly. "I ran all the way back, Mother." With a quick curtsey, she held out the card to the Princesse.

The Princesse read the card and flushed scarlet. *Lu et refusé*, read and refused, was written in a steady, elegant hand across the back of the card. "She's refused me!" the Princesse said in amazement. "*Lu et refusé!* Why she's mocking me! She's not refusing just me, and she knows it!" Her face was dark with anger. "Mocking me! The little baggage!"

"You mustn't think unkindly of her, Princesse. She sees no one here."

"But she will see me," the Princesse said sternly. "I insist on it!"

"Come now, Princesse. Calm yourself. Madame de La Motte is condemned to this prison, to be sure, but she is not condemned to receiving visitors—not even a princess of the blood—whom she is unwilling to admit," Mother Superior said with a satisfied smile.

Jeanne looked up from the long sewing table where she and six other inmates were stitching prison garments of coarse gray drugget, a heavy felted fabric so abrasive that the rough, torn skin on her fingers constantly oozed blood and pus. Across the dust-filled room she saw the slight frame of Angélique outlined in the doorway. Jeanne smiled to herself. Angélique had just finished her morning run of the kitchens, and no doubt she had stowed away in her apron pocket some special treat for Jeanne. Hardly a day passed when she did not turn up with something she had filched from the guards' kitchen or the sisters' refectory. A tiny creature with round, astonished eyes and an occasional stutter, Angélique had a way of slipping around the Salpêtrière without calling attention to herself.

"What's that you're hiding in your apron, Angélique ?" Jeanne said with mock severity, keeping her eyes on her sewing.

"Comtesse!" Angélique whispered.

When Jeanne saw the frightened look in Angélique's eyes, she was filled with foreboding. Any day now she expected to be hustled away from the Salpêtrière and sent to a country convent, buried alive and silent forever.

"What is it?" Jeanne said.

Angélique poked her hand around the pocket of her apron and motioned for Jeanne to follow her to the doorway.

"Last night . . . no, it was more like this morning though not yet light, one of the sentinels on night watch in the courtyard, you know, the big one with boots that smell like a manure pit, well, this sentinel poked the barrel of his gun through the bars of my cell and kept jabbing and pushing at me until I woke up, scared as I could be, though I didn't scream or make any noise."

Angélique spoke in such a low voice that Jeanne could scarcely hear her above the din of the vast workroom.

"What did he want?"

"As soon as I sat up in bed, he says, Are you not the young one who serves Madame de La Motte. Yes, I am, says I. And then he shoves some pieces of paper, a pen, and a pot of ink through the bars. Now don't be afraid of me, he says. Give these things to Madame de La Motte with this letter, and tell her that she can trust me! And then he disappeared. If I hadn't been sitting there with the pen and ink and paper, I would have thought I had dreamed it all."

"Where is the letter?"

Angélique patted her apron pocket. "Right here. I came as soon as they unlocked the doors this morning."

"Come to my cell after supper. Keep the letter until then, but don't let anyone else know you have it."

Jeanne looked back at the huge workroom where a few heads had lifted and were watching them. She had a terrible feeling that she was being led into a trap. Too many people were asking her to trust them. It set her nerves on edge.

44

It was raining again in London, a drizzly December rain full of agues, and Nicolas de La Motte had a very bad conscience. Dublin had eventually bored him; so he had returned to England where he had grown fat, leading the good life, most of the time dizzy with pleasure, but now it was all spoiled. Everyone he met made a point of giving him yet another grisly detail about the punishment inflicted on his wife Jeanne. The executioner cut off her nipples, someone had told him the day before, and he had had a blinding headache the rest of the day, thinking of how vain Jeanne had always been about her breasts. Twin peaks of perfection, his friend Rétaux de Villette had described them once. Possibly. The Comte confessed to only a vague recollection of his wife's breasts. A British lord at a gaming table had even insinuated that the Comte must be little short of a poltroon, letting his wife suffer the punishment of the damned while he disported himself in grand style around the pleasure haunts of London.

La Motte lowered his umbrella and furled it tightly before entering the French ambassador's waiting room. The usual crowd of French émigrés, many of them La Motte's boon companions at the gaming tables around town, were milling about the room, exchanging the latest gossip. Without so much as a nod La Motte boldly walked past them into the ambassador's office.

"The answer is still no, La Motte," Comte d'Adhémar, the ambassador, said, looking up from his papers. "I don't know how you ever came up with this hare-brained scheme. Parlement has no intention of allowing you to come before them to justify your actions. And those of your wife. You're condemned to the galleys in absentia, if you'll recall. You are a convicted criminal."

La Motte sat down opposite the ambassador's desk, pulled out a handkerchief, and loudly blew his nose, a mauve-red beacon of distress. "Parlement is making a mistake. Versailles is making a mistake. They are leaving me no choice in this matter."

"What do you mean, no choice?" Comte d'Adhémar had given orders to his assistants to admit Comte de La Motte to his office at any time without delay. The ferocity of the anti-royalist rumors flying around Paris, some of them implying that a plot was underfoot to help the Comtesse de La Motte escape from prison, worried d'Adhémar. The ambassador regarded La Motte as a wild card, a man who must be humored, an unpredictable threat to the King and Queen.

"Unless my wife is set free and allowed to come to England, I must go to the press. I've had many an offer. *The London Morning Chronicle*, for example. I shall publish an exposé in which the Queen and the Baron de Breteuil will be rudely compromised, believe me."

"You wouldn't dare, La Motte! That's nothing short of blackmail!" Comte d'Adhémar's said, his mind churning with plans to get a courier to Versailles and back with a decision by the King before La Motte could carry out his threats.

"Nothing of the sort. You must insist that the King act promptly. I yearn to exonerate myself and my wife before the French nation." La Motte languidly caressed his long, fleshy nose. "I should point out that my exposé will be substantiated by a very revealing packet of letters which Providence prompted me to take from a secret compartment in my desk before rushing from my home in Bar-sur-Aube. These are not idle threats, Monsieur le Comte. No indeed."

The French ambassador's pleas notwithstanding, on December 29, 1786, the *London Morning Chronicle* carried a letter from the Comte de La Motte announcing the imminent publication of an exposé promising to satisfy the world's questions about the Comte and Comtesse de La Motte's involvement in the notorious necklace affair.

"I shall make a clear and concise account," the Comte wrote, "of the whole diamond necklace transaction and tell what actually happened to the necklace itself by making special mention of the Party in whose hands it presently reposes—the Party who, while making my wife a gift of some of the lesser stones, which I later disposed of in England, retains by far the most considerable portion of the gems, which might easily be worn by that very Party today in revised design and settings without ever being identified by anyone, not even the jewelers. I shall relate in full how my wife and I were inhumanely sacrificed by this Party."

❦

At Versailles where the vast, gilded rooms now echoed with gloom, the Duchesse de Polignac stood looking out at the gardens, sullen in the late afternoon mists.

"I shall miss the Cordon Bleu fêtes," the Duchesse said, frowning, pulling her cashmere shawl tightly across her chest. "Ah, but what does it matter, if I can render a service to my dear sovereign?" She turned and smiled sweetly at the Queen, red-eyed, her long, thick hair loose and disheveled, for she had spent the day in bed with a trying winter cold.

"It's a question of time," the King said. "We must get possession of those letters before this fellow La Motte sells them to a newspaper."

"Dear God, I never thought it would come to this," the Queen said, and she began to cry.

The King threw himself clumsily into a chair at her side and took her hand. "Please, my dear. It will be all right. The Duchesse will go to London as soon as she can make ready."

"What if he won't negotiate?" the Duchesse said, and the Queen gave a small cry of distress.

"Why shouldn't he? He wants money; that's what he's after," the King said.

"I suppose he's a low fellow," the Duchesse said, lifting her lip with distaste. "Are you quite sure that I will know how to make him come to terms?"

"Dearest Yolande, you're the only person in the world I would trust with this affair!" the Queen said.

"You will simply offer him whatever it takes to get that packet of letters into your hands," the King said.

"That could mean a great deal of money," the Duchesse said.

"Whatever it takes," the King said firmly, as the Queen squeezed his hand.

45

Jeanne turned the letter over again, feeling the texture of the superb, expensive paper, examining the elegant handwriting, word by word and letter by letter.

"What is it? What does it say?" Angélique asked, nervously twisting a corner of her apron. "You look queer."

"Just let me think for a moment. I feel as if I might fall over in a dead faint." She read the few words again. "*Unfortunate lady, hold this letter up to the light. C'est entendu.*" It was the phrase, *C'est entendu* that took her breath away. That was the smart, new catch phrase of the Queen's crowd! Agreed! All right! *C'est entendu!* had become something of a password in that little circle of the Queen's favorites.

"I don't have a candle!" Jeanne moaned. "I'm supposed to hold this letter up to the light, but I don't have a candle!"

"Here," Angélique said, pulling a small disk of a votive candle and a match from her pocket. "I pinched it in the chapel yesterday."

Jeanne laughed hoarsely and with shaking hands lit the candle and held the paper up to its glow.

Madame, the letter read, *Your friends are working day and night to ameliorate your unhappy fate. We urge you not to abandon hope, but to try to build back your strength to undertake a long and arduous journey.*

"That's exactly what Father Tillet said only a few weeks ago!" Jeanne cried, incredulous. "He told me to get myself ready for a long journey."

Advise us what disguise will be needed, and indicate the day you wish to set out. You will find a boat and two oarsmen waiting beyond the King's Gardens, at the riverbank. Seek to procure a pattern of the key used to unlock your corridor.

Put all your trust in the messenger who brought this letter.

"I'll go with you, Comtesse!" Angélique cried. "Oh, do take me with you, out of this hell hole forever!"

"Shhh. Wait! Let me think. The messenger, was that the sentinel? The one with the smelly boots."

"Yes. I got a good look at his face today. He's young, trying to grow one of those big mustaches."

"I'll write a letter right away, and you can give it to him early in the morning after he comes on duty. And then . . ." Jeanne caught her breath and groaned. "The key! How in God's name can we find a pattern of the key?"

"We'll make one," Angélique said.

"What?"

"We can draw one. I see that key every day, dangling from the chatelaine at the warder's waist. Nobody ever pays attention to me. I'll keep my eye on that key until I know every notch by heart! You'll see."

But Jeanne's soaring hopes had collapsed. "My head aches. I'm going to bed," she said, folding the precious letter tightly and stuffing it into her stocking.

"But aren't you going to write a letter to give to the sentinel?"

"Not tonight," Jeanne said.

As days and weeks passed, Jeanne's initial euphoria gave way to a despairing torpor despite Angélique's tireless efforts to inspire her to snatch at this chance at freedom. From time to time she wrote letters to her "secret correspondent," expressing gratitude in a formal, sentimental kind of way that indicated that she had no real hope of ever escaping from the Salpêtrière.

In late January Angélique came to Jeanne's cell as soon as the inner doors were opened at five o'clock. She pulled from her pocket a dirty piece of paper on which she had drawn a facsimile of the corridor key with every jagged indentation reproduced.

"Wh-wh-what do you think, Comtesse?" Angélique said.

"Angélique, my child!" Jeanne said, after studying it. "I think it's a miracle! I think that I could open that damned door with just this drawing. Oh, my clever little friend!" She could not take her eyes off the little scrap of paper. "How did you ever do it?"

"I told you. I looked at that old key until my eyes almost fell out of their sockets. I know it's right. I finished it days ago."

"Dear, dear child!"

"I'll go with you, won't I? Oh, please say yes, yes, yes, Comtesse!" Angélique's pale, pinched face strained forward in the candlelight.

"Naturally you will come with me!" Jeanne said. "I'm being rescued from this pit, Angélique! Think of it!"

"It's the Queen, Comtesse, for a certainty it is."

"Of course, who else could it be? *C'est entendu*. As soon as I saw that phrase, I knew it had to be the Queen."

They could hear the heavy tread of the courtyard sentinel beginning his round. Jeanne quickly snuffed out the candle and motioned to Angélique to sit next to her on the bed.

"The next question: our disguises. I could be a society lady touring the prison. Or the wife of a magistrate visiting . . ."

"But you would look too much like yourself," Angélique said. "I can dress anyway I like because nobody ever looks at me. I can dress as a maid, some kind of servant. You ought to dress so that even if someone looked at you, they wouldn't think about you."

"You're right. I'll go as a man. Why not? I'm tall enough. Here, hand me the pen and paper. I'll write the letter now, and you can slip it to the sentinel with the drawing of the key when he comes on duty in the morning."

"*Oh, blessed deliverer*, she began, *you who have shed a tear of pity for this unhappy Valois . . .*"

🙥

On February 15, 1787, a bitterly cold day when patches of ice on the cobblestones of the courtyards glinted in the dull light of dawn and the nostrils of dray horses straining with their loads up the slippery banks of the Seine were stiff with frost, the sentinel with the foul-smelling boots pushed the barrel of his gun through the cell bars and awakened Angélique. Without a word he held out the key made from her sketch.

As soon as the cell doors were opened for the day, Angélique went flying to find Jeanne. All day long they waited for a time when they could be alone in the corridor leading from their courtyard. At last, when everyone else was busy sweeping down the workhouse and making up beds for the night, they escaped to the corridor. With trembling hands, Jeanne reached out and inserted the key into the lock, and, magically, the key fit, it turned, and the door swung open.

"Seigneur!" Jeanne whispered, awestruck. She quickly pushed the door back in its place and, pulling Angélique after her, ran to her cell. There she hid the key behind a loose stone in the wall.

Ten days later the sentinel began to pass through the bars pieces of their disguises. For Jeanne he brought a blue redingote, a black vest and breeches, yellow pigskin gloves, a high round black hat, and a cane. For Angélique he brought a working girl's simple striped dress and a plain kerchief.

Two weeks later the sentinel brought a letter with final instructions for the escape—*a boat and oarsmen would be waiting on the riverbank at the third plane tree beyond the King's Garden. Madame is kindly entreated to name the date and the hour convenient for her departure* . . . the note read.

Angélique squealed with delight as Jeanne read aloud the note.

"Just to walk out of here and be free!" Angélique said, bringing her clasped hands to her chin. "What's the matter, Comtesse? You're looking queer again . . ."

"I don't know, it's all going too smoothly for my taste. I smell a fish. Look at it this way, why would the Queen, who didn't turn a hair while they beat me and burned me and threw me into this damned hole, well, why should she come forward all of a sudden and hold out a helping hand?" Jeanne's eyes flashed with dark, bitter anger. "They have sent me a key and a disguise, but it may very well be that when I make my dash for freedom, even if I find that promised boat and the oarsmen waiting on the riverbank, how do I know they are not cutthroats hired to murder me before I cross the Seine? *Hein*? Ever thought of that? What if someone is offering me escape only to make sure that my mouth will be shut once and for all by slashing my throat from ear to ear?"

Jeanne shuddered. "We're going to wait and see, that's what we're going to do."

46

As the days lengthened and softened and the old stone walls of the courtyard warmed in the midday sun, Jeanne was tormented by the key's promise of freedom from the sour bondage of prison. To keep the key secure and on her person, she had sewn it to her undergarments, and its presence was a constant reminder of the world outside the Salpêtrière.

But the key also stirred up deep misgivings. Had Angélique's drawing really been good enough to reproduce a prison key? Jeanne could barely remember the drawing, and certainly there was no way to compare the drawing with the actual key. Now the ease with which the key was produced seemed to her far too improbable. Like magic, like a miracle, Jeanne had thought at the time. But in the depths of the Salpêtrière there were few if any miracles, and Jeanne knew it.

It was all a matter of trust, wasn't it? Why should she trust Father Tillet and his sugared advice to escape? Wasn't he a little too quick to be irritated with her when she chose to wait and do nothing? Jeanne cast back in her memories to reckon the number of those she had put her faith in. Not many. There was the Bishop de Langres, she had trusted him all right. And what had that amounted to? A stomach big with child and a ne'er-do-well fool for a husband. And dear Beugnot, earnest, cautious, plodding, absurdly, unnecessarily, honest, what had he done but walk out on her when he saw that she was a lost cause. Love didn't amount to a hill of beans with the scrupulous bourgeoisie. Beugnot was not one for taking chances. She had trusted the goodness, the nobility of the Cardinal. Memories of the Cardinal-Prince weighed like a stone on her heart. What good times they had had! Her chest tightened at the very thought of the food, the merriment . . . the sweet, silken luxury! But in the end, the Cardinal, too, had failed her. Why hadn't he settled with those wrought-up jewelers before the whole affair exploded into such a stink? He had not turned out to be the man she had supposed. Somehow or other she was the one who always managed to end up paying the price.

In early June, however, despite her fears, she gave a letter to the sentinel-messenger setting June 8 at eleven o'clock in the morning when the huge prison would be bustling with inmates, workmen, visitors, and nuns for the time of her escape. Jeanne was at the end of her rope. Why not make a run for it? And so what if it were a trap? There were all kinds of deaths, she knew now, and the kind she endured every day at the Salpêtrière made it easier to embrace another.

"We'll change into our clothes in Father Tillet's confessional after six o'clock Mass," Jeanne said to Angélique. They stood off to one side of the workroom, leaning on their stick brooms and watching a fight that had broken out near the doorway. Two stringy women, their arms spread wide for balance, stomped and kicked a woman on the floor with their heavy wooden clogs as if she were a nasty insect.

"Yes. And then we can go out the side door into the small corridor to the courtyard," Angélique said.

"What side door?" Jeanne said.

"The one that leads out of the confessional."

"Dear heart! I do believe you know every nook and cranny of this old pile of stones!"

Once Jeanne had made up her mind to go, she planned every move with precise detail and infinite patience. She asked her correspondent for money to bribe guards and inmates and got it right away. If the efficiency with which her demands were met alarmed her, she fought off her anxiety by thinking of soft, satiny new gowns and sweet soaps and clean linen bed sheets and all the comforts awaiting her in her life outside the prison gates.

On the morning of June 8, Jeanne and Angélique, their heads bowed, remained on their knees after the benediction and waited until the small chapel was silent and empty. They had both hidden their disguises in a tight bundle between their legs.

"You go first," Jeanne whispered.

Angélique sprang to her feet and hurried into the confessional. After a few minutes Jeanne followed.

"Oh, *merde!*" she cried. "I'll never be able to walk two feet in these boots! They're too small." The waistcoat, too, was a tight fit, revealing her very unmasculine form.

She opened the side door and made a few tentative steps. Angélique, distraught, watched as Jeanne hobbled down the corridor to what was called the Red Gate, the gate leading from the women's courtyard to that of the superintendent. This would be the first gate to be cleared of the nine courtyards that separated Jeanne from the freedom of the main entrance courtyard of the prison.

"The key works perfectly," Jeanne sighed. They carefully eased the gate open and crossed the courtyard.

For weeks Jeanne had been watching the gatekeeper at the Red Gate and knew that she was in the habit of going twice daily to fetch her bowl of soup. At eleven o'clock that morning, when the gatekeeper left her post to go to the kitchen, a prisoner named Dubois, whom Jeanne had bribed the previous evening, stopped the gatekeeper and begged her for a piece of bread. With that delay Jeanne and Angélique had time to slip through the Red Gate and the two beyond it. Coming into the fourth courtyard, they crossed a throng of workmen and servants, who merely nodded at the young man and the servant girl and went on about their business.

As they progressed further and further from the ninth court-yard, where Jeanne and Angélique had been confined with the hardened criminals, Jeanne could see that the surveillance grew slacker.

Jeanne took a deep breath and smiled to herself. It was so much easier than she ever could have imagined. If only her feet did not ache so much, she would actually be enjoying herself. Just as she was coming out of the courtyard, still preoccupied with the chatter of the workmen behind her, she looked at the corridor ahead and panicked. No Angélique. Where could the damned girl have gone? There was no one in sight. Jeanne's throat went dry. What if Angélique were in cahoots with the phantom assassins, the cutthroats and villains who had peopled Jeanne's nightmares for months? She leaned against the wall of the corridor, breathing hard. Of course, she could see it clearly now. She had been lured into a trap by Father Tillet and Angélique, who had never ceased to pester her until she yielded and agreed to escape. That stupid charade with Angélique expertly drawing the key to fit the corridor lock!

Jeanne wiped her wet palms against her trousers and tugged at the ill-fitting boots. Something crashed with a loud explosion in the next courtyard, and she could hear workmen swearing and squabbling. Jeanne walked as fast as she could down the corridor and across the courtyard, where workmen crowded noisily around a heap of collapsed scaffolding.

Jeanne came out into the sunlight of the next courtyard. Still no sign of Angélique. But perhaps Angélique, who knew every twist and turn in the Salpêtrière, had simply darted off on a short cut to the main entrance, thinking that Jeanne was close behind her. Jeanne looked around in alarm, uncertain what to do. A workman turned his head and watched her. After a moment's hesitation Jeanne forged ahead, and in each of the succeeding courtyards she slipped a tip to the gatekeeper and passed through unquestioned.

At length Jeanne came out into the enormous courtyard in front of the prison where throngs of visitors on a sight-seeing tour of the Salpêtrière were milling about. She looked around desperately for

Angélique. There were so many people in the courtyard that Jeanne could not see the main entrance gate and had no idea where to find it. She was afraid that she would attract attention to herself if she tried to push her way through the crowd. She took a few steps forward and melted into the crowd, letting it carry her along with it into the somber old church off the courtyard. No one paid any attention to her when she knelt and prayed as fervently as she ever had in her life. All would be well, she prayed; she thought of London and people making odd sounds as they spoke, and the excitement of strange smells of food, and the rich gowns she would buy and the soaps and scents.

She got to her feet, and, again, following the crowd, went out of the church and—it was like a miracle—walked straight to what she had been praying for: the main gate of the prison, the gate to freedom.

Once in the King's Gardens she stopped dead still. Should she turn to the left or to the right to reach the river? The sun was high in the sky. It had taken almost thirty minutes to clear the prison and reach the King's Garden. Already the alarm would be sounding in the women's courtyard signaling an escape.

She turned quickly to the right, and no sooner had she taken her first step than she spied the river—and Angélique, looking small and abandoned, waiting for her. Jeanne caught her breath and joyfully began to run toward her. The boat with the two oarsmen lay alongside.

Without a word, fearful that her voice would give her away, Jeanne scrambled into the small boat behind Angélique and turned her back to the oarsmen as they crossed to the Right Bank. Her heart lifted with joy. Paris looked like a city in a dream, softly golden, bright with blue skies.

The oarsmen grunted a little as they stroked the water. They moved swiftly, gliding past other boats, outdistancing the ferries lumbering back and forth between the riverbanks. She had a brief glimpse of the bulky dark fortress of the Bastille and averted her eyes. She had had enough of prisons to last her a lifetime.

The boat plowed upstream. The oarsmen said nothing, but Jeanne could feel their eyes on her. As they approached the Arsenal, the boat swerved toward the bank and pulled up under a stand of willow trees. Vivid green willow branches languidly swept back and forth in the muddy water along the shore. Farther down the river a man struggled with his horse as he led it down to the water to drink. All was quiet and peaceful. The riverbank was deserted. Jeanne and Angélique stood up, and without having exchanged a word with the men, stepped ashore. Jeanne did not look back.

Epilogue: Beugnot

I thought I had the whole diamond necklace flim-flam figured out until Jeanne escaped from the Salpêtrière. Less than a year after she was carried into the prison more dead than alive. I've been in the Salpêtrière prison many times over the years, and every time I was taken back to the inner prison where hardened criminals were kept—and Jeanne was incarcerated with these—I was struck by how impossible it would be for anyone, under ordinary circumstances, to escape. There were nine courtyards, and she was buried back at the ninth.

Word of Jeanne's escape got out right away, and there was no doubt in anyone's mind that certain parties in very high places had come to the Comtesse de La Motte's assistance. It was hard for anyone to avoid that conclusion.

You see, after the ghastly flogging and branding of Jeanne, an irreversible revulsion against the King and Queen set in. Having Jeanne imprisoned right there on the Left Bank kept the public's memory of the whole shabby business enflamed. I can see why the King and Queen would want Jeanne out of the way. But, good Lord, what a disastrous mistake for the monarchy her escape turned out to be!

Of course, the Orléans faction at court could have been responsible for helping her. Many at the time thought so, because the Duc d'Orléans had for years been lusting to wrest the throne from his Bourbon cousin. In any event, we can definitely rule out the Cardinal, who had been pretty much buried alive in his Abbaye de la Chaise-Dieu in Auvergne.

The point is that there was, without question, a powerful helping hand that day in June when Jeanne and her little friend walked out of the Salpêtrière. Think of it: the two of them walked through Paris and out the Porte de Vincennes, where they hired a coach to Provins. All of this was reported some time later in the newspapers, down to the color of the waistcoat Jeanne was wearing. From Provins they got a ride to Troyes on the wagon of a young farmer, and from Troyes they proceeded to Bar-sur-Aube, where they spent the night in a quarry just outside of town. Jeanne sent her friend into town with a note to Monsieur de Surmont to come to her at the quarry. Ostensibly, all of the La Mottes' earthly goods had been auctioned to the benefit of the King's privy purse, but apparently, the Surmonts, following Nicolas de La Motte's instructions, had shrewdly hidden many of their valuables, jewelry included, under a manure heap on Farmer Durand's property! I love the cunning! Naturally, Jeanne wanted Surmont to sell a few of the costlier pieces discreetly and send the money to La Motte in London.

Surmont wisely declined. His formidable wife would have had his head on a platter, had he agreed to associate himself further in any way with the "blue-eyed hellion," as she called Jeanne. Somehow or other, my father, that enduringly besotted man, got wind of the fact that Jeanne was hiding in the quarry and went to her, fat, heavy purse in hand. And do you know what? Jeanne declined his money, absolutely refused to take a single coin. Oh, truly she was a dashing woman, full of amazing gestures! Just thinking of her can still make my old heart sing.

From Bar, Jeanne and her friend went on to Switzerland, and again, one wonders how someone as notorious as Jeanne could have crossed so much French territory without being recognized somewhere along the line. Furthermore, the investigation into her escape from the Salpêtrière was perfunctory at best and totally superficial. I ought to know; I've looked into the matter pretty thoroughly.

When Jeanne eventually arrived in London—I think it was late November of 1787—she had to deal with that godawful husband of hers. All things considered, he was just about as destructive a force in her life as her obsession about her Valois blood. The problem, as always, was that he had run through all their money, which as I understand it was a considerable fortune. By the time, Jeanne turned up in London, he was up to his ears in debt with creditors clawing at the doors at all hours of the day and night.

I don't know what it was: he wasn't a stupid man. Well, he wasn't all that stupid. But he was the kind of fellow you could read like a book. A book in bold print. Every single thought or attitude stood out crystal clear on his face. For that reason, he was constantly being gulled out of his money by this one and by that one, whores mostly and then London lawyers of one stripe or another.

That being said, I have to admit that La Motte was a genius when it came to extorting money from the King and Queen. That's another point I have never been able to figure out: if the Queen had nothing on her conscience, if she had never laid eyes on Jeanne, as she claimed, and certainly never took her to her bosom—which, quite frankly, I believe to be true—if she had absolutely nothing to do with the purloining of the diamond necklace, then why, in God's name, did the King and Queen try again and again to keep the La Mottes quiet? La Motte was able, apparently with the greatest of ease, to milk the royal purse time and time again, especially after Jeanne took up her poisonous pen in London and began to write the story of her life.

Throughout her memoirs Jeanne insists that she was forced to tell her side of the story to vindicate herself, though she does admit, quite plaintively, to be sure, that she desperately needs the money as well. Oh, and did the memoirs sell! The first volume came out in May of 1789, and I totally agree with Mirabeau—a hero in my own personal Pantheon. I shall never forget his speeches to the Assembly; he has been called our "Shakespeare of eloquence" which, in my opinion, doesn't go far enough in describing his superb gifts of oratory—well, Mirabeau believed that the Comtesse de La Motte's voice alone brought on the horrors of the razing of the Bastille on July 14, 1789, and of October 5, when the so-called Women's Army stormed the palace of Versailles and took the King and the Queen prisoner.

Mirabeau certainly had a point, because in the insurrection of October 5 the Queen was directly targeted. Eight or ten thousand "women," some of them with suspiciously muscled forearms and a faint shadow of a beard showing beneath their wigs and bonnets, stormed through the gilded gates of the palace, past the guards, screaming obscene threats to tear out Marie Antoinette's heart to make a stew and her liver and gizzards for the cockades to trim their bonnets. They swarmed in and slaughtered the Queen's guard. It was a terrible moment for the Queen. Her ladies-in-waiting managed to bolt the outer doors and to hustle the Queen, barefoot and in her nightdress, through secret passages and back corridors to the King's suite. The King and Queen were taken back to Paris to the Tuileries, their long cortège of over a hundred carriages moving slowly along, the delirious mob swarming around them brandishing the bloody heads of the Queen's guard on pikes.

Call me an old fool, but I've never had it in my heart to be proud of the Revolution. Perhaps if Mirabeau had lived, he could have restrained the Robespierres and the Murats who set loose the howling jackals over our fair land.

Without question Jeanne de La Motte's memoirs fed the fury of those jackals. In the entire Revolutionary arsenal her memoirs were the deadliest weapon of all, because Jeanne, even in the written word, had a tremendous gift of persuasion. There was a floodtide of books vilifying the Queen, but the other books were trash, so outrageous and exaggerated they convinced no one who had a mind to think even halfway objectively of the King and the Queen. But Jeanne's memoirs were genuine poison for which there was no antidote because Jeanne was a scion of the royal blood, she had consorted with the highest level of court society—whom had she not consorted with, I wonder. Throughout the years the list of her lovers has grown longer and longer. Why, it turns out that the Marquis d'Aligre, the President of the Parlement during the necklace trial, had been one of her most ardent lovers during the time of her prosperity in the rue Neuve Saint-Gilles. But—that is neither here nor there.

There was a ring of truth about Jeanne's memoirs that had a devastating effect on the Queen's already crippled reputation. Don't think for a minute that those in power did not realize the political value of Jeanne de La Motte. Robespierre and his radicals tried repeatedly to induce her to return to Paris for a retrial of the Diamond Necklace Case, which would have put Jeanne on the witness stand with her "mortal enemy" the Queen in the dock.

In the midst of the turmoil of the Revolution, at the first sign of an all clear, Nicolas de La Motte hopped on a boat to France and was soon ensconced in a luxurious suite of rooms at the Palais-Royal—who paid his bills if not the Orléans faction?—with a renowned Parisian courtesan archly known as La Belle Impure.

Jeanne, however, stayed on in London, haunted by the notion that sooner or later she would be dragged back into the dread Salpêtrière. The Bastille might be in ruins, but the Salpêtrière still stood, and she apparently was not in the mood to chance being thrown back into that hellhole of a prison. She saw secret agents and conspirators all around her. She dodged from lodging to lodging and went out mainly at night to avoid recognition. And, being Jeanne, she took on lovers, the more noteworthy being her old chum from her Versailles days, the Marquis de Calonne, the former minister of finance, himself in flight from the Queen's wrath.

As a matter of fact, Madame Campan maintains that de Calonne assisted Jeanne in writing her second volume of memoirs. She claims that she came upon the King and Queen reading the manuscript, the Queen in tears, vituperating against "that snake Calonne," whose corrections of Jeanne's egregious errors of court etiquette were scattered all over the margins. The manuscript held by the King was supposed to be the only copy, purchased at great price from the La Mottes. Not surprisingly, the second volume of memoirs, resplendent with sixteen pornographic engravings of the Queen and her female harem, appeared in October of 1789 despite the exchange of stacks of gold coins from the King's treasury.

It was a hopeless situation for the King. He tried everything possible to keep Jeanne's increasingly vicious publications away from the French public.

The worst fiasco, of course, was the Sèvres porcelain factory incident. La Motte wrote to the King, informing him of a whole warehouse containing the French edition of the latest installment of his wife's memoirs and invited him to purchase them. The King's agents paid La Motte fourteen thousand francs for the copies, then closed down the royal factory at Sèvres for one day so that the ovens could be used to burn the memoirs. Naturally, suspicions were raised. But that was the least of it. The King's intendant, for whatever reason, simple curiosity I would say, kept aside one copy of the memoirs for his own perusal. Imagine what went through the King's mind when that copy was found, and swiftly rushed to the printers, who put thousands of copies into the hands of the booksellers of Paris! Poor King Louis, the more he tried to suppress the flood tide of invective flowing from Jeanne's pen on the other side of the Channel, the more he looked a fool and the Queen a guilty voluptuary.

Royal intelligence agents infested London to keep an eye on Jeanne and, most probably, to make sure that they got their hands on her before the revolutionaries or the Duc d'Orléans faction could bring her back to Paris for their own political exploitation of her.

Oh, Jeanne was a trump card, all right, and she must have gloried in that fact. She was a woman cut out for mayhem, the wilder the better. The Cardinal, on the other, shied away from lending his name or his presence to the gathering anti-royalist storm. A few months after the fall of the Bastille, he came out of exile to take a seat in the National Assembly. Since Revolutionary heroes were few and far between in those early times, there was a feverish rush to enshrine the Cardinal as a victim of a despotic monarch and court intrigue. He would have none of it.

I was a delegate from Bar-sur-Aube in those days, and I would often see the Cardinal, alone, without his fawning retinue of the old days, stride briskly through the crowds at the Assembly and take his seat on the bench. He always sat in the same place, near a window where his gaze could stray to the courtyard below. I sometimes wondered if he were thinking of Jeanne and the awful brutality of her sentence, the red-hot branding iron burning into the white breast that he had so often caressed. You see how tenacious jealousy can be . . .

He was still unnervingly handsome; he seemed taller, less virile, though far from broken. He spoke rarely and stood listening with a kindly patience, the result no doubt of his impeccable manners, to any fool who came along.

When it came time to swear to the revolutionary Civil Constitution of the Clergy, the Cardinal refused and divorced himself from the Revolution—and France—forever. He withdrew to his estates at Ettenheim across the Rhine from Strasbourg, where he welcomed multitudes of dispossessed clerics fleeing the bloody chaos of the Revolution.

"The Cardinal became truly saintly," the Abbé Georgel told me the last time I saw him—that was years ago, shortly before he himself retired to his native village of Bruyères, a charming place where the peasants make a delicious little goat cheese, I forget what it's called. "I know you may find that difficult to believe, Beugnot. You were always so hard on the Cardinal. I never could understand why," he said. "In Ettenheim the Cardinal lived through the terrible Revolution quite meagerly, sharing everything he had on this earth with his fellow clerics, his ambition long spent, his only concern the caring for his fellowmen. Think of it, the foremost prince in the realm, living like a lowly monk! Don't you see? He gave it all up, his country, his exalted birthrights, in defense of Mother Church! What courage!"

Georgel was faithful to the Cardinal to the very end, and I admire that, I truly do, though the practical side of me contends that this scruffy old abbé in his smelly soutane was amply rewarded for his loyalty. Perhaps too amply, if the gossip be true.

When the Cardinal passed over to his Maker in 1803, I felt a nostalgic longing for Jeanne's lavish parties in her grand apartment, the Cardinal looking noble and enigmatic, Jeanne at her devilish best, flirting, mocking, La Motte in his outrageous costumes, Rétaux de Villette, preening himself in front of Jeanne's admiring eyes, and Count Cagliostro, braying his incomprehensible cant.

I can still see them as clearly as if it were yesterday. I revisit those scenes more and more now that I am a doddering old man, scribbling away at my memoirs, trying to remember my past importance and to forget how useless I've become. Giving the gardeners a good scold is about as much as I have to show for myself at the end of the day now.

That I should feel any nostalgia for that disastrous circle shows you how far gone in my dotage I am. Look at what happened to Cagliostro. After the King threw him out of France, Cagliostro never found a refuge anywhere in Europe but dragged from country to country with his wife Serafina, her fabled beauty gone. Their money sources dried up to the point that he made the fatal error of returning to Rome. In Rome toward the end of 1789 the papal government imprisoned him and put him on trial before the deadly serious Inquisition court, intent on punishing him for his republican, freemason activity. The trial dragged on for two years, and in 1791 Cagliostro, broken in spirit, was imprisoned in the appalling Castel Sant'Angelo. Later, fearing popular unrest, the Inquisition authorities moved the poor man to a still more hideous confinement in the remote and almost inaccessible Castel San Leo, situated high on a rocky cliff near Montefeltro in the Apennines. Castel San Leo is a fortress carved out of solid rock with old dried-up cisterns converted into dungeons. Cagliostro was placed in one of these cisterns, totally cut off from human contact except when his jailers raised the trap door to lower food to him. Remarkably, Cagliostro survived in these dreadful conditions for three years and died sometime in 1795, not quite ten years after the Diamond Necklace trial and his return home to his wife in triumph on the shoulders of his multitude of admirers. Had he lived, Cagliostro would have been carried home in triumph again, being widely regarded in France as a great martyr to the cause of liberty, equality, and fraternity, the rataplan of our revolutionaries.

Rétaux de Villette ended up in Italy as well, in Venice to be exact. In 1790 he published his *Mémoires historiques des intrigues de la cour*, very much the mirror of the man: frivolous, self-serving, boastful. In his memoirs he calls himself the victim of a corrupt century and of a court steeped in intrigue. He whines a great deal about having betrayed Jeanne as if we were meant to admire him for his whining. He whimpers endlessly about having no money and no prospects of any.

Rétaux de Villette and La Motte were a matched set. Without Jeanne they hadn't the slightest idea of where the next franc would come from. Time after time, La Motte came to me with his hand out, and I would put him into figurehead positions that would bring him some money. I gave him the managership of the Théâtre de la Porte St. Martin at a salary of three thousand francs a year, and at another time, a prize plum of a post as a supervisor of gambling houses in the Palais-Royal. But La Motte would inevitably make a mockery of the position by failing to put in an appearance.

La Motte was a thoroughgoing parasite. After Jeanne's death in London, or rather after the "news" of her death in 1791 shortly after the royal family's abortive flight to Varennes, he tacked Valois onto his name, as if it might be a magic talisman, becoming thereafter Comte de La Motte-Valois. He lived on well into this century, vegetating idly in the capital, poaching meals from the dowager duchess set where the name Valois was still good currency. He would sit around their tea tables looking archaic in his outmoded clothes. They called him Necklace La Motte, and he became quite a conversation piece.

Necklace La Motte . . . well, it certainly was the scandal of the century, a fact that wouldn't shame Jeanne at all. She was rather the sort to take her glory anywhere she could find it. A moment ago I mentioned her death, and a sordid one it was, too, if the newspaper accounts are to be believed. The details are vague, but the gist of it is that three or four men showed up at Jeanne's lodgings with orders to take her away. Now, these men could have been agents of the Duc of Orléans faction or of the King. Or they could have been simply her creditors. Jeanne reportedly took fright, fled to the house next door, where she was cornered by her pursuers. As they pounded on the door, she crawled out a window and clung to the ledge, hoping no doubt that the men would go away. Instead, they broke down the door, whereupon Jeanne let go and fell three floors to the pavement below. According to reports, broken and bruised, she lingered near death for three weeks in the house of a neighbor before succumbing. They say she is buried in the churchyard of St. Mary's Church in Lambeth.

But is she really? What are we to make of the stories coming from as far away as the Crimea, where there is talk of an aging woman by the name of the Comtesse de Gachet (a pun on "ruined" or "wasted"?), who one day playfully showed a little boy a bag full of diamonds, diamonds so big and so brilliant that they made his eyes blink. And late one afternoon they say she slipped her gown off her shoulder and showed the little boy a scar on her shoulder in the shape of a "v." This woman lives at Artek, a place settled sparsely with Tartars and illiterate Greek fishermen.

You know, I don't altogether discount these rumors. Wouldn't it be just like Jeanne to concoct a story of her death and then slip away to another life? Or perhaps it's just an old man's fancy. At any rate, it does me no harm, sitting in the afternoon sun down below the fountain in the garden, and imagining Jeanne in some exotic place, easing peacefully toward death.

Jeanne was always a survivor, and so am I, though there have been times when I have had my doubts, such as during those awful months I spent in the Conciergerie, that rank, stinking antechamber of death. Back in Bar-sur-Aube, I was known as a progressive young liberal, and the crowd I ran around with preached egalitarian notions that made our fathers blanch and our mothers weep. But in Paris after the razing of the Bastille, you couldn't keep up with the extremism that kept sweeping over the city in tidal waves. For what reason I'll never know, I was arrested one night in October 1793 by the Jacobins in my section and thrown into the Conciergerie.

It was just after the Queen had been guillotined, and the scythe of the Terror was swinging wide and striking deep. There was a veritable harvest of death that October. When my name was being registered in the great hall, I turned my head aside so that I wouldn't have to look at the Little Pharmacy, that miserable, dark hole where they kept the Queen before her execution.

I remember the Emperor Napoleon remarking one day as he stood at a window staring out at the towers of the Temple, where the royal family had been incarcerated, "The Queen's death—and the death of the monarchy—must be dated from the Diamond Necklace trial." And none of us in the room that day would have disagreed with him, even had he not been the Emperor of France.

It was the trial that signed Marie Antoinette's death warrant, and when I am feeling really low, I think about how Jeanne de La Motte's obsession with living like a royal princess cast a queen from her throne and into the rickety tumbril of the executioner. And how the blood poured all over this land after the Revolution gained its foothold. Somehow or other, I survived the Conciergerie. That year I had married—and married rather well, actually—and my wife's uncle managed to get me out of prison a step ahead of the executioner.

After that experience, I tried to keep out of harm's way as the Revolution roared to its brutal finale. I was not at all unhappy to see Napoleon take over this shambles of a country. I was sick and tired of chaos. The Emperor named me as one of his prefects, and I was extremely touched by his high opinion of me. He wrote from his exile in St. Helena that when I served him, he could always count on me for the truth. I don't mean to brag, but the Emperor esteemed me greatly.

After his banishment, there were those who privately sneered when I was taken up with such enthusiasm by Louis XVIII after the Bourbon Restoration. I am not ashamed to say that I have always tried to serve my country, whether it be a republic, an empire, or a monarchy. I was given a title, Comte, which would probably rankle Jeanne not a little, and I held one portfolio after another with King Louis XVIII and his brother Charles X. I was Minister of the Interior, Treasury, Marine, Police, and Postmaster General. Most people would call that an illustrious career.

So you see, I have a great deal to scribble about in my memoirs. I've already finished five volumes, though the sixth doesn't hold my interest as much as it should. I've lived a tidy life, and with any luck will have a tidy death. I've begun to make my arrangements. My good friend, the Archbishop of Paris, has agreed to come here to my chateau at Bagneux to celebrate my funeral Mass. Some would find that arrogant, given my humble origins as a mere bourgeois from Bar-sur-Aube. There's no accounting for envy.

Oh, yes, I've survived all right. But like every survivor I've made a few enemies along the way. Why, just the other day when I was discussing my memoirs with a so-called friend, he opined rather maliciously that history will remember me only because of my association with the La Motte woman and the infamous Diamond Necklace affair. I've given that remark much thought lately and have reached this conclusion: *c'est possible.*